Choice

Also by Neel Mukherjee

A Life Apart
The Lives of Others
A State of Freedom
Avian

Choice

Neel Mukherjee

Atlantic Books
London

First published in hardback in Great Britain in 2024 by
Atlantic Books, an imprint of Atlantic Books Ltd.

1 2 3 4 5 6 7 8 9

A CIP catalogue record for this book is available from the British Library.

Hardback ISBN: 978 1 80546 049 7
Trade Paperback ISBN: 978 1 80546 104 3
E-book ISBN: 978 1 80546 050 3

Printed and bound by CPI (UK) Ltd, Croydon CR0 4YY

Atlantic Books
An Imprint of Atlantic Books Ltd
Ormond House
26–27 Boswell Street
London
WC1N 3JZ

www.atlantic-books.co.uk

Christopher

I

There cannot be a right life in the wrong one.

– Theodor Adorno

1.

He slips in between the twins, as he does every time it is his turn to read the bedtime story. Tonight's project is a little complicated and they have had to set aside for the time being the novel they have been reading: *The Wind on the Moon*. He has told the children that instead of plain old reading from a book, he is going to show them a film on his laptop. They are restless with excitement. He has fended off a dozen questions – 'What is the film?', 'Is it a cartoon?', 'Will Miss Piggy be there?', 'Will the red truck come with the sun rays on his face?', 'I want the smiley digger, Baba, I want the smiley digger' – with a patient 'It's a surprise, so I can't say anything.' Tonight, there isn't the usual drama of reluctance to settle down, the playful scrapping involving who gets how much of the duvet, who gets to cuddle with which stuffed toy. He finds that he is nervous; his heart rate is up. They snuggle up against him, Masha on his right, Sasha on the left.

Now is the moment. The camera is jerky. The children are ready with their usual 'What is this?', 'Where is this?', but fall silent when the pigs appear. It is not clear to Ayush that they are paying attention to the commentary that announces the location, the purpose behind the breaking-in and filming.

'Oink-oink piggy,' Masha says. Sasha has put his thumb in his mouth, the gesture that indicates he is now becalmed and

3

is concentrating on what is unfolding in front of him. Ayush knows that Masha will soon follow suit.

The number of pigs held in the pens is so large that the animals are seen climbing over one another. If you squeezed your eyes just so, the creatures could be a close-up of thick, rolling clouds. The voice-over says, 'They have no space to turn around, to move forward, back, sideways. The dirt on them that you see is their own faeces. They are kept like beans packed in a jar.'

The children are unblinking. Ayush cannot know if what they are seeing through their eyes is the same as that which he is witnessing through his.

'What are the piggies doing?' Masha again.

'They're in a place that is like a pig prison. They cannot get out. You'll soon find out why,' Ayush says.

Occasionally, they see pigs that appear to be asleep until another animal bites one such creature's stomach and starts chewing. The sleeping pig shows no reaction – it is a dead pig. A sow, with hanging, swinging teats, is struggling to stand in her farrowing crate, but it is too small to allow any movement. The camera lingers on her, unmoving. Ayush wants to chew the edge of the duvet covering him, his willing her to succeed is so intense. Instead, her hips get trapped in the bars. She continues to struggle, each successive movement more confined than the last as her lower third gets lodged more firmly. Soon, she cannot move at all except to stamp her hooves. She cannot even turn her head. There is a brief shot of her eye rolling, as if she is trying to slide it right back to see and understand what is obstructing her so that she can find a way to free herself. But that will only arrive, in a different form, when a human intervenes.

There is a badly executed cut, and the next shot moves to a different area. It is not clear to Ayush how these images were filmed or whether editing has given it the feeling of continuity. There cannot be any unity of location, he thinks, but there is no disputing the *verité* feel: the jerkiness, the sudden blurs, the momentary impression of someone running with the camera lens pointing at a speeded-up succession of random unidentifiable out-of-focus objects. Then back to tiled walls sprayed with blood.

Ayush looks at his children sideways without moving his head. They seem hypnotized, as they would be with any other film. There are dark-red cherries, with a tiny rectangle of white on each to represent their sheen, on their duvet cover. The night light on the bookshelf opposite the bed has heated up enough to turn the pinwheel inside the shade in a steady, fast rotation. The images are of seashells, seahorses, starfish, stripey fish, coral, all in pretty colours against a blue background. Ayush forces himself to turn his eyes back to the computer screen.

The tiled walls have gone. This seems like a small room in a warehouse, almost a cubicle. The walls are red. No, they are not; only on close observation do they turn out to be a dirty, yellowed white. The splatter and drip of blood looks as if a gleeful cartoonist has been at his merry, unrestrained work. The threshold, raised by an inch or so above floor level, is so caked with layers of old solidified blood and fresh new infusion that it looks like a large wedge of fudgy chocolate cake. At the centre of the screen are slaughtered pigs. Again, they look as if a painter, on a whim, has chosen to depict them as red instead of the usual flesh-toned animals. The camera catches the bristles of their coat already stiffening with the drying blood. It's a contained sea of densely packed red cushions and pillows. Then the camera moves. No, it's not the camera that moves. It's a pig. It stands up in the stew of bodies. Somehow, they have missed him. He has been showered so thoroughly with his companions' blood that it is difficult to make out his tiny eyes of contrasting colour. The chocolate-cake threshold is inches from his maroon snout. But there is no attempt to escape, no looking around at the scene that embeds him, no sniffing. He stands still and looks at the threshold. This time the camera really does move, back an inch or so. There is a closed iron door on the other side of the threshold. But he is not even looking at that. He is actually looking at nothing.

At this point, Sasha gives out a hoarse cry: 'Baba!'

Ayush gulps. His mouth is dry as straw. No reliable jokes about frogs in the throat – he cannot make a sound. He cannot even turn to look at the children or hold their hands.

He feels Masha shudder before he hears the beginnings of her sobs. She buries her head further into his neck and weeps wordlessly. As with all things involving these twins, Sasha joins her a split second later. It's as if Ayush is a mirror-line and there is an identical thing on either side of him. He toggles to a different tab on the screen and reaches out both his arms to hold the children tight against him. He has to be strong now. He cannot bend, let alone crack. He still has not been able to utter a sound. On the Kill Counter tab, his eyes alight on the number for sheep that he had noted before bedtime. It has gone up from 408 to 13,056 in the last twenty minutes. He does some quick mental arithmetic to distract himself from the distraught children: $13,056 - 408 = 12,648$. The whooshing silence that is the constant murderous private soundtrack to his life surges now so that he has to raise his voice to hear the comforting meaningless words come out of his mouth – 'There, there, shush, shush' – and release him.

He lets the sobbing run its course, reassuring them that they need never watch 'it' again. The night light keeps its repetitive show going.

'Blood comes out,' Sasha says.

Ayush doesn't know how to respond.

Masha now: 'Why are they in that place?'

Ayush takes a deep breath. 'It's how we get meat. They're being made into bacon and sausages. All the meat that we eat, ham and chicken and mince, it all comes from animals. You have to kill them to make them into meat. What you saw was how our meat comes to us. From animals that are put into cages and then killed.'

There is silence for so long that he thinks they are on the brink of falling asleep. Are they trying to join the dots between an animal, with its usual form consisting of four legs, mouth, eyes, ears, nose, a particular call, hooves, an animal with its moving, breathing aliveness, and its transformation into a radically different form, that of a flat pink disc between two pieces of bread? Are they trying to bridge that disconnect? Surely all five-year-olds know this? Did he know it when he was their age? There's no way of establishing that. Should he sleep with the twins tonight? His feet will stick at least a foot out of the bed. What is going through their heads? Will they have nightmares? Luke is away in the USA on a conference, so it does not matter if Ayush sleeps here.

While these questions crowd his head, he hears Masha ask, 'Did that piggy escape?'

2.

Ayush has the less remunerative job, so he takes the children to school; as Luke says, 'Economics is life, life is economics.' As always, Ayush tries surreptitiously to scrutinize the faces of passers-by to see if some kind of knowledge imprints their faces, their eyes, when they pass him and the twins, a quantum of a pause, a double take, a second look to pull together a middle-aged South Asian man and two white-ish children into meaning, but no, he is spared today. After drop-off, Ayush takes the Tube to his office near the Embankment. He works for Sennett and Brewer, part of a vast international publishing conglomerate. Sewer, as it's commonly known, is a self-styled literary imprint, as opposed to an upfront commercial imprint, of which the parent company has several. Self-styled because that's the window-dressing. Behind the deceitful window, what everyone would really like to publish are celebrity biographies and bestsellers. But the performance of literariness is important and does vital cultural work (i.e. economic work): it pushes the definition of literary towards whatever sells. Ayush knows that the convergence, unlike the Rapture, is going to occur any day now. Maybe it has already happened, but he's still here, playing the old game because it still has residual value. Soon it won't. He is an editorial director at Sewer, second in command to the publisher, Anna Mitchell, a woman reputed to have 'a nose for a winner'; in other words, that nous about how the convergence can be more effectively achieved.

He has never been able to shake off the feeling that he is their diversity box, ticked – the rest of the company is almost entirely white; all extraordinarily well-intentioned, of course, but stably, unchangingly white. The very few people of colour there belong to the junior ranks of IT and HR, none in editorial, apart from Ayush, or in management. The way the system works if they make any diversity hires is to leave them imprisoned in junior positions for so long that they eventually leave. Diversity is a gift in the giving of white people; they pick and choose whom they should elect to that poisoned club. Ayush was marked for the same fate until chance intervened. After four years as a commissioning editor – and, before that, three as the office envelope-stuffer (official title: editorial assistant) – he had got lucky with an author he had acquired for a fifth of Luke's monthly take-home salary: Rekha Ganesan was shortlisted for the Booker Prize for her debut novel, *In Other Colours*. Not long after that, he had published, breaking the imprint's ostensible mould, an upmarket crime-fiction novel set in the Punjabi communities of Birmingham. That had become a runaway bestseller and had scooped up a CWA Dagger and a Costa Novel Award. He heard the words 'alchemy' and 'golden touch' used of him; he knew that it was not because he was publishing good, maybe even important, work, but because these books were selling. Economics is life, life is economics.

A predictable state of affairs set in after these successes. Until that point, around 30 to 40 per cent of the manuscripts sent to him by agents, he would say, had been by writers of colour. That figure jumped to nearly 90 per cent. Anna complained that she only got books by white women on motherhood, the market for which, both on the supply and demand sides, seemed to be inexhaustible. It was true that she had not used the word 'white', but Ayush knew that the word he had silently supplied was accurate and could be easily substantiated by data: white women believed that motherhood was both original and endlessly interesting; a form of cultural narcissism. When he told Luke that his submissions from white writers had tapered off to almost nothing, Luke had said, 'It depends on what was first coming through the pipeline. What was the proportion of POC and black writers you were getting before?'

'Um, I don't know. Maybe three to four non-white to six or seven white? Probably fewer.'

'Maybe the success of POC writers leads to agents sending more to editors? Or more POC writers submit work and that doesn't get ignored or buried. The market decides these things.' Then Luke had proceeded to give him a lesson on 'herding' and 'information cascades'.

'You mean stereotyping, when it's at home?'

'It's efficient, if you come to think of it.'

This had, of course, led to one of their usual rows.

Today, from 8:45 a.m. until 10, he has spent the time at his desk sharpening all the seven pencils – always odd numbers – to murderous points, moving them from the right side of the desktop monitor to the left, then back again, nineteen times, to achieve symmetry with the pen-holder – again, seven fountain pens – but the perfect arrangement eludes him, as it does most days, so he sets about clearing the entire desk and hiding the contents in the metal cabinet below. This is easily done as there isn't much on the desk in the first place. Then he feels the air around Rachel, who sits on his left, and Daisy, on his right, take on that peculiar charge when the young women make a special effort not to look in his direction. On his notepad, he sets down a bullet point and follows it with 'Which more water, washing single portion of strawberries or cherries, or w/ing entire punnet in one go?' He makes the mistake of looking at both Animal Clock and Kill Counter on his computer before he heads to the meeting room. His breath races with the rhythm and speed of the numbers ratcheting up, as if his respiration is in competition with it. The list is headed by fish, which is already in the seven figures the very moment he opens that page and advancing five figures, in the tens of thousands, every fraction of one second. What goes up every full second is buffalo, which is number 15 of 17 on the list, arranged in descending order of numbers slaughtered: from wild-caught fish, through pigs and geese and sheep and cattle, to 'camels and other camelids'. The clock begins the moment the page opens: it says, 'animals killed for food since opening this page'. Luke would be pleased: he believes in the truth of numbers over the truth of representation. Ayush closes the tabs to stop himself from hyperventilating.

Ayush acquires around ten to twelve books a year; for the last three weeks, he has been pursuing a submission, a debut by an author called M.N. Opie. The agent through whom the work has arrived, Jessica Turner, knew so little about the writer that she seemed surprised not to have an answer to even the most basic question about whether Opie was a man or a woman.

'I don't know,' she had said when he called her. 'The thought never crossed my mind ... I had assumed that he is a he, if you see what I mean. But now I'm not so sure. Let me find out.'

Each story in Opie's short-story collection is different in subject matter, setting, featured characters and the points in the social spectrum they are lifted from, and, notably and subtly, in style. There is one about Richard Johnson, an elderly Jamaican vegetable-stall owner in Brixton, and the steady, casual, unthinking abandonment he faces from everyone, from the bureaucrats in Lambeth Council and the local Jobcentre Plus to his grown-up son and white daughter-in-law, to his customers who begin to move their business to a fancy organic store a few metres from his shop. Only his ageing, arthritic, halitosis-ridden coal-black dog, Niggah, is faithful to him. Then one day the dog goes missing. On the final two pages of the story, the man walks the length and breadth of Brixton, from Coldharbour Lane to Loughborough Junction, down Railton Road to Brockwell Park, shouting 'Niggah! Niggah!' The passers-by take him to be yet another black person with mental-health problems that Brixton is notorious for. The page had blurred for Ayush as he reached the end.

There is a long story about a young Eng. Lit. academic named Emily – an early modernist, no less – in a London university who is in a car accident returning home from a dinner party one night. The driver of the car is not who the app says he is. A combination of inertia, procrastination, and maybe even an inchoate strategy only half-known to herself sends Emily's life in an unpredictable direction. Everything about the story is unexpected and it is not the plot. It is the inner voice of the protagonist, the representation of her world of work and her mind. Even this is not the most salient thing about it. Ayush tried, and repeatedly failed, to put his finger on the elusive soul of the story. Plot-wise, it seemed simple enough, but the more he thought about the underlying moral questions that propelled it, the more complex and troubling it became. In fact, entirely unwritten in the story was its chief meaning: how no escape was offered by making what one thought was the correct moral choice. That meaning appeared only in the echo of the shutting door after he had left the story's room. And that room itself: a trap, a claustrophobic chamber of the protagonist's mind from which there's no escape. The prose sat at the exact opposite end of the scale from the story of Richard Johnson and his dog Niggah.

Ayush had felt an urgency he had not experienced for a long time. It was a physical feeling, something in his racing blood and in his stomach, in the heat in his hands and feet. He used to be derisive of the passing phases of editors' rejection letters to agents – for a while, it was 'I loved it, but I didn't fall in love with it', then it was, 'It did not make the hairs on the back of my neck stand on end' – but now he understood that, behind the congealed bullshit, there might, once upon a time, have been a real physical sensation. He felt that sensation while reading M.N. Opie's *Yes, The World*. He had to publish this book.

Ayush has to get the book through the acquisitions meeting this afternoon and he needs to have all his cards ready. He has shared the manuscript with colleagues already – with Anna, of course, but also the director of the paperback imprint, Juliet Burrows, with the sales director of the division, the marketing people (all men), the publicity team (all young women) – and talked it up, making sure to tick all the necessary boxes instead of actually talking about the literary and, to his mind, quietly explosive qualities of the book. So he had discussed the collection in terms of comparison titles ('as thunderclap of a debut as *White Teeth* or *Conversations with Friends*'; he had really wanted to say *Lantern Lecture* or *Counternarratives* but he knew that he had to hit topical, buzzy books that were being talked about right now, for ten or even five years earlier risked blank looks), talked up projected sales figures ('I think we could be looking at a best-seller like *Queenie* or *You Know You Want This*'; the collection was light years away from those reference points in every imaginable way). Later today there would be the usual cavils about short stories, the usual deliberate confusion between what sells and what is a good book.

There are five other books presented at the meeting by other editors before it's Ayush's turn. One book, by a 'mid-list' American writer, is turned down because 'there really is no place for yet another quiet, beautifully written literary novel'. An Israeli writer, whose first three books in transla-tion they have published, has his fourth declined because the sales record is poor. Everyone has done his or her homework in the only domain that matters here: sales figures of past books. No mention of reviews, no mention of prizes, which, admittedly, have negligible traction on sales apart from one or two brands, no mention of reputation, the meaning of the work (this would be embarrassing to bring up), or anything that cannot be monetized (Luke would have loved publishing). Two non-fiction debuts are given the green light with almost indecent eagerness – one, a book on new motherhood, another on why the author made the 'life-choice' of not becoming a mother. Both by white women, Ayush notes; reproduction is clearly hot. The book on volitional non-motherhood is based on a blog, the commissioning editor says, and its growing popularity among younger millennials, attested by the author's Twitter following, should assure high sales. There are the usual formulae to talk about books: 'Come for *The Handmaid's Tale*, stay for *Bridget Jones* by way of *Derry Girls*', 'Kafka meets *Fleabag* meets anti Female Genital Mutilation social activism', etc. Some of these references pass over his head – *Derry Girls*? *Fleabag*? Such a fever of excitement, such hopes of having caught the zeitgeist by its throat. As he tries to dress the words inside him to demur in a way that would appear seemly at a meeting, someone else, someone junior, has the foolhardiness to murmur something, which Anna cuts short with her tart 'High-minded books won't butter any parsnips.' He feels that she is speaking pointedly to him. Economics is life, life is economics. Several years ago, during the company's Christmas lunch, Anna, after a couple of glasses of prosecco, had observed, 'We just throw things at the wall and see what sticks. This isn't a science.' She thought she had been making a joke.

When Ayush's turn comes, he leans forward and speaks of his book as the future of British publishing, the voice of a new demographic, diverse (the buzzy term used to be 'multi-cultural' when he had started out all those years ago), a voice as at ease with hip-hop and Brooklyn drill as with Dickens, a new voice, he repeats, 'looking back to *White Teeth* in its vibrancy and to *Ghostwritten* and *Cloud Atlas* in the way discrete, disparate narratives come together cleverly to make a unified whole that we call a novel', 'a big-L literary work that is also a big-P page-turner' – in moments of extreme despair, he has always fantasized about selling the last free corners of his soul and joining an ad agency – and it would be a terrible missed opportunity to let this book, 'so of its moment and so timeless at the same, erm, time', go to another publisher. If self-loathing had material form, like vomit, he would be an abundant fountain now.

'Is there other interest? Are there any offers already?' This from Juliet Burrows, Head of Paperbacks. Of course. No industry is run more by herd behaviour than publishing: we want this book because others want this book, so there must be something in it, but we are not capable of discerning first, we'll take cues from others. Would Luke have called this a signalling game? Two years ago, a novel Ayush had acquired for a substantial sum, a book everyone had been impressed with, had had its marketing budget reduced to nothing, effectively killing it, when the chief fiction buyer of the biggest bookshop chain had decided not to 'get behind it'. Whereas before, it was a book everyone had 'believed in', or said they had, it became, overnight, something like a leper who had walked in from the gutters and stationed himself in the middle of the office: everyone felt embarrassed, full of pity and aversion, and walked in a wide radius around the leper, refusing to acknowledge his presence.

Ayush is prepared for Juliet's question. He lies without the barest flicker: 'I think Jessica said there was strong interest from' – he reels off three names – 'but no offers on the table yet. I'd like to try a modest pre-empt.'

There is talk of upper limits and caps. The sales director tweaks the P&L to make it work. Just; Ayush will have to buy it cheap.

Ayush runs out of the meeting to go to the toilets, shuts himself in a cubicle, and throws up. Afterwards, he spends twelve minutes scrupulously wiping, first, the top-edge of the toilet bowl, the seat, the seat cover, then, worrying that some of that acidy toast-mulch must have sploshed outside, the floor, in circles of increasing radius around the squat stand of the toilet bowl. Then he thinks of the Edgar Allan Poe story, with the murderer wiping every surface at the scene of crime until the police break down the doors in the morning to find that everything has been polished to a gleaming high sheen, and stops.

3.

All night, he lies awake. At 3 a.m., he gets out of bed and puts the tube-squeezers that arrived in the post yesterday on their three-quarters-finished tube of toothpaste and on the children's strawberry-flavoured one. Then he has an idea and clamps one on to the tube of tomato purée in the fridge and feels a tiny squiggle of satisfaction run through him, over before it can be savoured. Then he has another idea. He takes the largest mixing bowl (4.8 litres), puts it under the shower, and turns on the timer on his phone and the shower simultaneously. While the bowl is filling, he runs down to the kitchen to fetch a pencil and a small pad. He notes down the time it takes to fill the bowl and turns off the shower. Now he has a problem – what to do with the 4.8 litres of water? Tipping it down the plug hole of the bath is unthinkable. The cistern is full (although less full than it would normally be because he has put bricks, wrapped in the plastic bag that Thames Water had sent, in each cistern in the house). Wait, he knows. He comes downstairs with the full mixing bowl, careful not to spill, and goes into the kitchen. Spencer has followed him; he looks up at Ayush curiously, wondering at this change in routine, wondering if there's a nice surprise in store – an unexpected exploration of the night garden or something culminating in a chase and a treat. Ayush says, 'Shhh, we're not going out. You stay here, OK?

Stay. Sit.' Spencer obeys. Ayush sets down the bowl on the countertop, unlocks the garden door, turns back, lifts the bowl, takes it outside, empties it into one of the two water butts, and returns to the kitchen, very quietly shutting the door behind him but not locking it this time. Spencer is consumed by curiosity – the smells of the outside have flowed in – but also content to sit where he has been told. Something is afoot; he'll find out in time.

Ayush repeats all his actions, from the collecting and timing of water to disposing of it in the garden. His pad fills up with figures in two columns: time and volume. He lets Spencer out for a wee, then worries that this one-off toilet break will confuse him. 'Come in, now, come in,' he whispers, 'back to bed, sweetheart. Bed. Come on.'

Then he goes to his study and begins the calculations and research.

By the time Jessica reports back, four months have passed, Ayush has formally acquired the book, and even the contract has been executed, not something that happens quickly. 'I emailed to ask Opie for a phone number,' she says. 'He wrote back a very polite but firm note to say that he'd like all communication to be via email. I even asked about preferred pronouns, but that point was not addressed. I don't know how to put this, but there was a wall somewhere in the email – it gives off a thus-far-no-farther vibe. I'll forward it to you now.' Ayush knows exactly why she is treading a fine line between feeling troubled and trying to appear to be breezy and unconcerned.

'But what about publicity, when the time comes?' Ayush almost wails. 'I might get into trouble if I agree to this now. We aren't getting ourselves into a JT LeRoy kind of thing, are we? Although, if this is a Ferrante kind of situation, we may get lucky.' He finds himself walking her fine balance too and hates himself for letting *This could be a gift, a new kind of publicity* flit through his head.

'What's his or her name?' he asks instead, tamping down his polluted thoughts.

'Oh. M.N. In fact, another thing he made very clear in his email was that he preferred to be called M.N.'

'But what do M and N stand for?'

'He didn't clarify. He signed off "M.N."'

Ayush had already looked online, muttering, MNOpie, MNOpie, MNOpie. Nothing. A Catherine Opie in the US. *Did you mean Julian Opie? The search results show* ... etc. Then he had laughed. Of course. He doesn't mention any of this to Jessica now. Let it be his sort-of secret.

4.

It's a Wednesday, so Luke's turn to cook supper. Ayush always returns home early on Wednesdays to do the task of what he thinks of as pre-emptive damage control. He has had calculated by an amateur science blogger the difference in energy consumption between boiling water for pasta in a big pot on the hob and boiling several kettles for the same amount of water: kettle is greener. Ayush has measured out the pasta in a bowl and the exact amount of water to be boiled, the first of four batches, in the kettle. Left to his own devices, Luke would have set their biggest pot of water to boil, drained it all after the children's pasta was cooked, then repeated the same actions for his and Ayush's meal later – a scenario that keeps Ayush awake at night. Luke gives them sausages, diced into bite-size portions, and plain pasta with a curl of butter on top, and some petits pois (boiled in the same water after the pasta has been lifted out with a large-slotted spoon, not drained, since that water will be reused for the adults' pasta). In Sasha's case, the peas, sausages, and pasta are all served on separate plates since he does not like different foods to touch each other.

Spencer is under the table, as always, hoping for scraps. The children have refused to heed their parents' repeated pleas and threats not to feed him. It's a war that Ayush and Luke have lost, not with many misgivings.

Sasha pushes his plate of sausages away, taking great care not to make his fork touch the meat. 'I'm not hungry,' he announces.

Masha chimes in, imitating her brother, as she does in all things. 'I don't want this, I'm not hungry,' she declares.

'What's up?' Luke says. 'You love sausages. Do you want ketchup on it?'

They shake their heads in unison, toy with their pasta, then begin to exhibit the usual crankiness that comes with exhaustion. Later, Ayush will think that he was not paying any attention to what was really passing between them, so he is shocked, more by the speed at which the act is executed than by the act itself, when Sasha lifts the plate of diced sausages and tips it under the table. Spencer wolfs it down snufflingly before Luke and Ayush can react. When Ayush looks under the table, Spencer is looking up at the children's feet, his tongue out, gratitude and greed melting his eyes.

Luke, who never gets angry with the children, is puzzled first, at the swiftness with which things have happened, then irritated with the way he's been taken in. 'Why did you do that? Tell me, why?' He's trying to work himself up into a fury.

'He is canny-vor-es, he eats meat because he doesn't have a choice,' Masha says, looking unblinkingly at Ayush's face.

Ayush turns away, pours himself a glass of the mouth-puckeringly sour wine that Luke calls 'bone dry' and seems to like so much, and returns to washing broccoli, chopping garlic and chillies.

Luke still doesn't understand what's going on – he is like an actor who has been thrust onto the stage without having been allowed to see the script. 'How many times have I told you that you're not to feed Spencer? How many times? Do you understand that it's bad for him? Would you like him to get heart disease and die? Would you like him to get fat and ill and suffer and die? Would you? Answer me.'

The children look as if they're paying careful attention to each of his questions, which he delivers in a tone of calm reason, not anger.

'Fine, you'll go to bed without supper in that case,' Luke says, failing to enter into anger and inhabiting, by his characteristic default, especially with the twins, a reasoned gentleness instead. Ayush marvels silently.

'Bath time now,' Luke says, and chivvies them up to the bathroom.

By the time Luke comes downstairs into the kitchen, his bath-time and bedtime-reading duties behind him, he looks like a cartoon depiction of bafflement, his brows furrowed, his normally clear blue eyes clouded. 'What did you do with them?' he asks. 'They refuse to continue with *Charlotte's Web*.'

'What do you mean?' Ayush grates generous amounts of pecorino onto their bowls of steaming pasta with white-hot attentiveness so that not a single wisp of cheese falls on to the table. Let there be a hundred more years of a better, a healing world, if the tabletop remains untouched by a single particle of cheese. He will go blind with concentrating.

'They don't want to hear a story about a pig who will be made into sausage. I couldn't convince them that he is saved.'

Ayush makes some vague, non-committal tsks. He can tell that the children haven't said anything of consequence to Luke, but he knows that it's going to come in slow degrees. Now, Luke makes half a joke out of it: 'If the kids turn vegetarian, you are dealing with their meals.'

Ayush says nothing. In the space of that silence, Luke works something out. 'Wait,' he says, 'are you behind all this?'

'What do you mean?' Ayush repeats.

'Are you indoctrinating the kids?'

Ayush takes a deep breath; if it has to be done, why not begin now. 'I wouldn't call it indoctrination. I think we should teach them about choices and their consequences. Certainly about things that don't appear to be choices, things that are given to us as natural, things we fall into with such ease, such as what we eat, what we are trained to eat. I'd like them to question the so-called naturalness of that.'

Luke is silent for a while, assimilating. Then he says, 'Sure. But it can't become costly for us.'

In their twenty-odd years of being together, Ayush knows 'costly' is the econ-speak for not just the literal meaning of the word, but also for anything that is inconvenient. According to Luke, people simply won't do things, or at least not in any sustained way that would make a difference, if you make it difficult or inconvenient, i.e. costly, for them.

'There are more important things than convenience. If we all thought a little bit less about convenience, not a whole lot, god knows, I'm not asking for much, if we gave up just a tiny bit of our convenience, then maybe we wouldn't be in the state that we're in now.'

'Whoa, whoa,' begins Luke.

Thank god, he hadn't said, *What state are we in?* Ayush thinks. 'Most of us can agree on something,' he says, '– the badness of eating meat or Facebook – but why are we unwilling to pay the private cost of giving those up? Why has the responsibility for action been shifted to the never-arriving public policy or, in your thinking, market solutions to make that large change? Where has the idea of individual agency gone?'

'Because individual actions are low yield. Policing how much loo roll you use, going on marches, these things achieve nothing. The change needs to be on a different scale.'

'You think American Civil Rights protests, for example, were low yield? Market solutions brought about the end of that discrimination, at least on paper?'

Luke hesitates. Ayush notices the gap and rushes to fill it in: 'We are all so willing to follow the "no pain, no gain" dictum when it comes to improving our bodies, looking good, about all things feeding our general narcissism. What about "no pain, no gain" for the weightier matters?'

You must change your life.

'The end of that line of thinking is good old socialism – everyone should have enough; if you have more, we'll take it away and give it to others who have less.'

'You've made several leaps, but I cannot see a moral argument against that principle.'

'But a scientific argument there certainly is – there is no evidence to support your system.'

Again, Ayush has learned, over time, that this is a gussied-up way of saying that the arc of human nature bends towards capitalism and its foundational principle of 'everybody wants to have more'. But 'human nature' is a term that's unsalvage-able, and in any case too fuzzy, too humanities-inflected, for economists, so they hide behind the more sciencey-sounding 'evidence'. Evidence from where? What experiments or data or observation? How many people? How many experiments over time? In every country in the world or just the USA, the one country that has become the standard, especially in Luke's discipline, from which everything about human nature is extrapolated? What *is* evidence? Isn't it always already selective? They have clashed on these matters numberless times, and every single time Luke has pointed to socialism's bloody history to clinch his argument, or rather, the argument he thinks Ayush will understand. It's straying there again, the conflict of economic systems, the insistence that capitalism is science, not an ideology with its own very special, and unfolding, history of blood. Ayush, too tired to retread those paths, just says, 'But greed isn't turning out to have such a great history, is it? Besides, resources are finite – how long are we going to sleepwalk through life like this? Where has all your tribe's fetishization of growth got us? And anyway, who's talking about socialism?'

'Not again, Ayush, not bloody again. Bleeding. Heart. Liberalism. May I remind you that the foundation of our discipline is to work out the allocation of resources, which we know to be finite.'

'May I remind you who used the word "costly" a few minutes ago? I have to take Spencer out.'

That whooshing silence in his ears again. Ayush does not remember its origins, nor whether it began with the sound, as he hears it now, or with the accompanying image, which crosses his mind's eye when the sound begins. A spherical cosmic body on fire, hurtling through the blackness of space, like a burning coal thrown against a pitch-dark background. The soundtrack, perhaps simultaneous with the image, is a simulation of what that ignited hurtle might sound like, what Ayush imagines it might sound like – like a whispering, a low susurration, a sighing of breeze, with the barest hint of a crackling here and there, almost imperceptible. Is that really what burning sounds like or is it an imagined stylization of the real thing? An approximation which is touched up and tweaked to seem real? Everything is approximation. This is the silence he hears in his ears, so different from the real silence of the world, which is not the absence of sound at all, but just a momentary stilling of the foreground while planes, buses, cars, people, pigeons, sparrows, dogs, children, construction, all with their specific sounds, carry on in the background.

Outside, in Crocus Park, Spencer and Ayush walk the perimeter of the pond, then Ayush begins to feel confined, and they head towards Herne Hill. The traffic is minimal on Half Moon Lane at this time of night: only one number 37, with its overlit interior. Spencer is surprised and overjoyed; this is going to be a real walk, longer than his usual final toilet break, a curtailed, half-hearted thing, whereas now he can smell the night and its creatures, almost present, shimmering and immediate, behind the undergrowth, not their dying traces in the daytime. Ayush too thinks of the flowers working at night, smelling different, more intense, more liberated, more obscene, somehow, than their polite, corseted daytime selves. There's the enormous spreading pillar of the jasmine adjacent to the front door of number 41, which it seems to want to devour. The little bells in the small but spreading colony of lilies-of-the-valley near the steps leading to the door are now brown and over. The honeysuckle is out on the low front wall of number 43. Like Spencer, he wants to push his head into everything – even the foxgloves and geraniums and cistuses seem to smell, or want to smell, if he could only just shake off his human form and lower his head and nose into them. In the last available light, the sky is a shade of the ink his father used to call royal blue. Ayush can make out the briefest flitter of a bat across the jagged-edged canvas of that blue strung out between the dipped roofline and the fractals of treetops before it disappears into the orange flare of the streetlamp. The flowers are working to summon their friends, the big hairy moths and other insects of the night. A whole secret world, invisible to him, to other humans, thank god, a world awake with spinning, weaving, rustling, hiding, killing, devouring, fucking, spitting, marking, secreting, eating, a wild, violent world where, to put on Lukey's hat for a moment, self-interest and unintended benefits and costs are inseparable, suffered or enjoyed asymmetrically, by different parties. Spencer can hear and smell the night's dominion. There he goes, sniffing that low mound of fleabane growing out of a crevice in the boundary wall between 51 and the garage with great, slow intent, then raising his leg and sprinkling it with his piss. What would the moth coming to visit it think? What would it think, what would it think? Pay attention, pay attention, *pay* attention. How funny, that the verb for the only agency we have, the only thing left to us, the act of noticing, should be one of cost, as if you're buying something in exchange. Lukey would be privately smug about it. If Ayush can step on every alternate slab on the footpath and get to the junction of Half Moon Lane with Milkwood, Norwood, and Dulwich Roads and Herne Hill without one false or extra step or break in his stride, then. If he can get to number 153 without a single vehicle going up or coming down the road, then. His breathing ratchets up. For here there is no place that does not see you. You must change your life. If the traffic lights ahead stay green until he hits the front door of the pharmacy, if Spencer doesn't mark the lamp post whose base he's sniffing, if, then, if then. Many years ago, before, before … before what? Anyway, many years ago, Lukey had once tried to explain to him how economists modelled the world, and Ayush still remembers the bit about how any proposition opened up a palette of possibilities – not Lukey's phrasing – and then economists went down a series of *if this, then that*s, proving or disproving them one by one.

When Spencer and Ayush return home, Luke is in the bathroom, cleaning his teeth before getting into bed. He has left the tap running: Ayush can tell because he can hear the boiler in the kitchen humming. He whips out his phone and sets the timer – he'll have to add a handicap, or whatever the term is, for the lost minutes before he entered the kitchen and before the idea to time the hot water struck him, say an extra minute or two – and starts cleaning the kitchen table to take him away, however feebly, from the threshing inside his chest. He wipes down the placemats with a damp dishcloth, sets them against the backs of the chairs to dry, each mat assigned to its own chair, then wipes the kitchen table in great sweeping arcs, equal number of arcs for each quadrant. He waits for the table to dry, then repeats the wiping exactly, the same number of sweeps, which he has counted (seven), for each quadrant. The boiler stops its music. He leaps to his phone: 2 minutes 38 seconds. Plus two (handicap or reverse-handicap?): 4 minutes 38 seconds.

Luke calls out, 'Oh, I didn't hear you come back' – to which Ayush wants to say, to scream, to bellow with all the power in his lungs, 'Because you've had the fucking tap running for nearly five minutes', but concentrates on arranging the table – as he comes into the kitchen to find Ayush measuring the distance between each placemat with a plastic ruler so that they are equidistant from each other and in perfect symmetry.

'Are the children asleep?' Ayush asks in his calmest voice.

Instead of answering, Luke turns back to go upstairs, then thinks twice before re-entering the kitchen. He comes very close to Ayush, reaches out his right hand, and very gently brings it to rest on Ayush's hand that is holding the ruler. Ayush can smell Luke's toothpaste.

'Please,' Luke whispers. 'Please. Can I help you stop this? It's easy to get help for this, you know.'

Ayush feels too tired to fight back.

'I've read up about it. It's one of the things you can actually make better. Trust me. Tell me what I can do.'

Ayush is afraid of uttering a single word.

'And,' here Luke pauses, 'and if there's something underlying, and this is just the expression of that, it's best to find out.'

That 'underlying' brings Ayush out of his enclosedness. Inside, his bitterness wells up into a very brief laugh, almost a snort. Something underlying, yes. He hears Luke saying, 'If you're unhappy at work, you can look for some other job. I want to help you. Please tell me how I can help you.'

The only way Ayush can stop Luke going on is to lean into him and let himself be enfolded.

5.

The day starts with a spreadsheet called 'Daily Figs': not the fruit, but numbers, figures. Economics is life, life is economics. A meeting to review Q2 sales figures, then straight to a meeting about metadata. Half an hour in between meetings to look at 231 emails. A meeting about sales-rep streamlining in spotty markets. Emails (this time about half of them between colleagues two desks, or one floor, or eight desks four metres two right angles away). Divisional targeted ads rationalization meeting. He thinks he has perfected clenched-jaw-shut-mouth-flared-nostrils yawns to a degree that no one will notice that he's suppressing them. (During the Zoom Era, he had caught himself stifling a yawn on his square of the screen, and it had looked so obvious that he set himself daily practice sessions to perfect it.) Emails (including from two authors asking for their sales figs, which they could find on the company website's 'Author Portal' it had taken seven meetings within four hierarchies to design, and yet, now, Ayush needs to send a memo to ask this to be raised at the next Editorial & Publicity meeting to decide to inform all authors upfront so that it doesn't eat into Editorial's time). Meeting with the Production Manager to go through the coming year's books. Jacket meeting to discuss new cover briefs with the team; Ayush never stays for other editors' books, running out as soon as he has finished presenting his own. Meeting to discuss comparative digital revenue advantage over scaled-time sectors. Wow, someone from Editorial asks a question. The answer is a succession of PowerPoint slides with blue, green, pink histograms. A joke about data visualization; everyone laughs in a way that the only salient thing is the sound's lack of energy and sincerity. Emails. Meeting for discounts for volume sales in online distributions. Meeting for distribution optimization in the bookstore chain. Recently, unconscious bias meetings, at which everyone looks at the floor, their inner selves caught up in a frenzy of eye-rolling, and Ayush feels a strange sensation, both superiority and a kind of low-stakes paranoia, as he imagines all his white colleagues hating him for the temporary edge his brown skin gives him at these meetings. Publicity meeting about emerging social media platform targeting. A different stripe of herd behaviour obtains here. Publicists work hard for authors who are already successful, well known; in fact, the more famous an author is, the more publicists work for them, the more attention these writers get, the more famous they become, in a nice, cosy circular feedback loop. Ayush had once dared to ask, in the years when his star was in the ascendant at Sewer, whether it wouldn't be more equitable to redistribute publicity budgets. While everyone had instantly and in unison, as if directed by a choreographer's cue, looked at their papers on the table, trying to find the meaning of life in them, Anna had declared, staring at the whiteboard with a kind of truculent energy, 'We are talking about taking things to another level, not throwing good money after bad.'

Another level – that has stayed with Ayush. His work life has been an education in a recalcitrant knowledge: that publishers and authors are separated by an insuperable line. How can butchers and pigs be on the same side? As Lukey would have put it, 'The interests of the two groups are not aligned.'

Many people loathe the jobs they have. Some go through with it thinking of the paycheque at the end of the month and all that they stand to lose without the money. Some go a step farther and delude themselves by learning to love the job, or certainly to perform a kind of love, becoming zealously supportive of the industry they are in, giving no sign or murmur of dissent or criticism, certainly not to those on the outside. Then there's him, at war with wherever or in whatever he finds himself, never settling, or settling down, with what is given. Shouldn't existence be a quarrel with all that could be better but isn't? But what does it mean to not belong to your own side, to be at perpetual war with them, to remain perpetually on the outside? For him, it's the only way to be, and the costs, as Lukey would put it, are enormous.

Meeting to discuss meetings about meetings. The real work, the work that Ayush had thought, years ago, he was getting into, the work of reading and editing, the work of ideas, of conversation – that work is no longer within work hours; it is part of his non-work life, which old-school Marxists, with what looks now like touching naïveté, used to call 'leisure'.

Ayush is getting the children ready for school. Nothing is straightforward, least of all time.

He has put Cheerios into their bowls and two mugs of chocolate milk on the side before they've sat down at the table. Sasha tries to pour milk into his bowl, misses, and sploshes a generous amount on the table. It creeps and begins to drip down to the floor. He tries to move his bowl and spills half his cereal in the process, some of which lands in the milk on the table. Ayush goes down on his knees to wipe up the spill on the floor but Spencer takes care of it.

'May I have sugar on my Cheerios, please, Baba?' Masha asks.

'Try it without, you like it,' Ayush says.

'I want sugar,' she says.

'I want sugar on mine too,' Sasha follows.

'What about a banana, sliced into rings? So you'll have the big banana rings, fewer in number, attacking the army of small Cheerios, which are greater in number. Then you can decide who will win.'

'How?'

'Whichever gets eaten first wins,' Ayush extemporizes.

They nod but lose interest after the first couple of mouthfuls.

'Can I have sugar on mine, please?' Sasha says.

'No. Finish it without the sugar.'

'May I have toast then?' Masha demands.

'Finish your cereal first.'

'I don't want cereal, I want toast.' Sasha instantly piggybacks on the demand.

Ayush takes in the half-eaten banana, its peel already blackening, the blue bowls, with a painted yellow hedgehog, now drowned under milk and soggy cereal, in their centre, the small off-white puddle on the table, and suddenly remembers that his tea has been steeping for nearly fifteen minutes now. He removes the infuser, pours the tea from the pot into a mug so that it is half-full, tops it up with water from the kettle, then microwaves it for thirty seconds, watching the timer-clock count down from 00:30 to 00:00. There are five beeps. He takes it out, stirs, pours in a splash of milk, stirs briefly again, then says, very slowly and clearly, 'What would you like your toast with?'

'Egg, egg,' says Masha. 'I want toast soldiers to dip into the yellow of the egg.'

'Jam,' says the boy.

Ayush waits for one of them to change her or his mind. 'Are you sure, both of you?'

They nod.

'I'll give you two more minutes in case you want to change your mind, OK?' His breathing is even.

He puts a saucepan with water to boil, takes out an egg, butter, strawberry jam, egg cup, more cutlery, plates for the toast, thinking about and concentrating on each object in turn, almost letting himself flow into each of the things. This act can save him, if only temporarily. He can hear Sasha saying, 'If I put strawberry jam in your egg and you mix it, it will be yellow and red,' and Masha responding, 'Eww, jam and egg cannot be mixed.' Very soon it enters the usual scratched-LP mode of 'Yes, it can'/'No, it can't'. Ayush will have to look at the time when he sets the timer for the egg. He thinks of the story his father used to tell him when he was a child: when his father was a boy in Calcutta, he was made to stand outside the principal's office for an hour if he was late for school, as punishment; a mild form of public shaming, and a very effective one, his father had added. Chronic, repeated lateness would involve incremental disciplining, summoning of the parents, even culmination in a short suspension from school.

'Baba, Baba, can you eat egg and jam mixed together?' Masha appeals to him for arbitration.

'I wouldn't do it,' he answers, putting two slices of bread into the toaster. The water comes to a boil. He sets the timer on his phone for five minutes and gently drops the egg in. He turns around to see Sasha pouring orange juice into his cereal bowl. Masha watches with equal parts thrill and fear that make up the territory of vicarious transgression. Part of the juice slops outside the bowl. The toast pops up. Ayush turns back, butters both slices, cuts one into soldiers, and spreads the other with strawberry jam, puts it on a plate, and places it in front of Sasha.

'What does one say?'

'Thank you, Baba.'

Luke comes into the kitchen, dripping water, towel wrapped around his middle, cursing. 'The bloody shower's stopped working. The water's just stopped.'

The children look at each other, delighted shock on their faces.

Luke opens the door to the boiler cupboard and fiddles for a bit. 'Can't see anything wrong here.' He goes to the sink and turns on the hot tap. It emits an untroubled flow of water. 'What's going on? This is working. Oh, fucking –' then bites his tongue.

'Daddy swore, Daddy swore!' the twins sing out, unable to hold back any longer.

The timer goes. Ayush lifts out the egg, puts it in an egg cup, cracks the top, and slices it off. He places the toast soldiers and egg in front of Masha.

'I'm sorry. Please forget the word. Don't use it. Ayush, what's going on with the shower, do you know? Has it happened to you? Can you call someone to come have a look?' Saying this, he runs upstairs to get dressed.

'Daddy, you swore, you said bloody, you said the f-word.' Masha, beside herself with joy, shouts at his fleeing back. She gesticulates with her arms and sends her mug of chocolate milk flying across the table. Part of it splashes on to Sasha's plate with the nibbled, unfinished slice of toast on it. He cries out immediately, 'It's touched the toast, it's touched the toast', and pushes his plate away. His chin begins to quiver and his mouth to pout, then follows an explosion of a wail. He lifts up his plate and flings it against a cupboard. Before Ayush can get to him and try to calm him down, the boy leans forward on his chair and sweeps his hand across the table, spilling everything within his reach – glasses, cups, salt and pepper cruets. His face is like a tomato on the point of bursting. Ayush cries out,

'Stop it, stop it right now,' but Sasha is firmly locked inside one of his fits. Ayush picks him out of the chair as the boy tries to hit him and scratch his face – there is no restraining him without some damage, so he lets the child down on to the floor, where he lies on his back and screams and screams and screams. It seems to come not just from his throat and lungs but from his navel, from the very centre of his being. Masha sits on her chair, trembling, looking down at her brother, then she begins to whimper too. Spencer is frozen looking at Sasha become someone else.

Luke rushes down the stairs and enters the kitchen. 'My god, what mayhem at this hour,' he says. 'Ayush, what's brought this on? Sash, Sash, darling, now, now, tell me what's wrong and I'll whoosh it away, like magic, sweetheart, just stop crying and tell me, if you can't put it into words, I won't be able to use the magic,' he says, crouching on to the battlefield soil and trying to scoop up his son in his arms. Sasha is not giving an inch; his fists are balled, his arms are bent at his elbows and held tight against him, and the screaming issues out of him as if from an infinite fountain.

The invisible Ayush watches his visible self embedded in the scene from a corner of the kitchen ceiling, as if he's a spider, a camera, a satellite, a god: chrome-yellow dots of congealing egg yolk on the table; the collective-nouns placemats with their realistically depicted watercolour birds (a chime of wrens, a charm of goldfinches, an exaltation of larks); smears of jam; spilled water; a dozen cups and glasses in play, for milk, chocolate milk, water, juice, coffee and tea for the adults; stains on clothes that need to be wiped with a damp cloth; breadcrumbs and grease on countertop and tabletop; the growing pile of washing-up tottering in the sink and outside it; a confluence of the separate streams of chocolate milk, water, and milk on the floor to one side of the table; a child in an unyielding paroxysm; another looking on in despair; a parent trying to mollify.

'OK, looks like it's another of those,' Luke says calmly. 'I'm running late, I need to go. I'm sure it'll settle down in time.' He gives Masha a quick kiss on her head, squeezes Ayush's upper arm, kisses Spencer's ear, and is out of the house.

A non-fiction proposal on submission that contrasts the German reckoning with its twentieth-century crimes with the willed British oblivion about its empire. Not only oblivion, but also a stubborn denialism, Ayush thinks; the pages seem to read his mind and, in a blistering section, go on to address the history of this denial with rigorous details and evidence. Where the book becomes urgent, urgent enough to want to publish it, is in its explanation for the British phenomenon: the crimes of empire happened elsewhere, far away from home soil. *Foreign* people were oppressed, killed, ruined, not its own, like in Germany. A small plaque with a name engraved on it on the pavement outside a house in Berlin from which the named family was taken and sent off to be gassed in Buchenwald or Dachau has one kind of impact, especially cumulatively, when those tiny plaques, once seen, become unignorable and proliferate like daisies in the grass in springtime. A plaque outside a house in Murree in Pakistan that says 'Here was born Reginald Dyer, the Butcher of Amritsar', or one on a building in Berkeley Square in London, noting 'Here lived Lord Robert Clive, leader of the pack responsible, through their looting, plundering, and tax policies, for the Bengal Famine from 1769 to 1773, which wiped out a third of the population', would have a different kind of ring, if any at all. The very soil of Germany is bloody. The ghosts of empire are far away; the British need never see nor hear them; the land of Great Britain is clean, unhaunted. The bad things are for other people, far away, in different countries – India, Kenya, Malaysia, Palestine – to deal with.

A quick search reveals that the writer, Claudia Pilikian, is white. This strengthens his hand in the acquisitions meeting: it means that newspapers and magazines will be interested in running think pieces on the topic from her. Had the writer been brown or black, they would turn down the publicity team's pitches, because a) they are not interested in yet another writer of colour being angry, and b) they think writers of colour are good for adding, well, colour, with immigration stories, family suffering, family sagas, colourful cultural stuff, but not for contributing to intellectual history, or theories of practices which are the domain of white people, or even their property. Ayush had had this experience a few years ago when he published a smart novel by a Sri Lankan writer. The publicist got nowhere pitching pieces to the liberal and halfway-intelligent sectors of the press. The essays were on topics he would have thought were exactly the kind of thing they ran on a weekly basis in their books pages: an article on the European models behind the novel (impossible for white publications and their reviewers to see in a Sri Lankan work unless spelled out for them); an essay on Guy Debord and the ways the subcontinent torques the aspiration of life to the condition of the spectacle; a piece on Michel de Certeau and the legitimization of a certain kind of political power in the writing of history. Not only were they all declined, but the literary editor – a white woman – had got in touch with the publicist to ask if the Sri Lankan author would consider writing a piece on his country's food, which had become, with the success of Hoppers, so popular this year. Meanwhile, Ayush noted, its pages gave up not its usual one but a full double-spread to a white author – published by Thomas Cotton, Sewer's sibling imprint – for a trailer-essay explaining the theoretical inspirations (data,

Derrida, Baudrillard, Deleuze) behind his new novel. A lefty newspaper, of course; the enemy, as always, is within. The job of gatekeeper is perhaps the only job in which there is the biggest gap between talent and power. But that was then. Now, enough black people had been murdered by the police in the US for these good white people, who think of themselves as the good, the best, to hang on to the coat-tails of a newly imagined civil rights movement in a country they genuflected to on all matters and signal 'Look, we're progressive, we're forward-thinking, we're with the oppressed and the downtrodden. Look how good we are, look, how right.' It requires them to change nothing, do nothing, except the thing they have always been extremely good at: signalling. But mask is one thing, and the skin it cleaves to, not too tightly, is another matter: the chances are favourable that Claudia Pilikian could be got through the gates these trustworthy people guarded. He also thinks that he is beginning a trend. Brown and black writers are readily cor-ralled into the pen marked 'Colonialism' from where they can shout and bleat but they are safely and effectively contained there, a demarcated space that will not contaminate any place else so that they can be easily ignored and everyone else can carry on with business as usual. For the British to pay atten-tion to colonialism, white writers needed to tackle the subject. Maybe Claudia Pilikian could be a beginning.

Ayush is sitting opposite one of his authors – *A History of White Condescension* – and hoping that the time has come to ask her the question he always asks when he thinks their guard is down or they are relaxed or trusting enough to give him a halfway authentic, true, from-the-guts-and-soul answer.

'Why do you write?'

Shocking him, she is saying, 'You must know this – I wrote a novel a few years ago, set in my home country, Bangladesh, and about its seemingly incurable diseases. All the social ills stuff. They – the lefty newspaper, of course; the enemy, as always, is within – got the same white professor who was fucking me in creative writing school all those years ago to review it. So quintessentially English, no? Incidentally, also the newspaper that was going to jump most assiduously on to the #MeToo bandwagon a few years down the line. I was his student; apparently, it was a habit with him, a new student each year. And this Dead White Male – well, he's all but physically dead, nobody reads him, he's forgotten in his own lifetime – put the boot in. Dickens was the closest thing the DWM could come to because, you know, if you're writing about social injustice, the model *must* be Dickens for us because the last hundred years haven't happened to us brown people. Nothing has changed for these gatekeepers and chatterers – they're still embalmed in vindictiveness and the sense of entitlement, keeping their busy cottage industry of rewarding white mediocrity churning away: laureateship, knighthood, chairing of headline prizes. Again, so English, no?'

She takes a gentle sip of her Pinot Grigio, in absolute counterpoint to the contents of her speech, and continues, 'I write to let them know that I'm not going away.'

She is breathless and her eyes are flashing and any moment the stem of the wine glass that she is holding is going to break. Ayush is riding a wave of pure, electric exhilaration.

Of course, none of this happens. He imagines the scene, as he does several such conversations with his authors. It always begins with the same question: 'Why do you write?'

6.

All five of them are going for a long walk in Epping Forest. Ayush sells the idea to the twins in a different way from the usual 'we're going for a picnic' story: 'There are huge trees there,' he says. 'They're all hundreds of years old, can you imagine that?'

'Are you hundreds of years old? I am five, I will be six on the thirteenth of October,' says Sasha.

'I will too,' the boy pipes up.

'No, I'm not hundreds of years old,' Ayush says, helping them get dressed, put their shoes on, fill their water bottles. 'Human beings don't live for so long. But trees do. Think about it – they stay still in one spot for hundreds and hundreds of years. Standing still. And they look over everything, they see everything – the forest floor, their neighbours and friends, which are other trees, all as old as each other. They talk to each other through a network of fungi, which are something like mushrooms that grow under the ground and connect all of them.'

'Do the mushrooms talk?' Masha asks.

'Not in the way we do. But they have their own language, their own system of signals.'

'Can we hear them talk?' she asks.

Their curiosity has now been aroused.

'No, you can't. Their conversations are not made of sounds. I'll say more in the car. Daddy's waiting.'

As they are making their way through Bethnal Green, then Bromley-by-Bow, Luke asks, 'Ayush, what's up with the shower? And the effing' – the last word in a sort of undertone – 'lights yesterday evening. They kept going phut in the living room, the bathroom, while I was reading to the children. Basically, every room I was in. I tried replacing the one in the kids' room, no joy. All this home stuff needs seeing to.'

Outside, a series of cash-and-carries, grim 1930s houses with sooty fronts, an Art Deco apartment complex, a Victorian terrace interrupted by a fried-chicken place, a Tesco Express, a petrol station, another small string of shops. There was once a forest in Waltham; no longer, but the name has stuck. Like Lavender Hill, Saffron Walden. Ayush shuts his eyes and opens them again. The world has not disappeared. He seems to be squarely in it. He says, 'The passive voice. All this home stuff needs seeing to. You actually want to say, Why don't *you* see to the home stuff? Well, go on then, say it.'

'Eh?' Luke hasn't been quick enough to follow where Ayush has gone.

'Say it, say: Ayush, can you sort out the home stuff? Please? Thank you.'

'You're getting into one of your moods. Careful, the children are with us.'

'Say it, Lukey, say: I have the more important job, the better-paid job, the job that's saving the world every day, so it's your job to do the menial domestic stuff.'

'Well, if you insist on putting it that way, it's only efficient.'

Ayush cannot tell from Luke's tone if he's taking the piss, deliberately needling him, with the red-rag 'efficient', or whether it's his idea of a joke to defuse the situation.

'Efficient,' Ayush repeats. 'Efficient. Of course.'

'You got rid of the nanny against my wishes when we all had to work from home, but never asked her to come back when everything returned to normal. I've still not understood why you did that. It's not as if we couldn't afford her.'

Ayush notes the slide between 'you' and 'we'.

Luke continues, 'If we still had her, maybe things wouldn't seem too much to you. You just wanted to make life difficult for yourself.'

Ayush has got his teeth and jaws into efficiency and he won't let go. How quickly everything that begins as an innocent discussion, a basic human need to talk, exchange information, use the facility of language to deepen and enrich social bonds, becomes a conflagration, bringing down the roof and the walls. 'Yes, my job is not grand, I won't dispute it. I don't go about life thinking what I do is important. But, maybe, just maybe, in my whole working lifetime, I'll publish one book, or two, that's going to be read in fifty, or a hundred, years' time. But you, Lukey? You'll co-author a hundred, two hundred papers, each of which is going to contribute to making fancier, cuter models of maintaining the status quo.'

He knows he's lying – nobody knows better than he that publishing hides behind the myth of the nobility and indispensability of literature to conduct what is ultimately business. They could be selling something, anything, else: coffee, bras, iron filings, cupcakes. The business model is at its heart, as it is at the heart of everything in life, everywhere where humans are, everything that they have touched. Not a nation of shopkeepers but a planet of shopkeepers. Where did we take the wrong turning in history that made us put that as the central ruling principle, its soul of meaning, in our lives? And how comfortable, how settled, how at peace we are about it. How unquestioning. Imagine the reckoning at the end of life: *What did you do? – Oh, I ran my life on the business model*. Happiness, well-being, goodness, morals (Goodness! Morals), community, health, summum bonum – all run using sophisticated P&Ls. Didn't we do well? Didn't we prosper and thrive and make our lives and those ours touched enriched and worthwhile? Got us and them where we and they wanted to go, to *be*? And for that, too – the business model, that is – who do we have to thank but Lukey's tribe? 'Dismal', as they were once described by one of their own, seems to be the kindest, most generously affectionate word one could use of them, something their mothers would use. The rest of us need a new vocabulary.

Luke had once said to him, 'You have a real problem with money, you know. You need help.'

Ayush had said, 'No, I don't have a problem with money, I have a problem with the *centrality* of money, its foundational-ness. It has a habit of pushing other, maybe more important, things away. It blinds us, puts blinkers on us.'

Luke asks now, 'What status quo?'

'I had a plumber come and install cut-offs for all the water we use. Also, timers for lights.'

Three side roads off the M11 pass by before Luke spits out, 'What?' It gives Ayush a minor frisson of triumph that, quite apart from the twins' constraining presence, Luke is in the driver's seat and cannot turn to confront him. Their clash will be truncated, in however small a way.

'But why did you do that?' Luke is spluttering. 'Why did you not tell me?'

'Saving energy is the short answer. We use too much. We consume too much. Unthinkingly. As if it all belongs to us. As if it's all infinite.'

'And you think these little choices made by little individuals is the way forward? Defeating climate change by taking bottles to the bottle bank?' His voice is ice-cold, but Ayush knows that the key lies in that second 'little'.

'You'll of course recommend leaving it to the market to sort out, right? As it has everything. While some have laughed all their way to the bank and you've tinkered around with incentives. Well, we're waiting for the market to sort it out.' He keeps his voice steady and pleasant, as if he's talking about a routine gardening task like deadheading the geraniums.

'You're spoiling for a fight, aren't you? I don't know what's going on. The children are in the back seat. I'm driving, I can't do this now, I just can't.' Luke's voice breaks pleadingly over the last three words.

The air in the car has changed. The children are suddenly quiet; in the rear-view mirror, Ayush can see a quality of alertness to their faces. It'll soon become a stricken look. Instead of pulling him back, it drives him forward.

'Your tribe's great sleight of hand,' he continues, 'has been that anything you can't pour into the paradigms and principles of your discipline, you rule out as unimportant or irrelevant or non-existent. The rest is deniable. Indeed, there is no "rest". It's a kind of gaslighting – everything is in the domain of our study; there is no outside outside our discipline. There cannot be anything that we don't or cannot understand.'

'And what do we not understand?'

'Human nature –'

'No, it's *you* who doesn't understand. You're ignorant. You're ignorant of how sophisticated our tools are, of how much we can capture, model ...' Luke is shouting now. The children in the back seat have noticed, Ayush can tell from their frozen faces reflected in the rear-view mirror.

Ayush carries on with the list of shortcomings as if Luke hasn't spoken: 'Power. Morality. The erasure of ideology.'

'What power? What morality? Morality is an arbitrary, bounded-rationality thing –'

Ayush hoots with what he means to be laughter.

45

'You're the worst victim of the humanities I can think of,' Luke shouts to the windscreen. 'All your bullshit about left, right ... What left, what right? We do science, there's no left or right in that.'

'Meaning you do whatever keeps you on the side of the powerful?'

Luke lifts his hands from the steering wheel and brings them down on it hard, twice, his teeth bared. The horn beeps twice in response to the bangs. He shouts, 'Your politics belongs to the high-school debating society. It's puerile, *puerile*.'

The car swerves across one lane of the M11. Irate drivers zoom past blaring their horns in long-held notes of irritation. The children in the back, so far cowed into silence by the display of hostility, now scream, 'Baba! Daddy, Daddy!'

Ayush laughs hysterically. The children are now utterly confused. Spluttering, almost choking with laughter, he says, 'Remember you told me about that professor who you once TA'd for, the one who said, *You have to do math till it hurts*, the one who set up a cottage industry by making it obligatory for the hundreds of students who took the course to buy the textbook that he wrote? Remember? The one to whom all the students had to certify with the barcode of the book that they'd actually bought it, not cadged an older version or borrowed from the library? I suppose grifting is great because you're maximizing your utility, no? If I were the right age, I'd say "lmfao" now.'

Luke, taken aback by this sudden digression, struggles to say, 'How come a matter of private failing demolishes our whole discipline?'

'Because, as an economist, you could have thought about the poor students in your class who could not afford the three-figure price-tag? Because professors shouldn't be making money off their students in side-schemes? Because if I were to confront you with that, you'd bluff me off with some kind of market explanation for why this is, how do you put it, optimal, ah yes, optimal for all parties, or some bullshit about matching or whatever? Because there are no rights or wrongs, only market solutions? Because wrong is only something that you can't get away with?'

There are flecks of his spit on the windshield. The children are beginning to whimper in the back. Spencer licks their faces, then positions himself gingerly down into the well and stretches the length of his body out there. Ayush has noticed this before: whenever he and Luke argued, Spencer left the room, but if the argument was in the children's presence, Spencer, never far from them, took up what Ayush could only call a guard position in front of Masha and Sasha, sometimes laying himself out flat, as if to indicate *You'll have to climb over my body in order to get to them* or to make himself the landing cushion should the children fall from the sofa on which they sat. Watching Spencer take the protective stance now in the car takes Ayush out of himself.

As if a switch has been flicked, Ayush says, 'Oh, look, exit here, Luke, Epping Forest. *Ragazzi*, we're here. Aren't we going to have a fun picnic in the forest?'

Among the great trees, Ayush and Spencer, on his leash, walk several feet ahead of the rest. The chatter of Luke and the children is almost inaudible. Ayush looks back to see Luke kneeling at the base of a giant beech tree with something in his hands, probably some burrs, explaining something to the children, who are listening intently. In an effortful attempt to note something positive about Luke, Ayush thinks: *He knows about beechnuts. Very few economists do. I must not forget that. He knows that beechnuts provide food to deer and pigs. He knows that if a novelist sets a sex scene under a beech tree, that novelist knows very little about nature since the shade under a beech tree is the most uncomfortable place to lie upon because of its carpet of burrs. It's the worst nightmare for the princess in 'The Princess and the Pea'. I must remember that he knows this too.* He swallows hard, once, twice. Spencer keeps turning his head to see if his full pack is following. A biscuit-gold creature, darting, leaping, alive, his tail like a pennant in a Renaissance painting, moving through the still, stationary, alive green. Two different manifestations of time and motion, one visible, one not. The great trees are breathing; Ayush wants to still his heart to hear them.

Spencer sniffs at the great roots, lifts his leg under a hornbeam and marks it, then turns his head to sniff at some undergrowth. He occasionally lets his tongue hang out in a doggy smile. The world is a whole map of smells. He follows them and thinks, Ha, a squirrel has been here, and here there is the faintest trace of a fox, the Upright following him, the leader of his pack, will know it too, but he is lagging behind, looking up, looking ahead, what a strange thing, when the world lies below and under him, on the ground. The other three Uprights of his pack are farther back. Why don't they hurry up? He cannot contain himself: he must run back to round them up.

The trees look down and ahead and in all directions. The hornbeams and ilexes and oaks in this sector of the forest know each other intimately. They look in all directions, feel and see the birds sitting or landing on them, the humans and squirrels and dogs and the dozens of other creatures below flitting by, so quickly that their passage should be imperceptible. Would humans register something that flickers across their senses for the tiniest fraction of a second? The trees' unit of time is so great that the smaller calibrations of time among other living things, the creatures that move through the forest, should mean nothing to them. They think of the seasons, of all the work they need to do, relentlessly, to stay alive and to propagate – the stomata under their leaves opening to let out oxygen; the auxin gathering in the leaves during the autumn and turning them red and yellow; the water going up the xylem, the sucrose going down the phloem to be circulated everywhere. But, wait – do they actually think that? Do human beings think – Here's our heart pumping blood, whooshing out through the ventricles; here it goes down the veins and arteries to carry oxygen to all the tissues and cells and organs? No, they don't. It would make a good children's book to make trees think about their biological processes. Surely, there must be several already? There's moss on their bark and maps of lichen archipelagos. A stand of towering lime trees is perfuming the air. What a strange flower – you stick your nose in the blossom and it hardly smells of anything, but, amassed, they create a cloud of the most astonishing fragrance.

How much longer will they be here? he thinks.

How much longer? Spencer thinks, looking at the woodland stretching in every direction.

How much longer? think the trees.

7.

Who is he? Is it even a he? Is it an implicit bias that Ayush thinks of Opie as a man? How *does* Ayush imagine the author? What is the mental image that forms in his mind's eye when he reads one of his stories? Is that a valid or even empirically correct way to think? When we read a hunting scene in which the actors are two Russian men, Levin and Stepan Arkadyich, a dog, Laska, some roding woodcocks, what do we imagine – the marsh, the streams, the aspen copse, the two men, the dog, the flying birds, or the white-bearded, intense, slightly deranged-looking man who wrote it and whose face we know from a photograph or two? Who has an image of the author in their heads rather than of the imaginary characters when they're reading fiction? Perhaps no one, but what terrible ideas the author photo and the author bio and lit fests and all the attendant shitshow have been. How can you read an author's book after you've heard her speak? Wouldn't that real voice get in the way? Is it a good thing, then, that Opie refuses to show himself, thereby liberating Ayush into a bigger interpretive field where he, the reader, can run and sing and dance and turn somersaults and roll and kick a ball or sit still or lie down or or or? And that mental picture of Opie? It changes from story to story: sometimes it's a black man, sometimes a white woman, at other times a black woman ... an

Indian woman. Academic. Caribbean (woman, no, man, no, woman, again). British Jamaican. White British. British Asian. Migratory bird. Not British at all, just a naturalized Caribbean or Asian. Not naturalized. Immigrant. Guest. Foreigner. Traveller. Temporary leave to remain. Opie is not there; there's no author photo, nothing online, no biographical detail, nothing he will yield, so you're free to picture him however you want: it's a mirror held up to your own face.

Should Ayush put a blue line under 'caliginous gloom'? Certainly ask for more details about London, its ever-morphing sights and smells and sounds, to be scattered throughout the story of the early-modernist academic: 'What does the air smell of here?' and 'What does she see littered on the pavement?' Also: 'acceleration – the simple dynamo of fiction. Think about this?' And then an intuition, perhaps inspired, although there wouldn't be any way of knowing for sure: what if he were to ask Opie to create a sort of diagonal semi-connection – a dotted line rather than a complete line – between the project the academic is contemplating towards the beginning and the newer one that she feels impelled to write about as the story progresses?

8.

The head teacher of the children's school sends an email, requesting a meeting, to both Luke and Ayush. On the appointed day, Mrs Bennell tells the fathers that Marielle and Alexander have been miming being sick over other children's lunchboxes and causing some to become disconcerted by their stories of blood and of animals screaming and dying in pain. 'Ham comes from blood and the pig screams and screams and dies and looks at you.' That is apparently what Alexander had said to one child at lunchtime when she was eating her sandwich.

'Was it a ham sandwich?' Luke asks.

Mrs Bennell carries on as if she hasn't heard. While of course the school warmly welcomes children of widely different backgrounds and cultural practices, indeed it is their mission to be as diverse as possible, it is also their aim, as enshrined in their charter, to instil in the children a spirit of tolerance and understanding, of mutual respect, and she is sure that the fathers, she means parents, of course, parents … Ayush instantly wonders if an outsider can notice, now that the children are growing, their East Asian features, and if this is what made the head teacher stumble, not the gay parenting.

Luke breaks the silence after they have left. Walking down Brixton Hill to the Tube station, he comments, 'That fool. Do they come from central casting? Is this how they're taught to speak in teacher training school?'

Ayush is surprised – he was expecting Luke to reprimand him for putting ideas in the children's heads. Ayush has prepared himself for an argument, which, in line with all their arguments, will move swiftly to the big questions about individual choices and agency, about efficiency and effectiveness and the superiority of market solutions, yadda yadda yadda.

Luke is saying, 'What a waste of fucking time. Do you think she thinks this is the best use of my time? And yours?'

Ayush knows that Luke does not accord their times equal weight, but he says nothing. Equality is a lie. Nothing is, can be, equal, not by any objective definition. All the lies that we live by. Such as Brixton being a poor, edgy place, it occurs to him yet again. The gentrification must have happened when he was not looking. But all these roads off Brixton Hill, with their classical names, their Victorian terraces, are not exactly urban poverty material, have never been. A lettings agency, a bookmaker's, a Nisa Local, then a shop that sells organic chicken, organic rhubarb, upright bundles of asparagus tied with purple silk that oddly look like the fasces on the flag of Mussolini-era Italy, chef's hats of cronuts at £6.50 each. On the other side of the road, the locksmith is still there but flanked by an artisanal pizza place and a hipster coffee shop, which also sells microbrewery beers and ales and has a sentimental-kitsch mural by a bestselling children's author on the outside wall on Arodene Road. A number 159 coming in their direction seems to list towards the pavement; Ayush and Luke instinctively move inwards. The bus stop has a changing display board, which at that moment is advertising a council-sponsored exhibition on the history and contributions of LGBTQ+ people in Lambeth. Then the display shifts, with a whirr-and-click, as they walk by, to a new broadband company's offers. They cross Brixton

Water Lane and walk down the path through Rush Common, the fifty-feet-wide strip of green island between Brixton Hill on the left and the council estates on the right. This long park has always felt like a surprise to Ayush, tucked incongruously between a trafficky road and ugly public housing. In March, the ground is a patchy carpet of violets cleaving tightly to the grass, like purple embroidery on a green scarf, and the unmistakable fragrance, which never fails to remind him, inexplicably, of nail varnish, drifts in and out of existence. Spencer had once rolled amongst the flowers as a puppy, trying to bury his face and straightened-out body in the sunny grass, thinking he was hidden completely from Ayush's view, then leaping out to surprise him: *Looky, looky, I'm here.* His silky golden throat and chest had smelled of violets for a brief second, then the scent had disappeared. Ayush had sat on the ground, sniffing Spencer's chest for another hit of that elusive perfume, but it was gone. And here is another incongruous thing – an urban orchard at the crossing of St Matthew's Road and Brixton Hill, full of giant fountains of silver-grey cardoons, a triffid of a sunflower here and there, small mounds of geraniums, nepeta bushes, tall artichoke plants with their punk heads erupting in tufty violet hair, mallow, salvias, and, miraculously, about a dozen apple trees, enclosed in chunky wooden enclosures, the wood all blackened with time, arranged higgledy-piggledy along two sides of the orchard's perimeter. One apple tree, on the far side, near the wall separating the orchard from the houses, is a Beauty of Bath, Ayush knows. The same variety that Dr Henry Selwyn gave to the narrator and his wife, Clarissa, in the first section of *The Emigrants*. And now M.N. Opie's sad Richard Johnson comes to mind: did he pace this very green, distraught, halfway to being broken, calling for Niggah, with the world swerving away from him in fear and repulsion?

'So, will you, or would you like me to, or shall we both, but at different times?' Luke is saying. They're at the station. Beside the entrance, an incense seller is burning some of his samples – the smell of something artificially floral-chemical hits Ayush's nose. Bang opposite the stall, next to the traffic lights, a man is shouting into a handheld megaphone, 'And I say unto you, ask, and it shall be given; seek, and you shall ...'

'Have you been listening to me at all?' Luke asks, a little piqued.

'What? What? Yes, yes, of course, I will, don't worry about it, your, um, opportunity costs are greater,' Ayush extemporizes, having no idea what Luke is talking about. It is only when he is changing to the Northern Line at Stockwell that he understands that Luke was urging Ayush to talk to the twins. He has no intention of doing that.

Months have passed in trying to get something out of M.N. Opie. Nothing. Polite replies to emails from the publicists, asking for the author questionnaire to be filled in, ending in polite but flat refusal. To Jessica Turner's increasingly firm emails, a reply that ultimately bares its teeth: 'I am afraid I'm beginning to find that these communications are putting a lot of pressure on me. I'm very happy to move my representation elsewhere if these importunate messages do not cease.' After which Jessica can do nothing but let Ayush deal with the matter; she is relieved, he can tell. His own entanglement is more complex, edgier: he does not want heavy air hanging between editor and author before the editorial process is completed, but at the same time he is inwardly thrilled that a writer, a class of people not exactly renowned for their reluctance at being whores, is refusing to play the game, and he does not want to discourage Opie in the stance that he has taken. But this thrill is multifaceted, for Opie's refusal gives

55

Ayush an ally in his own eternal truculence with his professional world: he is forever, always against his own side and for his authors', therefore for Opie's.

The editing process itself is, surprisingly, rewarding. There are real conversations, by email, of course, since Opie won't show himself. For someone who feels that the medium has been a kind of drowning and that the best people can manage on a regular basis, just to keep their heads above water, is to send unsigned, often unpunctuated messages saying 'OK thx' and 'Cc-ing in X, who is leading on this', Ayush finds it easy to modify his habits and treat this exchange as a form of letter-writing. He had begun the process with the usual formal note accompanying an attached Word document containing a list of editorial comments and suggestions: please see this as the beginning of a conversation rather than as prescriptive guidance, etc. It was Opie's careful, considered, expansive, and immensely literary reply that had brought out a long-repressed side of Ayush. All that long academic training before he decided to turn his back on the humanities and enter publishing; he had had to beg Luke to stop saying, 'If you're so unhappy in the publishing world, you should think of reactivating the academic side.' Of the many replies Ayush could have given to this, he had chosen the most minimal, that it was not possible to change one's career more than once, and he had already done it. But editing Opie now, Ayush draws on his distant literary training to respond; soon it becomes an intellectual exchange between friends. A mention of an observation about a Coetzee story leads to a bigger discussion about reference points for fiction: when journalists are busy beating up novels for failing at this or that, surely they must have a reference point for what works and how it works? What about the kind of philosophical fiction to which Coetzee turned in his late career? Could you have long stretches of dialogue that argue out opposing philosophical or moral positions as long as the dialogue is not (as it is not in Coetzee) expository, what they call an 'information dump' in creative writing courses? What if the characters are involved, in a way organic to the story, in such discussions or arguments? *Can ideas be discussed openly as ideas, or do they always need to be disguised under drama and action and emotional development and all that rubbish, like vegetables smuggled into food for children?* Opie writes. Ayush has no meaningful answer to give. Through years of habit of keeping editorial conversations on the level of enter-taining anecdote instead of literary-critical discussion, maybe inserting a comment about how X and Y are just names on the page, not fully-fleshed characters we can believe in, or how the dialogue here says too much, there too little, he now finds himself succumbing to that old anecdotal gravity and telling Opie about the time he, Ayush, accompanied an author to a literature festival at which a very well-dressed novelist – she seems to be known for this – on a panel despaired about what awful hair Penelope Fitzgerald had when the late novelist's name was brought up by a fellow-panellist. That is all that the sartorially dazzling novelist can say, effectively shutting down any literary conversation, because who would want to talk about, or even listen to anyone talking about, books if there can be chit-chat about hair?

Opie and Ayush get down into the weeds about the sequen-tial order the stories should follow in *Yes, The World*. This, more than any other among their numerous exchanges, gives Ayush palpable pleasure, something he experiences, almost physically, as an expansion in his chest. In an industry that secretly hated books and writers, for its captains to describe themselves regularly, and with defiant pride, as 'not an intellec-tual' or as 'a tart, deeply shallow', Ayush feels that he, like a few others, a very few, has to hide his passion for that unspeakably

57

embarrassing thing, literature, to put a lid on arguments based on literary criticism, not commerce. Economics is life, life is economics. But no more, at least not in this instance. Opie's range is daunting: he – he? – begins the discussion on sequentiality with references ranging from Spenser's *Amoretti* and Sidney's *Astrophil and Stella* to Claire-Louise Bennett's *Pond*. How does arrangement confer meaning?

    – *Can one leave the different strands that constitute a story or a novel* seemingly *unknit and hope – trust – readers to bring them together into meaning?*

    – Why not knit them for the reader? But Ayush deletes the question.

At the end of the editorial process, just before the proofs are ready, Ayush sends a note requesting a meeting: It has been such a wonderful conversation, a rare one, that it would be a great pleasure and privilege to meet you, etc. A curt reply, *I would much rather not, if you don't mind.* Ayush is a little wounded – after all the back-and-forth, from formalistics, the idea of coherence and collocation, to a comma shifted or deleted, and the querying of certain points in Caribbean English, the conversation lasting months and constituting a kind of romance, the best sort, this brush-off? At least a few more words could have been expended to soften the blow, some explanation, however fictitious, offered? He sulks for a few days, then gets the publicist to write. The reply is prompt: *Thank you very much for your email. I'm afraid that, for various reasons beyond my control, I shall have to decline doing any publicity-related activity, except for the odd Q & A conducted over email. I hope that this does not cause you any inconvenience. With apologies,* etc. There is nothing that they can do after this. In fact, it's an undisguised blessing for publicity: it saves resources and allows them to move on to the next thing, of which there are several, with a clean conscience.

Two weeks after a PDF of the page proofs is emailed to Opie, Ayush receives it as an attachment with all the corrections taken care of, but the body of the email is empty.

Nineteen months after the meeting in which Ayush acquired *Yes, The World*, the book is published. It gets one review, in a round-up of five new releases in *The Times*. The reviewer has nothing to say except how some of the stories are too long to fall under the category of short stories. It does not even get the usual 'darkly comic and sharply intelligent' treatment, nor the sentence-fetishizers' obligatory para of picking out holes and infelicities in the prose that they think passes for book-reviewing. Nothing. The publicists say that they didn't have a 'hook' – no author bio, no photo, nothing to pitch to the media, no help from the author, no endorsements from other writers, nothing.

What the publicists do not know because Ayush has not told them is that he had written to M.N. Opie to ask his writer friends, if he had any, to provide a few words of praise to put on the cover. Three days later, an email reply had arrived:

Mercilessly brilliant and life-changing – Philip Roth.

Reading it is like feeling new life being breathed into you – Toni Morrison.

A book that is alive, changing and growing as you read it, and changing you too in the process – James Baldwin.

It had taken Ayush a few seconds to work out, after which he had felt winded with ... with what exactly? Was Opie taking the piss? My god, the cheek. But after the shock had subsided, the understanding had come to him in a sudden revelation, while he was dissecting the episode in his head during a spell of insomnia. Yes, of course, the action was of a piece with what Opie stood for. And, as always, Ayush, breaking all norms, norms that mean nothing to him, can only be on Opie's side.

So here they are, Ayush, the publicists, the eminences at the morning meetings to discuss figs, looking at yet another book they have to write off.

9.

'Can you help Daddy make dinner?'

The children nod in unison.

'Will you spin the salad leaves and dry them for Daddy?' Luke knows they love doing this; the excitement of pressing down on the knob on the spinner lid and setting off the whirring below never seems to fade. Sometimes the twins have a competition to see who can make the container spin faster. Luke calls it incentivization. He has even fine-tuned this incentivization by explaining to them that the faster one can get the contraption to spin, the drier the leaves inside get. A nice, clean triangulation of competition, incentives, and efficiency, Luke had once boasted. Watching the children activate that hamster wheel again, in all innocence, makes Ayush's mouth feel ashy.

'Could we not bring them up without all these terrible wirings – greed, competition, consumption, incentives?' he had once asked Luke, to which Luke had replied, 'How? Relocate to Mars?'

'You think these things are inherent to humans and their functioning?' Ayush had said. 'Are they like the laws of nature, like gravity, or time?'

'You want a long answer or a short answer?'

'Short, please.'

'Yes, they are like the laws of physics. We don't make these laws, we study and try to understand them.'

'You don't make these laws? You seriously believe that, that your theories don't make the world as it is?'

Luke had sighed – a clear indication that he did not want to get embroiled in another 'Econ 101' war with Ayush – and said, almost in resignation, 'You want them to live in the greater world, don't you, not be like hermits or holy fools or children forever? They must know the ways of the world.'

And here they are, learning, unbeknown to themselves, that economics is life, life is economics. Ayush decides to concentrate on every ticking second of doing the washing-up – this is his version of meditation, an almost Zen-like space he enters by throwing himself into the task at hand in all its particulars so that his mind is drained of everything except the minute acts of pouring washing-up liquid on the sponge, sudsing, scrubbing, rinsing, turning a pot this way and that, turning on the hot water tap, the cold water tap, getting the temperature just right, a second scrub after the first rinse to get everything sparkling clean. It does not work now. He is aware of what Luke is doing (peeling and deseeding butternut squash, chopping garlic, mincing sage, preheating the oven). He can sense Spencer feeling happy; his entire pack is here. He cannot decide between sitting in one place, basking in the company, or getting up, grinning, tongue hanging out, tail thumping and waving, moving from one human to another, just to acknowledge their presence, his presence, all bound up together. Ayush can hear the children.

'I push stronger than you,' Sasha says.

'No, no, me, me. Look, I show you,' Masha counters.

'When I press, it moves very fast. When you press, it moves slow.' The slightest hint of italics in the personal pronouns.

'No. I'm faster. Give it to me, I'll show you.'

Ayush has his back to the kitchen table, where they are seated, so he cannot say what exactly makes the salad spinner, which is supposed to have a non-slip base, fly off the table, dispersing the washed lettuce leaves all over the floor in the children's corner of the kitchen. Spencer immediately obliges by sniffing and nuzzling and even licking some of them. Ayush has wheeled around and taken in the stricken look on the children's faces, Spencer's snuffling, felt Luke's steadying hand on his back – just the briefest of touches – before he sublimates everything inside him to 'Spencer, no, NO!' in a whipcrack tone that makes the dog look up, puzzled, hurt: he has never heard this kind of a sound from Ayush; all this in a second or two. Luke bends down to pick up the leaves, keeping up a patter of 'Wow, wheeee, they all went flying, didn't they? Wheee! Don't worry, don't worry, we'll wash them, and you can spin them again ... Now, Spencer, Spencer, naughty doggy-woggy-woggy, off, off, shoo, off you go. Don't worry, nothing to worry about, guys, nothing.' Ayush turns back to the sink and tries to focus again on the washing-up. Luke places the salad spinner with the leaves next to the sink and continues in an unbroken thread, 'I can do it if you move for one second, just one sec, no problem at all, I can do it.' Ayush looks at the soapy wine glasses and thinks of breaking one under the surface of the water in the sink with the force of his hand, just pressing on the glass balloon very hard so that the shards can dig into his palm. Without waiting for Ayush to move away to make space, Luke turns on the cold water tap, swishes the leaves in the spinner, empties it, repeats everything, and hands the twins the job again. The children's temporary phase of feeling subdued begins to lift: as soon as Luke says, 'Oh, yikes, the dog hasn't been fed,' both of them sing out, 'I'll feed him, Daddy, I'll feed him.' 'OK, only the kibble, you know where it is. Only half a scoop, all right? Both of you do it, no fighting,

63

both of you,' Luke says and turns to check the progress of the butternut squash in the oven. Ayush has barely rinsed the big yellow Le Creuset pot and turned sideways to put it on the draining rack before he simultaneously hears, and sees in his peripheral vision, the sound and sight of a ten-kilo bag of kibble spilling on to the floor as both children, trying to lift it up to pour into the dog's bowl, cannot manoeuvre that huge weight and control the stream of dry dog food as physics and the unmanageable sack get the better of them. Spencer is so beside himself that he doesn't know whether to guzzle it all up or wait to work out what is happening, if today this bounty has been spread out for him to eat unrestrainedly. He tries to make his way over to his bowl, now with a brown, granular mound in it, over the patchy rug of spilled kibble on the kitchen floor tiles. Ayush, uncontrollably, lets out a cackle that sounds like a staccato yowl: seriously, if this had been happening in one of his authors' books, he would have written 'RE, take one out, you can't have both, esp. so close together' in the margin with his blue pencil – 'RE' is 'Repeated Example' – but this is not a book and reality does not have to satisfy certain conditions of realism, which is, after all, a highly artificial model of the mess that is life. All this goes through his head as Luke rushes over to the children, pulls them into his arms, and says in his tenderest voice, 'Oh, sweethearts, you were trying to help, weren't you? You were trying to help, my loves,' as he strokes their heads, kisses their cheeks, and placates their tremulous lips and red faces. Ayush is suddenly held in the beam of an illumination: is this, then, what it takes to grow up comfortable in your own skin, comfortable and at ease with the world, the knowledge that there are no negative consequences, however trivial, that you are entitled to kindness and forgiveness and love regardless of what you do? The understanding in which he is held leaves him, like the beam of a lighthouse, and he is left looking at the detritus which is everyday life.

'Will you come with me? Just this once?' Luke asks Ayush. He can tell Luke is nervous, that it has taken a lot for him to get to this point of posing and articulating this question.

'I know you dislike us, our tribe, I mean, but it'd mean a lot to me if you could be there,' Luke rushes on. 'Just for an hour. Just come and smile and make small talk, which you're so good at, then we'll leave, and I'll take you out for dinner to the Delauney, or wherever you want to go. Please?'

Ayush feels the inside of his chest being wrung: it has cost Luke so much to say this to the man he is married to? What does Ayush see in the mirror that Luke has just held up to him? Ayush averts his face, as if from the imagined reflection, and says, 'Yes, of course, I'll come. Happily.' Radiating relief, Luke almost leaps to kiss Ayush on the mouth, but his burning face is still averted.

The Xanax Ayush takes half an hour before he and Luke make their entrance at the donor-schmoozing party in a private room in Gymkhana is working like a dream. After several minutes of smiling, saying hello, shaking hands, sipping bubbly, Ayush feels Luke's mouth at his ear, whispering, 'I have to go talk shop. You want to mingle or come with me?'

'I'll be all right. You go do what you have to do. Come find me when you're done.'

It is unimaginable to Ayush that British academia has money to burn on an evening like this. Clearly, someone in charge of the purse strings is certain that the gamble will pay off, that the donor being courted is going to endow the economics department with millions. In all the years of being with Luke, Ayush hardly knows any of his colleagues. He has heard some recurring names, but apart from one or two, he cannot match them to faces. An eager, bright-faced American man comes up to him, says, 'Hi, I'm Alex,' and extends his hand. 'Are you an economist?' Ayush feels the handshake loosening as he confesses he is not. The bright-ness fades a little, or maybe it's the artful low lighting in the room. Then the forced question, 'So, what do you do?'; Ayush cannot help feeling that it's really 'so what on earth *can* you do if you're not an economist' that Alex is asking. The Xanax insulates Ayush from everything; he feels indifferent, removed from the action. 'I'm a publisher,' he says, apologetically. 'Oh, that's awesome!' Alex performs. 'Amazing. What do you publish?' 'Books,' Ayush says, and is ready to turn away, when an Indian woman comes up to him and says, 'Luke just pointed you out to me. You're Ayush. I've heard so much about you from him. I'm Ritika, Ritika Santosh.' Then with a slightly sideways look, 'Hi, Alex, so nice that you're here.'

'You've heard about me from Luke? What have you heard?'

She smiles and says, 'Well, I've read some of the books you've published. *In Other Colours*, of course. Also *A Question of Honour*. Then that book on the history of statistics.'

Ayush feels tempted to say 'awesome' and 'amazing' too, with sincerity. He smiles – he hopes humbly – and mutters a thank you.

She continues, 'Luke says you're not a big fan of us. Of economists.' There's a generous, indulgent smile on her face, but no trace of condescension.

Alex is now interested. 'Oh. Really? Why?'

'That's going to be your opening conversation gambit?' Ayush says to Ritika with the most dazzling smile he can muster. 'Here, I have a better one: what kind of an economist are you?'

'A damn good one, I hope,' she says, laughing.

66

Ayush feels an immediate connection with her. Is it the Xanax? Or the fact that they're the only two non-white people in the room, as far as he can tell? Or even that they're Indians?

'Of that I'm sure,' he laughs too, 'but you know what I mean.'

'I'm a development economist. I work on poverty.'

'Say more? It's a huge subject. The only subject, one might truthfully say.'

'Here? This is an odd setting to talk about my work, or any work. We're supposed to mingle and keep our conversations light and fluffy,' she says. Her eyes are sparkling.

'But I'm really interested.'

'OK, let's make a deal. We go out for drinks one day, and I tell you about my work, and you tell me about your problem with economists. Because, you know, I may not be entirely opposed to your position vis-à-vis us.'

Ayush's eyes widen. He is now hooked. 'Done and done,' he says, in a slight daze.

10.

'Daddy, Spencer's not coming up to bed,' Masha complains.

Spencer always looks mournful at the children's bedtime because he knows that he is going to be without their company until morning. Both Luke and Ayush let the dog come into the bathroom during the twins' bath time and sniff around and soak up the human company, as if he needs to store it up for the parched hours of the night. After bath time, he leaps onto his bed on the landing outside the two bedrooms, the twins' and Ayush and Luke's, on the top floor, to wait out the dark hours.

'Stay guard, doggy-woggy-woggy-woggy,' Sasha says every night, kissing the dog goodnight.

'Look after us through the night, O faithful friend,' Masha always adds. The unchanging routine of secular prayer. Ayush forgets where Masha picked up the vocative address. But tonight, Spencer seems to have forgotten the routine.

'What do you mean, not coming up?' Luke says.

'He's standing at the bottom of the stairs and not following us up like he does at night.'

Luke comes out to the landing and sees Spencer stationed there, looking up at the staircase then looking away.

'Spencer, old chap, what's wrong? Come up, come on up,' Luke says and climbs down then up a few stairs as if to lead by example.

The dog turns his head away, as if mildly embarrassed.

'Come on, sweetheart, you're a big boy, come on. What's the matter?'

Luke comes down and tries to lift his front paws on to the second step, coaxing him. The children scamper down the side and stand at the mezzanine landing, looking down and urging, 'Doggy-woggy, come to bed. You have to stand guard while we sleep. Good dog, Spencer, come now.'

Spencer looks up and heaves his bottom up to stair number three, pauses, looks away, tongue out, then lumbers up to step four, pauses again.

'Ayush,' Luke calls out, 'Ayush, come here, please, for a second, will you?'

Ayush comes out of the kitchen. 'What's going on?'

Luke says, 'Look at Spencer. Have you noticed this before?'

'Noticed what?'

Ayush watches Spencer do his climb-stop, climb-stop movement for two more steps and understands immediately. He swallows all the exclamations that sprint to his tongue and says instead, 'Lukey, can you lift him and take him to the living room? I'll bring his bed downstairs after I settle the children.'

In the children's bedroom, Ayush says to the puzzled faces, 'Spencer's getting old. He can't climb the stairs as nimbly as he used to. Now, I think it's even better that he stands guard in the living room downstairs, don't you? That way he'll catch anyone right at the entrance, at the very beginning. He won't let them come up. What do you say?'

Ayush finds their slow, silent nods listless. It is worse to witness another's deflation than feel one's own.

Downstairs, Luke is sitting on the floor, his arms around the dog. Ayush puts Spencer's bed in the corner between the bookshelf and the window. 'Come on, sweetheart. Come, your bed is here now. Come on, good boy.'

The dog has trouble standing up and getting over to his bed. He gives Ayush's neck and ears a 'thank you' lick and gingerly steps over into the hollow of his cushions.

'Have you noticed this before?' Luke asks again.

Ayush sits on the sofa and lowers his neck on to Luke's and whispers, 'No. No, I haven't. You?'

Luke reaches up and puts his hands on Ayush's face, his neck. 'No,' he says, after a long time. 'So sudden. Or I've just not been very attentive. I'm not teaching the day after tomorrow. I'll take him to the vet's.'

'I'll come with you. I'll find a way to get out of work for a couple of hours.'

The young Bulgarian vet, Vassilena, confirms that it's arthritis. 'It's so common among retrievers his age. He's nearly ten, it's to be expected.' Her voice and manner are kind, caring, not rehearsedly so, as she takes Luke and Ayush through medication, diet, exercise, practical arrangements of what to do if Spencer finds it difficult to lift his leg to pee, to squat while shitting, if he wets his bed, if he becomes incontinent, if the side effects of the drugs manifest swiftly.

They come out with a stash of Rimadyl. Ayush, concentrating on the lichen-blooms of ancient chewing gum on the grey pavement but seeing nothing, says, 'You take him home, I'll be back a little late. Give the children supper. Tell them whatever you feel like.' He squeezes Luke's arm and makes his way to the Tube.

An important meeting, flagged up for weeks with frequent emails, about some momentous announcement and involving the presence of the MD of the division and the CEO of the company. Everyone, of course, thinks of redundancies and cost-cutting and restructuring, but plays the game: 'How exciting, what can it be?' they say, but there is no hiding the slightly high-pitched anxiety behind the words. The announcement turns out to be of a new imprint 'dedicated to Diversity'. From the press release: 'An imprint to reflect the enormously rich and enriching diversity of our times, to enable and encourage a whole new generation of writers, change-makers, and thought leaders, to find new voices that will create new understandings, new meanings, a new society.' They have paid a management consultant hundreds of thousands to come up with a name for the imprint: Together. The logo is three hands clasped in a circle; the hands are uniformly beige with black outlines. Ayush can imagine exactly the conversations in which having one black hand, one brown, and one white – or two black and one white, or all black, or all brown – was discussed and shot down. Three people are going to be hired to run the imprint, and, 'to be a microcosm of our fabulously diverse society', they will all be 'people of colour'. There is vigorous nodding of all the white heads at this junction of the presentation; self-satisfaction, like a gas released into the room, makes it difficult to breathe. Ayush's face burns.

He stands up and walks purposively to the dais. No one seems to be surprised even as he positions himself at the lectern – maybe this was part of the surprise script the MD and the CEO have drawn up, this imminent speech by their one non-white editor. Who knows, maybe he is going to head up the new imprint, and this is the speech from the new head. Ayush begins: 'This is not the way to go about things. I don't need to remind this gathering what good intentions pave, but I do want to say how ill-conceived they are and how they can only result in further polarization, further ghettoization. Quite apart from the corporate black- or brown-washing that the creation of this imprint is, another predictable act of tokenism and virtue-signalling, everyone will treat the books and authors of Together as the "special needs" children at school. It will also have the effect of funnelling out all the non-white writers that the other imprints publish, making them whiter still. Did you think about this? Did you deign to consult a non-white *writer* during the hatching of this bullshit idea? Did a management consultancy outfit tell you what to do? Will you *ever* wake up?' His voice rises higher at each question. Horror and embarrassment mark the very few faces that are not looking at the floor or at the handouts everyone has been given.

Stewing in his seat, his whole body now aflame, his heart a piston, he allows the fantasy to wash over him, leaving him stranded, like a wave that could have swallowed him alive but decides to spare him instead.

11.

'No, 9 can be broken down into 3 times 3, so it's not a prime. You know what factors are. So, a prime number can have only two factors: the number itself and 1, because anything multiplied by 1 is that number itself.'

Ayush can only hear not see them in the other room, so he imagines, from the silence that follows, that the children are either puzzled or processing what Luke has just said. Wasn't eight years in any case too young to be learning about prime numbers? Luke had begun to teach them about numbers during the lockdown and, finding that he enjoyed it, had continued.

Luke's gentle, confident, reasoning voice again: 'OK, let's do this. What are the factors of 12?'

'6 and 2.' Masha.

'Very good,' says Luke.

'3 and 4,' pipes up Sasha.

'Very good. You're both correct. Now think again. Can any of those numbers – 6, 2, 3, 4 – be broken down further into factors that are not 1?'

Such calm kindness, such patience. They spring from a mysterious source of love. Did everyone have it, something lying dormant, awaiting the arrival of children to be activated? Ayush remembers Luke melting while looking at the twins in their crib when they were only a few months old, trying to swallow their fists or eat their toes, giving both adults a gurgling beam or an inexplicable grin, while he, Ayush, had noticed only the nappies and was insulated from their uncalculated charm by the mental arithmetic of working out how many nappies per week, per month, per year until the children became continent and potty-trained.

From his study window Ayush can look down on to the garden. It's too cold and windy to sit outside, but the clematis – *Clematis montana* var. *wilsonii* – is a white froth over the boundary wall with the neighbour's house. Will the children learn about the things that really matter in both life and in the living of a life, things such as plants and flowers and insects and birds and trees, not just about prime numbers, and market forces, and resource allocation, and preferences? What matters more, the surface of the world that one experiences or the forces under the surface? There is an intrepid magpie sitting on one side of the steeple under the chimney breast on the roof next door. The wind blows the bird's long black tail up in an enthusiastic tick-mark as it tries to balance. The bird doesn't give up, clutching at the mossy bricks as the gusts buffet him. Then he admits defeat and hops off on to the gentler gradient of the slate roof, where he appears to feel less precarious, but also less heroic to Ayush.

These sights take him elsewhere, places where he thinks he can live forever. He is doing a tranche of his regular weekend chore – or it should be regular – of four hours of reading manuscripts that are on submission. The four hours are spread out over the day, as they would have to be since he and Luke have long not been a self-contained family of two in control of time and its management. Time. He had once read a memorable line in a review of a Per Petterson novel: 'The only true problem of the realist novel is time.' After the instinctive reaction, not entirely frivolous, 'Of that other realist thing called life, too, my friend', he had returned frequently to that sentence, so dense with meaning, in his mind. He now thinks that so much of the frequent articulations of impatience and boredom with plot and plotting by writers is nothing more than an inability to know what to do with time, its representation, the modelling of its passage in 200 or 350 or 600 pages. These writers, all enthralled by the self, are hectically caught up in signalling the breaking of new ground when, in reality, they are just trying to dress up their limitations as cool, daring, new, adventurous.

But life, too, to go back to his first response: why is the abiding experience of life a struggle with time; why is this experience so pervasive, and so acute of late? All the stuff at the foundation of Luke's discipline, which commands the world and all the lives in it, such as efficiency, outcome, productivity, growth – what are these but functions of time? How much can you get done, how much can you produce, in a given chunk of time: that's the dynamo at the heart of everything, from the smallest to the biggest. Giving children breakfast, getting them ready for school, getting them to put their shoes on (has someone aggregated the hours of a life lost in getting them to put on their shoes and jackets and coats?), replying to thirty-two emails between 6 and 7:20 a.m., three manuscripts to read before lunch, a PowerPoint slide: in the last year, ebook sales in the first and second quarters were up 7 percentage points compared with physical book sales while in the third and last quarters physical books showed etc. Another slide: across imprints and divisions, revenue fell by an average of 6.34 per cent for three etc., etc. And how would the day's calibrations be for Lukey? 'Revise and resubmit' due last week, finding two extra hours in the week to write reader's reports on three journal articles, two extra hours to write letters for students, 588 calories burned in 60 minutes, three extra hours to reply to all the emails that keep mounting up if you don't reply to twenty an hour every hour every day every week every month every year. The only accurate descriptions of life as they live it in the first world are all metaphors: a treadmill, a hamster wheel, a perpetual-motion beltway, a non-stop carousel going round and round and round. The clock's running, running out, running down, time is flowing, flying, snapping at your wheels, its chariot is behind you, rushing to run you over, run you down, run you under its wheels, run run run to keep ahead, till you are a hit-and-run statistic, roadkill, as we are, always already are. Time, time.

His eyes close.

Ritika is saying, 'So the only way to understand what works is to actually do a kind of lab experiment but in the real world. A kind of intervention in the real lives of real people.'

Ayush is agog. 'How does, how would, that work?'

'Say, you have a theory that X, an asset, might diminish poverty. When you give the ultra poor that asset, it may pull them out of their poverty trap. You conduct a controlled experiment to check if asset transfer can truly alleviate poverty.'

'But how? Like, what asset? Something that will generate income indefinitely? And who gives it to the ultra poor? The government?' He is still at a loss to understand.

The waiter comes out with their glasses of orange wine, which he has described a few minutes ago as 'unfiltered and funky'. Ayush and Ritika are sitting in the outdoor space – the pavement, in reality – of a wine bar called Diogenes the Dog in Elephant and Castle. If someone had told Ayush last week that he would be in a wine bar, which had extraordinary and unusual wines from unexpected places on the menu, in

Elephant and Castle he would have laughed, but even this stretch between Walworth and the Old Kent Roads has been gentrified beyond belief.

'Something like, say, knitting machines given to women in an area we are studying. Or – here's a recent example from a successful intervention – giving cows to rural women,' she says.

'Cows? You mean, the animal?'

'Yes, the animal. Cows generate income, in answer to the question you asked. You sell the milk, use cow dung to make fuel cakes to sell, etc. But the experiment has to be set up carefully and, most importantly, has to be randomized.' She takes a sip of her wine, looks at him, and says, 'I hope you're not going to think I'm being condescending if I ask you whether you understand what randomization means. Or what it entails, in this kind of an action. It's essential that you get this part of the experiment.'

Ayush shakes his head. 'Not really. Is it like trials for medication and things like that?'

'Absolutely. But how do you control for other causalities in a field that is not a lab but life? How do you nail the fact that it is *this* particular asset transfer that has worked? How do you measure success in this experiment? That's the beauty and challenge of this method.'

'Can you explain using an example? Like a real trial that you did in what you call the field? I find it easier to understand with concrete illustrations.'

Ritika takes him through a recently conducted experiment in which random women in randomly selected villages in a district in West Bengal were each given a cow to improve their lot. It was a stupendous success: consumption – the metric used by economists to measure well-being among the ultra poor – went up and continued to hold up at the raised level two years after the asset transfer.

Ayush absorbs all this thirstily. It must be nice to work in a field in which success is evident, tangible, in which measurable good can be done in the world. He feels at once enthused and slightly deflated. 'Wow' is all he can say, like a callow teenager.

'And it was a success with all the women you gave cows to?' he asks.

Ritika narrows her eyes and looks at him in a pointed way. 'Why do you ask that?' She stumbles a little in getting the words out.

'No reason. Just like that, as we would say when we were children.'

Ritika looks down at her glass. She peers into it as she says, 'No, not all the women. But over 99 per cent of them.'

'What happened to the tiny fraction that was not a success?' Something has just begun to take shape in his mind.

Ayush takes the children for a walk to Brockwell Park on a sunny Saturday afternoon in late May. The park is crowded, but not as heaving as he had thought it would be. The daisies are like discrete, dense constellations in a green sky.

Ayush asks the children, 'Do you know what a comparison is?'

They look at each other, then Sasha says, 'It is when you compare something to something.'

'And what is compare?' Ayush knows it's a difficult question to answer – all things that we take for granted as part of our foundations of understanding are difficult to express when faced with a question like that – but he wants to push them a little.

'It is when,' Sasha begins haltingly, 'when there is one thing and there is another thing and.'

'And,' Masha takes over, 'and the two things are' – she brings her hands together, palms open and facing him, as if she's miming curtains or doors closing.

'Yes, correct, I know what you're thinking, but do you want to try and put it in words? Try?'

'And, and,' Masha tries, scrunching her eyes tight shut with effort, as if she's got bad constipation and is straining, 'one thing is like the other thing.'

'Very, very good. One thing is like another thing. We compare when we bring two things together and see how similar they are. That is called a comparison. Now, think about this: can we set two things side by side and they're both a little bit similar to each other, but also different from each other?'

They look at each other and turn their heads back to him and – he can see the thought passing through their heads – think about nodding but don't quite do it.

'Let's find some examples, shall we? Look at the daisies in the grass. Do you see the little white flowers? Here, and here, and here' – he points to the ground. 'These little white flowers are daisies,' he says. 'Do you know where the name comes from? They used to be called day's eyes, as in the eyes of the day. You open your eyes first thing in the morning, right? These flowers open first thing on a new day, so they're called day's eyes. So, from day's eyes, to dayseyes, daysyes, daisyes, daisies. Do you see?'

The twins nod but he cannot tell if they have understood or are even interested.

'Now, comparison. Look at this other flower' – Ayush points at a yellow dandelion in full bloom – 'that's called a dandelion.' He pauses, thinking whether he should subject them to another etymology of a flower name, and decides against it.

'I know, I know,' Masha chirps out, 'we do phoo phoo phoo on it and it blows away and that's a clock and we can tell the time.'

Time, again. It's always time. 'Well, yes, but you'll have to wait for a little bit before this flower turns into a clock. Now, look at the daisies. And look at the dandelion. Can you now compare the two? Are they similar? Are they different?'

'One is small and white, the other is bigger and yellow,' the boy answers.

'Very good. We've noted the differences' – he emphasizes the word – 'now what about the' – slow again – 'similarities? How are they the same?'

So hesitantly that Ayush almost expects the interrogative uptick at the end, Masha says, 'They are both flowers.'

'Very, very good, again. Now, let's move a little sideways with this game. Sash, you noted that the daisy is white and the dandelion is yellow. Can you think of other yellow things?'

A few seconds of thinking, then the boy says, 'Egg-yellow.'

'Yes, good, egg yolk.'

Masha says, 'The sun is yellow. My yellow colour pencil. Lemon.'

'Excellent, well done. Now, can we say *The dandelion is as yellow as an egg yolk*? Do you understand what I did there? I compared two yellows – the colour of the dandelion and the colour of egg yolks. Clear?'

The twins nod.

'As yellow as. Or you can say *The dandelion is like an egg yolk*. Clear?'

Again, the children nod.

'Now, pay attention to how I said it – I used *as* or *like*. One thing, in this case a yellow flower, is *like* another thing, in this case egg yolk, because they're both yellow. They are similar in *colour*. This kind of comparison is called a si-mi-le. S-i-m-i-l-e.' Very slowly, the spelling out.

If he starts this early, will it become a kind of hardwiring in them? Again, *pay* attention: if the cost is high enough, would they cherish the thing bought? He doesn't have much time, three, four, maybe five years if he is – they are – lucky, before time enters their lives and lays everything to waste. Will this remain in their memory, make them look up and out, make them notice, and, much more importantly, notice again, slowly and carefully and deeply, counting bracts and sepals, the number of spots on an insect's chitinous shell, the different cohorts of pink in different species and hybrids of perennial geraniums, all useless knowledge, all untradeable, all a waste of time, which must always be used to yield something, but what if noticing becomes, if nothing else – god knows, he's not going to make any big claims for it – a haven, a small one, like a dot of a calm island in tempestuous, destructive seas that would swallow them alive and never spit them out, what if it gives them something, however small, that cannot be poured into readymade vessels of understanding, what if noticing is something they retreat to inside themselves and find and find –

'It's like smile, but with one more *i*,' Masha says.

'Yes, it is. Good. Now, we'll step forward to another game. I'll give you one thing, say, a colour or a quality, such as hot or cold or good, and you will find as many similes as you can. Like we did with yellow – yellow as egg yolk, but you can add to that, yellow as the sun, yellow like lemons. Right? Do you understand?'

There's a brightness on their faces. They nod convincingly.

'OK, let's go. Black. Let's find similes for the colour black. I'll do the first one, OK? *Black as ink*. Now you go.'

They've stopped near the old stone water trough which is now used as a planter for Mexican fleabane, campanulas, geraniums, lobelias. The children are thinking hard. They consult each other in whispers, which gives Ayush a little hope that at least wherever competition reigns it hasn't found hospitable soil in them. Not yet. Masha looks expectantly, encouragingly at her brother, who says, a little tentatively, 'Black like your hair.'

'Goo-ood,' Ayush tries to skate over his own tentativeness. 'Masha?'

'Black as night.'

'Great.'

'Black as clouds,' the boy says. They are on a roll now, and clearly enjoying themselves.

'Brilliant. You've learned similes now. Shall we move on to something related called metaphor?'

'What's meta for?' Sasha asks.

Life. Living. Fiction. Lies. Modelling. Representation. Numbers. Words. Data. Everything is metaphor. It rules your life. You understand everything, in so far as you do, because of it. Should he weigh them down now? Simile was enough for one day, he decides.

'Let's get very good at this simile business, then we'll do metaphor another day. How does that sound?'

They nod. Now, he hears the piercing song of a blackbird and looks up. The male blackbird population of what seems to him like all of South London has learned the same tune, the one with a pleading, cajoling four-note up-down-up wave that ends the song before the coda begins. There, on the topmost branch of a lime tree, sits the singer.

They are near the corner where the path bends right along Cressingham Gardens Estate on the other side. He kneels down to their level and asks, 'Do you hear that bird singing? There, do you hear?'

Notes drop like silver through the clear air. The twins nod.

'If you look up, you can see him. He's a blackbird.'

'Black like a blackbird,' Masha says and looks at her father for praise.

82

'Well done. Now, look up, look where my finger is point-ing. Now, look beyond the tip of my finger, in the same direction, in a straight straight line, like an arrow. There's another simile: *straight as an arrow*. There. Do you see? Can you see him? He's sitting on the top branch, right on the top.'

The children look up and nearly topple over backwards. Sasha spots it first. 'Yes, I can.' As if to reward him, the bird lets out that silver stream again. Then the girl sees him too.

'Why do they sing from the top of a tree?' the boy asks.

'Good question. They sing to attract female blackbirds who will come to them, lured by their song, then they will build a nest, lay eggs, and have baby blackbirds together. He is sitting on the top branch so that it's easy for a female blackbird to see him and think, *Oh, this is a lovely song, let me mate with the singer. Now where is this wonderful singer, where is he? Ah, there he is.*'

Wonder is easy to read on a child's face, but Ayush cannot interpret the expression that flits across the twins' faces, simul-taneously, as he finishes his little speech about courtship rituals.

'Did you sing for Daddy?' Masha asks. 'But Daddy is not a female.'

He has already said, with a little laugh, 'No, that Daddy is not', before he pays attention.

'Neither of us is,' he adds. There seems to be intent, it appears to him, in the way the twins are not looking at each other. Or does it appear to him later, when he is running and rerunning the reel in his head?

'You and Daddy are two males,' Masha says, looking at the grass, but not at Ayush, not at her brother. The words seem like a mumbled aside.

'Yes, you've known this forever, no?'

'In school, Elizabeth and Sanjeev said it is wrong,' Sasha joins in.

Ayush feels a brief rushing in his ears. He cannot, will not, believe that this aria-duet has been rehearsed by them beforehand, that they had it all planned to bring it up on this walk.

'Did they, now?' A surface as calm as a mirror. Another simile, but he doesn't point it out to them since it is internal to him; they wouldn't understand what he was talking about.

They nod in unison. Is it true that twins think the same thought together in time, that there's an invisible arc connecting their brains?

'Yes. They said that everyone has a daddy and a mummy,' Sasha explains. 'Having two daddies is wrong.'

'But you don't have two daddies' – calm as before, and now, even playful – 'you have a daddy and a baba. See? Magic!' The blackbird is continuing with its infernally repetitive song; he wants to wring its little neck.

'No, but you must have one daddy and one mummy,' Masha says. 'One man and one woman. Not two men, and you and Daddy are two men.' Clear, unhesitant, like something learned by rote, delivered without thinking, like a slap.

In that same playful voice, Ayush says, 'Well, some things are wrong to some people, and to others not. Let us take an example. You, Sash, and I think that eating meat is wrong, but Daddy doesn't think so. We can live together happily, with each of us, or groups of us, thinking different things, doing different things, but loving each other. Do you understand? Things don't have to be the same. In fact, it's better if things are all different, it keeps everything interesting. What is better, only one colour, say, blue, blue sky, blue trees, blue grass, blue birds, blue dogs, blue skin, blue water, blue everything, or what we have now, all different colours to different things?'

He sees them nod almost imperceptibly and thinks he also sees a knot inside them that is beginning to loosen. The difficult bit will come later.

'Also,' he continues, 'the idea of a family as a mummy, a daddy, and two children has changed over the years, many, many, many years. Don't you think Spencer, who is a dog, is part of our family of human beings? In many countries, daddy, mummy, and children live with daddy's parents or mummy's parents. But we don't do that here. That doesn't mean that we are wrong or the people who do it are right. Or the other way around –' Then the rushing in his ears returns and the energy and conviction behind the performance leach away, leaving him stranded. The fucking blackbird is still going.

He has to confront the difficult bit now, and he has to do it, not Luke. He tries out several drafts of the phrasing inside his head before he asks gently, in his most Luke-like impersonation, 'Did Elizabeth and Sanjeev call you names?'

They shake their heads in unison.

'Did the other children call you names?' He cannot ask all the things that he wants to ask in order to establish an empirically sound he-said-she-said-then-they-did account for fear of putting fears and anxieties and ideas in their heads.

They shake their heads again. Ayush cannot tell if they are hiding something. From his own childhood he knows that bullying, especially at their age, can be the most difficult thing to talk about.

A slightly different question this time. Over lunch at a Middle Eastern place in Soho, Ayush asks Emily Zhao, whose debut novel, *Disassembled*, he is publishing next January: 'And why do you want to enter the literary world?'

A shrug of her shoulders; no writer this young should be subjected to the question he has just asked. Despite that awareness, Ayush continues, 'Do you know what you're letting yourself in for?'

She does not understand what is being asked of her, whether there's a right or a wrong answer, and she's too intimidated by her first lunch with her publisher, so she shrugs again, waiting for him to answer his own question.

Ayush obliges. 'Misreading,' he says. 'Pure misreading. Or deliberate limited reading. They'll be like horses with blinkers. You're not white, the blinders will go on immediately. So much of what one finds in a book is what one allows oneself to find in it. Conversely, it's possible to trivialize and mock and be negative about any book – *Lolita*, *Anna Karenina*, *Beloved*, which a much-loved hack called a "hysterical ghost-story". They go in already prepared to find range, intelligence, allusion, formal innovativeness, Marx this, Agamben that, in any number of white writers, because they think it all belongs to them, but that won't obtain with you. You could signal the whole world in your text, but in your case, they either won't see it or they'll call it extraneous, straining for learnedness or relevance, the polemical sitting uneasily with the fictional, that kind of bullshit, you see?' There's a devil inside him. 'A white writer will just have to drop in the word Marxist in an ironic description of, say, a floral arrangement in the foyer of a Philippe Starck hotel, or not even in her work, but in an interview that she's given – every writer or freelancer reviewing the work will write paras about the profound entanglement with Marxist thought that's going on in that writer's work, the political utility of the novel this, the querying of atomized labour under late-capitalism that. But your book? No. Never. Not in a year of thirteen moons. Are you ready for this? The sheer wilful blindness, the illiteracy?

'Do you want to publish under a *nom de plume*? Under a neutral – by which I mean white, of course – a neutral name? Emily Smith? E. Smith? And no author photo or bio?'

Emily looks stricken, then alarmed. She holds the table as if trying to force herself to remain seated.

Of course, this conversation doesn't happen.

What does happen is this: he puts a small phrase in the jacket copy of *Disassembled* – 'exposing the ever-renewing, more hectic forms of erasure of labour under late-capitalism' – just to give her book a small fighting chance. A vanishingly small one.

12.

At the entrance to the cool basement of the restaurant in The Strand, Ayush and Ritika, out for dinner, bump into one of Anna's authors, novelist, historian of cartography, even a frequent radio pundit, now in his impressively august seventies. The current chair of the Royal Society of Literature, he seems to be heading a group of five or six, mostly writers and literary types, Ayush can tell, although he can vaguely put a name to only one of them, maybe two. The chair of the RSL recognizes Ayush, just, and says hello, so Ayush feels compelled to say what a coincidence, what brings him and his party here.

'Oh, we just had the most wonderful event at the society on an Italian writer. Just fascinating. So well attended. Such great speakers. Really terrific evening.'

'Which Italian writer?' Ayush asks.

Just the barest microsecond of a pause – beyond calibration, Ayush feels; besides, it could always be his imagination; it *is* always in your head, isn't it? – before the answer, directed, with a slight turning of the head, at the air six inches to the side of Ayush's head, 'Primo Levi?' Another pause, an infinitesimal fraction longer than the previous one. 'You know, *The Periodic Table*?' It's not upspeak – he belongs to a different generation altogether – but a genuine interrogative.

Both Ayush and Ritika look at the floor. A waiter comes and escorts them to their table. Not a word passes between them as they both fall into a careful study of the menu, as if it were a manuscript, or a dataset, until Ritika looks up and says, 'I'm sorry.'

Reading to the children at bedtime is now a twice-weekly treat instead of a daily occurrence. Every time it's Ayush's turn, he cannot help but cast his mind back to that night two-and-a-half years ago, maybe a little longer, when he had shown them the underground animal rights film. Do they think about it when it's him instead of Luke reading? Luke had taken over bedtime reading entirely for months after that incident. Who knows how long memory persists, or how sharp it is, at that age? How do children process it? Could it be buried deep and have a pervasive, ongoing effect on their lives, a spring oozing unstoppably, or could it lie just under the surface, ready to break out into blood, to hurt, yet not be deep and damaging? Could it be both?

Ayush allows himself to notice consciously something which has been developing right under his nose: the children are beginning to express their Thai features. They are very subtle – an olive shade to their complexion instead of the wholly English milk-and-roses (Ayush used to call it 'blotchy' until he had been corrected by a friend at university); an upturn to the outer ends of their eyes, as if an artist had, with utmost delicateness, moved the brush up the barest stroke while holding his breath in – but once seen they cannot be unseen, not at least by him. And he feels cold fear toll through him again like a bell. They are not going to be at the receiving end – hopefully – of the kind of behaviour that is the usual content of mental images sparked off by the word 'racism': someone calling them chinky, or saying they have Jap's eyes; that kind can and will be easily laughed off, more or less. The kind he is worried about is the one that takes the form of white liberal inclusiveness and its regular need to be fellated: come and be the one non-white judge on this book-prize jury because, look, we're so diverse; come and speak at our famous literature festival, but only to its ethnic chapter that happens at a different time of the year from the main festival.

'Baba, Baba, what story, what story? Are there pictures?' Masha asks while brother and sister are getting ready to go to bed.

'Only little children want pictures in their books,' Sasha says. 'I can read, I don't need pictures.'

'I can read too,' Masha says.

'It is a story about a prince,' Ayush offers gratefully.

In the bedroom, the usual entanglements about duvets and blanketies, about which stuffed toy's turn it is to sleep with whom, about who decides tonight when the rotating scenery of the night lamp has hit optimum speed. Ayush lets every-thing wash over him, hoping that conserving the energy that otherwise might have been expended on his own responses to the children's chatter will at least not exacerbate his exhaus-tion. He has a blurry memory of complaining to Luke about the sheer, inexorable boredom of parenting … or has he thought about it so much inside his own head that the false memory feels real now? When the children are at last settled down, Ayush can barely lift the fifty-page book and turn its pages. He takes up his usual position between them, propped up against a big pillow, and starts to read.

'Many years ago, in a town called Lumbini, in the country that is now called Nepal, there was born into a noble family of kshatriyas a prince called Siddhartha Gautama.'

'What is sh-shu-sh-shat …?' Sasha begins.

Ayush was hoping for plain sailing. He repeats the word 'kshatriya' a few times then attempts a version of the Indian caste system for eight-year-olds. He is dreading all the follow-on questions, but the novelty of the material seems to have turned that switch off, at least for now.

They continue unimpeded until Siddhartha, protected in a cocoon of wealth and luxury by his father, witnesses an old, dying man one day who says to the prince, 'Suffering is the lot of humans. Everyone suffers and dies. You, too, Prince, are subject to that law.' Siddhartha replies, 'I am subject to no laws, I am a prince. I give out the laws that rule life.' But something in the encounter snags at the prince's mind, some inchoate notion that there might be a life outside the palace walls that is different from the life that he knows …

'He calls out to his charioteer, "Chandaka, harness Kanthaka, my horse. Prepare my chariot,"' Ayush reads.

'Why do they have such names?' Sasha interrupts.

'What do you mean, such names?' Ayush asks. He knows exactly what the boy means, but he wants the child to articulate it better.

'The horse has a funny name. If I had a horse, I would call him Spencer.'

'No, you numpty,' Masha chirps, 'Spencer is our doggy. How can we call the horse and the dog the same name? What will happen if we want to call the doggy, and say "Spencer, come!" and the horse comes?'

She is on a roll. Ayush debates whether to interrupt and give them a lesson in diversity and why people have different names or whether to use this little debate between the children as his stepping-off point for the night. He is, however, puzzled by the question about foreign names – hardly any child in school has a traditional Christian name, given that their parents come from all over the world. Off the top of his head, he can think of only non-Christian names of the children's friends: Reza, Fissaha, Shumi, Daljit, Ayad, Zuneera … It was a kind of joke that Sasha and Masha, with their white English and Thai genes, should carry the first names that they did: Alexander and Marielle. Ayush had been given the privilege of naming them – since everything else had been Luke's preference – and Ayush had activated his lifelong obsession with Russian diminutives, inspired by the novels that ruled his inner life. He had worked backwards, settling on the diminutives first, Sasha and Masha, then moving to their original forms, Alexander and Marielle (Marielle because Maria was too boring to even consider as an option). Here they are, named after literary obsessions, with their mongrel heritage, asking why a horse in ancient India around the fourth century BCE is not called Spencer.

After some half-hearted 'Come, now' and 'OK, that's enough' from Ayush, the children stop their bickering. The story will now deal with the four great scenes of suffering that Siddhartha witnesses on this ride in his chariot: poverty, sickness, old age, and, finally, death, sending him into such a deep introspection about suffering and the causes of suffering that he will renounce his material life, his wealth, his wife, his little son, his life of a prince, and repair to meditate under a bodhi tree, where he will find enlightenment and become the Buddha. This much Ayush knows from books he read in his childhood and in the class on 'World Religions' when he was ten or eleven. What appears instead when he resumes reading is totally unexpected: the writer has united all 'four sights' into one using a dead, dried-up river as the cohering force to string them together. The drama of poverty, sickness, a miserable old age, and an even more squalid death plays out along the banks of the river that once gave life and prosperity and health. Now, the pictures of earth fissured into irregular geometric shapes, dead trees, rotting animal carcasses with the ribs exposed, hungry, grieving people, dead children all render a portrait of such communal anguish that Ayush has to turn his head away from the page and stop reading. Here he is again, immersing his children in the intractable foundation of human existence, this time without having intended any such thing. He is aghast. On the page, a child looks up at an old man, who appears to be saying something to him. The words underneath the image tell of a river that the child never knew; he asks the old man 'What is a river?' and the answer that results fills up the page with the river's life-giving history. In the child's eyes, Ayush reads bafflement – how to understand someone else's grief for a thing one didn't know oneself? Ayush feels a warm pressure behind his eyes and sits up straight. It is time to kiss the children goodnight and turn off the overhead light.

'I'll stay here for a little bit while you fall asleep, OK?' he says to them. He can see their eyelids growing heavy. He goes and stands at their window for a long time, looking out into the garden below, as the July evening turns bluer and bluer, edging towards black but never quite falling into it. The white globes of the hydrangea are lamps in the increasing gloom outside. When the darkness devours everything under and around them, they are still visible, looking like closely clustered bobbing heads in dark waters, floating for survival.

He can no longer bound to the door, tail a wild weathervane in the breeze, squeaky toy in mouth, squealing with joy (impossible to tell sometimes whether the squeal is his or the toy's), turning round and round in erratic half-circles and circles as if wanting to be stroked and touched on every part of his body all at once, surprised by joy, impatient as the wind, when any member of his family comes in. Now it's a lifting of his head, a bark, his doggy smile, and the repeated thump of his tail on his bed or, on rare occasions, a slow arising and a cautious walk to the door. Movement, restlessness, speed, in all this is joy, not in this measured, halting slowness.

'Sweethearts,' Luke says to the children, 'be gentle with him, OK? He's getting old, he cannot tumble around with you any more.'

'He's only ten-and-a-half years old,' Masha replies, 'so two years older than us.'

'Yes, that's right, but dog years are different from human years,' Luke says. 'His first year is equal to fifteen years, his second year is equal to nine years, so can you tell me, quick mental arithmetic, how old he is in human years when he is about to turn three?'

'Five plus nine is fourteen, carry over one, one plus one equals two, twenty-four, he is twenty-four,' Masha says, doing the calculation with her fingers.

'Great, Masha, well done. OK, now something a little difficult. Every year from his third birthday is five human years. Can you tell me how old he is now in human years?'

Luke will handle this brilliantly, Ayush knows. He slips out of the living room.

Ritika gives a short laugh before she says, 'But I wouldn't know how to go about writing a whole book.'

Ayush says, 'I'll help you. You know how to do it, you just don't know that you know it. Trust me, I'm an editor.'

'But what on earth am I going to write about?'

Ayush has given this some thought, but faced now with the direct question, he feels as if he's going to flub his lines. He takes a deep breath and says, 'About the biases and elisions and blind spots of your discipline. About the collusions and orthodoxies and limitations of your priestly class. All the bullshit – trickle-down, Laffer curve, wage-price spiral, incentives in healthcare markets – all of which have had, continue to have, such oversize destructive effects on the lives of ordinary people. The ways advances in behavioural economics are being used as tools to wring every last drop of blood out of workers and, generally, fuck over the labour side of things.'

'Wow. Ayush.'

'Can you write me a book about that? About the human cost of that? From what I've heard from you ever since we met, it seems to me that you're unhappy with your lot too.'

'But you want me to tell a story. Our work is quantitative, data driven. Data rule everything. It's not easy to make that into a book readable by the general readership.'

'But human beings are at the origins of data, if you see what I mean. You take certain aspects of real human lives and stylize them into data. There must be humans, embodied, feeling, alive human beings, standing at the beginning and at the end of what you do, no?'

'Yes, true, but that stylization, or abstraction, is the key. Unfortunately, data are faceless, not individual. Life is not data. For that, you have to go elsewhere.'

Ayush is silent. He cannot rebut this argument.

'Why do you want me to write this book?' Ritika asks.

'I'm a publisher, I'm always on the lookout for interesting books to commission.'

'Is that the real reason? The *real* real reason?'

Phone held to his left ear, Ayush paces the living room, aligning exactly the corners of the books with the bottom left corner of the coffee table. He counts the number of steps he takes in each direction – seven – along the wide black margin of the rug, his feet stringently within the margin. He doesn't want to hear her answer her own question. Instead, he says, truthfully, 'I want you to write this book because you too are at war with your own world. You, too. You know that it's the only war worth fighting.'

13.

The children are in school. Ayush is working from home – the only way to get what he considers his real work done. There's a brief text from Luke: 'Are you at home? Stay there, I'm coming back.'

He's found out. Ayush also knows why it has taken Luke so long. In fact, the reason why Ayush knows is because Luke long ago had explained some point about behavioural psychology to him, something about how and why most people procrastinate and ignore certain unpleasant tasks, or leave them until the last minute, or even beyond: deadlines, of course, but also filing tax returns, opening bank statements, looking at credit card bills. Eight months after the deed Luke has opened one of his email updates from the brokerage company that manages several of his – their – investment funds.

The knowledge doesn't defuse the anxiety at the imminent confrontation. Luke comes straight to the top of the house, to Ayush's study.

There's no beating about the bush. 'I spoke to Peter Dirks at Gaveston's,' Luke launches in. His lips seem oddly white. 'Is it true that you took out £200k from the children's education fund?'

'Yes, I did.'

'Why didn't you tell me?'

Ayush is struck by the fact that this is the first question, not the one he thought would open the discussion. 'Because you wouldn't agree. Because it would defeat the whole purpose, telling you.' He's quivering inside. With every human being, regardless of how well you know them, of how much, how unquestioningly they love you, you can cross a line.

'What purpose? If you needed money, why didn't you ask me?' Only after this does Luke ask, 'What did you do with it?'

'I gave it away to three different climate change charities.'

Luke's face wears an expression Ayush has never seen before: the struggle between shock and disbelief is so picture-perfect that a column of laughter begins to build up inside him.

'Why? Why? I don't believe this, this is fucking insane. Are you mad? Have you taken leave of all your fucking senses?' His voice is low, hoarse, and suddenly Ayush realizes that this is what the rage of a calm, patient, even-tempered man sounds like.

'We have so much. So much to consume and waste, and forget that we even have so much, we just take it for granted ...'

'That was for the children. All the consultancy that I do on the side, all that money goes into that portfolio. You robbed their future to give to charity, where the money is going to make zero difference. Zero. Nada.'

'They're not going to have a future anyway.'

'And you were trying to make it cast-iron certain that they don't. What were you thinking?' This comes out in a whisper.

'I'm going to pay it back.'

'How? With the pin-money that they pay you in publishing?'

Before he can answer, Luke moves closer to Ayush, lifts up the heavy brass Nataraja that he has on his desk, and hurls it at the window. There is a disfiguring snarl on Luke's face as he does it, teeth bared, white lips in a thin rictus. The statue shatters a windowpane and flies out. In a second or two, they hear it fall with a splash into one of the water butts in the garden three floors below. He sweeps his right arm across the table, cleaning it of the stacks of paper and the laptop, the pen stand, the notepad in one clean move. The computer, open like a butterfly, lands with a clunk in the strip of floor between the desk and the bookshelf. Several sheets of A4 follow it in a flutter. Ayush stands frozen: who would have thought that crossing that line could be transformative in this way, for this is a different, a wholly new, man he is watching. He feels no fear, no distress, just wonder. In the odd, dissociative calm that has settled upon him, he worries about putting all the pages back in the right order, the edited ones face down on a pile, the unedited ones in a different stack, facing up. He feels that thing again where he is perched somewhere on the upper levels of the floor-to-ceiling bookshelf and looking down on himself looking at Luke, thinking about ordering the pages of the manuscript he is editing, and Luke standing in a ridiculous pose, knees bent, arm not yet fully retracted, mouth open, as if frozen by a mistimed click of a camera, watching, the tremor running through him now visible.

The moment unkinks and time flows again. Luke collapses on to the sofa and puts his head in his hands and clutches his hair. After what seems a very long time, Ayush says, 'I have to get the children from school.'

Luke looks up but not at Ayush. To the broken window-pane he says, 'I'll get them. I'll take them to my parents' for the weekend.' He gets up to leave, then turns around and says to the scattered paper and sharpened pencils on the floor, 'I'd like you to think about what you've done.' Ayush thinks Luke has finished talking, that he'll leave the room now, but he keeps standing. 'You think I don't know that you showed them that abattoir film when they were little?' Luke says. 'You think they didn't tell me? What are you trying to do? I'd like you to think carefully about that too.' Then he's gone.

Ayush can hear Luke move downstairs, opening drawers, closets, going into the children's room; presumably throwing things into an overnight bag. Now that Ayush is alone in his study again, he feels frozen in the aftermath of what he has witnessed. He cannot get out of his chair to retrieve the laptop and check if it's damaged, gather up the pages of the manuscript, sweep up bits of glass on the floor near the window. That division he had felt earlier is now gone, leaving him entirely trapped inside himself, sealed, unitary.

All weekend Ayush speculates about the reasons, apart from the obvious one, behind Luke's decision to get away for the weekend to his parents' in Gloucestershire. Luke's family is wealthy – his father is a former banker, and there's money stretching back generations in his mother's family. While Ayush understands how Luke's father has made money, he has only ever received vague, airy non-answers from Luke about where the wealth from his mother's side originates. Maybe the real reason for Luke's impulsive decision is to strategize about how the money appropriated by Ayush can be best recouped? Or whether they can give him a temporary loan until he has made back the sum in consultancies? If this is the reason that Luke has taken off for Gloucestershire, Ayush simply doesn't know what the exact contents of these conversations would be, what details they would entail. His soul feels burned enough after each acquisitions meeting for which he has to produce a P&L for the books he wants to take on. Then a corollary to this path of speculation occurs to him: in the unlikely event that Luke tells his parents why the twins' education portfolio is short of £200k, what kinds of thoughts and judgements about Ayush would be going through his parents-in-law's minds? He cannot prevent himself from falling into the rut of this rumination. Unbidden, and surprising him, the thought of M.N. Opie suddenly visits him. Ayush can understand some of the many reasons for a person to want to disappear from his own life but what were his author's? A stripping away of the self or the necessary insulation of hiding? The former is the highest definition of courage, but who is to say that the hiding is cowardice? It could be an act of defiance, two fingers to the world, or an act of desperation. When Ayush emerges from the churn of his mind, he has managed to banish any misgivings, any feelings of residual guilt, about his small act of redistribution; if anything, he is adamantine in his defiance of any opposition, real or imagined. He is not sorry.

On Sunday afternoon, he gets a text from Luke: 'I'm sorry. Will buy you a new computer. Back by six.' Then, as an afterthought, or maybe an invitation to note its standalone salience in a separate message: 'xx'. Ayush knows that Luke is not just apologizing for his utterly out-of-character outburst and the material damage he has inflicted, but also – perhaps chiefly – for that spiteful dig at how low-paying Ayush's job is. In their twenty-five years together, Luke, with the charitable-ness of the comfortably powerful, a power that springs both from his intellectual discipline and the money he makes, has never brought up money or earning differential simply because he hasn't needed to: to believe, and articulate, that 'economics is life, life is economics' is enough. The rest can be filled in by others. In one of their frequent – bitter and tense – clashes about economics, Luke had said, with touching candour, 'I'm pretty confident about the way I view the world and its workings'; only a certain kind of power can speak like that. Whereas he, Ayush, is left out, will forever remain outside, of that charmed set of people who have achieved equilibrium – comfortable in their skins, comfortable in the world, comfortable inside their heads.

They can only get into the same bed together after Friday's row in the study because Luke doesn't bear grudges, doesn't let things play on in his head. Ayush lies wide awake in the dark. Time behaves the way it does during insomnia – small increments seem of enormous passage. He feels like he is in the open ocean, right in the middle. The only path left is drowning. Luke's hand, in his sleep, comes to rest on Ayush's shoulder. It takes the barest increase of pressure for him to register that there is intent in it, that Luke too is lying awake. A car passing outside creates a thin moving wand of light on their ceiling through a tiny chink in the curtains; no amount of magic is going to mend things and make the world whole again.

Luke says, 'What is it? Tell me. Let me help. I can't bear to see you like this.'

It's easier to say things to the darkness in a room. Ayush moves his hand up to put it over Luke's. They lace their fingers and squeeze. Ayush has to revise his opinion about Luke's tendency not to stir the same fetid pool in his mind.

'It can't be easy for you either,' Ayush says.

'It didn't begin like this. What happened? I feel you're struggling with everything.'

'I am. I'm at war. I can't explain very well. I feel we've taken a wrong turn at some point and it's too late now and we can't get back to the right path.'

'We? Meaning us? You and me?'

'No, no, the whole world, I mean. Everything. We're in the wrong life.' That's the tip of the iceberg. Underneath roils, unarticulated, a lifetime's belief bordering on an incurable disease: that everything in the world, from Lukey's discipline to Ayush's own second-hand domain of fiction, everything hinges on the individual, the rational agent making choices, exhibiting or hiding preferences, the character and her destiny, unfolding over time, developing, changing, reaching a point of fulfilment or its denial; everything in the world makes one think that the solution lies within private choices, personal responsibility, that it is the individual at the centre of things, that personal agency is everything – taking antidepressants, going running, going to the gym, going for therapy – that these actions, within a person's power, are going to solve everything, because the problems are at the level of the self, the self is everything – look at the chattering monkeys' unceasing din about the zeitgeisty, crapulous 'autofiction' ... But what if this centrality accorded the self is entirely misplaced, erroneous, or, as a scientist once joked, not even wrong?

Luke lets out a long breath. 'You can't be at war with everything. You'll be destroyed. Can't you pick your battles? I mean, can't you let some things go, reconcile yourself to them? Isn't it exhausting, for you, I mean, to keep at this pitch of conflict with everything around you?'

You mean, be more efficient, Ayush thinks, but doesn't say it aloud. Luke has never spoken with such eloquence. Could it be the dark, the fact that he can't see Ayush? He remembers a Coetzee story in which the narrator says that it is easier to speak difficult truths in a car because the driver and the passenger are unable to look straight at one another. Again, the thought crosses Ayush's mind how wrong he has got Luke, or at least this aspect of his personality. To have assumed that he thinks only in terms of incentives and costs and benefits and utility, or has no ordinarily human side to him, the part that worries, knits knots, furrows the same path over and over again in his head without reasoning it all away with the formidable intellectual tools at his disposal – that assumption is not true for all cases.

'It could be that you're unhappy with one very deep thing that you're not facing, or cannot face,' Luke continues gently, almost whispering to himself, 'and it's bubbling up in all these smaller things spread over a bigger area.'

Ayush is both amused and dismayed that Luke, the rock of rationality, has taken to spouting psychobabble bullshit, but Ayush knows a related theory from editing – often, the problem on page 172 is not a problem on page 172 but something that needs fixing on page 46 and the issue on the later page is no longer a problem.

'I mean,' Luke whispers, 'the problem could be me. Or us.'

It seems to Ayush that Luke has stopped breathing. He is too unpetty to blame Ayush by going through examples to illustrate this point, to say, 'You're like a bomb all the time, about to go off any second', or 'You're sabotaging all our lives', or 'That day when I said – and you said –'. No, Luke does not do finger-pointing. How come some people's personalities run so clear? Happy childhood? Knowing one's place in the world from the very beginning, never having to fight for it or to constantly prove oneself? Following an intellectual discipline that can explain, explain away, or understand the world? More importantly, having faith in that discipline? Many years ago, Ayush, at the beginning of his journey as a humanities graduate student, had thought his intellectual discipline too could account for the world. How quickly that confidence had burnt away, leaving behind the ashes of a politics of resentment. Luke believes in his discipline with zeal and knows its indispensability to the world as we understand it. Ayush realizes that he has been drawn again into his usual hostile slipstream, at a moment when Luke is offering him sympathy and, crucially, understanding. But can any understanding be in the spirit of the other person's mind, not one's own? Does Luke, perhaps unconsciously, pour everything into his overwhelming paradigm for the world, economic theory, and think of that as understanding? There Ayush goes, pulled inexorably by the defining gravity of his life.

'No. No, that's not it,' Ayush says at last and squeezes Luke's hand. 'No. The thought has crossed my mind, of course, but it can't be.'

'It took you so long to say that?' There is a catch in Luke's voice.

'I was thinking.'

That wrong turning – could it be that he had taken it, ignored the signs that had perhaps always been there, unable, at the time, to read or interpret them? Where could the error have been made? The fiction of a unitary moment, a single explanation, is tempting even to him. What about that long bank holiday weekend on the Suffolk coast nearly twenty years ago, a time that resides in his head as having been spent almost entirely in bed, the bedlinen towards their checkout time at the Aldeburgh bed and breakfast almost steaming with their mingled juices? Such a different time, such remote actions that even the memory of them is faintly unappetizing. On a rare venture outside for a walk along the pebbled shore, the sky the colour of oysters, and the water like an infinitely dimpled stretch of wet grey marble seething with life underneath, Ayush had picked up a small collection of beautiful stones, polished smooth by the waves, each one unique in shape or design or colour. He had recited Auden's lines to Luke, 'If equal affection cannot be / Let the more loving one be me', and had meant it, or thought he had. Luke had been baffled by the lines, by the sentiment behind them. Ayush had tried to explain and interpret but Luke simply could not understand why anyone would want to be the more loving one. Of course, he wouldn't have, Ayush now thinks. Many years after that incident, which he had almost forgotten but now thinks of as some sort of a key, he understands that in the columns and tallies of give-and-take that was the foundation stone of Luke's discipline, and therefore formed his understanding of the world, giving more of something meant having less of that same thing and was always a negative. Net cost, in his words.

A silence has now descended; there is no way of telling for how long. To Ayush, it seems unending, until Luke breaks it with 'It's the children, isn't it?'

Ayush cannot answer this, so he remains silent.

Ayush had never wanted children. He had grown up as part of a generation for whom the idea of gay parenting was, literally, unthinkable. That boundary was surmounted only in the noughties. It was puzzling for him that Luke had pushed for having children. Ayush had taken on the mantle of a faux-economist to try to argue Luke out of parenthood. How can you think the benefits will outweigh the costs when the advantages are conspicuously so few, some of them unknown, some even unknowable, while the costs are enormous, lifelong, and all too visible? What is the utility, however expansively you define it? Time, money, leisure, travel, available energy, the slack and the buffer zones that make life bearable – Ayush had thrown everything he could think of at it, and one by one Luke had argued against his points, or been stubborn in refusing to acknowledge, often doubling down on his mulishness. Net cost, Ayush had shouted, you wouldn't hesitate for a moment to dump it into the basket called net cost. The devil can quote scripture for his purposes. And what about Spencer? We just got Spencer, he's only a year old, I thought that was going to be it, you, me, and the dog, I thought that was our family, two adults and Spencer. Luke had professed bafflement that Ayush should have thought of the dog as a child substitute. Ayush had wondered then – and wonders now – if Lukey was being disingenuous. And climate change? What about climate change? Wouldn't they be contributing to it: from extra washing-machine runs to extra consumption on all fronts to adding two more humans to the great crushing weight on the world's finite resources? Luke had dismissed this as ... as what? Ayush doesn't remember now; something about multiple equilibria, or another snazzy term that served one's own interest well under the guise of a cute mathematical model, something that Ayush wouldn't have the wherewithal to argue against. What about the future of the children in a burning world? What kind of life were we going to be bringing them into? Ours is the very last generation money might be able to cushion, but what about theirs, even if we leave them well-off? They would be living in gated communities, walled cities protected by private militia, in a world of permanent war, permanent movement, of migrants hunted down to keep the have-nots from sharing the spoils of the rich. He had floated all kinds of dystopian scenarios, with all the eloquence that he could muster, but Luke had remained immovable because he could only be convinced by arguments based on real economics, made by real economists, not by fiction. But it was not as if the vision he evoked was some time in the future; they had already begun to live it; not to know that was akin to not having a firm visual image of the outer shape of a house because one lived inside it.

Where was this baby-hunger coming from, Ayush had wondered. If that question could have been answered, if Luke had even approached answering it, Ayush would have conceded; reluctantly, of course, but he would have given in since it was not possible to go to war on something that was so central, so consuming in a partner's life, without breaking up. Really, what remained of the very few advantages of homosexuality if gay people were in this frenzied rush to close the gap with the heterosexual world by opting into all its conformities and oppressions – wedding, wedding frock, wedding list, reproduction? Parenting as a consumer lifestyle choice, like buying into the Instant Pot craze or 'this season's must-have' fads; they have it, so we must too. The fight for equal rights turned out to be a revolution to have the right to change nappies and have months on end of interrupted sleep. But Ayush also knew that deep inside he had a fundamental discomfort about gay parenting, gay parents. He hated to admit it – it made him a conservative in his own eyes – but he had dug it up and thrown it at Luke as his last bit of ammunition.

Luke, who knew Ayush better than anyone else, had been wrong-footed at having been unable to imagine that the man he had married would have misgivings about gay rights. But he had recovered quickly enough to lob it all back at Ayush.

'I thought that you, of all people, would have pushed back at this prejudice.'

'What do you mean, I, of all people?'

'You know, growing up in this country, what exclusion is, what prejudice is. Do you not want a different life for the next generation?'

'It is exactly because I know what it is that I do not want these children to be at the receiving end of it. You think this country has changed? Why can't you understand my sheer fear of what these children with two fathers, one of them even brown, will go through in school?'

'I thought you wanted a better world. Someone has to begin the process.'

'But, don't you see, we're performing this big experiment on the children? They have no choice in the matter. We cannot imagine what damage it might do them. How can you be so optimistic about the outcomes?' Ayush had slowly acquired Luke's vocabulary and jargon to the extent of using some words unthinkingly, even unironically.

Could Luke not see? Ayush had thought then. Did Luke want the children to become like Ayush, a consumed, jittery, unsettled creature? When he was five or six, he had discovered a cat hiding behind the big, dense growth of oleander against the back wall that formed the boundary between his parents' home and their neighbours'. Ayush had approached it with the intention of luring it out and perhaps, eventually, indoors for the longer term, not just as a visitor. The cat had growled and hissed and spat, but not budged; Ayush noticed that in the space where one of its eyes should have been, there was only an oblong of concave white-red jelly. His father had warned him not to go anywhere near the cat – the wound had made it feral, and it could attack anyone within striking distance. 'Byathay hingsro hoye gechhe,' he had said; Ayush still remembers the phrase: 'It's gone feral with pain.'

Luke had won, if it could be put like that. Ayush had simply given up the fight one day. He has a cloudy memory of what the proximate reason was. Was it indulgence on his part, in the days when affection could give rise to something like indulging a loved one? With that tide gone, and surrounded now by the detritus left behind, it seems difficult to summon the memory of the feeling that must have resulted in giving way to Luke's wishes. Maybe it was a gift that he had given Luke; an expensive present, given by Ayush, true, but purchased by Luke. Money had never been a problem for him – his trust fund had taken care of the three-storey Victorian terrace on the border of Dulwich and Herne Hill, and his consultancy side-work had paid for the surrogacy.

Once Ayush had acquiesced, an overjoyed Luke had even floated the idea of a milkshake baby, but Ayush had drawn the line at that: Luke could have the full pleasure – and conviction – of being the biological parent. When the twins arrived, Ayush was revolted at his first sight of them, two red, puckered, insect-like faces, but soon what swept through him was relief that the Thai phenotype from the mother appeared, at least at this point in the babies' lives, to be minimal. It was fear on his part that had made him not want children who would not manifest whiteness.

And what had happened between then and now? He thinks of it as a steady diminishment, an attrition. Standing on the shingled beach in Aldeburgh on that dirty romantic long-weekend getaway, he had picked up a smooth piece of grey stone, marked with an entirely inset map of milk-white that reproduced perfectly the stone's shape. The map had two concentric rings of light grey around it, again, in the perfect shape of itself, as if it were a section of a diagram showing iso-therms or the way the depth of the water shaded in deeper and deeper bands away from the shore. He keeps it on his desk at work. It had begun as a reminder of a time of togetherness, then of a fading time, but that too had disappeared, leaving it silent and marooned as just a decorative object. Thinking of its earlier roles caused Ayush slight discomfort, even embar-rassment. But of late it has started speaking to him again, with the exact words it had used at the very beginning: 'I shall be your good luck charm, for you have saved me from the fate of millions of my brethren, which is getting caught by wave after wave after wave, then dashed on to the shore, unceas-ingly, over and over and over, until everything is worn down to finer particles of themselves, or until the end of time. No sooner have you thought this is the last dragging-and-flinging, that you'll be out of reach of the next wave that comes along, left to rest with those who have also been liberated, than you're sucked back up again and thrown down. No rest, only motion, motion forever. Here I have perpetual rest.' But now the words mean something entirely different. He often stares at the stone with something tending towards longing, even envy. Had Luke planned the whole children thing so that he would have something to hide behind, an excuse, a reason, an armour, all of those together, when love and desire ran out, like they always did? How heterosexual of him, if he had. Or maybe, putting into practice what he knew from his theories

109

of changing preferences, reference points, multiple selves, or whatever they were calling it nowadays and declaring it a great breakthrough in understanding, he had obtained a kind of insurance for one possible, perhaps only, route the future could flow. Whereas he, Ayush, well, he didn't foresee the inevitable, who does, even though everyone knows it with the rational part of his brain, and everyone thinks that he is going to be the great exception to the greater laws of inevitability, but he has always been prepared to come to the end of something and look down the precipice into the void far down below. Or maybe it wasn't a precipice and a void, but just a sea of grey you stepped into, and it enveloped you in the way the air had previously done, and you just lived in the new element. That was all. He doesn't need any insurance for that.

14.

It's a raw November new moon night, dry and cloudy. Ayush has already cut up his debit and credit cards, his Sewer expenses card, and buried them in the far bed where the three ferns, the photinia, the rampant honeysuckle, and the ceanothus live. Luke is sleeping like an angel, helped by the Clonazepam drops Ayush has added to his dinner wine; no ordinary sounds of the night, nor anyone moving about, not even a minor burglary, can disturb his peace, at least not for several hours. Ayush goes to settings in his phone and cleans it of everything. He has had to consult IT at Sewer to help him with this. He gets out of bed and tiptoes to the children's room. The diorama the sea-creatures night light casts on the inner surface of the frosted glass globe is elongated and diffused to pale sheets of moving light on the walls, in eternal, unchanging repetition. In that light, surprisingly bright, he can see their sleeping faces. What are they dreaming? They are where he cannot accompany them; he feels a mild envy, then liberation – he cannot go there, so there is no need to try. Each of them is unyoked from the other in this passing moment.

Tonight, Siddhartha slips out of his princely bed and looks at the sleeping faces of his wife, Yasodhara, and his son, Rahula. She has her arm around their son and his face is pressed to her breast. They are peaceful, innocent, and ensnared. He leaves the room and moves through the halls and corridors of the palace until he reaches the front door. The guards bow and open the gate for him. Chandaka is waiting outside, in the courtyard, with Kanthaka, already harnessed.

'To the Anoma River, Chandaka,' Siddhartha says.

They had reached up to this point in the story. He tiptoes downstairs, careful to avoid the creaky bits of the stairs. In the living room, Spencer gives a very hushed bark; a quiet 'hello' so that it doesn't disturb anyone. Ayush moves towards him, puts his arm around his neck, and whispers in his ear, 'Come on, sweetheart, we're going.' The dog's breath is bad, and he takes so long to assemble himself into the right arrangement to get off his bed. He is mystified by this untimely activity, so out of routine. What are they doing? He doesn't want to go anywhere. The door opens, so he must follow, but why? Where? He is beckoned to get into the back seat of the car. Ayush has spread a plastic sheet over its entire length and covered it with a candlewick bedcover to protect the seat from Spencer's incontinence. 'Come on, come on, let's go. Come on, good boy,' Ayush whispers. Spencer, arrested by his joints and his puzzlement, cannot move. Ayush picks him up – not an easy task, especially to do delicately, as he must, since he cannot cause Spencer pain through clumsiness – and gently deposits him in the back seat, then stands up, panting slightly after the exertion.

At a red traffic light approaching the Hammersmith flyover, he opens the car window a crack and flicks out the SIM card – already separated from the phone back at home; home! – with all the force that the two-fingered action can muster. He rolls up the car window and takes the right at Fuller's Brewery gently to prevent Spencer from sliding around on the plastic. The contrast with the wisp of cold breeze that entered the car earlier makes him now smell Spencer's sickness in the trapped air inside. For here there is no place that does not see you. You must change your life. Even at this hour, traffic on the M4 is a steadily flowing stream of red tail lights in one direction and the measured onrush of headlights on the other. Just beyond Heathrow, he cranks down the window again and flings his phone out with one easy arcing movement of his arm; he cannot tell from the sound he has peeled his ears to hear if the gadget hits the road or the ground beyond the hard shoulder on the other side. No doubt some camera has picked this up and will regurgitate it in a bluey pixelated blur later, much later, but what does he care? His mouth is so dry he can barely swallow. Near Marlow, he pulls over at a lay-by and gets out of the car. The traffic is still steady. Where are people going, what are they fleeing? He opens the back door and tries to usher out Spencer, but he doesn't want to move. Even in the dark, Ayush can read his imploring look – can you not leave me alone now, in the cage of my pain and old age? Everything has to happen swiftly now, in one clean motion, like the way an executioner's axe has to come down and sever in a swift single stroke. Ayush lifts the substantial weight that is Spencer, judges a gap in the traffic, runs across to the median metal strip, and deposits Spencer on that border – whichever way he chooses to cross, his slow, arthritic body will be in the full flow of fast-moving traffic. Then Ayush leaps across the highway with cars heading in the opposite direction, towards London, jumps over the metal boundary, and runs and runs and runs, across woods and fields and streams, across towns and cities, over the sea, until he runs outside time.

II

I thought how all of us are always trying to imagine what someone else is doing, eating our hearts out trying to find the truth and moving about in our own private worlds like a blind man who gropes for the walls and the various objects in the room.

– Natalia Ginzburg, *The Dry Heart*,
translated by Frances Frenaye

People were leaving one by one, or in couples, with long intervals in between: the end of this dinner party was not following the exodus-en-masse rule. First, the pair who had to teach tomorrow: Marcus and Eleni, both economists. This was the eleventh pair of economists she had met; they tended to marry each other. She entertained her hypothesis about this again, silently, but decided against bringing it up now. That topic had a tendency to go in unintended directions, all unwelcome. Next, the furiously bright but mostly quiet graduate student, Carla. It had been Rohan's idea to invite her: while working for a PhD on 'The Novel in the Internet Age' she was also taking some poetry creative writing classes, taught by his colleague Leonie, but the more interesting fact for Rohan, he had told Emily, was that Carla was already a published poet – *Poetry Magazine*, the *NYRB*, the *LRB*, the *TLS*, even one in the *New Yorker*, and all this in the second year of her PhD; according to Leonie, Carla had 'arrived fully formed' to the class. Other than Emily, Carla had been the only person to have arrived solo to the dinner. Two other couples, Liam and Brenda (philosophy and English, respectively), and Katrina and Avi (mathematics, linguistics), left within half an hour of each other, until Emily was the last guest left. She could tell that Rohan had enjoyed this staggered leave-taking. Noam, Rohan's partner, knowing that Emily and Rohan would now need to dissect the party, left them to it and retired upstairs. Noam, a shy, self-contained, somewhat otherworldly man, was an astrophysicist at Imperial. Quite early on in the two men's relationship, when she had been introduced to Noam, she had asked him politely what he did, and he had said, 'I model tides in stars and extrasolar planets.' Wonder had shut her up, not disinterest; she didn't know how to move further with the conversation. Rohan had once said to her, 'He tries to explain something called N-body dynamics, or is it M-body, anyway, whatever, N-body or M-body dynamics of dense stellar systems when we're stuck in a traffic jam. How sexy is that? His head is really in the clouds. I was going to say "literally", like the kids, ha! He'll take a curve on a highway and tell you how because of M-forces some cars will take the curve faster than others.' Emily had been brushed by awe again. What did the two talk about other than physics? What did their shoes, in the shoe rack just inside the front door, say to each other?

While giving Rohan a hand with the clearing up, Emily asked, 'Why didn't you get Carla to bring somebody with her?'

Rohan said, 'What do you mean, bring somebody?'

'I mean, someone, a friend, a boyfriend, whoever.'

'I didn't know she had a boyfriend ... but why?'

'It might have been less lonely for her. You know, a single grad student amongst faculty, everyone nearly her parents' age ... She was so quiet.'

'We're more an older sibling's age than a parent's.'

'Anyway, it was just a thought ...'

'You don't think she enjoyed it?'

'No, no, it's not that at all,' Emily said forcefully. 'She was so eloquent and seemed so relaxed and confident when she spoke.'

Emily knew that she hadn't really offended Rohan. Their friendship went back to secondary school, nearly two decades, so they could take certain liberties with each other.

Besides, she was being sincere about Carla's eloquence: much of the conversation, initiated by Rohan then taken over, out of genuine interest and enthusiasm, by the three literature scholars, including Emily, had been about poetry. In fact, Rohan had been curious about Carla ever since Leonie had told him that a student of hers had written an extempore sestina in class the previous semester. The dinner conversation had been about technically difficult forms (sestina, villanelle), about favourite poets, about how poetry was, or even possibly could be, workshopped and edited. Rohan and Noam, ever the sensitive hosts, had tried to involve the economists and the linguist and the mathematician by changing the subject frequently, but the gravity of the evening had been directed towards poetry.

Little had Emily known, when she had started out as a keen early modernist, that an academic job would be the most hostile ground for the flourishing of a love of literature. The new cornucopia of contemporary times, email, the gift that could be relied upon to keep giving, and giving in plenty, forever, until she was no more, had thrown a heavy mantle over Emily's first love, poetry, and consigned it to a locked, dust-sheeted room in her mind. This evening, she had been led up to that forgotten room, given a key and a promise. How come she had never heard of all these American poets who Carla claimed were 'transformative'? George Oppen? Carl Phillips? Philip Levine? Gwendolyn Brooks? Even memories of Bishop and Lowell and Muldoon and a few others were hazy now. How had the sixteenth century devoured it all? How come she knew Spenser backwards but not a line of Marianne Moore? In fact, it was not the sixteenth century that had devoured it; had that been the case, she would have been doing something right. But here she was, transported to some balmy oasis, created by magic for a fleeting few hours, in a little side lane off the desert that was academia, watching poetry flourishing and flowering, *living*, in the way she had forgotten it could. She felt a column of pressure in her chest not unlike an effervescence. She kept it from Rohan; a private thing that she had just been promised possession of.

By the time she left at around 1:40 a.m., it was surge pricing; seven minutes, her phone screen said. Karim, 4.9 stars. When the map showed he was only 400 metres away, Emily kissed Rohan goodnight and stepped outside. The rain, which had been the weak garden-sprinkler type that's characteristic of the London winter, was now strafing the pavements as if wishing to perforate the solid asphalt: there was a steady mist of spray rebounding from the street. In the orange bath of the street lights, the scene looked like a film set, created perfectly, waiting for the action to begin.

She heard it before she saw it – a screech and then a grey Nissan taking the corner of St George's Square and whatever street it was on her left at unacceptable speed. Was she drunk? She got in, said 'Hello', and added, 'It'll be a slow journey to Victoria Park in this rain', hoping he'd get it. She couldn't make out his face in the rear-view mirror, only a pair of coal-black eyes with lashes that made them look as if they were lined with kohl. Did he even return her greeting? She was jolted forward then thrown back on her seat as he set off. Either she must be drunk, she thought, trying to find the clasp for her seat belt, or the driver was a madman, or intoxicated, or a total amateur. How much had she had? Two Campari-and-sodas before dinner, then she lost count of the glasses of wine. Then Rohan had got out the Armagnac and she had had what he insisted on calling a nightcap, although they were clearing up and loading the dishwasher and debriefing when they had started on it. She could ask the driver to slow down, but she was suddenly self-conscious about speaking – what if she slurred her words? And did she smell of booze? He … he must be Muslim, what would he think? But no, it was nothing to do with the alcohol – he really was speeding. Everything was going past her in such a whizzing rush. The river cleaved close to them one minute then snaked away the next, only to reappear and keep them company, dark and oily for stretches, then gleaming with shivered lights, steadily rippled with rain, for what seemed like minutes. There was the tower on the right; the river had been left behind almost immediately after. Whitechapel was deserted at this hour, but still looked dense and squalid under the steady rain.

They were going down residential side streets now, with frequent swings right and left that made her head swim. Had they crossed the canal? It should be a straight road with one right turn – why was he zigzagging so much? And, god, at such speed. She couldn't recognize where they were – Victoria Park-ish? – so she took out her phone. The car lurched sideways, and the phone slipped out of her hand and slid under the front passenger seat.

'Fuck!' she fairly shouted. Without thinking, she unbuckled her seat belt and bent down sideways, almost on her knees, head bowed between them, her right hand groping under the front seat. There, she could touch it with the tip of one finger but otherwise could get no purchase on it. Then the car bounced as if it were trying to take a series of speed bumps at a hundred miles an hour, bumped and hit the road like a spinning top flung down from high by a capricious child. Within the duration of those movements, her neck gave an audible crack, she shouted, 'What the fuck', and then her head crashed so hard against the door that she screamed. She felt the car swerve, heard the screech of tyres. She dug her nails into the seat and pulled herself up. For a fraction of a second everything went black, except for the pop of colours behind her eyes, and she felt a strange sensation of tingling inside her head, like pins-and-needles in her brain. The car had stalled. Something made her turn around. Through the back window, she could discern an animal – a dog? – lying in the middle of the road, black and shiny with the rain, beside another heap. The bigger heap was trying to get up: it was a boy; even at this distance, and in this white-and-sepia illumination, she could tell that his front and hands were stained. He stood up for a few seconds then fell over the dog. With another violent jolt, the car started up, causing her head to spin. The scene receded farther and farther but seemingly in one flash, then the car turned a corner – the boy and the dog belonged to another street and, she felt for a moment, to another order of things, things that she had imagined, not seen.

The car was speeding, and she was shouting, 'Stop! Stop, just fucking stop! Let me out, I want to get out.' The next minute she was outside Gascoyne House, the mid-century modern estate that contained her flat. The familiar reasserted itself before she could react – she was out of the car, standing in the cold rain, shaking, watching the car flee.

Later, she thought – and still thinks, to this day – of her decision not to text or call Rohan, or someone, immediately and wondered if that was where the crossroads lay. It was not even a decision, not a withholding, but a momentary inertia that ripened, without any intention on her part, into something weightier. Sunday passed in darkness: when she got out of bed in the afternoon and managed to force herself to her desk in the study, she stared at her inbox, as if mesmerized, for hours without opening a single email, and let the deadline of an important conference in North Carolina (on imitation, authority, and authorship) slip past because she couldn't bring herself to send the abstract of her paper on Spenser's reading of Virgil. The following wet, grey morning, only a few shades paler than the darkness that was going to swallow it in around six hours, she walked the thirty-five minutes to the department, hoping the walk in the cold would clear her head. The decision not to take the bus was foolish: her insides were rinsed by waves of nausea, and the beats of a headache kept time with them. She taught a graduate seminar on Spenser and the complaint tradition during which she kept losing the threads of so many arguments and lines of interpretation that she caught one of her five students in the middle of a furtive eye-roll to another. Back in her office, she pulled out the wastepaper basket from under her desk several times because she thought she was going to be sick; she couldn't face the curricular committee meeting. The walk to the meeting room along the corridor would give her a view, three floors down, of the sculpture of the horse's head in the tiny, entirely enclosed inner courtyard, and today she would have wanted to throw herself down into that well. At the Sainsbury's on Mile End Road, she sleepwalked along the aisles, looking at nothing, and left with a packet of pine nuts, a bag of carrots, a one-and-a-half-litre container of Persil Non Bio liquid, and some candied orange peel. She boarded a 425 and got off at the roundabout after Victoria Park; she didn't know how she would manage the ten-minute walk after that. At the corner of Victoria Park Road and Guinness Close, she kneeled on the sodden earth under a sycamore tree in the strip of green between the two roads and discreetly threw up the hummus wrap she had forced herself to eat before class. Her eyes felt as if they were being pushed out of their sockets by the pounding inside her head. She could taste the spirituous tang of Armagnac pushing up with the burn behind her breastbone, even a note of the fiery tomato rasam that Rohan had served in dainty teacups before the first course ('to wake up your liver', he had said). She retched again. Her knees were cold. Yellow light spilled out from a window on to the dusky pavement on the other side. A car drove past her then another seconds, maybe minutes, later. No one slowed down to check on her, if only out of curiosity.

She left the bag of groceries by the door after she entered her flat, flickering in and out of short, intense bursts of dizziness. Her phone had become something radioactive – in the early hours of this morning she had swiped away the request for the star rating of her driver and not looked at it again. She had missed calling her mother at some point over the past weekend. She could hear the phone's muffled rings occasionally and fear washed over her. She allowed herself to think of the incident as an arachnophobe would think about spiders, hoping that volitional summoning to mind would nibble away at the fear, ultimately reducing it to nothing. There were so many things which she could have done, could still do. Call Rohan. Get in touch with the ride-share app. Read their page on safety. Call the police. Call the doctor. Go back to the ... the term that jumped into her mind was 'scene of the crime'. The headache, like the dizziness, was a fickle visitor, but when it was present, it seemed like that was the only thing that focused her attention. The word 'concussion' floated up in the murk of her thoughts then sank down. She got up several times in the night to retch – mucus, bile, then nothing. She heard what she thought were foxes on the common. The glow of the street lights got in through the space between the curtain rail and the wall. She hadn't looked at her email for over twelve hours; the twinge of anxiety was not hers, she felt, but someone else's, someone she was observing.

The feeling persisted in the metal-grey morning. Who was that with dark circles under her sockety eyes looking back at her from the bathroom mirror as she made an immense effort to put on some make-up, if only some concealer, with shaking hands?

There were only one or two people walking across the common on this raw morning as she left for work. Lost inside herself, she made the sharp turn left at the entrance to Gascoyne House to walk to the end of Well Street Common. She did not see the man following her until she had almost reached the People's Park Tavern. She heard someone call out from behind, 'Excuse me.'

She turned around. A stranger with most of his face hidden by a scarf that reached up and nearly covered his entire mouth and a skull-hugging woolly hat lowered to his eyebrows. Bloodshot eyes. But even if his face hadn't been so muffled, how could she have recognized him? She had only seen his eyebrows and his eyes in the rear-view mirror two nights ago.

They couldn't have sat in a peopled café to talk, and Emily couldn't – wouldn't – invite him to her home or her office. Throughout their aimless walk, slow, arduous, first in Victoria Park, then hopelessly, in an attempt to head towards her department, in Mile End Park, both of them avoiding, by tacit complicity, retracing any part of the route his car had taken towards the end of their journey, Emily found herself struggling to find the appropriate public face and tone for this encounter. Ridiculously, given the context, she thought that Hamlet's tragedy had been his inability to find a congruence between his inner self and its outer manifestations with the people in his life. How should she be? Just angry or outraged? Cold and stern? Cutting? Threatening? Formal, reserved, with all judgement suspended until she had heard him out? But what was there to be heard? This wasn't a matter of differing viewpoints or interpretations. Reality couldn't be budged. But here she was, concentrating on how to dress her affect and wondering if it wasn't a problem of tone and vocabulary, of what words should come out of her mouth and how. She knew she was, habitually and by intellectual training, focusing on the trivial, but she also knew that very big things could only be made sense of through more manageable related, yet marginal, things: black holes, say, reduced to equations. The map was never to be confused with the territory.

Later, she will remember the external geography of the revelations, such as when he said his name was Salim, not Karim, her bafflement had the setting – objective correlative, in her thinking – of the broad avenue running diagonally across Victoria Park, with the Old English gardens, nestled inside topiaried walls, on their left, the expanse of the manicured parkland stretching out in front of them on either side of the avenue.

'So ... so who, who is Karim?' She felt the stupidity of her words.

'He is brother.'

'Why were you driving it?' She heard that dull-wittedness again; did he too?

'Brother sick, no drive,' he said. 'Sick, very sick.'

Something kicked in and Emily asked, 'Are you insured on that car?'

'Um ... say again,' he said then added 'please' as an afterthought.

'If your brother is the registered driver, then the insurance is under his name. Do you have insurance to drive that car?' She knew she was doing the classic English thing of raising her voice and articulating each word slowly while speaking to a foreigner, and she hated herself for doing it now, but the need to get information, reach some kind of understanding so that the subsequent steps could be taken, drove over social niceties.

On Grove Road, traffic moved slowly. There were shrieking seagulls wheeling around above Wennington Green, some landing on the alopecic earth to look for something only they could see and squabble over. Why were they here, so far from any stretch of water? The red spot under the yellow beak of one just a few feet away from her on the pavement made her want to retch again. That information about correct ownership of the car – or was it the incorrect one that was the admission? – wore the face of the Jehovah's Witness hall on the other side of the road.

What haltingly emerged – and Emily wasn't sure that she had understood fully – was as soiled and spirit-lowering as the scavenging patch of the out-of-place gulls. Because Karim was too ill to drive, and because the family couldn't afford to forego the money his driving brought in, Salim had stepped in. And Emily's impression was that Salim hadn't insured himself, or even declared to the app company that he was taking over from his brother. Repeated and increasingly pointed questions, ultimately to the extent that only clear 'yes' or 'no' answers were possible, or so Emily would have thought, had elicited ambiguous responses, or answers that left her in doubt that her questions had been comprehended. Wild solutions darted through her head like electrical impulses. Get hold of an interpreter – but which language? Arabic? Which version of it? Where was he from? Somalia? Eritrea? Ethiopia? – and don't let Salim go until he replied, in writing, to all the points she will have put on paper. Surely she could just drag him now to the Arabic department? Did the Mod Langs department even offer Arabic? Do a citizen's arrest – did that work or was it a liberal myth? – and take him to a police station. Or, better still, call the police right now. Call someone, anyone, to take over and tell her what to do. Tear off the veil of language between this man and her. For the first time it occurred to her that Salim had come to test the waters, to see if she had already spoken to someone, taken some action, or was considering anything along those lines. Fear had brought him here. She realized that he had not asked a single question, instead had let her do all the talking, thereby revealing her hand. The thing was that, unwittingly, she had not given anything away; not that she had a strategy, but he didn't know that.

Later, she was to think that the flurry of seemingly purposive activity at the end of their walk, although it gave her some necessary information (his phone number, the fact that he lived in Stockwell), was anti-climactic compared with how much more she could have found out or even done. But found out what exactly? What good would more information do? In any case, what she wanted was not his to give. She should have simply gone ahead unilaterally and acted; speaking to a police officer should have been her first action. Instead, she had stood outside her department building, lamely saying 'yes' to his questions, 'You work in this building? You are a teacher?', and appearing petulant to herself by turning away with what she had hoped was a stern 'I shall be in touch' and not 'Goodbye' or a handshake (surely inappropriate?).

Once in her office, she shut the door and fished out her phone. It was out of charge. She plugged it in and tried to focus on her emails but within two minutes the phone came back to life. She keyed in her password. Even the minuscule amount of attentional effort she had to devote to this returned her to a temporary darkness. But what good was giving in to that? And from this moment onward, she wanted to do good, wanted an unravelling followed by restitution.

The pressing things were missed calls and several messages from Rohan, but she allowed herself to defer setting this decision in motion by calling her mother first instead of him.

'I'm sorry I didn't call over the weekend,' Emily said. 'I got caught up in things, and then it was too late. Sorry.'

'Oh, don't worry about it, I know how busy you are.'

The conversation ran down familiar routes. It was the emptiness that was comforting, not the familiarity, not the time-honoured connection. Emily and her mother got along just fine – it was a slightly formal, slightly buttoned-up relationship one could imagine with a work colleague who was liked enough but who one knew would never graduate to becoming a friend. It was a relationship that had no weather fronts, no shadow areas, no possibility for either damage or succour. It was a habit that had lost along the way the interest in which habits usually originated. The only thing that held it back from falling into entirely mindless practice was a tiny but growing desire, even hope, on Emily's part: she wanted to mine her mother for information for a project that had been taking shape in her mind, a small, personal, intimate book, no more than seventy or eighty pages, on the fiction that was memory but played out in the domain of oral family history. It was the colonial strand in her mother's family that had aroused Emily's curiosity: her maternal grandparents had lived in British India during the high noon of the Raj. In fact, her Scottish grandmother had been born in a hill station in South India. There were handed-down stories of a tea estate somewhere, and refractory native labour, and tales of bomb- ings and assassinations told to a child agog with wonder and terror. She recalled shreds and patches of these; they were like thinning mist, about to dissolve; she wanted to see and feel them again, record them to represent.

But what emerged now was a different question altogether.

'Mother, did you get rid of Teapot when I was away at school?'

The question threw Emily herself, but if her mother were taken aback by it, she didn't give any sign because she wasn't the kind to express any emotion, not even one of surprise, unless the unusually long silence that appeared as a punctuation mark at this point of the conversation constituted one, but, Emily later thought, this could have been just the time required by someone to process an utterly unexpected question in order to establish its referents and meaning in the first place. A missing cat from more than a quarter of a century ago, probably never mentioned in conversation for nearly that length of time, and now suddenly, without any build-up, any context, any embedding, lobbed into the conversation as a non sequitur – a silence lasting a few seconds was the least her mother could have given it, Emily tried to explain away, even as those long-buried doubts asserted themselves and rushed out in the form of the question. Time healed nothing.

'No, darling, I didn't. What a thought,' came the calm, unassertive reply, as if her mother had been asked if she had put the kettle on or signed the postal-voting form.

No exclamation of surprise or indignation, no hesitation in placing the event, no fumbling during recall, no question about why Emily was asking such a question after so long, not a single misstep except the seconds-long pause; Emily couldn't help but admire the flawless performance. She could yet learn a thing or two from the older woman.

Teapot had been an unpredictable tabby cat. She could be affectionate and friendly, wanting to sit on your lap and purr away peacefully as you were stroking her, then suddenly she would get a mad look in her eyes and viciously bite and scratch the hand that was petting her. Only Emily could tell the lightning-fast shift in mood and read that changed expression. Teapot had bitten her mother three times, once scratching her close to the bone near her wrist. One Christmas Emily had returned from school to find Teapot gone. Even now she could see in sharp detail the nine-year-old girl standing under the stunted apple tree in the garden that the cat had liked to scratch and calling her heart out. The light had gone, and the girl simply couldn't be brought back inside. Teapot never came back. On a number of occasions, Emily was discovered in the garden in the blue light of moonlit January nights, barefoot on the frosted grass, with her Miss Piggy duvet like an overstuffed sack containing her imperfectly, calling out for the cat in a whisper so as not to disturb anyone. It was only much later – Emily did not remember when – that she ascribed meaning to her mother's tight-lipped parsimony with explanations and consolatory fictions. Or was that meaning itself in the nature of fiction or incorrect interpretation?

Now, though, for the purposes of carrying on their weekly conversation, which normally involved Emily giving an abridged version of her days, she decided not to tell her mother anything about the recent event. After the call was over, she took a deep breath, held it for a count of twenty, exhaled, inhaled again, then tapped on Rohan's number.

'Hello, stranger – did I poison you Saturday night?' he launched in.

'Rohan, can we talk?'

'Correct me if I'm wrong – I thought we were doing exactly that?'

'No, I mean talk talk, as in meet up.'

'Yes, of course. Is everything OK? Can you give me a little sneak preview?'

'I was in an accident returning to my place that night from yours.'

'W-what? What accident? Are you OK? Oh my god. Where are you? Can I come see you right away?' in one rush-and-tumble.

She smiled – so Rohan – and, ridiculously, felt her eyes pricking at the same moment. She steadied her voice enough to say, 'I'm fine, absolutely fine. Don't worry. Unscathed. But there are, um, complications.'

Unusually for people in this city, they managed to meet within an hour, the time it took for Rohan to take the Tube to a café near Stepney Green. They spoke like conspirators in a public place, her perception of her own soul as a dirty thing. Rohan followed his writing-workshop rule of 'no interruption' as she told her story but she knew she was going to be in the dock. While stringing the events of that night into a narrative, she withheld Salim's visit that morning out of some vague instinct.

'Have you called the police? Or reported him to the company?'

She shook her head.

'Why? You must do that immediately. You witnessed a hit-and-run.'

The concern, the sympathy, were all there, but also, now, something hard, a perceptible change from his over-eloquent persona. 'I ... I can't be sure of anything that evening,' she said. 'In the car, I mean.'

'But you saw it, right? The child and the dog, the blood?'

'I ... I think so.' Pause. 'I don't know.' Had she dreamt it all? The nausea paid a kissing visit to her insides and was gone before she had a chance to grip the sides of the table. She turned her head to get out of her line of vision the brushstroke of jam and the scatter of sugar on the plate that had held the doughnut Rohan had just finished.

'Why didn't you call me immediately? What took you so long?'

Yes, she was in the dock. 'I think I was a bit in shock. I also have headaches, nausea, I just couldn't face the phone.' They were still speaking like assassins after a successful mission.

'But why haven't you called the police? OK, if you can't be sure, why not go check on the road where it happened?'

'And do what? Knock on doors to ask if, if ... someone, if there's been ... Or look for, um, evidence on the road?'

'Which street was it?'

'That's what I can't be sure of.' Pause. 'I think I was drunk, the journey felt too long.' Pause. 'No, too short, no, actually, both at the same time, if you see what I mean. There was the river on our right for a long time, then he kept zigzagging and taking side streets. It's basically three long straight lines from Whitechapel to my place, maybe a very tiny wiggle at the end, so I don't understand why he was doing that. It ... it was on one of those side streets. It felt like I was at home almost immediately after that. I think.'

'What do you mean, I think? Let's go and look! There will be a police sign for witnesses to a hit-and-run.'

Alarm seized her face. 'You mean now?'

'Yes, while it's still light. Come on, let's go.'

'I ... I don't think I can face it,' she said desperately. 'I don't know where it was.'

'It's in the receipt they mail you. There'll be a map of the whole route he took.'

Emily didn't know this. She opened the map on the receipt – there it was, beginning time, arrival time, the black line of the route, which she magnified to see the names of the streets towards the end. Salim hadn't taken a wiggly road, the map said: the straight line of Well Street, a very gentle right on Cassland Road, then a sharp right on Gascoyne Road. The zigzagness had been entirely in her head. The map gave the lie to her experience. If she shut her eyes, she could still feel the jolts and swerves of the car and even the attendant head spins and brief moments of nausea. Were they all imagined?

Emily and Rohan took the 277 to Victoria Park, then began to retrace the last leg of her car journey, her arm in the crook of his held close against her side. The one prominent thought among the dozen colliding in her head was: I shouldn't have told him, or not in the weak, helpless, hesitant way that I did. She should have been breezy and confident, emphatically implying that this whole business was in the past, closed, come, let's go get a negroni at Le Bateau Ivre for a debriefing, gosh, what scrapes one gets into. Instead, this; macabrely, the cliché from an adolescence and youth consuming crime fiction that had occurred to her earlier flitted through her mind again: a murderer always revisits the scene of the crime. And that nausea again – she clutched Rohan's arm fiercely. But no, this was head spin, not nausea; had she just made what they called a category error? She wanted to run away. The tightened clasp made Rohan say, 'It's going to be fine. There'll be a big sign the police will have put up on the street. There'll be a number to call. It's going to be easy.'

No, nothing was easy, nothing was ever going to be. Where were they headed? There were no signs on Cassland Road.

'Are you sure it was here?' Rohan asked.

'I can't be sure of anything. I was convinced that he took several turns in the last five, maybe ten, minutes of the journey, but the map shows that I am wrong. Could the map be wrong, somehow?'

'I don't know. I don't think so. Shall we check some side streets, just in case?'

She led like a pack animal, with an unthinking focus, with no choice in the matter: King Edwards Road, right on Clermont Road, back up then left on Tryon Crescent, back to King Edwards Road, then left on Alpine Grove ... it was endless. She wanted to kick him into the road. Wouldn't it be wonderful if the church that formed the island on the crescent fell on to him? And on her too, while they were at it. Then they were on Cassland Crescent, and she kept swallowing down the bile, the column, the nothing that was rising in her. Even in this state, on this mission, she could not fail to appreciate the quiet splendour of the Regency terraces on either side of the small public garden. On Poole Road: which one of those houses was in shock and grief? On the Victorian terraces on Queen Anne Road ... maybe one of the houses on their right side was in mourning? But she had seen the boy and the dog charging out from the left, hadn't she? She was certain it was from the left since the car had been moving up the street in the direction in which they were walking now; it was a one-way road. She disengaged herself from Rohan to slow down and turn to look back then ahead and repeat the movement.

'Is this the road? From which direction did the car approach your home?' Rohan asked.

She nodded, but said, 'I don't know.' The uttered words were instinct, a kind of cultural and behavioural wiring, at some distance from empirical value. 'But it can't be – it's not on the route in the receipt.'

'Oh. Shall we walk down the parallel-ish streets anyway? Maybe it was a street or two away? There doesn't seem to be a police sign here anywhere.'

'But we just did,' she said, indignant now. 'How could it be a street or two away? The map says clearly Cassland then Gascoyne Road', but she felt compelled to do as Rohan suggested. She felt numb and nauseous. On Balcorne Street, a block west, modern terraces presented themselves. Was it this one then? How could she know? She was desperate – she looked down at the street to discern traces of blood – it was blood that she had seen, the dark blooms on the child, hadn't she? On the pavement, a pair of chopsticks and the empty tiny plastic fish, its red plastic mouth missing, of soy sauce from someone's sushi takeaway. No sign from the police tied to a lamp post on the pavements here either. On Terrace Road, a block east, the situation repeated itself. If she had known the child's name, or the dog's, she would have rent the air calling them out; now, she could find nothing around which to give form to the scream that was building up inside her. How many streets east west north south of the first one that had looked promising – ha, god, promising! – would they have to cover? What about knocking on doors and inquiring? Vote canvassers did that, didn't they? Everything looked similar, everything looked different. She shut her eyes and opened them again. This felt unreal. Like a dream she was struggling to wake up from, the here and now.

'Rohan ... I'm, I'm ... let's go back.'

'Wait. We're here. It's just a matter of finding the street on which it happened. I have an idea – why don't we walk from Whitechapel all the way down the route he took? What do you think?'

'I'm ... I'm not feeling great. And it's very cold. The light will go in an hour or so –'

He interrupted, 'Wait! I have a better idea. Why don't we do the route at night later this week? Tomorrow or day after? Everything will look a lot more familiar, don't you think?'

In a novel or a film, she would have fainted at this point. Instead, miraculously, the blooming-and-closing flower of nausea inside her transformed to one of relief.

*

Over the next fortnight, Rohan rang with ideas – a drive from his place to hers to replicate 'that' evening even more authentically; calling the police to establish if there had been a hit-and-run on the night in question; getting in touch with the driver of the car 'in the first instance'. (She felt the piston begin behind her breastbone at the last suggestion even as she snagged over that 'first instance' – what happened after that? What was the last instance? What were the stages of progression?) Lunch, coffee, Rohan continued; she dodged and parried and feinted for nearly a week; she didn't go back in to work. Soon, she knew, he was going to try another tack or get confrontational ('because moral issues are at stake') or walk away and surround himself in a cloud of froideur for weeks.

At nights, she found that she was unable to turn off the infernal motor of her mind. Six hundred and thirty-eight unread emails – the only information she could glean from scrolling up and down was that several were repeated nudges to respond to pressing matters: graduate admissions committee duties; departmental bursaries and prizes committee meeting; field chair meeting; TeLSOC assessment meeting; inclusivity office meeting; agendas and minutes that needed reading; an email from a journal to which she had sent an article; student queries; student work; revision of diversity committee staffing rules. She opened one at random; read it three times, forcing herself to concentrate on the final reading; still couldn't understand a word. Did concussion manifest in this form? Even the worry couldn't land properly on the surface of her mind, which felt grated raw with tiredness. Like deer flitting in a forest from the pillar of one tree to another, silently and very fast – the boy and the dog. But not fast enough. She lay in the dark, sensing more than seeing the diffuse inner glow from the lights outside. In a poem attributed to Ovid, two people enter a wood, but two animals emerge – it is never made clear if a transformation has taken place or whether the entrance and exit of the different creatures are unrelated. The woodcut accompanying the sixteenth-century text showed only birds flying above a copse on a hill. How lonely, how isolated that black clump of trees. It was from childhood, that purity of solitude. It was usually light that did the trick – the way the afternoon sun fell on the side of a building, making a tracery of the shadows of tree branches on the ember-like bricks, or a yellow-and-rose midsummer evening, and she was back immediately to a light-filled day, a sharply delineated, particular day, of childhood, every detail intensely alive, but most alive that sense of utterly pure solitude, as if she had then existed in a world before time, before all turmoil. Why did that picture achieve such a teleportation to the stillness at the heart of everything? She fingered it in her memory as one would worry beads. The past was settled and parts of it could be visited for succour, for hiding in; the future was a narrative one believed one was free to construct – it was like a childhood game with building blocks. But the present tense was always a drowning; recalcitrant and uncompromising. She had to do its bidding; there was no other choice. She felt grit under her eyelids. She remembered a piece of advice for insomnia she had once read online: get out of bed and do something else, such as read or write or cook or whatever takes your fancy. She lay in bed, turning the advice over in her mind for an hour. Then she roused herself and typed 'Homerton hit and run', 'Well St Common hit run', 'Well St Common car accident', 'Homerton boy car accident' into the search engine. Nothing. 'Homerton police hit run report'. Nothing, again, although this did give her the option to report such an incident. How could this be? Had she really seen the boy and his dog being hit by Salim's car or had she just assumed it, seeing them on the road like that, her neck craned back and the distance between her and what she saw increasing so fast that all of it could well have been a flash of mis-seeing which her imagination had augmented? If it had happened, why was it not online yet? Had anyone complained? She felt a tug of relief, even joy – if it wasn't online, then no one had reported it, and that's because there was no incident to report. Her eyes and mind and memory had played tricks. She could return to poetry without feeling guilty. Dickinson and Heaney were the only two non-work poets on her bookshelves. In her ongoing to-do list, she wrote 'Buy poetry', as if it were apples or a coffee grinder. Above it was 'FINISH MVIOPOTMOS ARTICLE BY SUNDAY, LATEST'. That was ten days ago. A clarifying indifference washed over her. She could feel the links of something loosening – it could have been a rope fraying, but a rope in use, a rope being a rope, not lying in a snaky coil in the corner of a shed or the boot of a car. *What I do is me: for that I came.* God, she hadn't forgotten it all. Was a human being just a lull between choices? She felt the euphoria of exhaustion and, alongside, something else, the beginning of a shift. She knew that when it finally arrived, it was going to be without warning: and then the inevitable string of metaphors and similes – like a change in the weather, knocking on her door in the morning, or treading in the bus on her toes … No, she hadn't forgotten it all. It was three a.m. She dialled a number. He picked up before the first ring ended.

After hours of indecision, she had picked Sunny da Dhaba, 'a Punjabi dive', in the words of the friend who had recommended it, on the Holloway Road because it seemed to defuse all the imagined criteria – class, race, sumptuary laws, pricing – on which she might have conceivably given offence. But even here, Salim, with his military-green puffer jacket and red woollen cap down to his ears, neither of which he took off in the overheated restaurant, looked incongruous. It was something about the sheen of the parachute-type material of his jacket. His eyes wouldn't settle on anything, but on the one or two occasions that she managed to look into them straight and hold his gaze, she thought how she would never have considered that such eyes could be shifty. She even imagined that she caught a child's mischievous gleam in there, as if he'd done something transgressive that he might be told off for but which he was proud of anyway. She read many things else – tiredness, radically insufficient sleep, anxiety, even an unnamed grief, but perhaps most of all hunger, a basic, physical hunger for food. She over-ordered; how she was going to face the food, she had no idea. In her head, she had put together a set of questions she was determined to ask him, no matter what his strategies for deflecting or stonewalling were, but she found herself beginning with the wrong one: 'Are you still driving your brother's car?'

'What?'

She repeated herself.

'No.' Pause. 'No, no.' Longer pause; she had come armed with the decision that she wasn't going to help him out. 'No, he now drive.'

There was only one way she could verify this. 'So, is he better now?'

Again: 'What?'

How could his responses be anything other than stalling for time? 'Is. He. Better. Now.'

He flashed his impossibly white teeth; he knew that she knew.

'Better, yes, yes. Good, he good.'

Which didn't mean anything at all. She decided to begin again when the food started to arrive. There was no space on the small, wobbling table to fit all of it. He must surely know that she hadn't done anything yet about the accident. Her stomach turned at the smell and sight of food. She tried to focus on his face, which now had an unreadable expression – bafflement? Pain, even? What if she was sick, right at the table? She took a dainty sip of water. His gaze seemed to be elsewhere although his eyes were on the food.

'Excuse me, I have to –' she said, and got up.

When she returned, it was immediately obvious that he hadn't touched the food.

She said, 'Where are you from? How did you come to this country?'

Surprising her, he gave a direct answer: 'Eritrea. You know?'

'Oh. N-no, I don't know … I mean, I know where it is on the map, but I don't know, meaning I haven't been there.'

She persisted, 'How did you come to London? When did you come here?'

Again, without any game-playing, he answered, 'Three, four years.'

Then, amazing her, a stream that she felt as a torrent: 'I was soldier. Many years. I run away. They follow me to kill. But I run and run and hide. I go Sudan. I go Libya. I work and have money. I give men money to go Sudan. But … but …'

'But what?' She could not lose this, not now.

He looked at the food. She kicked herself for not having understood quicker. She tore off a corner from a pillowy naan and spooned some black dal on to her plate. As if waiting for a signal, he pounced. She averted her eyes; her stomach was roiling. Again, that feeling of slight bathos – she had expected him to set about devouring everything, but, as if in competition with her, he brought a graceful thrift to how much he served himself and ate. For someone who assumed that she had the upper hand, she found herself feeling that he bested her all the time, or at least found herself lagging behind in understanding, as if she were playing a game whose swiftly changing rules were being set by him.

Eventually the food defeated her. They had not managed to make much of a dent. She said, 'We can ask them to pack it for us. Please take it all, I don't want it, I'm out for most meals this week …'

'Yes. Yes.' Pause. 'Thank you, very kind.'

'What happened in Sudan?'

'Sudan?' As if he'd never heard of the country.

'Yes, Sudan. You said you gave money to someone to go to Sudan. Who did you give money to? What did you do in Sudan?'

'I ... I worked in building.' His gaze was firmly fixed on the table of food.

'And in Libya?'

'I give money to men to go Libya.'

She was thoroughly confused but she pushed ahead. 'What men? How much money? Why did you leave Sudan?' Even while speaking she wanted to rein herself back, but his revelations had changed her original questions and now she had to make up new ones, run to stay in one fixed spot. The smell of curry and oil and spices in the air was solid, like a wall closing in on her. She knew that she would have to get under a hot shower and wash the clothes she was now wearing the minute she got home. Horizontal rain pelted the glass wall that separated the restaurant from the road and ran down in swift diagonal rivulets against the glass.

'I tell another time, it is long, many time,' he said, indicating the expanse of time by throwing open his arms.

'You can make it short.'

'It is difficult. I run away in boat on sea. Many people in small boat, many days in sea. Then boat dies and police boat find us and we are in Italy.'

She clutched both sides of the table with her hands. Either the food would rebel or she. Or the weather might walk in and carry everything away in its wet vortex.

'I am refugee there.' Silence. 'Then I run away to England from Paris. I am refugee in England, they try send me back Italy. They try and try and try. I die before I go to Italy.'

A waiter came to ask how they were doing. Emily could not answer. The past was a desert of quicksand; she had to keep pushing forward forward forward, and that would all turn to treacherous terrain as well, ready to suck her in.

'And how did you go from one place to another?' she made her voice say. Also, 'Yes, please, if you could put them in boxes for us, thanks very much.' Turning back to face Salim, she added, 'What do you mean, you die before you go back to Italy?'

The waiter was transferring the food from their plates into Styrofoam containers. 'Thank you,' Emily said, again and again. Then, 'Yes, he'll take it all' to no one in particular. In the face of Salim's gentle demurral, she said, 'No, I shan't hear of it, I have so much food waiting to be eaten, it'll all go off,' as she handed her card to the waiter.

The thread was broken. She knew it by her own reluctance to pursue with her questions, not by his to answer.

Outside, the rain, which had let up for a moment, came down with gleeful force as they started walking to the Tube. They got drenched running to the nearest point where they could take shelter, the awning of a bicycle shop.

She couldn't – wouldn't – call for a car; how could she? And where was that … that car, was it being driven by his brother, had he got a lift here? After barely five minutes of battling the rain, the paper bag in Salim's hands turned into a rag and fell away in large, soggy patches. The look on his face was priceless. She laughed and, still laughing, dug into her handbag to fish out a plastic bag. He took it and it was as if the bag conducted her laugh through her fingers to his, then to his mouth and eyes. Even through the curtain of drifting rain between their two heads, she could see those eyes light up. With an unexpected jolt, she realized that she had never seen him smile properly, never seen him look anything but serious and burdened. Yes, burdened, that was exactly it; he could have had a stoop or a bent back, the metaphor literal-ized, and she wouldn't have been surprised one bit.

A rare bright morning. Feeling upbeat for some unknown reason, she thought she would take a detour on her walk to work. Just to see, she told herself. The sun made the route

Salim's car had taken on that night seem normal, unweighted with incidents, in the same way that daylight makes a child's night-time fear of shadows in corners appear fanciful and ridiculous. Before she was near enough to read it, she knew what it was: on Cassland Road, the metal board asked for any information on a hit-and-run. The date and the time were correct. Why had it taken them so long, nearly three weeks? There was a flare inside her chest that manifested as an itch she wanted to scratch. She looked around to see if anyone had seen her reading the notice. Her hands shook so much she couldn't get her phone out of her bag. A picture. If only she could take a picture, she could look at it later to reassure herself that all this was real, that what she had seen on that night was real. She would then call the number on the 'appeal for witnesses' board and everything would be taken out of her hands and she would be made whole again.

They argued on the phone for a while before Rohan finally raised his voice and said, 'You're a classic PTSD case and you're in fucking denial about it.'

'That's cheap. Trauma is sooo easy to come by these days. What I can't believe is how *you* are espousing this trauma crap too.' Things had been on a rolling boil in her for some time during the call – she understood this only after she had spoken the words.

'Now *that* was cheap, and you know it.'

A torrent came to her – about the steadily increasing mollycoddling of younger generations, of their essential narcissism, their foundational self-absorption – but its elements had been weaponized by the enemy, an enemy common to both her and Rohan, so she bit her tongue. Besides, the target was wrong – this British Asian man, her oldest friend in the world, tempered in the forge of the needling, condescending, no-fingerprints brand of educated middle-class English racism, was the last person she should attack for posturing and nombrilisme. But she had to say something; she couldn't let him win with that weak non-shot.

'Sure, if you say so, but true,' she said.

Rohan too must have had a private reckoning to pull back from the precipice: he only said, 'You're having a delayed reaction to this, you've not acted in any kind of rational or intelligent way. What are you hiding?'

It was probably a throwaway, unthought comment, but it resonated enough to bring the boiling inside her to stop.

'Hiding? What do you mean?' She too was using Salim's trick to stall for time; she hadn't told Rohan about seeing the 'appeal for witnesses' board.

'I don't know. I just get the sense that you're not telling me the full story. You're leaving something out about what happened that night.'

'You're being ridiculous. I've told you everything.'

'Why haven't you called the doctor? These headaches and nausea ... you have a concussion, it could be serious. Shouldn't you at least check?'

A worm of a different kind of anxiety now; she was evasive for a while then gave in: 'Yes, I'll call them now, the doctor, I mean. I've been putting it off.' What she really was procrastinating on was calling the number to report the accident. It occurred to her only now that she had not thought about the boy and his dog, whether they were dead or alive, when she had seen the sign because she had been devoured by a shock almost approaching fear.

'Let me know if you want something?' he said.

She heard a door closing in those words, as he had intended her to. Oddly, she felt only liberated.

'Of course,' she said. 'I'll let you know about the visit to the doctor.'

In the end it turned out that she did have concussion. The process was not as simple as a single visit to her GP; it also involved an MRI scan, after a six-hour wait at A & E in Homerton UH, then another appointment with her doctor. It cut up her days in an annoying way. Emily's interest in, or anxiety about, the diagnosis, however, was secondary compared to what she felt was pursuing. 'Dear Eleni,' she wrote, feeling only a niggle at disregarding the doctor's injunction not to look at screens, 'you may not remember me, but we met at the dinner party at Rohan's and Noam's a few weeks ago. Please forgive me for writing out of the blue like this, but may I pick your brains about something? I'm trying to understand something about the business model of ride-hailing apps, especially the labour side of things, and you're the only person I've met who I think might be able to help. A quick look at your research interests on your department's website makes me think that you'll have all the answers. I can drop by the café in your department at a time convenient for you one day – please let me know what suits best? Many thanks in advance.'

When Eleni's reply arrived, within three hours of Emily's email, she calculated that she had three days for some quick research. She remembered that Salim lived in Stockwell, but that was all she had: no street name, no number, nothing. What was she going to do when she got there? Aimlessly walk a random two or three or four square miles of it? Maybe a bus? She felt defeated at the very outset.

During their meeting, Emily tried to switch off the usual internal voice which made itself known whenever she met anyone in the sciences, the voice that said, 'They think you humanities people are all fools, or at least involved in pursuits that have no purchase on the real world and its millions of questions, that you are just engaged in a frolic of your own. They are humouring you when they talk to you, being guile-lessly condescending, as they would with a child.' The voice made her a certain kind of person that she hated. Could Eleni tell? Emily must not show any signs. Not a single question on her part must give away the contestations and pre-emptive warfare inside her.

'Surely if the fares are so cheap, either the company is not making any money, which must be part of its long-term strategy, like, say, Amazon's, or the drivers must be getting next to nothing,' Emily said and instantly regretted it – she was convinced she had allowed her ideology to show.

Eleni said, 'I was surprised to learn that the drivers get a much larger cut than I had assumed, but, yes, you're right, you must have seen how these companies are not allowed to operate in certain cities because they define themselves, and their drivers, as something other than the obviously intuitive so that they can get around certain regulations governing the licensed taxicab industry. Tax arbitrage, in short.'

Eleni talked of how attractive it was for economists to see 'a freely clearing, frictionless, two-sided matching market with vol-untary participation and no intermediation', and the efficiency of price surges and putting more drivers on the roads during times of higher demand. Emily couldn't quite bring herself to raise the question she really wanted to ask, for fear that it would appear naïve, or naïvely lefty, the standard bugbear of economists.

She tried another tack. 'Is tax arbitrage the only problem?' she asked. 'Are ... is there room for improvement in, in, in the labour side of things?'

'Oh, yes, of course. Inadequate protection of drivers' rights, issues of liability and insurance, and now, of course, we're beginning to understand how these companies are using advances in the behavioural sciences – basically, psychological tricks – to push their workers' buttons. I can send you a couple of links if you're interested.'

Emily's heart gave a leap. She had spent the better part of three hours yesterday looking at the company's pages on safety, insurance, vetting of drivers, and other related matters on its website and had found herself being led on an empty, circular dance. There were no phone numbers given so it was impossible for her to call and talk to an actual human being about a matter that did not fall exactly within the possibilities imagined by the company. Almost absent-mindedly, she had undertaken a basic prac crit of the bland, meaningless, consumer-fellating discourse, which was a textbook example of the kind of large-scale locutionary act – she forgot the exact term for it – that misdirected, made you think one thing while, behind the words, it was engaged in doing exactly the opposite. Nothing here that Barthes hadn't excavated last century; the surprise was how the collusion between producer and consumer worked so well. Predictable stuff. Her real problem navigating those pages was how they kept returning her to the one page that could have been the most useful – the one on reporting an incident – but that she could not bear to look at, and this she could not pin on any corporate behaviour but only on herself. How could she have filled out a form that required name of passenger, date, time, and location of incident, 'additional information', her email address?

So here was Eleni instead, unknowingly providing Emily with information that would help her navigate her own peculiar path through the woods. The wood of silence, she thought, with three rooks flying above it and no humans anywhere, just the wood itself, contained and singular and pure in its itselfness that needed nothing else.

Lulled by her own reverie, she let her self-censoring guard down and found herself asking Eleni, 'So why do so many people sign up to be drivers? There seems to be an endless supply of them at all hours.'

'Flexibility. Say, someone wants to do two hours before his daughter's school pick-up and only those two hours. Plus, better than no job or worse job.' Pause. 'The ideal that we're all looking for' – Emily noted the use of the plural subject – 'sometimes is difficult to come by, so you make do with what you can because the alternatives are worse. What I'm saying is this: the choice is not always between good and bad, but more often between worse and better.'

Emily nodded. Yes, the world divided into two kinds of people, the ones who dreamed loftily and sometimes immolated themselves to bring about change, often taking down their surroundings with them, and the ones who were patient and bullish, tenaciously nibbling away at the mountain they wanted to move, and one day, they and their likes got it done without destroying themselves and half the world order. Her kind wanted everything razed so that the pure new order could be built; Eleni's kind waited, worked, waited, had jaws of stone to absorb all the punches aimed at them, waited, and then, one day …

'I should get back,' Eleni was saying. 'Do let me know if you have any further questions on the subject. We should try and arrange a dinner soon – Marcus and I have been meaning to have you all over.'

And with that she was gone, leaving Emily, on the short walk back to her office, tolling back and forth, back and forth, between the polarities she had isolated in her understanding of the world.

'Mother?'

'Goodness, this is early. I mean, not too early for me, of course, you know I get up with the birds,' she chirruped.

Emily had to say only one word and they were instantly in the territory of this game of good manners, of the elaborate play of not giving offence. How had this come about? She must have been as equal a participant as her mother otherwise it wouldn't have survived for so long. It couldn't have been caused, in whatever manner, by Emily's father, whom she remembered as a demure, silent, almost invisible figure, tiptoeing around the margins of everyone's lives, and not because his wife was a more powerful and assertive person. On the contrary, they had both played the role of weak, insipid English people to perfection, and after her father's death, Emily's mother had continued with it. It was only now that Emily saw in this unswerving, dogged attachment to the ordinary and the low-key a kind of steel, of bloody-mindedness even. Her father had died when she was away at university, in her second year, and the words used by her mother to break the news – 'Darling, your dad is no longer with us' – had made Emily immediately think 'Was he ever?' before the weak sense of loss had briefly descended, like precipitation from quick-moving clouds.

'Well, I missed our call last week, so I thought … and … and I can't seem to go to sleep,' she said, then added, 'too much work suddenly, I don't know how it's all piled up.'

This liberated her mother, so she continued to talk about how focused and intense Emily had been as a child, how the signs of insomnia had manifested subtly but early.

'Mother, it's not insomnia, just a couple of nights working late. What are you doing?'

'The cyclamen is just coming out. Very pretty. I'm bracing myself before going out to the garden to do some pruning. The salvias need cutting right back. I have to ask Trevor to come and put in an arch for the Mme Alfred Carrière in the corner – it's got very lanky and top-heavy. I could barely manage to stake it last summer.'

Emily knew that her mother could carry on in this vein without interruption and Emily would normally have let her. For the second time that week, Emily tried and failed to put her finger on the correct linguistic term for a speech act, this time for one that had no information or emotional value. But perhaps the emotional value lay in exactly this obvious lack of informational content? And surely there was a term for that too, or she could coin one?

She came out of her little maze to hear, just on time, 'So, will you be coming home for the Easter break? It's early this year.'

'No, no, I'm staying put, I have a lot of stuff that needs to be done. Mother, I wanted to ask you about Grandpa and Granny. Do you know much about their life in India?'

'A little, not very much. They hardly ever talked about it.'

'Oh. I remember all these stories from childhood – a tiger entering the tea estate, blue hills, frequent strikes in the plantation, bowl-shaped pancakes and when you peered in there was an egg inside.'

'I'm surprised they talked about strikes. You couldn't have been that old.'

'So you knew about them?'

'Just as something mentioned in passing. Barely touched upon. I haven't heard about the tiger or the egg pancakes. Maybe they were making up colourful stories to entertain their granddaughter?'

'I remember many more, but I can't join them up in a' – she wanted to say 'narrative' but paused and picked different words – 'continuous story with a chronology. I seem to remember lots of stories about conflicts and fighting and bombs going off.'

'What were they doing, telling a little girl all this?'

'I think that I must have revisited the stories when I grew up a bit and saw them for what they were – stories of the fight for independence from colonial rule. Political conflict. Turned into stories for a child.'

A beat or two of silence, then her mother said, 'Are you sure you're not confusing them with what you read? I mean, stories that you read in a book?'

'No, I remember some of the stories they told me very clearly. Didn't you grow up with them?'

'No, they didn't talk about their time in India, I told you. Not that much. And my memories are very vague. I also got the sense, god knows from where, that they didn't like to talk about it, or think about their life there too much, but maybe that's something I just made up. What's brought this on suddenly?'

'Do you know if there are any papers? Or diaries, letters, something?'

'Gosh. I don't think so. I wouldn't know where to look.'

'Did you not find anything when Grandpa died?'

'Well, I wasn't looking. And your grandma looked after all that.'

Emily's grandmother had died a couple of years after Emily had moved to the USA for graduate school, but Grandma, ravaged by dementia, had been in a care home for several years before Emily's departure, so contact, or any content to those contacts, had been minimal. Grandma had been unable to recognize her own daughter by the end. Emily felt defeated but ploughed on with her questions; she knew what the answer was going to be.

'And did Granny leave all her stuff to you? Could there be something in there?'

'Among the papers, you mean? No, I don't think so. I did go through them. It's all the usual stuff, you know, banks and portfolios and birth certificates and wills. The usual.'

'No letters, no cache of photos, no pictures or mementos from their time in India?'

'I would have remembered if there had been any, I'm sure. Do you want to go through them when you're next here?'

'Oh, yes, please. Thank you.'

'I think you'll be disappointed. There's not much. You might get something from the school they founded. If it still exists. But it was all such a long time ago ...'

For a few seconds she did not understand what her mother was saying. 'School? What school?'

'Oh, pardon me, I thought you knew about it. They set up a school for the children of the tea-estate workers before they returned to England. Surely you must have known this? There was a charity or trust fund for some money they had endowed. Not much, I should think.'

'Mother,' she nearly screamed, 'this is all totally new to me. Why didn't you tell me before?'

'But ... but I thought you knew.'

She said, 'Oh my god,' then collected herself immediately. 'No, I didn't. This is the biggest surprise to me. What school? Where? What's its name?'

'The estate had a tongue-twister of a name, many *m*s and *r*s, I'm sure I'm going to get it wrong. Varugam? Varagaram?'

Emily clenched her teeth, then thought, How come *I* don't know the name? Did I ever ask Grandma or did 'tea estate in India' suffice?

'The school must have been named after the estate,' her mother continued, 'but I don't know for sure. It was for children aged five to nine, if I'm remembering correctly. It was all well before my time. It doesn't seem likely that the school is still going, unless others put up more money. The trust money wouldn't have lasted more than a few years.'

'Do you know how much money? And the name of the town? Why did they do it, did they ever say? Odd thing to do if they were leaving the country forever ...'

'I have no idea how much money. I don't know the name of the village, I'm sorry, only the name of the estate. Perhaps the Internet will tell you?'

'Was it the kind of thing that the … the British did, set up schools and charities before' – a heartbeat's delay in the flow of her words – 'giving independence to a colony?'

'I wouldn't know. I suppose they wanted to give back something or leave something to mark their time there. Or do a little bit of good.' Pause. 'It's such a poor country.'

It was the pause that did it. 'What do you mean by "a little bit of good"?'

Her unsuspecting mother replied, 'Oh, you know, some kindness … after all, it had been their home for so many years.'

'A home stolen from its own people, you mean?'

'I … I …'

'A poor country, you just said. Maybe poor because we looted and robbed and plundered it dry for two centuries?'

In the silence that followed, Emily imagined the journey of her words through the air, bouncing off trees or passing through them, like light through glass, flying over fields that looked like a patchwork quilt, over ancient woods of oak and ash, over motorways like clogged veins and arteries, hitting tall buildings, arcing over them, looking down on pitched roofs, then realized that her understanding of the mechanics of sound transmission through mobile phones was totally wrong.

'I'm not … I don't quite … understand. It was some time ago. We gave them the railways …' her mother began.

Whatever regret for her own aggressive words that Emily may have had a chance to form in the silence was now scotched for her by that 'we'; she was back in the grip of the demon.

'We? We? Well, *we* tell that railways story because *we* don't want to know the truth, *we* don't teach it in our schools, *we* have strategically encouraged and built this amnesia, *we* have never had any reckoning –'

'Emily. Dear.'

The words arrested her shaking. She was flooded with shame; for what, she couldn't have said. Where had the possession come from?

Later, she went online to track down the tea estate. The correct name was Varugaram, now part of Veritea, an umbrella company constituted of half a dozen plantations, all in the Nilgiri Hills in South India. The head office was in a town called Coimbatore. They had a decent enough website: lush pictures of low green hills, slopes green with dense rows of tea bushes; the usual corporate branding and marketing language, all performatively labour-centred and green consciousness vision values community yadda yadda, to describe the company, its mission, and its products; even pictures of past and present CEOs and the present CEO's email; a contact tab. Emily didn't know why she was expecting something shabby and unprofessional. What she wasn't expecting was the lethally effective dispersal of Western bullshit, like spores of some malign fungus, to the other side of the world and finding welcome soil there. There was a little history thrown in too – its first chairman was a British man, Sir Reginald Hartley, who founded the company, then named after the one estate it owned, Varugaram, in 1898. The page said: 'He dabbled in many an industry – cotton mills, coffee plantations, tea, coffee curing, motor works, and tyre retreading. It wasn't only industry that interested Sir Hartley: he was a man with a commendable sense of social responsibility. As early as the 1800s he had set up a couple of schools, taken on the chairmanship of the city council of Coimbatore, and was soon conferred the title "Kaiser-e-Hind". And in 1960, this company passed into the hands of Mr Balasubramanian.' Passed into. An entire history of oppression, resistance, bloodshed, independence elided over in a phrasal verb that made it sound as easy and natural as the flow of water. And such a large gap between British founder and first Indian CEO, an erasure of the period into which Emily's grandfather fitted.

There was a tab called 'CSR' and its short drop-down menu included health care, children's home, and education. Education. She read the short sections on each and had a mild plummeting feeling: the school was set up in the late 1970s, an orphanage in 1986. The dates were all wrong – her grandparents had left India very shortly after Independence in 1947. So, either her mother had misremembered some detail, or something had been lost in the transmission of anecdotes. The school page, for example, said that it had been set up in 1979 for children of the plantation workers and managers. The medium of instruction had been Tamil, but in 1986 it had affiliated with the Central Board of Secondary Education and switched to becoming an English-language school, now serving not only the children of all the estates that formed Veritea, but also those from 'surrounding villages'.

The only way she could find out more was if she wrote to them and they bothered to reply. She composed a brief note to the CEO (surely an account monitored, if at all, by a secretary?), then spent half the night worrying about whether she had got the tone right, whether the CEO, if he ever saw it, wouldn't think that this was phishing, or that a person claiming to be a descendant of their English founder was getting in touch to assert some kind of legal or financial claim. Every twenty minutes she got up to tweak, rewrite, add, subtract, copy-and-paste; her mind couldn't move on to anything else. If only she could get hold of something … anything from their colonial lives would do.

Where had it all gone, Emily continued to fret through the sleepless blue-grey hours, because there must have been something: people leave traces, they accumulate, they have memories that are material, the concept of 'memorabilia' attesting to that very materiality, they have *things*. Where did they go? Got rid of in a clear-out, donated to charity shops, binned, set on fire? What happened to them? She could not settle. She found other bitter fruits to gnaw at and unearthed a few lines of solace – the rare gleams on the Internet that could take one by surprise – while looking aimlessly for new poetry, here they were: 'About what's past, *Hold on when you can*, I used to say, / *And when you can't, let go*, as if memory were one of those / mechanical bulls, easily dismountable, should the ride / turn rough.' What had led her to these unexpected depths? Typing in 'poem' and 'memory'? Algorithm moves in a mysterious way / His wonders to perform etc. And wonder it was that filled her, at the poet's sinuous enjambed stream, a silver curve through the dense and forever-changing forest, like the Wood of Error in Book I, of an individual's history of emotions. Flick, flick, changing the inner and outer weathers like a magician shuffling cards. Then that final flick, almost an apology, an admission, an irreducible residue in the crucible of a relationship. In the lightness that insomnia brought on, the feeling that not only she but everything around her, the whole embodied world, would begin to levitate any minute seemed now to be dented and bent by a new gravity, as if a black hole had materialized in her universe. Why should he text or call her, she tried to reason; it was ridiculous to have even allowed that thought to flit through her head. He was afraid, watching her every move, like a prey watches its predator, or a sapper regards a bomb that he's defusing. To run with the simile, shouldn't she be doing the defusing by calling him? The feeling of levitation, again. They didn't say it was a side effect of concussion, did they? At half-past three in the morning, she started to put on make-up, just as a way of reminding herself that she could still do invisible make-up, the kind that had given her boyfriend in university such a shock when he had seen her face the first morning after, when all of it had been scrubbed off rigorously. Oh god, what had he said, something like, 'You look like a different person', poor lamb, and she had asked, 'Better or worse?', and he had made his indelible mistake, something that had set a foundational pattern to their relationship as long as it had subsisted. Now, trying to dust her face with the brush, she feared that she would make herself look like a painted monkey, a circus clown, if she strayed even slightly beyond the boundaries of her minimalist cleanse-tone-moisturize-SPF routine. 'To be born woman is to know – / Although they do not talk of it at school – / That we must labour to be beautiful.' She wanted to drop the little wand of Touche Éclat and punch the air – she hadn't forgotten it all or, as she was now beginning to reckon, sacrificed it all to admin and committees and league-table fuckwittery. When had she first read that poem? Must have been for mods in her first year. Then, sure as death, the *basso continuo* of guilt-laced anxiety: all this time rushing past her that she would never get back and the work, undone, mounting mounting mounting. Halfway through wiping her face raw with micellar water, she went to her study and looked at her email tab. She had been aware for a while that her life was in the prison of acronyms but had not accorded it due weight and salience; the bars now closed around her. The majority of communications was from DLTC (Department Learning & Teaching Committee), SEOC (Student Experience & Outcome Committee), CQAC (Curriculum Quality Assurance Committee), TeLSOC (Teaching, Learning & Student Outcomes Committee), TESTA (Transforming the Experience of Students Through Assessment), TESEP (Teaching Excellence & Student Engagement Plan). The neoliberal university was not about knowledge and its flow. Those who talked about the marketplace of ideas actually meant only the first half of the phrase, the only one that mattered to them. In the ideal university, she would be contemplating how unprepared she was for the graduate seminar on Wednesday and the 'Forms: Pastoral, Romance, Epic' lecture on Friday, thinking about how any time-management scheme that she drew up now would have to prioritize finishing the two articles-in-progress (one on Lodowick Bryskett, a 'revise and resubmit' from *ELR*, and another, yet to be sent out on submission, on a textual matter in *The Countess of Pembroke's Arcadia*) and a chapter, vaguely titled 'The Pastoral, Interrupted: Spenser, Guarini, Milton', that she had been thrilled to be asked to contribute to a festschrift for her late thesis supervisor. How profoundly the interest in these matters had run out, like water escaping in a rush after the plug in the sink was removed; a mighty gurgle, a brief vortex, then nothing but a wet residue. This compulsively irritating habit of life to assert itself as more interesting than, say, literary-ideological agendas under the surface of an early modern writer's reading of the classics. She could hear one of her bolshier students posturing, 'Like, yeah, whatever.' The intellectual is no match for the lived, for the process of living. Model versus mess – what chance did the former ever have? Weren't they all fools to think so and to persist nevertheless like blind donkeys? And which self-respecting woman – person! – called a man, who was almost a stranger, at four o'clock in the morning? What would he think of her? What kind of signals would she be sending? But in the vivarium of regrettable ideas that this hinge between the night and the morning was, she had one that she hoped would salvage something: resisting the pull of a somewhat inappropriate text that was beginning to take over her, she instead sent an email to Rohan.

On a murky grey March mid-morning, the sky like a lid about to press down on the petty business of humans scurrying about, Emily and Rohan met outside Stockwell Tube station. Embarrassment helped them get quickly out of the way all the difficult things, apologies, gracious acceptance, articulating that the contretemps was behind them and forgotten, by not going through them at all. Bits and pieces of these things could be alluded to in the interstices of their conversation and the essential work would be done. Emily had set it up in such a way that she would come across as needing his help – the email had explicitly said that – and Rohan, adept at that same code, would instantly understand it as her way of saying sorry.

'So, this is what I have in mind,' she said. 'I need to feel out this area for some research.' She was certain that he could detect the lie, and her voice, she thought, sounded different, but she consoled herself with the thought that they both knew they were playing a game and had to abide by rules that had a different truth-value.

'What research? I didn't know that you had leaped from the early modern to the contemporary,' he said. With that, she knew that he knew. Everything could proceed without any glitches.

'Well …' she feigned shyness, 'I'm, I'm trying my hand at something more, how should I put it, more creative, and for a while, I didn't tell you because it's, it's so new and you'd be sceptical about it, rightly, of course, it goes without saying, but for a while my mind has been gravitating towards fiction, and I thought that perhaps I should, I could, give it a whirl …' She amazed herself. Where lay the wellspring from which this flowed with such ease, such guile? Her mother? Why did she think that? It had its own momentum, own pleasures, she found, as she let it blossom more fully: 'Besides, I felt awkward and shy about telling you, of all people, a feted writer ...'

'Feted-schmeted.' Emily knew that this was no false modesty: Rohan genuinely wore his two Booker shortlistings lightly; 'Nothing to wear,' he would have said, 'hundreds of second- and third-rate writers get on that carousel and are quickly forgotten.'

'So, what exactly are you, we, looking for?' he asked, looking on his phone for a route to chart.

'Um, I don't know ...'

'What do you mean, you don't know? A particular street or set of streets, landmarks, shopfronts ... I mean, what do you want?'

'Just a general feel of the place. I think.'

'General feel. Ah. Yes, of course. But what is the story about? Wait, I know, sorry, scratch that, terrible question to ask anyone. Let me rephrase that. If you feel like saying anything more about this ... project, you have a keen listener standing next to you.'

Admiration took her breath away and silenced her for a while; two certainly could play at this game. The world around them insisted on attention, if only for the sake of her performance, which hid an ulterior truth that only she knew, or could eventually feel her way towards. Rohan planned out a circular route, with a number of small detours into the interior of the circle. Seven years in London had familiarized her with the discrete-villages model of the city but had not made her a Londoner; there was still the novelty of the unvisited areas, a sort of mild shock of the new. On Stockwell Road, a long stretch of council estates and tower blocks, with sodden earth in front and in the lots. A small public garden that looked municipal to the last blade of struggling grass and an enormous straggly clump of St John's Wort. Even accounting for winter, this was a place still and stultified with the lack of colour. The grey-white and grey-red of the building fronts, the grey of the wet roads and pavements, the grey of an empty park, with its abandoned play area, the wet grey of mud and the grey of concrete, the mud-brown of the wet bark chips in a bare garden, all aggregated to a non-colour, so that when they came to a stylish second-hand furniture store, Loved Again, the orange mid-century leather recliners in the display window had the effect of blood in a crime scene. There followed a small string of delis, cafés, and restaurants.

They walked past a skate park, with its diminutive hills, valleys, and canyons, every available inch profuse with graffiti, and suddenly, like a radical scene change, unmistakable Caribbean Brixton arrived. They turned back and started exploring the side roads off Stockwell Road. Stockwell Park Road and Stockwell Park Crescent, with their Victorian detached houses and semi-detached terraces, gave off the odour of money, of long ownership: doors with lead-bordered coloured stained glass, a shiny imitation of a Victorian coach lamp in brass positioned above it; gardens in the front letting you know that their bigger versions lay at the back; a house with two huge tree palms standing sentry in the stone courtyard on either side of the short flight of stairs leading to the front door. Her walking pace picked up past these homes, slowing down again when the scene changed to council houses on Lansdowne Way and South Lambeth Road.

A sense of deflation was building up inside her; was that a contradiction in terms, like this purposive meandering, which could conceivably yield nothing? What was she expecting? There followed another moment of being read as Rohan asked, his eyes focused mercilessly on the road in front, 'Still not found what you're looking for?'

No, she hadn't. The streets were resolutely unyielding in their response to the absurd demands she had made of them

– that Salim should come out of a walkway in the Mursell Estate, look for a moment up and down the street, *his* street, before turning the corner and walking to Rooster's to pick up several orders of family-sized fried chicken and chips for the new members of the family who had come to visit them ... yes, that was what she wanted, a sense of the plural, of others, a family, better still, a community, a community of Salim's own people, seeding a garden they could one day perhaps call their own in this cold, grey corner of a foreign world, or even better, she wanted to see a whole big family, rambunctious children, stately dowagers, patriarchs, sons, wives, Salim, all emerge from a restaurant owned and run by one of their own community, like the one they had passed, Asmara, on Clapham Road, a little earlier in their walk.

'A penny for your thoughts,' Rohan said.

'Gosh. Never thought I'd hear that expression again. My grandmother used to say that to me. Did yours?'

'My grandmother wasn't English, she wouldn't have known what it meant.'

'I don't think I've ever used that expression in my life. Do you think that's how these things die, or die out, I suppose – the next generation, while understanding their meaning fully, just stops using them, for whatever reason?'

'I would guess so. So, you didn't find anything in Stockwell that would be useful?'

She remembered reading, a long time ago, in a Coetzee story, that it was easier to speak – and hear – unadorned truths in a car journey because the driver and the passenger looked straight ahead, not at each other. Could that not be the case during a walk as well?

'No, actually, yes, I'm just absorbing, it all helps, local colour and all that.'

'Local colour. Ah. So it is set in these parts?'

'You seem to be quite confident about the route. You must know this area well.'

'I have no idea. I'm just wandering aimlessly, waiting for you to sing out "Here, stop right here, this is exactly what I need!"'

'Here, stop right here, this is exactly what I need!'

They stopped in front of Stockwell Tube station, smiled at each other, then took the escalators down. The edge inherent in any game-playing was now blunted; they became easier with each other, but she didn't come clean.

'Dinner next week?' he asked, turning to her, as the train approached Pimlico.

'Yes, that would be nice. Thursdays, Fridays, and Saturdays are good, as you know,' she said, meaning every word.

Back in her office in Mile End, she began working on a plan that could politely only be called coasting – how to survive the semester doing minimal work without being caught out. As for the cost to her research, which meant other, more serious consequences for the mid- to long-term arc of her academic career, she thought about it distantly, disengagedly, not with the expected rising tide of anxiety, as if they would all happen to someone else. In fact, they *would* happen to someone else; she knew she would be changed; she was changing, changing utterly.

And then, the English spring, temperamental, refractory, magical. The temperature remained unchanged – in fact, maybe even fell a little – but in one corner the sky dazzled with a blue that was stolen from a Renaissance painter's palette and in the other it was the slate of rain-washed roofs. The banks of daffodils along the edge of the common outside her living room and bedroom windows raised their kitschy heads, reminding her, inevitably, of some of the worst – and best-loved – lines in English poetry. In the concrete courtyard outside her door, the three cherry trees around the car park and the six-feet-by-six-feet children's play area with one slide and one pair of swings were going to burst into blossom any minute. A little later, she knew, there would be a large colony of lily of the valley in the house at the top end of Harrowgate Road – someone who lived in that house had taken great care to plant a vast number of bulbs that stopped passers-by at this time of the year. She always took a small detour to walk past it on her way to and from the department in late April and early May.

And sometimes, she was reminded why she knew the names of flora, why it was almost unthinking on her part, as natural and as unnoticed as breathing: it was an early and abiding gift from her mother. As a small child, Emily had been made to prick out seedlings, using a pencil and always holding them by their true leaves, never by their stems, from the shallow trays in which her mother had sown seeds. She had also taught her daughter how to pull out weeds with equal fastidiousness and care, reasoning that a child's natural obsessive bent could be harnessed for use. In the process, Emily had learned how to distinguish a blue-grey poppy seedling from a weed such as Herb robert or wood sorrel. Sometimes she felt an unnameable twinge, as she did now, passing the waking cyclamens: *That's an honesty seedling. Do you see their big true leaves, with crinkled edges? Darling, look here, these, not the seed leaves here, the true leaves above them, do you see? That's how you can tell them apart from a weed. It's called honesty because it has these beautiful, nearly transparent seed cases through which you can see the seeds. I'll point them out to you in the summer and then you'll see what I mean. Maybe you can take some to 'show-and-tell' in class next year?*

There were days of unseasonable warmth during which students sat in the sun with their coffees, phones, laptops, lunches, headphones, but rarely, if ever, any books. This was not the English spring of her early childhood, when the sun would disappear for half an hour, and everyone was sent scurrying indoors by a squall of hailstones or icy rain, only for it to come out again, smiling, saying, 'Fooled you!' Now, people enjoyed this ratcheting warmth while feeling fear, in the back of their mind, at the radically wrong clock. This was the spring of southern Europe, not of England.

On one of these sunny days, she sat on a wooden bench at a café in an allotment garden in Stepney with Salim at her side. His shoulders were hunched, and he sat on the edge of the seat, shifting frequently, but never leaning back or relaxing into his pose. His latte, which he barely sipped, was placed in front of him as if it were a grenade; the leaf shape, which the kitchen staff had made with foam on the top, was becoming amorphous. All around them, greenery frothed up from the black soil. She could see a rhubarb patch in a corner, a lane of green tops of onions, ruby-veined beetroot greens, the bushy fountains of carrot tops. A blackbird flew out from a branch of the newly green horse chestnut tree opposite them like a freed note from a musical piece scored in black ink. His eyes followed the bird; she read both wonder and exclusion in them. Perhaps his life had not featured, until today, sitting under a tree just coming into leaf, watching birds fly out. For one crazy second the thought passed through her mind that she could explain to him that this moment they were in would be an instance of *otium* in pastoral poetry, but dismissed it, with mild horror, immediately. He had his sheeny military-green puffer jacket on, fully zipped up to his chin, and she wondered if it would be out of order to suggest taking it off; he must be hot under it. Years of making these kinds of microcalculations with students and worrying that any personal statement could be interpreted amiss had made her into a self-censoring machine.

'Why were you driving so fast that night?' *In medias res.* Best to catch him unawares. She was watching him like a peregrine would a quivering rabbit.

He didn't play for time, didn't play the fool. The reply was instant: 'My brother ill. I only man who drive him to hospital. I come to pick up you, I get call.'

'What is wrong with your brother? I hope he's all right now?' She was going to pretend to be as unfazed as he was.

'Keed-ni.'

It took a few beats for her to decipher this. 'Kidney?' she asked, tentative herself.

He nodded energetically. 'Yes, yes, kidney. He need new kidney.'

The answer to her original, almost non-sequitur of a question had been so quick that she wondered whether he had mentally rehearsed this story, perhaps in collusion with his brother. Then shame filled her till she could taste it in the back of her mouth: the promptness could be equally marshalled as an argument that what he had said was such an inalienable, ever-present truth that no preparation had been needed.

A repeated five-note call ending on a trill rose above the sound of all the human lives going about their business, the traffic, the voices. She looked up in the direction of the sound. There, on the top branch of a still bare tree, he was perched.

'Look, follow my finger,' she said, 'look up, there, do you see it? That's the blackbird you saw fly up from the tree a few minutes ago. There, do you see? Right on top, on the very top branch.'

She touched his head and tilted it up, then moved it slightly to the left.

'Do you see it now?'

As if to help them both, the bird sang out again; that escaped note from the score asserting its independent existence.

'Yes, yes. Bird,' he said and looked at her quizzically. He was not interested; she had misread the look on his face earlier.

'Never mind,' she said, covering up her own disappointment. 'Tell me more about your brother?'

'He go to hospital two, three time a week to' – here he made a series of gestures with his hand, involving the inside of an arm, the area of his love handles, the air near his side, that she couldn't interpret – 'to clean blood.'

Here he was, again, unperturbed, while undulating the very ground under her with what he was saying, and she, under pressure from some unidentified, unacknowledged source, only caught up hectically in an internal debate about how to arrange her face, how best to respond so that she would appear to be doing the right thing; all the right reactions frittered away in the struggle to identify what the appropriate response should be. And her suspicion of his possible duplicity: where did that come from? Working for that company, he, or his brother, must know that she could report him any time, regardless of when the incident had occurred. He must know that she could hold this over him forever. Why did he choose to reply to her messages, sit in a garden and talk to her, go out for dinner, and not bring up the terrible thing, the only thing, that connected them? The sole explanation she could imagine was that he was trying to befriend her with a view to somehow neutering that connection, making her passively resigned to it so that she would never want to act on it. You'd have to be extremely confident, or extremely risk-loving – 'same difference', as Rohan would have said – in order to go down that route, and he appeared to be neither. 'Appeared': the word gave her pause. *Seems, madam? Nay, it is. I know not 'seems'.* All the usual strictures against asking a near-stranger 'What are you really thinking?', and similar barriers the other person would have to surmount, she imagined, in order to answer the question truthfully, held her back.

Until one day, she did, a slightly different question, a direct one in which she left no shadows where he could hide: 'Tell me about your life before you came here.'

He was from Keren in Eritrea, and in 1997, when he was fifteen or sixteen, he was forcibly conscripted by the army and sent off to fight in the Eritrean–Ethiopian War that began in 1998. He was told by the commander in charge that his military service was going to last for a mere six months, but those six months proved to be elastic: they became six years, years of being moved from camp to camp, fighting against Ethiopia, against Djibouti, until Salim summoned up enough courage to confront his commander about his broken promise, for which Salim was first detained, then confined in an underground prison. The prison housed nearly four hundred men, and after one year twenty of them, Salim among them, dug their way to escape. Soldiers fired on them, but Salim survived, and after walking for one month, he entered Sudan illegally, without any papers.

Salim was in Sudan for eight years, and the narration of his time there was sketchy, the account perfunctory and skated over quickly.

Whatever the reality of the matter or the accuracy of the finer details, one salient point emerged from the Sudan chapter: Salim worked – illegally, in the black economy (*as what?* Emily wrote down as soon as she got back home) – in Sudan for those eight years and saved enough money to pay a thousand US dollars to a trafficker, Omar, to get him to Libya, where he was promised a regular job, a better life, papers.

Salim belonged to a group of thirty men who were driven, all tied to a big truck, for four days until they arrived at a border town where they were sold to rich Libyan men. It was here that Salim realized what the racket was: slavery. The

Libyan man, Ahmad, who bought Salim, took him to the desert to look after sheep. Salim joined a group of eight such 'shepherds', all of them housed in a bunker in the middle of nowhere. He worked there for six months without any pay; there was nowhere to escape – he was in the middle of the Sahara. (*Sheep? In the middle of the Sahara?* she had written on the margin of her hastily scribbled and abbreviated notes as she was stringing them together into a more coherent copy.) The hard calculation that led Ahmad to return Salim to Omar, the racketeer boss, after six months remained opaque to Salim, but when he asked Omar for money for his months of labour in the desert, Omar said that there was no money for Salim, and if he dared to ask again, he would kill Salim himself.

There was nothing for it, so Salim travelled to Benghazi without his money and from there to Tripoli, where he stayed for a year, working odd jobs, in construction, as a handyman, as a porter, lifting, carrying, and saved up enough money to pay a further sixteen hundred US dollars to yet another trafficker who promised him and eighty-four others – sixty men and twenty-five women – a new life, a better life, a decent working life in the paradise across the waters that was Europe. Yet again Salim fell for it – what could be worse than this life as an illegal low-grade labourer in an alien city? Better to cross the Mediterranean to life in the wealthy north, the land of hope, of jobs.

The inflatable dinghy was eleven metres long. Eighty-five humans were packed in it. The traffickers pointed out the cylinders of fuel, then picked two men to drive the boat, showed them how to operate the engine, then pushed the dinghy into the waters. It was the dead of night. After a few hours, the passengers discovered that the dinghy had holes in its bottom. For one day and one night, they took turns bailing water out of the boat until the engine sputtered and stalled in international waters. They bobbed and floated, bailing water, on the vast open seas for four days. Then they were spotted by a Tunisian fishing trawler. The fishermen could not repair the dinghy's bust engine but what they were able to do was call the Italian police, who arrived first in a helicopter, then a big ship, which saved the refugees.

They were taken to Lampedusa where they were finger-printed. This was an important moment, both an arrival and the beginning of a kind of imprisonment, but Salim did not know this yet. This was a new life but not in any way he had imagined. He would find out. The refugees were taken to the camp near Catania. Fifteen months passed as Salim's application was processed by the Italian authorities. At the end of this period, he got his five-year *soggiorno* and was released from the camp into the freedom of Italy. The new life began.

He had no money, no home, no job, no benefits, no Italian, nothing. For nine months he slept on the streets, ate from garbage bins, sifted through rubbish heaps for clothes, a stray dog among humans. He was sick, frequently. He moved from city to city, from Catania to Palermo, Rome, Messina, begging, foraging, homeless, until he fetched up in Milan and managed to board a train to Calais and join the 'jungle'. He lost his Italian documents and phone in a Portaloo and reported the fact to the Calais police. On each of the twenty days that he was in the 'jungle', he tried to jump on a Eurostar – on the open truck carrier of the train – headed to London. If only he could get to London, where his brother was (*ask him how his brother got to the UK*), all the broken bits of his life would be pieced together into one new whole again. One day in July he got lucky – he managed to give everyone the slip, hide under a truck on the Eurostar, and get to Dover. He immediately sought asylum at the border. After two months in Dover, the Home Office decided to deport him back to

Italy: under Section 4 of the Immigration Act, he was eligible for refugee status only in the European country where he first disembarked and was fingerprinted, which was Italy. He was not allowed to 'shop around'.

Salim refused 'very strongly' to board the flight and was taken to an immigration removal centre near Gatwick. Every few days, the Home Office cancelled and reissued tickets to Italy and he was carted off to the airport and even on to a plane. On one occasion, the pilot refused to fly with a forcible deportation case on board his flight. On another, a nineteen-year-old Swedish activist, alerted by her group that there were 'removals' on the plane, refused to sit down, so they couldn't take off. Salim and four others eventually had to be escorted off the plane and back to their detention centre. Then, in accordance with new rules about moving refugee applicants to different parts of the country, Salim was relocated to Manchester. He had to report in person to the local Home Office outpost every two weeks. At any of those visits, he was liable to be detained and removed to Italy. On the way to one of these appointments he managed to throw off the minders who accompanied him, discarded his electronic tag, and began the walk to London to be reunited with his brother, whom he hadn't seen for maybe fifteen years, the brother who had managed to claim refugee status in the UK successfully.

And the reason Salim did not want to be returned to Italy? Quite apart from the life of a street dog he had there, there was one thing in his narration that kept echoing in Emily's head: 'I no see difference between Eritrea and Europe – I not free in any place.' That line.

As a child of eight, Emily had visited the Natural History Museum on a school trip. Dippy the diplodocus stood in Hintze Hall, amazing everyone into silence by the impossibly long, gently curving line of his skeleton. But what had awed

Emily was the light from the high windows streaming through his body, thick, dust-moted shafts of them piercing him through, pouring through his ribcage, the holes in his neck, as if he were a pane of glass. There was no flesh, no body to stop the light, only a skeleton that configured, it would seem, holes, gaps. Lacuna was a word she learned in her undergraduate years: lacunae in the archival evidence; lacunae in the manuscript record. Here, now, was an exemplary skeleton, profuse with holes and gaps: what did they use to bail the water entering the dinghy through the holes? What did they talk about when the engine died in the deep sea? How had he saved a thousand US dollars in eight years in Sudan or, more importantly, sixteen hundred *in one year* in Libya? How did he hear of the traffickers? Who told him that the Mediterranean crossing would be the way to get into Europe, especially if he had a brother in London? What went through his head as he tried to smuggle himself onto a Eurostar train every day for twenty days and was caught every single time? How many attempts did he give himself? After which attempt would he think, 'Enough, I'm never going to make it'? What was the one-month walk from Eritrea to Sudan like? What did he eat during that time? How did he travel between towns and cities in Sudan and Libya? What was the network of people keeping him alive, allowing him a toehold in the black economy in foreign, unknown countries? Why had he kept up his sleeve the existence of a brother in England? Was that why he was desperate to get here? Why did he say that he would rather kill himself than go back to Italy? What was it like to arrive in a new world and find it to be exactly the same in substance and soul and impossibility as the old?

And then, once the questions began to press, her notes were nothing; the story that was alive, the person that was alive in the story, lay in the answers to the hundreds of questions Emily wanted to ask at every turn. She wanted to know, to imagine, every single detail: from the food he ate in the shepherds' hut in the middle of the Sahara, the exact nature of what looking after sheep entailed, to how much money he made a day on average begging in the streets of Italian towns, what he and his compatriots used to dig out of the underground prison in Eritrea. Eighteen years in different kinds of confinement or on the run escaping from them, trying to find some measure of freedom, and failing each time, with every turn of the story, a seemingly eternal repetition of the pendulum swing between hope and the crushing of the hope.

The more she read her notes the more she noticed that sometimes the arithmetic was not quite accurate: the date of birth changed, the number of years on the run or in hiding or moving from one place to another could be variable, the accounts contradictory or inconsistent here and there. Things didn't add up properly. She would have to represent all this very carefully and truthfully, with as much responsibility as she could muster to shape the material. The thought of the research ahead was both challenging and exciting.

What do we want from the world? A point of rest, security, the tacit assurance that one will be able to live the full trajectory of one's life, from birth to death, without any shock denting or cutting short that arc. More, perhaps: a home, enough to eat, freedom from illness and disease and the capacity to get treatment for them when they afflict us.

Another small thing to want from life: to be free. And yet it was everything, not only to the ones escaping, the ones displaced, but to the rooted, too, who they hope will save them.

And what did the world want from the people in search of a point of rest? Nothing.

*

In the last few lectures before the summer break, she tried to get herself to inhabit fully the subject she was teaching – the seemingly infinite side-branches that opened up along the main narrative road of medieval and early modern romances. It had resonated once, got her enthused and bright-eyed. Now, sitting at a faculty meeting, her attention far away from the business being transacted, she thought about the key nodal points of luck turning a life around, without which a life could be something but not become anything much more. An inspiring teacher, a lucky scholarship, a break from the run of the ordinary everyday, a person who decided to take it upon himself to do something good for someone else, selflessly, generously, as a matter of course, without putting in too much thought or deliberation. Had she ever needed such a person, turning the winds of fortune around by blowing back against them, or had she lived in an order where a cushioned existence did not necessitate such things, where life flowed in well-ordered, predictable, predictably comfortable runnels?

It was someone else speaking through her, as if she were possessed, when she said, 'I'm on leave the first half of winter term next year, I think.'

Chloe Burford, department head, not one to allow herself, even in the thickets of soporific admin work, to be blunt, peered up above her bifocals, brows furrowed with surprise. 'What do you mean you think? This is the first I've heard of it.' She looked around the table. 'Does the AP Committee know?'

'No. Not yet. But they will, immediately after this meeting ends,' Emily said, trying to channel the perfect perpetual equipoise her mother presented to the outside world. All that concerned Emily now was the bureaucratic headache she had so unthinkingly, on the spur of the moment, inflicted upon herself and on the faculty academic planning committee. Yet again, she felt this detachedly, as if it were happening in a film she was watching.

'Come for dinner? It's been a long time,' she heard Rohan's voice say from her phone.

It had been six months ago, yet she felt the briefest visit of nausea. Saying no was not an option. Saying yes would mean taking a taxi back at night; the idea was unthinkable. And making excuses to leave early so that she could take public transport halfway across London would have been seen through by Rohan instantly or, at the very least, triggered a cascade of searching questions. There was no way out of it. Even the fact that there had been a half-year wait for a dinner invitation, when these had once occurred more frequently, held its own meaning. There really was no way out of it.

'I thought you'd never ask,' she said, and hoped that he could imagine her smile but not the calculation behind the words.

'That took you a little while, didn't it? Time was when I took your yes for granted,' he said, then sighed dramatically, trying to make a joke out of it. It was only a partial joke; the other part hit home.

'Why don't we go out to celebrate the end of the semester? It saves you all the chore ...'

'Since when were cooking and entertaining chores for me? But, fine, if you want to go out, so be it. Shall we bounce some dates?'

She had her way, then, but why did it feel like he had scored all the points?

Emily had missed the message, submerged as it was under the daily torrent and the inevitable feeling of exhaustion when she checked her emails. Only while cleaning up her inbox, a kind of displacement activity, in any case, did she notice the sender

176

and open the message; she had almost forgotten her query from three months or so ago. 'Respected Sir,' the email began, 'Veritea thanks you for your kind enquiry. Here at Veritea our aim is for the best customer satisfaction ...' She skimmed down to where a real answer might be found after the template froth. In a different font were a few lines: 'We can find no record of a school before 1979. There is no one called David Colebrook, the company is fully Indian. You can contact the Coimbatore Record Office for historical documents. In tea estate here there are no paper or records. We are sorry for the inconvenience caused.' Then the earlier font returned with: 'We hope we have been of help to you. We are at your service', etc. etc. It was signed by a George E. Perumpalliyil, 'Secy, Corporate Affairs (Ext)'.

So that was that. Short of calling up the CEO, Emily surmised, or showing up at the estate and interviewing people, tracing a chain of employees or their relations from now to then, this was the end of the road. But she didn't sense the usual plummeting feeling inside her – a feeling she knew well – when faced with a cul-de-sac at the very beginning of some research. Instead, she caught herself feeling uninterested, indifferent, even relieved. Unbeknownst to herself, she had lost interest in her grandparents' colonial story, or rather, had transferred her interest to another project, which would demand much more of her imaginative powers. But the noose of the Research Excellence Framework tied around the necks of every academic department in the country had strict rules about what publications coming out of humanities departments contribute to its research excellence and, therefore, to the flow of government funding. Neither of her projects was REF-able, she thought now, in this moment of understanding the shift, and chided herself for still being tied to the habits of thought of what she was coming to view as the old ways.

She took out her phone and looked at her photos folder. There it was, the picture of the board asking for any information about the hit-and-run. She deleted it with two taps.

At eight o'clock in the morning, the A & E department of St Thomas' felt only like a moderately busy airport departures concourse, not the seething chaos that she had been led to expect from the headlines in the gutter press she occasionally caught a glimpse of in the newspaper stand of her local Sainsbury's. But her business was not here. She took the lift to the twelfth floor, to the dialysis centre. She instantly spotted the two men sitting next to each other. She knew from Salim that Karim was twelve years older, but he could easily have been double that number. The brothers' eyes were similar, as were something about the chin and mouth and a way of looking sideways first before they subjected anything to their full gaze; she would have been hard put to distinguish their filiation if she hadn't known about it already. Her first thought was 'This man a warrior, even if he hadn't been broken by renal dysfunction?' Salim had told her about his brother's brave and distinguished past in their country's long war of independence and how he had had to escape, seeking asylum in England. This story, too, had been vague, certainly in Emily's understanding of it, she who knew nothing of the history of that conflict. Looking things up online and browsing the two books she had bought on the subject had only led to more questions, not clarity: had Karim been one of the tegad-elay, a veteran of the Eritrean People's Liberation Front? Surely he was too young for that? Even if he had joined the EPLF as a teenager of sixteen or seventeen, he would have caught only the tail end of the war of liberation. But why had he decided to flee his new country and seek asylum in the UK, a country whose position had been strikingly pro-Ethiopian?

She didn't know how to begin asking the larger historical questions about politics and events and warfare – as Rohan always said, 'To speak two things, one needs to know four' – let alone the personal ones. Maybe they were going to be answered without her striving for them, just as this hospital visit had fallen into her lap, with Salim suddenly inviting her to accompany him and Karim to his twice-weekly dialysis at St Thomas'. What had he been thinking to have asked her to come along to something like this? She had tried to ignore the immediate answer that had occurred to her, but no amount of shame could push it down: he had asked her to a dialysis session as a matter of insurance, to show her that he had not lied about the circumstances of his life. She kept returning to this matter of insurance; to her it was like a silent, strong stream under every conversation, every interaction they had. It was invisible, inaudible, but it provided the unity and coherence to everything between them that was above the surface.

Karim said hello without getting up from his seat. 'It is kind of you to come,' he added, then leaned back, as if uttering those few words had exhausted him. It seemed to Emily that even keeping his eyes open was an effort. His English was better than his younger brother's. How much had Salim revealed about how he and Emily had met? Or even – and this was where she kept stumbling – how they had continued? All those walks in Hyde Park and Kensington Gardens, asking him about his life, in cafés, taking down notes as he spoke, discussing his brother's condition, how he had come to England ... throughout those meetings, she had wondered what kept him agreeing to walk with her, have lunch or tea, talk about himself, his life, his brother. He had never asked a single question about her, nor about the calamitous origin of their ... she quickly discarded 'friendship' for 'interactions'. Once, she had even thought of showing him the photo of the 'appeal for witnesses' board, but had refrained. She pushed all that away now and shook Karim's hand. There was nothing to do except ask inane questions: When are they going to see you? How long does the process take? Do you have a long wait today? The usual English taboos held her back from asking about his illness, the symptoms, their progression, the procedure about to be performed now. Flinching inwardly at the possibility that she had been invited to actually witness it, she suddenly felt trapped in the corridor by the lifts. A sense of desultoriness washed over her. Why was she even here? She stood up and said to Salim, 'I'm going to go get some air. Can I bring you anything? I'll be back soon. If you're inside when I return, I'll wait here for you, OK?'

Outside, the river was the colour of coffee with too much milk in it, and even at this hour, humid warmth seemed to rise from it instead of the freshening breeze that she had hoped for. On the opposite bank, the Houses of Parliament looked like a child's model that had been set down by cranes for a film and would be dismantled, piece by piece, as soon as the shooting was over. The motion and sound of traffic over Westminster Bridge were unbroken. There was a stationary barge farther downstream. She walked south on the Embankment to the coffee van near Lambeth Bridge, bought a latte, then retraced the short walk back to Westminster Bridge. Joggers ran past her. She found a bench, took out her phone, and typed 'dialysis' into YouTube, then smiled at the weak postmodern joke of watching a representation on a screen while the real thing was taking place somewhere a few metres behind and above her. It reminded her that Rohan's phone's ringtone was a recording of his voice saying the words 'Ring, ring' blandly and affectlessly. At the time they had thought it was a great po-mo joke. She wondered if he had tired of it by now. She crossed the bridge and at the sight of a lengthening queue for the London Eye retreated to the hospital. She took the lift back up and kept her eyes firmly away from the doors with porthole windows on her right. After ten minutes, Salim came out of the dialysis room.

'When is he going to be out?' she asked, followed by the real question: 'Do you need me to be around for anything?' As if he hadn't done this unaccompanied for god knows how many years.

'Maybe half hour, maybe one hour.'

If she had expected him to read her circuitous English manners and release her, she was mistaken. She would have to do it herself.

'Oh, I see', she said, then added after a seemly beat or two, 'Salim, I need to go, I have a lot of work waiting for me. Do you mind?' Should she squeeze his shoulders? His hand? She felt dizzy for a moment; a madness was passing through her.

He looked up and said distractedly, 'Yes, yes, goodbye, see you soon.'

She felt her deflation keenly; the madness was still not done. As she walked to Waterloo Station, her mind awhirr, she thought that her GP would have to be her first port of call. She did a quick calculation: if Karim was out of action for two to three days a week because of his dialysis, and Salim, too, as his brother's carer, then the income from driving was, in effect, earnings from a part-time job. From Salim she knew the number of people in that household: Karim; his wife; their two children, now presumably grown up, but still living with them; Salim; the men's mother; Karim's parents-in-law. She also knew that they were all dependent on the two brothers. Actually, one, she corrected herself; Salim was illegal, so under the current dispensation of what was being called a 'hostile environment' for immigrants, he would have great difficulty finding a job, or seeing a doctor, without the proper papers.

The arithmetic was simple; the lived complexities, not so much. But she could hardly demand, or even request, a visit to observe how they lived, give them a questionnaire, make intrusive inquiries. She just had to speculate, imagine, and take a risk. It would be her Pascalian wager.

Emily had always felt a good vibe about her department. Bar one or two bitter and malicious academics, almost every faculty member was kind, generous, collegiate, helpful. The head, Chloe, led in this; she knew that while institutional change and real power were in the hands of bureaucrats, a chair could make a difference to the spirit and soul of a department, to the energy and morale of all the academics and staff. There could have been a shrewd calculation in this – what better way to get the best from people? – but Emily didn't think that this was where Chloe's centre of gravity lay. Besides, Chloe, also an early modernist (Tudor, Elizabethan, and Jacobean drama; Shakespeare, Donne, Marvell, Milton; literary theory), had been the head of the selection committee that had hired Emily and, she thought, perhaps instrumental in giving her the job. So sitting opposite Chloe now in her office, all prepared to deceive her, did not fill Emily with uplifting feelings. Chloe was older, wiser, much more experienced with people and institutions; the least that Emily hoped for was that she wouldn't be caught out.

'But why did you leave it till so late?' Chloe was asking, trying to keep her voice level.

'Well. I was in an accident in January' – she saw Chloe widen her eyes and hastened to add, 'nothing serious, really, no injuries, nothing, except' – here Emily drew a deep breath – 'except I suppose I underestimated the seriousness of the concussion. I was hoping it would just go away, or fade to nothing over a couple of weeks or a month or something, you know, but … but here we are in the summer, and I'm kind of still having trouble concentrating and in doing any kind of sustained reading or looking at the screen …'

'Oh my god, Emily, I'm so sorry. Why didn't you tell us in spring term?'

'Because I honestly thought it would go away. The accident was so … such a non-event.'

'What happened?' Pause. 'May I ask?'

'Oh, I was in a taxi, and it was in, in, in a sort of mild collision, yes, that's what it was, but my phone had fallen and slipped under the seat, so I was bent down, trying to retrieve it, and I twisted my neck, only a little bit, a sort of whiplash, I think, then I hit my head. It was a lot less serious than it sounds, but … but the effects are not yet gone.'

'Oh, Emily, I'm really, really sorry. How awful.'

On the wall behind Chloe's head was a large framed poster of a horse, two young men, and dogs in what looked like a darkish corner of an orange grove. The preening horse, decorated to the nines, took up most of the picture, but what drew Emily's eye was how the lower half of the poster was a dense, bristling forest of legs – horses', humans', dogs'. The tail of one hound ended exactly at the diamond pattern on the stockings cladding the shapely legs of the man at the centre so that the tail looked like a curled arrow with a large head. At the bottom of the picture it said 'Andrea Mantegna, Camera degli sposi, Palazzo Ducale, Mantova'. Directly below it were the bookshelves. The New Arden editions of all the Shakespeare plays, the facsimile edition of the first folio, the Oxford edition of the complete non-dramatic poems, the seven-volume Cambridge edition of the complete works of Jonson … There was no way she could avoid the crunch. It was so near her now. She could see its teeth.

'So, I spoke to my GP several times over the last month,' Emily said, 'and he thinks, he advises that some time off would be helpful. And I wasn't sure whether the summer break would be enough to sort things out, so, in a way, I'm being, uh, sort of risk-averse by asking for a, a leave.'

'Yes, I see what you mean. And presumably you're asking for it in, let's see, seven months' time rather than right after the summer break because you wanted to give us enough notice?' Pause. 'Or because you thought that there was no way you would have got autumn semester off at such short notice.'

Emily found herself admiring the way in which the older woman had, in two sentences, told her off, put her finger exactly on the aporia of the case Emily was trying to make, and offered her a kind let-out. Chloe could easily have decided to make things difficult for Emily by choosing to run with the first two of those stances, and Emily found herself moved by the option Chloe decided to take.

'It would have made sense, health-reasons sense, I mean, for you to apply for autumn off. In for a penny, in for a pound,' Chloe said, looking up at Emily over her glasses, her eyes twinkling. 'Anyway. Warren is already having a nervous breakdown about rotas. Will you give us a note from your GP? I'll see what I can do.'

'I can't thank you enough.' There was a lump in her throat; she felt foolish and ashamed.

'Hold off that until it goes through.'

Emily looked behind Chloe's head at the face of the hunting dog in the poster. The creature was dwarfed by the horse, even the marginal humans, yet the arrangement of all the elements in the fresco was such that it made the dog the centre of attention, indeed his could be the point of view for Mantegna's famous *sotto in sù*. She took a deep breath and said, 'Well, fingers crossed.'

*

When they finally arrived on the outskirts of Assab, it took them nearly a third as long to reach the six berths for the ships as it had taken them to come down from Adi Nefas, where the air smelled of rotting human flesh, the rotting of their dead enemy combatants hastily buried in shallow graves dug by the agalay as they retreated, and Salim and his comrades saw wild dogs and occasionally hyenas with bones in their mouths, barely bothering to run away from human presence, and the dry, dusty, wind-swept soil was littered with what looked like white stones that turned out to be human bones, picked clean by the animals and bleached by the sun and the wind. The southern and eastern sides of the harbour at Assab, the road to Ethiopia, that is, had been entirely dug up with trenches, but the overflow of soldiers, tanks, artillery had made even their approach from the west a prolonged business. Besides, it was too hot to do anything after ten in the morning, so the commander of their unit had decided that they should travel only at night. It did little to mitigate the way they all smelled. Salim had never been bothered by the rank smell of his comrades – and of his own, since he must smell like them – but something in the air of Adi Nefas had given birth to a new sensitivity.

At dawn, they had stopped by roadside vendors selling beles – these sellers used to be Tigrayan women before the war began – and gorged themselves on the fruit. Medhanie had said, 'Careful, the stones will bung you up, then you'll need to be unclogged,' the last action accompanied by an elaborate gesture. Several tittered, but no one held back from stuffing his face, even the unit commander, Fesseha, whom they did not trust one bit but had no choice except to obey unquestioningly. Salim would never forget the time when Fesseha had caught a group of them – Salim, Abu, Dawit, a young Somali from Ogaden – sneaking in roadkill to their barracks to cook and eat. He had reported them to the other, more senior officers, who had then confiscated the bloody rabbit and eaten it themselves. In the end, it was the constant monitoring of how much Salim and his fellow-fighters ate that wore them down. How could they fight wars if they were kept on the brink of starvation? Dawit had said, 'When they wanted to recruit us, it was warsai this, warsai that, the fate of the nation depends on the bravery of the warsai' – he had mimicked the lieutenant commander who had conscripted them – 'but these old soldiers are jealous of us, of our youth. They starve us to keep us under their control. They suffered during the liberation war, so they'll make us suffer now. Don't you see how a shadow falls across their faces when they see us, how their lips become thin with resentment?' Salim had nodded in agreement. As Fesseha had kept eating beles one after another, like a man possessed, Salim had thought, 'You are afflicted by the same hunger as we are,' then Medhanie's joking warning had reminded Salim of his grandmother's remedy for constipation resulting from eating too many beles – having berbere water squirted up the bottom – and the image of Fesseha's hole on fire from the berbere water had brought a fleeting satisfaction.

But now, in Assab, Salim and his unit were confused about what they had been brought here for. It was not as if they were the real warsai, trained at Sawa, as all these soldiers in the trenches around the port seemed to be. They, on the other hand, had been plucked from their homes and thrown into the war, ordered to do their bit for the hard-won country. In fact, there was never a time when Salim hadn't known war. All through his childhood, there was the war for freedom that seemed like the long birth pangs of his nation trying to be born. He hardly remembered a time when the television was not blaring out

186

martial music, songs from the freedom struggle, footage of war-riors. Every year, his school organized a trip to Asmara to see the gigantic shida, a memorial to the EPLF martyrs. Martyrs' Day was barely one month after Independence Day. And now they were in the dark about what their next mission was. There was only one ship docked in the harbour; all the busy trade for and with Ethiopia had come to a halt, like the metal limbs of the cranes, all frozen in mid-air. There was a big sign on the side of the ship: USAID. Later, Medhanie would tell them all what it meant, but Salim let the fancy pass through his head that they had been brought to Assab to be put on the ship and sent away to … here his imagination failed him – shipped where? If they were going to be put on a ship, it was only going to be to another place to fight, to clear dead bodies, rob the Ethiopian dead of their papers and anything else that was worth stealing, whereas Salim allowed himself the cruel luxury of fantasizing that the ship was going to take him away to freedom.

And then began, again, what was Salim's most abiding experience since being conscripted – not fighting, not killing, not hiding, but waiting. Killing time. One of the training exer-cises they had endured early on was to stand straight with their arms stretched out in front of them, loosely, palms upwards, and have heavy objects – small sacks of salt or cement, boxes of bricks – placed on their hands. Then the weight had been increased – one sack, two, three … you had to keep standing erect, and you couldn't drop the weight. If it was more than you could bear, you had to bend down slowly and put the sacks on the ground without curving your spine. But there were few who hadn't dropped the whole ratcheting load when it got too much. In between all the action, they had learned that they were subjected to a similar exercise with time, with all the waiting, all the lying about, all the inaction, and time got heavier and heavier but there was no way it could be dropped.

They talked, they slept odd hours, they went out in twos and three and fours, they even had the radio on all the time, which mostly broadcast patriotic songs and speeches from the tegadelay and current commanders, they sat or lay down, looking at nothing, and time got heavier and heavier, but they couldn't drop it, and their insides filled up with an unending scream.

Six days after arriving at Assab, Medhanie told them what the sign on the ship meant, but where he had picked up the rumour that it was aid for Ethiopia, no one knew. Soon after that, the cranes came back to life and began to empty the ship of its contents: hundreds if not thousands of sacks, all marked with the blue-and-red sign that was also on the ship's side, sacks containing rice, wheat, flour, sugar, and who knew what else. Salim had not been aware that his instinct had known what their unit's orders were going to be, but when they did arrive, he felt a sense of recognition, of something confirmed: the men were to form a relay line to convey the cargo from where it had been placed to the trucks waiting to take it away. It was to be done from ten at night to four in the morning; the official reason for this was to protect the men from the deranging heat of the day.

So that was what they did: Salim, eighteenth or nineteenth down a line of forty or so men, spent six hours every night turning left to receive a sack then immediately turning right to pass it along to the man next in line. It was done in two days. He had lost count of the number of sacks; there were times when he felt that the amount of staples could have fed a whole country, then there were times when it seemed to him that he had become a machine, which could not think or feel, let alone count, so he had done nothing because to do something one needs to have the awareness of doing that thing and a machine part has no such knowledge. This, then, was war – looting, in however orderly a fashion, food aid sent to the enemy country. A strange satisfaction filled him, the joy of a small accomplishment well executed, of having played a tiny part. He wanted it to be counted so that when the time came, they would say, 'You've done your bit, and done it well, now you're freed from the life of a soldier. Go.' It was at that point that he woke up from his reverie and felt the burn of ache in his buttocks, his back, his arms.

At Shepton Mallet, the week felt long; as it had never done before, Emily thought, but was quick to qualify that as a possible false memory, something invented by her present tense. After supper on the first evening, her mother said, 'I've had Trevor take out the boxes with Granny's stuff if you want to go through them. I had a quick root-around – nothing that would interest you, I think.'

There were three big cardboard boxes, a suitcase, and a large metal trunk. The trunk contained, surprisingly, clothes, some of them eaten to almost transparent frazzle by moths, although a faint cloud of mothball odour had hit her nose as soon as she opened the lid. Two shawls, clearly of very fine wool but now looking lacy with holes. Two silk sarees, one with an enormous golden paisley border. A lacquer box with a few pieces of jewellery, some Indian, most of them discoloured; Emily couldn't tell if any was valuable or if the gemstones were real, the dull yellow metal gold. Two suits, falling apart at the folds. A heavy wooden box with silver cutlery, all of it oxidized to a shade of pewtery grey. Under the silverware, a few photographs, some stuck together, all of them sepia, even burned in patchy white flares, with age. Not one person Emily could identify – wait, there was Granny, probably, when she was in her twenties, but that too Emily couldn't tell for sure; age made everyone entirely different people. Not a single Indian in the dozen photos: croquet on a lawn; large sun hats and bonnets; a long car; rolling low hills, densely vegetated, the colour of an English sky in February; but not one Indian in sight. The photos could have been taken in any English shire. Who decided to erase the Indians, the Indianness – the eye of the camera-holder or the camera's eye? Who selected what to represent? The suitcase was full of empty ledger books and crumbling browning receipts and invoices, some of them headed with 'Varugaram Tea Estate, No 7 Savithri Shanmugam Road, Race Course, Coimbatore – 641 027'. She knew from the printed name underneath, D.A. Colebrook, that the flourishing signature in fading royal blue was her grandfather's. The loose papers looked as pointless as the ledgers: why carry this junk all the way back to England? Unless there was some meaning there that she couldn't see, didn't have the background knowledge or training necessary to read it. That could have been the point of entry into her new project: lacunae, staring into the lack of material for a story, then the gradual illumination, an education in the ways the apparent absence could be read in the correct way to suture together a shape, a picture, legibility, just as in the stories she had read as a child in which notes written in invisible ink had to be held in front of a fire and the warmth awakened the writing and made it visible. It would have been, to her, a new way of writing a book – her first, *'Endlesse Worke': The Connections of Spenser's Epic Romance to His 'Minor' Poetry*, had been a conventional, straightforwardly research- and theory-oriented monograph – although the fields had been so furrowed and ploughed that no doubt this approach had already yielded superabundant harvest across several areas and disciplines. Except she couldn't even do that, for she lacked a master key, didn't know in front of which fire to hold her invisible letter. For all she knew, it could have been just a pristine, empty page, not a secret note. She lost all interest in looking inside the cardboard boxes; she had not embarked upon this search with much of it in the first place.

She and her mother spent a sunny day in Bath, which was seething with tourists. The blazing sand-coloured stone failed to charm her this time. Could she have brought Salim here? Would she have been less distracted, less detached from her immediate surroundings, with him around? What would her mother have thought? Emily would never find out because her mother would never say, never give a clue through any action, expression, passing shadow over her face, a perfectly timed pause preceding a word. What would he have made of it? How alienated, out of place would he have felt? She had come close to giving in to the impulse when she had joined him at another hospital appointment and he had asked, 'Why you do this?' She noted that he had never called her by her name. It was at that instant the words had nearly escaped her mouth, 'Salim, come with me to Somerset, I'm going to visit my mother for a few days,' and, as instantly his reply, imagined by her, had arrived: 'What is Somerset?' She had desisted, thank god.

'A penny for your thoughts,' her mother now said.

'How funny. A friend used that expression not that long ago. You know, Granny used to say that to me when I was little.'

Jostled by tourists, they ate ice cream sitting on wobbly metal chairs in a colonnade under enormous Georgian pillars, Emily put out by the crowds and wondering if that Mona Lisa smile on her mother's face was because she liked this bustle or whether she was just happy, easily happy, at the fact that she had company. There was a pink dot of strawberry ice cream on the tip of her nose; Emily did not tell her to wipe it off.

On another sunny morning, her mother drove them to a private garden, open to the public, in Cold Ashton. Emily did not offer to drive, but later thought that perhaps being in the driver's seat would have been fractionally less tense than being a passenger and immediately dismissed the idea as ridiculous. By mid-morning, the garden had begun to feel crowded too.

She bought her mother two Thalictrums from the shop, then they left, Emily murmuring, 'I don't see why we can't sit in your beautiful garden, which is free of crowds.' That is what they proceeded to do, eating fried halloumi salad and chasing away wasps. Emily went up to the apple tree when her mother had gone inside with the empty dishes and bowls. There, if you looked very closely, if you knew where to look, were scratch marks near the base of the trunk, about six or ten inches up, where Teapot had regularly sharpened her claws and pushed off for her climb up to the tree's lower branches.

But she was unsettled. In the in-between times of the day, she worried about the barrage of physical and psychological tests awaiting her on her return to London, and she wrote, or tried to write, managing no more than a constipatedly produced hundred or hundred and fifty words a day which she undid on the following. She waited and waited for the sensation of being in her childhood home, and the kind of regression to safety and security and mindlessness it promised, to wrap her in its cocoon, but it didn't arrive, not even when she was lying in her old bed, trying to summon that woodcut of three birds flying over the dark clump of a wood, that certain slant of light, but no, the comfort adamantly withheld itself.

'You're distracted, dear,' her mother said, during an aimless late-afternoon walk in the town. Emily had always thought of the place as shabby and down-at-heel, especially with its ghastly neo-Gothic market cross that added to the air of grubbiness, and nowhere near as picturesque as a market town in this part of the world could be. Now, outside the vintage clothing store at the bottom of Town Street, with its enormous planter of all the kitsch municipal plants – petunias, pansies, asters – she felt pity flit through her chest, pity at the name of the shop, an anagram of Shepton Mallet, pity at the place's provincial-ity, its attempts to spruce up while managing to achieve only something resolutely second-rate. She wanted her mother to hold her in this moment of sadness and say, like she used to when Emily was little and had scratched her knee or knocked her head, 'There, there, darling, it'll be all right, here's a kiss to make it better.' The moment passed.

'Oh, am I?' Emily returned to her mother's observation. 'It's nothing,' she wanted to add, but didn't.

'Is it because you're a bit disappointed that you didn't find what you were looking for in Granny's stuff?'

The question, so uncharacteristically direct and enquiring, even inquisitive, surprised Emily; she hadn't seen it coming.

'No, it's not that,' she said, and immediately withdrew it. 'Well, yes, a little bit, to be honest' – then looking at her mother and smiling – 'just a tiny bit.' The retraction would save her from more questions.

'I'm sorry,' her mother said.

'Don't worry, it's nothing, 'twas always thus with research,' Emily reassured her, speaking too much. 'Let's see if we can find a bottle of Mitsouko for you in this … little town.'

Inwardly, she mocked her own feeling that this visit had a somewhat valedictory air about it; how absurdly self-pitying – she was only going in for a more or less routine procedure, not undergoing a serious, possibly life-threatening, medical intervention.

In August, the only month of the year when some respite was to be had from the ever-grinding machinery of admin and email, when everyone went away on holiday having activated their part-wishful part-defiant 'out of office' auto-replies, Emily researched, imagined, and wrote, imprisoning herself in her flat, content to look out at the sentry-stand of giant plane trees and the dusty common behind it. The sun had never held any appeal for her; she was happier with its presence, to be sure, but that was only for the light, not the warmth. The unchanging and monotonous grooves in which her life shuttled back and forth, back and forth: were all lives, looked at closely enough, this boring? Was it fiction, the way things were selected to be represented, that led us to believe that lives were interesting, had legible shapes? Perhaps things were interesting only in the stylization, when they were narrated within the bounds of form, not in the living. In which case, the stylization, or the modelling, if you will, had a fundamental falsehood at its heart.

When the autumn term began, she realized that she only saw Salim nowadays in the medical context of hospital visits. (Her own phalanx of tests she showed up for alone.) Behind that understanding was a more melancholy, more shadowy one: her decision had put them both on a trajectory where seeing each other had become even more constrained by awkwardness, by an even weightier implied obligation than the accident – it seemed so long ago, as if it belonged to a former life that she could only dream about in fleeting flashes – had imposed upon them.

Was it four years ago or five that he had looked all around him at night and thought, 'This is a sea of sand. There's nowhere to run, like there's nowhere to run in the middle of the sea – the sand, like water, would kill you. Maybe one drowned in water faster, but sand promised the same fate, only a little more delayed.' All things were beginning to become what they were not: sand became water, water caught fire. They were all signs. And that's when you knew that your life had taken a wrong turn, and it was going to go on like this, on the wrong path, until your breath left your body. That's what Medhanie had said, all those years ago, so many that he felt all that had happened to a different person, so distant was that young man to what he was now. Crouched in the dinghy, he was reminded of those cold nights in the desert, the sky a black sheet stretched out far above him, except that it was not black at all, but with patchy smears and trails of what looked like dense whitish dust, as if someone had taken out an old black cloth and strung it up without shaking it out first. If you focused on the dust, you knew that they were stars, but if you allowed your eyes to swim a bit, they became dust again. No, not dust – it was like smoke, as if whitish smoke had got stuck to that black cloth and become like particles. And then he had that drowning, falling feeling again, except he didn't know whether he had fallen upwards and was drowning in that dusty sheet above or in the black sand under and around him stretching away forever and forever in all directions.

Now, in the boat, he had a similar sensation: the constant motion of the water, and of the boat bobbing on it, had brought a different kind of dizziness, but he felt he was again close to that falling, drowning feeling. It was a sensation low down in him, somewhere in the need to tighten his sphincter muscles. He knew the name of the one other Eritrean on the dinghy – Gebreysus, an older man, with the thin body of one who could have been a guerrilla fighter, or perhaps someone who was familiar with periodic bouts of starvation. He was shouting in Arabic, to no one in particular, to hold down the legs of the boy – no more than thirteen or fourteen – who was retching into the sea, half his body out of the edge of the dinghy. Several people had observed, while the boy was being sick, that the motion of the boat was causing it, but the motor had died last night, and the boy had not taken a rest from vomiting, although by the look and sound of it, there wasn't even the thinnest string of bile inside him to pull out. Salim now thought perhaps the boy had tried to bargain with fate, thinking, 'I'll settle with a stalled boat in the middle of the sea if only this agony will stop', but fate, miserly as always, had blindly granted one thing and not the other, so now not only the boy but also everyone else on the boat with him was in peril. Salim wondered if any of the women were thinking of this unequal exchange.

But now his turn in the queue arrived; he had to go to the other end of the dinghy, grab one of the empty plastic bottles, each with its top two or three inches cut off so that it had a much bigger mouth, and use it to scoop up the sea water that had begun to enter the boat last night from a hole in the bottom. All the men, arranged in a loose line, took turns, bailing water night and day, returning to the sea what was the sea's, until they drowned or were, somehow, saved. They had been given a pack of twenty-four two-litre bottles of drinking water by the men who had set them off to sea. The women on board barely touched it, Salim noticed, but even with rationing, they were down to eight or nine bottles now. The rest had been drunk, the empty containers put to use as a bailing implement. Salim thought of the absurdity of siphoning bottles of water into the sea … if the sea wanted to get in, it would; human effort was a pitiful thing. After the last ten years of trying to find a toehold somewhere, anywhere, it had come to this: drowning, any hour now, in the middle of an unknown sea. The boy was still retching. Salim, like many of them, he suspected, had silently pissed in his trousers. Earlier, a Libyan man had prevailed upon a few of the men to stand as a kind of wall in front of him as he balanced on the edge of the boat to shit into the sea. One of those men held down his legs, another pulled the Libyan's hands towards him, so that he didn't topple over. Even in the situation they were in, a roll of disgusted merriment went up. Perhaps people liked to laugh when faced with being extinguished. There was a brief stench, then nothing.

Salim bailed water and was reminded, yet again, of the trick Medhanie had used to get out of combat – shooting himself in the hand. The trick was to position a water bottle between the *gun and his hand so that the burn marks from a close-up self-inflicted wound, so easily identifiable, could not be detected. Medhanie had asked Salim to follow him, but his nerves had failed him. Now, faced with the open sea and a boat letting in water, Salim thought that hope was the thing that caused all the undoing. What hope of discharge from the army had made him avoid putting himself through a little bit of pain only to be ultimately confronted by this?*

*

She knows how the conversation is going to go even before she has picked up the phone, when the only information she has is his name showing up on her screen. Her chest feels, oddly, both constricted and expanding.

'Hi,' she says.

'Hi,' Rohan says, and adds, 'What news?', as if this were any old inconsequential conversation, as if she were still the old she.

'Not much. Still recovering from surgery.'

'Surgery? What surgery? My god, are you all right?' That old Rohan again.

'Nothing serious. I donated one of my kidneys. It's a routine surgery. You know, you need, one needs, I mean, only one. Did you know that?'

'I think I knew that.' Emily can hear him trying to recover. 'Is that why you went AWOL?'

No, he isn't going to ask. She debates whether to tell him, but in the time that she takes to consider it, a quantum segment of a second, it's as if her head has become clear glass and he, even separated by miles, can see her thoughts inside it moving like a line of insects, for he asks, 'So you donated it through the organ donation scheme, you know the one I mean, the NHS one, wait, is there an NHS one, or to anyone in particular?' Then carries on innocently, 'Like responding to an ad or, or I don't know how these things happen, did someone contact you or what?'

Emily interrupts him in his floundering. She understands his polite emphasis on the trivial, or trivial to him since he thinks he has more pressing, more awkward business to get over with on this call, and this chit-chat – in another person, she would have called it nervousness – buys them both time. She says, 'No, I donated to someone particular.'

'Oh. Someone you know or "particular" meaning not to a kidney bank? Are there kidney banks?'

'I donated to Karim, Salim's elder brother.'

'Who is Karim? Who is Salim?'

She takes a deep breath. 'Salim is ... is the guy who was, who is, was the guy driving the car that night.'

'Which night?' And then it coheres into meaning for him. Instead of the Rohan-like tumble-and-cascade of words and swearing expressing surprise, even shock, there is an odd, reticent formality to his tone when he says, 'I see. That night.' Then silence falls and Emily again has the image – wrong, she knows – of it filling the line, traversing the geographical, physical distance between Homerton and Pimlico. Who will blink first?

'Do you' – pause – 'know him' – pause – 'well now?' he asks, his voice controlled to the extreme.

'No, I don't. Not at all, in fact. But there are many people in that family, all dependent on Karim, on the elder brother's income, I mean, and he is ... was out of action for three to four days a week for dialysis. And Salim doesn't have any papers, you know, he's illegal, so it's difficult for him to get a job to help out, I mean, be another earning member, if you see what I mean –'

'I do see what you mean.' His words are a switchblade. 'So, you've made friends with him in the last however many months.'

'I wouldn't say friends, exactly ...'

'Are you fucking him? Is that what this is all about?' Tonally still absolutely controlled, as if he has mentioned an empirical fact, 'Petrarch was born in 1304 in Arezzo', to a class of students.

'That's a bit below the belt.' She feels too deflated and tired to take offence. She knows that in the past Rohan would have made a ribald joke of that idiom. She also knows that he will not do it now.

'I'm sorry you think that. What about the boy and his dog you ran over' – pause – 'that night?'

She can smell his fury in the choice of pronoun, in that pause, in that 'I'm sorry' – using good manners as a weapon, like any well-brought-up English person. She cannot answer the question he has posed; not only is it unanswerable, but whatever she says is going to be wrong.

'I don't know how to answer that question,' she says simply.

'No, you don't. Do you know how close I came to calling the police? Do you? But every time I was on the brink of calling them, I thought of Forster's trade-off between friend and country and decided in your favour. I feel soiled by my choice now. But we're not here to talk about that, in any case. I'm sorry I brought it up.' Pause. 'I read the pages you sent me. I was going to ask why you decided to tell this particular story, I mean, what was the compulsion behind it, but I think I know the answer now.'

She doesn't feel the usual dread one feels when a reader is about to give comments on your work; and not just any reader, but a successful writer to boot. Maybe it's a defence mechanism, maybe a deferred reaction to his earlier animus, controlled no sooner than it had begun or transmuted, by a sheer act of will, to something else, but she feels unreceptive, hidden tight in an armour of indifference.

'You haven't changed his name. Are you going to write it as fiction?' Rohan asks.

'Yes. Yes, I think I am,' she forces herself to respond.

'All right. I guess you've already thought about how to give him a back story – I mean, where he is, what his life is, and the world he inhabits, before the event that sparks off everything begins. I mean the illegal conscription that stretches on and on and eats his life. Because these few pages I have are only part of the story.'

'Yes, yes, that's right. We talked about this, remember?'

'I do, yes, but I did not know then whose story you were writing. You asked about it in very general terms. So, in chronological order: his past in Eritrea, then the years in the army, followed by being trafficked, et cetera, until he arrives as a stowaway in England. What happens from that point onward?'

'I … I don't know. I haven't thought that far. Is it necessary to know it from the very outset?'

'No, not necessary, but maybe useful. Or desirable. And you want to write the whole thing from his point of view?'

She suddenly understands that he is hedging, buying time, trying to find a way to pull on his gloves before he punches: it is clear that he didn't like the fifty-odd pages she sent him and is now leading up to the *coup de grâce* via this mealymouthed sub-prac-crit comments.

'You can be brutal, you know,' she says. 'I can take it.'

There's a very long silence before he speaks. When he does, what he says takes her by surprise; this was not the criticism she was expecting.

'Well, my first reaction,' he says, 'was, is: this is not your story to write.'

Something in her wakes up, something that could not be roused when he had asked about the boy and the dog. She says, 'No. No, it's mine. It's my story too.'

III

Data, n., pl. of **datum,** that which is given.

The truth is always concrete.

– V.I. Lenin (ish)

1.

She is to arrive in a tempo on an early afternoon in spring, when the weather has already turned too hot, but it is still a good while from the sowing of aus paddy. Mira and Sahadeb have been sitting since dawn in a patch of shade that keeps moving with the sun – they know she is going to come in a tempo today, and they are more curious about the tempo because they have never seen a motor car in their short lives. There are no roads in Nonapani. There are no roads anywhere near Nonapani: you'd have to go nearly twenty miles east, near the border village of Dhopabari, to see a tar-and-crushed-stone-chips road. How the tempo is going to come to the children's hut is a big question, but it doesn't occur to them. It evidently doesn't cross their mother Sabita's mind either, for she comes out of the hut frequently and, under the guise of chivvying the children, lingers outside on each occasion and looks into the distance, the way she does when she is expecting the children's father to return. In a way, she is looking for him, for he too is expected to arrive in the tempo. That's what he had said when he had left yesterday: 'We will return riding in a motor car, a big one, maybe a tempo, or even lorry, because a motor car would be too small.' He knows all these things because he works in cities and towns. He is gone for months and months, then comes back for a few days, occasionally for a few weeks, when he is in between jobs, then ups and leaves again. The children call him Baba, of course, and are happy when he arrives, largely because of the presents he brings – lawjens wrapped in shiny cellophane or plastic; little painted tin boxes that once must have held something, they do not know what; shirts and short pants for Sahadeb, frocks for Mira, clothes for both children too loose and big on them ('You'll grow into them,' he would say, 'better to have something ready for the future than clothes you no longer fit into and will have to discard in a few months; what a waste of money'); plastic balls and plastic dolls with pale pink-orange skin and red-painted lips; once even a wind-up tin rooster that stopped working after one day. These things brought excitement and novelty to the children's unvarying days, but they were formal and aloof with their father, shy, as they would be with a distant relative or a stranger. Their mother would have to say to them sometimes, 'Go, sit with your baba', or 'Go talk to Baba, he's here for only a few days, you won't see him for a long time after he leaves.' Mira and Sahadeb would try to get out of these directives, but when they couldn't, a sense of stilted dutifulness marked their actions, not easy affection.

Now they await Baba's arrival, but only as an effect – he will be arriving in the tempo with the gift that is meant for the whole family, but it is really the sighting of a motor car that the children are waiting for. They move to the outskirts of their hamlet. 'Outskirts' makes it sound grand; in reality it's only four dispersed huts away. From this point there are only flat fields and earth, nothing to obstruct their view. It is well after the sun has begun its climb down from the highest point in the sky that the children spy movement on the horizon. Mira starts to count, 'One, two, three, four', leaving out the cow in the midst of the advancing silhouetted figures. There is no tempo. Sahadeb runs home. 'They are coming, they are coming,' he announces to his mother, spinning around, 'but they are walking, there's no motor car.'

'You silly boy, how can they come in a motor car? There are no roads here.'

2.

She is the colour of milk, except around her budding horns where the skin looks as if someone has tried to rub off a spill of rust. She still wears the vermillion smear that Sabita had put on the creature's forehead when she had arrived and the now-withering orange marigold garland around her neck. She has enormous eyes that don't seem to be looking at anything in particular yet give the impression that she has seen and absorbed and understood everything around her, as if rapidly shifting and darting vision, the very notion of alertness, is a sign of lower creatures.

'What beautiful, deep eyes,' Sabita had said on the first day, 'just like the sea.'

'When have you ever seen the sea?' her husband, Pulak, had said.

'Oi aar ki, just saying, it's what people say.'

The children are mesmerized by the creature. They stand outside in their compacted earth yard and stare at her all day. Sabita says, 'If you look at her for so long, she'll put you under her spell and you'll become cows too.' Even this cannot deter them. Truth be told, they are all, including Sabita and Pulak, a little afraid of the cow – what if she charges at them? What if she kicks? Tries to gore them with her horns, small as they are? Stories of recalcitrant cows are all too common, although how they have come by these tales no one can be sure, since none of them has ever come in contact with a cow. Maybe it's a rural myth, cows and their dangerous horns and their propensity to kick.

When they were naming her, Sahadeb had piped up, 'Bilu! Mahadeb!', but he had been vetoed by everyone – 'These are all boys' names,' Mira had pointed out, 'and this cow is a girl.' So they had ultimately settled on Gauri.

And here Gauri is, placid as a pond's surface, lying on the earth, near the post to which she is tethered, looking at nothing, her mouth churning away, foam spilling out of it.

'It's as if she's eaten soap,' Sahadeb observes.

'No, no, silly,' Mira says, 'don't you remember, the people who gave us the cow said that they do this? They eat hay or grass then spend all day chewing it.'

A shed has been built for her: four bamboo posts supporting a straw roof. It won't keep her safe from the rains in the monsoon, but it can provide a little bit of shade during the summer. Straw has been spread on one corner of the earth to serve as a bed, but Gauri has already eaten most of it. They don't have any cloth to spare to bundle up and make it a nominal bed. In fact, there is no bed for anyone: when Pulak comes back from his construction work in far-flung towns, he gets the old, oily, filthy quilt to spread on the earth floor of the hut under him. The rest all sleep on madur that are coming apart. When the people who had decided they should be given a cow had totted up their belongings, the very short list had included that quilt, a low wooden stool, an iron sharanshi that was loose at the fulcrum, one dented haandi, a bonti whose blade, it felt to Sabita, had to be forever sharpened. The list-makers had not considered the family's very few clothes, their floor mats, the broom, and a few other utensils and odds and ends worthy of inclusion under 'assets', not even the red plastic comb so beloved of Mira. When Sabita had said, 'How can Gauri lie on the bare earth? I'll make her a bed with straw,' Pulak had responded with derision, 'Let be, no need for a bed for Gauri. No skin on your bum, yet your name is Hare Krishna! She's a cow, they don't have beds in the fields and in the open, do they?' The shed is behind their hut, not strictly on land that belongs to them, but in these distant outskirts of Nonapani, it's not as if anyone is going to check. There are a couple of fallow fields behind the shed, then a copse. After that, the paddies begin – irregular parcels of land, some as small as ten steps by ten steps, some larger. During planting season, Sabita works on some of these plots, standing calf-deep in flooded paddies, transplanting seedlings all day long. If Pulak is around during harvest time, he will also work there for a day or two when more hired hands are needed. For most of the year, Sabita works as a domestic help – cleaning, doing laundry, grinding spices, cooking, fetching water, and other odds and ends – in three of the bigger houses in Majharsharif, the town nearest to Nonapani, a two-hour walk away. She leaves the hut at six in the morning every day and returns around six in the evening. Sometimes, in the blood-drying heat of the summer months, she feels like she is not going to make it back home, or she is, but while vomiting blood, and she'll expire before one of her children can give her some water to drink. In the monsoon, the opposite problem – there are days when she cannot leave home because the sky is sending down sheets and sheets of water. The force of the water feels like it can perforate holes in your head. It is in the monsoon that she is sometimes fired from one or two of her jobs because of absenteeism; not per-sistent absenteeism, of course, but not being able to show up a couple of times a week for a month, or on three consecutive days, is enough. Then, in the rotting heat after the monsoons have passed, she has to walk around Majharsharif looking for other houses that'll take her, because being without her wages, albeit meagre, is unthinkable, especially when the timing of the money that Pulak sends home is so random, so unreliable – three hundred rupees one month, then nothing for another four or five or six.

And the children? Mira is now six, Sahadeb eight. When they were smaller, Sabita didn't work – she could hardly leave two toddlers under the care of the families who lived nearby. She did, once, with her first child, a boy called Bhola. She came home one day – they lived in a different village then, Nabagram, farther east, near the river and much closer to the country on the other side – to find that he had crawled off and drowned in the pond behind the house of the people with whom she had deposited him before leaving for work. When Sahadeb was born, someone suggested that he wear an amulet around his upper arm to ward off the pull his dead brother would inevitably exercise on him. The amulet had come off only after the family moved to Nonapani, which they took as a sign that they had left behind the radius of Bhola's influence. The ghost of a toddler is limited in its strength, while the ghost of a grown-up person is a different matter altogether. They had had Sahadeb's left ear pierced, and a small, thin, almost thread-like, metal ring put through it to replace the amulet. He wears it still, and when people ask him about it, he says, 'The brother before me died ...' That's all he has to say; people understand him immediately; it's as if he's a marked child.

Fiddling with that earring now, Sahadeb watches Gauri. In fact, that is what the two children have been doing ever since Gauri arrived, the thought of going to the pathshala in the village, already intermittent at best, nearly forgotten. Sabita and Pulak, both illiterate, had never had the thought of their children's education uppermost on their minds; enforcing the children's attendance in Nonapani's only pathshala was even further.

'The didimoni in the pathshala will know why the cow keeps chewing,' Sahadeb says.

Suddenly something occurs to both brother and sister – they haven't been there to tell everyone that they have been picked above everyone else to receive not just any ordinary gift, such as clothes or sweets, but the grand, majestic gift of a cow.

3.

Pulak is away again. Sabita had hoped that Gauri would keep him here, if not for the long term then at least for a while, until she had learned the ropes, but no, like the wind he was gone. They had fought before he left.

'How am I going to manage this on my own?' she had asked.

'They said they were going to come check on everything regularly,' he had answered.

'They said, and you believed! Well, more fool you. Maybe we'll see their pigtails in six or nine months, but I'll have to look after the creature every day. How will I go to Majharsharif?'

'You don't have to go any more – the cow will bring us more money than you get from being a servant. They said so. That is why they've given us the cow, not anyone else. It's to help us.'

'But how will it bring us money? She can't give milk unless she has a calf. To have a calf, there'll need to be a bull. Besides, she'll eat us out of house and home. Do you think *they* will bring us hay every day?'

'They said we could let it graze …'

'Graze where? Summer's coming, the grass in the fields is going to be scorched to ashes.'

'Just let her free, she'll find her own food. They're animals – do you think all the animals that you see around you are fed by humans? They find their own food.'

'You have wheels on your feet, you'll disappear in a couple of days, then it'll be me who'll have to look after everything.'

And disappear he did, exactly two days after she had asked him for help with Gauri. There is nothing for it, she must do it all herself. A hundred worries go through her head. What if she let Gauri free to graze and then she ran away? Or got lost? Would she have to pay the price of the cow to the people from the city who gave it to them? Several sets of those people had come in the past months, armed with clipboards, paper, pen, phones. They had asked so many questions – what do you eat for your main meal of the day, what things do you own, do you have a PDS card, what about aadhar, how much money do you make a month, do they give you food at the homes you work at in Majharsharif, do the children go to school, do they get a midday meal there, and dozens and dozens of others – that her head had begun to ring. After Gauri had arrived, those people had promised they would be back to arrange for regular delivery of food for the cow, to check on her health, to teach Sabita and her family the ways of cow-rearing ... What if those people come one day only to discover that Gauri had been sent out to graze and had not returned? The border with the other country, where they kill and eat cows, is not far – what if Gauri strays past the border? What if someone lures her over to the other side in a boat? What if the people from the city then ask her for the full price of the cow? Her head begins to ring again.

This morning, when she begins her walk to work, the only thing she has eyes for are fields and pastures where Gauri might graze. But who will bring her here and then back home? None of them has ever grazed a cow before. Would the city people know what to do? Then there is the added anxiety of what awaits her when she shows up at the homes in Majharsharif – she hasn't been for six days, maybe eight or nine, she has lost count – there may not be a job waiting for her, surely she has been replaced? Even this is less pressing than the concern that they could dock her pay for all the days that she has worked this month, then there would be a nasty argument, and she would have to forfeit the wages owed to her, as she had to do once before. They had made her come back for the fifty rupees owed her for four months, come back tomorrow, come back a week later, come in the afternoon, come after Thursday, they had put a rope through her nose and made her go round and round until she had lost all patience one scalding-hot afternoon and had stood outside their closed doors and shouted filthy abuse so that everyone in the neighbourhood would know what kind of lowlifes these people were and she had cursed that their family line would die out … Several months later the young boy, the heir of the family, had died after being bitten by a snake. Shortly after this, while Sabita was being given her wages at another job, the woman had given her an extra fifty rupees and said, 'They sent this from that house you used to work at, you know, the one where the boy died of snakebite.'

Sure enough, when she reaches Majharsharif, one of the families tells her not to come back. When she asks for money for the days that she has worked, they haggle with her and try to bring the number down, their seven against her eleven, but ultimately end up paying her for eight days, which is better than nothing. In the other two homes, she's shouted at: 'We won't pay you for the days you were absent,' she's told, 'next time you pull this one on us, you're out, be warned,' they say, but at least they don't kick her out.

Halfway through sifting the spent coaldust cakes to find a nice one to use for scrubbing the dishes and utensils, she tells the mistress of the house with shy pride, 'They've given us a cow.'

'They? Who are they? And what do you mean, given you a cow? Just like that? You expect me to believe this?'

'Yes, I'm saying, Boüdi, just like that. Some people from the town. Government people, maybe.'

'But why on earth would they do that? Did you pay for the cow? It costs a lot of money – how did you come by that?'

'No, no, they gave it to us. It's a gift. They said she'll make us money.'

'But how?'

'She'll give milk, then we'll sell it.' Here, Sabita becomes hesitant, and her words trail off.

'But that's a lot of work. Do you know how to do it? Who will do it?' Then self-interest hits the mistress of the house, and she says tartly, 'Well, you'd better let us know now so that we can look for someone else – if you want to look after cows, that's all you'll be doing, you won't be able to do your job here.'

'No, no, how can that happen?' Sabita mutters into the pile of stainless-steel plates and glasses and bowls, all grey-pink with arcs of gritty wet ash, awaiting rinsing. Her vigour in dealing with the dirty dishes abates. There is no getting away from what her mistress has just pointed out. Sabita then washes an enormous pile of clothes, wrings them and hangs them out to dry in the Chaitra sun baking the backyard. Only one thought fills her mind: who will look after Gauri? Boüdi has spread out cut-up green mangoes tossed with salt, turmeric, and chilli powder in the sun. Sabita is distracted and a corner of a mostly white block-printed cotton saree brushes against the mangoes, but she doesn't notice. There'll be shouts and threats when the mistress of the house finds out.

Her walk back to Nonapani smells of smoke from cooking fires being lit in the sprinkle of huts that occasionally dot the way, of the baking earth, brief drifts of the vegetal smell of weeds and their flowers. Telakucha, growing wild, is in flower; she must remember to pick the fruits right before the monsoon. There's a blue plastic bucket hiding in the thickets. A bucket would come in useful in any number of ways. Someone must have abandoned it – was it cracked or broken? She lifts it by its handle and turns it around and upside down then back on its base again. No, it seems to be intact, although the handle has slipped its slot on one side, something that's easily fixed. The unexpected find lifts the end of her day. And then she sees them, standing beside a pond, in the middle of a field, three of them, no four ... five! They look worn, their ribs are showing, their skin hangs in folds, the humps on their necks look like hillocks on their bodies. Three of them have enormous curved horns. Tentatively, she walks towards them to find out if this is what grazing is. What are they doing, standing and staring at nothing? They are not nibbling at the green around them. Are they about to begin eating or are they done and waiting to be led back to their sheds? She just wants to stand and watch them for a while and, maybe, learn something in the process. Who knows, the people who own them might suddenly appear, to take them home at sundown, and then she could ask them a few things.

As she gets nearer, full of trepidation, the one with the biggest horns turns to face her and lets out a loud 'Hum-baaa', then begins to move towards her briskly. Sabita thinks she's being charged at and runs and runs and runs, not stopping to look back. The bull wasn't charging at her – his head was not lowered – but only wanting to make friends and seek food that she might have been bringing. He is baffled and maybe hurt and stops still in his tracks. When Sabita eventually turns around to check if the bull is at her heels, she finds him stoically looking after her, standing some distance away from his friends or relatives, who appear to be as unmindful of her as they did before. A cow from the group lows and Sabita quickens her pace.

When she reaches her hut, she finds her children at the back, rooted to the ground in front of the cow, watching her almost without blinking. Something about the way they stand there tells Sabita that they've been more or less in that position for the whole day. For the first time she notices the odour of cow dung, then its source – pats of earth-brown, hay-flecked shit in almost circular formation, nearly a dozen of them, all in the same rough area, some pats even touching each other, since the tethered cow can only go so far. The heat, the hyp-notized flies on the dung, the heat that seems to have sucked the blood dry from her head ... she feels something rising in her. She asks the girl, 'Have you lit the unun?'

Mira shakes her head without bothering to look at her mother.

Sabita goes up to them, takes hold of the girl's bony shoulders, and slaps her cheeks, once, twice, shouting, 'So you expect me to do that after I have worked like a dog all day in this heat, huh? How many times have I told you to start on the unun before I return? How many times? And you' – she turns to Sahadeb – 'could you not have made yourself useful, you root of the rot?' She slaps him too, but he doesn't start crying like his sister. 'Standing here all day, looking at the cow, is not going to feed us. And what's there to see? You two have turned my flesh and bones black.'

The children run into the fields to get out of her way. Sabita continues to mutter and grumble as she lights the fire to cook. She does not have the energy to do anything beyond boiling rice. Besides, there's not much else to eat except a gourd. She will eat the rice with green chillies; the children will have to do with only salt. Something occurs to her: when she drains the rice, she catches the starchy water in another pot, then gives it to Gauri when it has cooled down. The cow doesn't bother to stand up, but she understands that something is being given to her, so she cranes her neck forward. Sabita, still a little afraid of the cow, stretches out the entire length of her arm and deposits the pot of starch in front of the cow's face, keeping herself a few feet away even though Gauri is tethered. The cow laps up the glutinous water and it's gone before Sabita has withdrawn her arm. Aha, poor thing, she was hungry, Sabita thinks. The bales of hay Gauri came with, as part of her start-off food, are nearly gone. She has no idea how to contact the government people, does not even know the name of their town. A solution has to be found, and she is the one who has to find it.

4.

It's not as if the village pathshala imparts any education to the children of Nonapani. A straw roof perched over mud walls, with a sizeable front yard of dust in the summer and mud in the rainy season where the children mill around when they're not in the only room inside, it functions as a kind of social centre for poor children in the general catchment area. The nearest free state school, in the town of Ranirhat, is too far away for the children of Nonapani. The pathshala has a total of two teachers, both addressed as 'didimoni' by the students; one of them is the fat didimoni, the other the thin. Very rarely are both present and, more than occasionally, neither is, so that the children make their way to the pathshala, drift about, wait a while for either didimoni to show up, and then leave desultorily. This means that there is no set, stable attendance on the part of the children either, and no standard age group; the children range from six to twelve, and all are taught the same thing, since there are no age-differentiated classes with lessons tailored accordingly. The informality extends else-where. There is no blackboard, no chalk, the children don't even have footwear, let alone paper and pencils and books, slates and writing chalks. When a teacher is present, and what counts for a class is in progress, they sit on the floor and recite in unison whatever poem the didimoni has chosen for the day:

she recites one line, the children repeat it after her, each line receiving three solo and three choral iterations. And so they progress through the poem: 'The little boy says a, aa ...' Like the buzzing of bees or the cooing of pigeons, this choir can lull you to sleep. Learning, in this mode of practice, is aural learning by rote.

Sometimes the didimonis try to teach the children the alphabet; the extent of written learning. The teacher writes the vowels on the earth in the yard with a stick, then the children trace over the letters with a twig or a stripped branch. When they have spent several days doing this – a way of filling up the time, since limitations of all kinds mean that it is impossible to move on to the next stage – the children are tested on how much they have learned. They are sent to the opposite corner from the one in which the primer is inscribed on the ground and each child is made to scratch out the vowels in the earth on his or her own, without any help, as a didimoni calls out, 'Aw, aa, i, ee, ...' How much the children progress from recognizing individual letters to words and sentences is open to question.

Today, for example, the children are reciting, along with fat didimoni, 'The python comes hurtling along / I'm going to pluck the mango and eat it ...' The children dutifully sing out after the teacher recites each line, but lacking the textbook in which they can follow the words with their eyes as they are speaking them means that they learn only aurally and cannot match the spoken to the written word.

Didimoni halts and raises her voice, 'What's all that whispering at the back?'

The class falls silent. Didimoni repeats her question, this time a little threateningly. The children fear her – she has a cane that she uses liberally.

'Who started it all, eh? Who?'

Sahadeb stands up. He is shaking slightly.

'What were you saying? Tell us all, we want to hear too.'

Sahadeb mumbles something that no one can catch.

'Is there a lock on your mouth that you can't speak up?' Didimoni thunders.

'A cow has arrived for us,' Sahadeb manages to say, still mostly inaudible.

Didimoni shouts, 'Say that again, loudly, so that we can all hear.'

Sahadeb repeats himself, the last two words trailing away.

'Cow? What do you mean "has arrived"? How did it *arrive*? It walked on its own to your place? Not surprising it recognized its own kind, you stupid ox. Now sit down. Right, next line, "The mouseling trembles in fear / Lest the eagle catches it".'

Sahadeb sits down, awash with relief. He has been humiliated, but it could have been so much worse. He has avoided a hiding. Along with relief, there's something else – a sense of deflation that no one else is caught up in the excitement of something as unusual as the gift of a cow. He had wanted to share it with everyone, feel the warmth of a different kind of attention, bask in others' silent, maybe even envious, acknowledgement of his family's move up in the world, for a cow could be the possession of only a rich family. But all of that had swiftly, suddenly trickled away. He had had such high hopes and had been unable to stop chattering about it with his sister on their walk to the pathshala. Maybe they would both be moved up to the front of the class – he had confided his secret ambition to Mira. And now this. He can barely look at his sister on the walk back home, let alone talk.

5.

Sabita scoops up the cowpats one by one and deposits them in the blue plastic bucket. A few of the fat blue flies are so reluctant to move from their feast that they get transferred with the dung. The rest buzz around her, adding sound to the cloud of stench. She quells her repulsion by thinking – This is cow dung, it is holy and purifying, it is smeared on the walls of huts to disinfect the interior, there is no harm in it. She doesn't know how she has learned that one always adds some shredded straw to the dung before mixing it all up to make the dough for fuel cakes, but the thought makes her ponder a trade-off: the hay is nearly gone, and using some of that dwindled supply of straw would mean that Gauri will have that much less to eat. Never mind; she can always give the cow some starch water, or even some grass or leaves, which she can ask the children to gather. She is careful to take only a little bit of the straw, which she shreds on the bonti, then adds to the bucket. Her gorge rises again as she kneads the mixture. She will get used to it, she knows; there's no harm in cow dung. When she feels that it's the right texture, she takes it to the side of her hut, the one that'll get the sun most of the day, shapes the mixture into a patty almost the size of her palm, and slaps it on to the wall. There, so easy. As she is shaping the second patty, the first one comes unstuck and falls off. Is the mixture too wet? How can she dry it? It's going to be impossible. She picks up the fallen patty, reshapes it, and presses it back against the wall. She repeats the action with a second and third patty, hopeful that they're now sticking. One by one all three peel off and drop to the ground. She curses loudly. A long, recessive chain of accusations unfolds in her mind, starting with Gauri at the base then moving up the ladder via her good-for-nothing children – why are they not here to help? – to their useless father and ultimately coming to rest at the apex, the terrible people who have cursed her by giving them, of all things, a cow. If they had really wanted to help, could they not have given her some money? Whore's eggs, all of them. She returns her attention to the aborted cakes, presses each flat against her palm, sticks them one by one to the dried mud wall, and waits before shaping a fourth. As she watches, they dislodge themselves once more. She lets out a wail and another string of dirty abuse. She picks up the cakes and hurls them against the wall. They fall off again. Her blood is now up; she *will* make them stick. She picks up a fallen cake and, hand shaking with fury, does a swift double-slap against the wall, so quick that it could be one movement, but it's actually broken into two. She stares at it, willing it to take. And it does. She doesn't dare try another one. More time passes and yet the cake, with finger-shaped dents on its top half and the impress of the hollow of her palm in the lower, remains in position. Chance or skill? It could have been that unique double-slap technique she had just used. Superstitiously, she repeats that motion with the second patty, then the third. Both of them adhere to the wall. So that was it, a trick to the slapping movement. She does three whole rows and just under half of a fourth line; twenty-seven in all, she counts. If she sells two dozen, she will have three left over to try out in her own unun tomorrow evening or the evening after that, depending on how long they take to dry.

It would have made sense to go to the main village of Nonapani to sell the fuel cakes there, but when would she find the time? How can she take a day, even half a day, off work at Majharsharif? She has no choice but to carry the dried cakes in a cloth bundle balanced on her head all the way to work.

'O ma,' Boüdi at the first house exclaims, 'you've started making fuel cakes too?'

'Yes,' says Sabita shyly, 'there's so much cow dung after the cow arrived …'

'That cow will be the end of you.' Boüdi laughs. 'Are you selling them?'

On this lucky day, both families that Sabita works for buy a dozen cakes each – 'They'd better be good,' the boüdi at the second house says, 'you're the one who'll have to cook with them' – and the whole maiden batch is gone. Sabita had not imagined that it would be so easy; an auspicious sign, she thinks. But the amount of money she gets for them is so small that she would have to sell hundreds, not two dozen, for the income to be of any use. With the money this lot fetches, she won't even be able to afford a large basket to bring them in.

On the walk back home, it occurs to her that to sell more fuel cakes, she'll need more raw material, and Gauri cannot be made to produce that on order. Also, to produce more, she'll have to eat more; in other words, Sabita will have to find more food for the cow. Her head reels, both from the sun and the inexorable calculation.

As she makes her way through the main village, a woman with a bundle of dried branches and twigs balanced on her head crosses Sabita's path, then stops, turns to her, and says, 'Ei, you're Sahadeb's mother, no?'

Sabita has no idea who this woman is, so she takes a while to collect her wits and answer.

'I hear you've been given a cow,' the woman says in a tone that appears to be calculating, assessing something.

Sabita is instantly on her guard. 'Who are you? How do you know?' she asks. Her second question answers the stranger's first.

'News like this cannot be hidden. Words move and spread in the air. So, do you know how to keep a cow? And Sahadeb's father? Where is he?'

Something in the woman's insinuating way of speaking raises Sabita's hackles. Her words come out in a sizzle: 'What's your business whether we know how to keep a cow or not? Why do you need to have your snout in every trough?'

'Cows are expensive things, gifts of cows are the business of the rich. Who would give a cow to the likes of us? It's difficult to believe ... Maybe the cow came to you by other means.'

This time, Sabita doesn't hold back. She descends to the lowest form of 'you' to address the woman: 'What's that to you? I can see you're sizzling with envy, burntface!' Having delivered this, she rushes past her and continues on her way. She doesn't turn when she hears the woman call out, 'Careful, who knows what ill might befall your cow, the border is not far away, they kill and eat cows out there, those dirty mollas,' but the heat in Sabita changes instantly to ice to hear her own fears articulated aloud by someone else.

When she returns to her hut, she is too preoccupied to have a go at her children. Mira, at least, has lit the unun, and has had the good sense to add the dung cakes to it. Sabita notices that her daughter has repositioned it so that the smoke doesn't blow in Gauri's way. The cow looks in Sabita's direction, not directly, but something tells her that the animal recognizes her. Poor creature, thinks the woman, maybe she's hungry, why not throw in some rice with the starchy water this evening? It's not as if they have anything to spare but one handful of cooked rice wouldn't be too much of a sacrifice.

Gauri seems to be expecting Sabita to bring her dinner – the cow moves towards the woman, then turns back as if to check how much rope she's allowed, faces Sabita again, and cranes her neck forward. Sabita's fear of Gauri has been replaced by the fear of any possible harm that might come to her. Almost without thinking she strokes Gauri's head before setting down the bowl of rice in its starchy water. Gauri laps it up in the time it takes for Sabita to breathe in and breathe out and looks up to see if she will give more. No, there doesn't seem to be more. Still, it's nice to feel the gentle stroking of her forehead by a human hand, although Gauri can't help thinking that the woman's tongue would have been better. She has never seen these humans lick each other: such an odd omission from life. And Gauri has smelled fear on them, a wispy cloud of sourness that's intermittent but they are never entirely free of it. Even this evening, as the woman strokes her head and makes a stream of sounds that Gauri cannot understand, there is still the tiniest trace of that sour enveloping cloud. She sighs and tries to lick the woman's lower arm.

Sabita strokes Gauri's head and neck and throat and says, 'Eeesh, bechari, how hungry you are. Let me change your water. I'll let you free from tomorrow so that you can graze. I'll get Sahadeb and Mira to take you to the fields in the morning and bring you back at night. No need to fear, everything will be all right. I saw some other cows grazing there. Maybe you'll meet others of your kind, then you won't be so lonely. Nothing to fear, I'll look after you. You are one of us now.'

The words seem to push back the stench of cow urine and soothe her; much needed, as the needle of the stranger's final words that afternoon has gone through Sabita.

6.

Sahadeb and Mira have been given a new task, an enormous one, in their opinion. Their mother has said to them, 'Nothing doing, all this pathshala business. What a waste of time. It's not as if you have learned anything. You'll take Gauri to graze from tomorrow. She needs to find her own food, we can't give her enough, the hay is all gone.'

The children are too young to understand that it is really their father who is the cause and target of Sabita's constant irritation with them. Still, it is as if they have been granted an unexpected, large gift – of spending sanctioned time with Gauri. It is not as if it's a holiday from a burdensome, hard-working school, but Gauri is new, and the novel will always win out, if only at the beginning, while it's still novel.

'What if she runs away?' Sahadeb had hesitantly asked his mother.

Exactly Sabita's fear, but she hadn't wanted to admit that to her son. Instead, she had said, 'Why would she do that? They are peaceful creatures, not flighty. And she's settled here – can't you see how calm she is, standing or sitting, chewing the cud? She's given us no trouble so far.' The words, meant more for herself, hadn't done much to allay her anxieties.

Mira added, 'But she's so big, and we are small, we can't –'

Sabita cut her short. 'Where will she go, do you think? Have you ever seen cows running?'

'But where will we take her?'

'You know the pond a little distance from where the paddies end? You'll see it if you keep walking. Not where you go to pick branches and kindling, but the other side. It's a little bit jungly out there. Lots of bushes and trees and green – just let her loose there, she'll find her own food. You'll see other cows grazing there. That's how you'll know you're in the right place.'

Sahadeb leads the cow by the rope. Gauri follows placidly but the children are apprehensive. Parul's-ma sees them walk past her vegetable patch and says, 'O ma, where are you taking the cow?'

'To graze.'

'To graze where?'

'Out there' – Sahadeb points south – 'near the beel, Ma said.'

'But graze on what? The grass is nearly drying in this heat, there'll be nothing but scorched grass in a few days.'

Sahadeb has no answer. What does he know of grazing, leading a cow to it and back, of the effect of weather on vegetation? He has just been thrown into the job, and he'll have to do it.

'Staring like an idiot won't help you,' Parul's-ma says. 'Ask your mother to give it the excess from her vegetable patch, and peels and scrapings. It's a big cow, it'll grow bigger, it has a big stomach.'

Sahadeb and Mira both nod their heads then head off towards the pond. Parul's-ma calls out, 'Orrey, the cow is ten times your size, how are you going to handle it? A swish of its tail is going to knock you over.' Then she bends over the makeshift cane roof for her gourds and mutters, 'Can't afford to fill their own stomachs, but they had to add a cow to it. Pah!'

The children, fearful, lost in the sea of their task, follow the path that they've been directed to take. The paddies blaze green in the sun. There are ducks in a few of them. Ordinarily, the children would have taken the narrow, raised aal dividing the plots, but they cannot do that with a cow in tow. Gauri is following where they are leading, peacefully, obediently. She is glad to have a change of scene, have the freedom to move more than the rope allows her back in the yard of these humans' home. Sahadeb asks Mira, 'Do you know what the name is for a boy who looks after cows and goats?'

Mira shakes her head.

Sahadeb says, 'Rakhal.' But he remains closed about where he has come across this word.

When they arrive at their destination, the sun is beginning the long phase of its unforgiving rampage. The pond, still and black-green, with a colony of pale green algae at one end, looks shrunken. It overflows its edges and floods the fields around it every monsoon but now it is a neutered diminutive of itself. The trees, weeds, clumps of undergrowth, even the denser areas of green that the children think are like a forest, are still flaring green. In the shadow of a giant mango tree, they see three cows standing. The animals show no curiosity about another of their kind approaching them. Neither does Gauri.

'Shall I take off the rope and let her go?' Sahadeb asks. Without waiting for his sister to reply, he unknots the rope with his child's fingers, getting stuck halfway through then having to doggedly work out which bit goes under what loop and which strand to loosen first; enough time to change his mind, as Mira watches in wide-eyed silence. At last it's done. He loosens it enough so that he can slip it off Gauri's head. Mira shuffles close to her brother's side, slips her hand through his and clenches it. Except for a brief movement of her head to look at the children and breathe on them, Gauri remains standing where she is. Sahadeb has always felt that Gauri looks in their direction but never sees them.

'Maybe she won't move until we do,' he offers. 'Let's see if she follows us.'

They walk a short distance towards a tall and spreading tamarind tree. Gauri doesn't exactly follow – she moves at an angle to the line the children have taken and walks diagonally to the shade of some trees. The other cows are busy nibbling what grass there is. Gauri, too, moves her mouth across a few inches of the earth, left and right and forward, then begins to nibble.

'Look, she's eating the grass,' Mira points out.

'What are we supposed to do now? Wait here with her until it's evening, then take her back? Evening is a long time away,' Sahadeb says. 'We'll die of thirst before that.' He doesn't dare mention food.

'Look, look, the other cows are getting closer.'

Yes, they are, but not in any purposive way: they are simply reducing the distance between them as they look for a new patch of grass to graze. Neither party shows any signs of curiosity or interest or even territorialism. But the children, expecting a fight – they imagine it as an almighty locking of horns, a fight which Gauri is predestined to lose since her horns are just about incipient – remain tense, watching every move of the cows' heads, their hooves, the movement of their tails, with unblinking gaze. But nothing happens.

Time passes. The children fall asleep under the shade of the tamarind tree. They dream of their cupped hands being filled with an endless stream of cold water and they're drinking and drinking and drinking … until thirst wakes them up – it grabs hold of them and won't let them go. Mira starts crying. Sahadeb feels he cannot leave Gauri alone here – although she seems to be fine, standing under the shade with the other cows, staring at nothing – while he and Mira go back home, or at least to the well, to slake their thirst. There will be hell to pay if the cow disappears – his mother would break every bone in his body and drink his blood to boot. But they'll die of thirst if they continue to sit here until sundown. In an instant, his decision is made. He says to Mira, 'Let's go home, we'll come back for her.'

They walk in stunned silence in the heat. Everything around them looks and sounds stunned too – the vegetation with its drooping leaves; the hush, with everyone indoors, sleeping; even the birds are silent. They stop at Parul's-ma's house and ask for water. Parul's-ma comes out, not too pleased to be woken up, and says, 'What a mother you have, leaving two wretched children to fend for themselves, and now to beg for water. You were born with burnt foreheads to have parents like that.' She would say more, but the sight of these two dazed, thirsty, shrivelled children goes through her heart. She tips the kunjo straight onto the cups of their joined palms and feels as if her pouring is never going to end.

In the second house in Majharsharif, Sabita sits with the bonti positioned securely under one foot, scaling and gutting a pile of pabda fish. Her mind plays a series of situations combining these elements: Gauri has run away; the children have lost her or lost control of her; the children are lost too looking for her; Gauri has been stolen by powerful people from whom she will find it impossible to retrieve her; the people who have given them the cow will arrive any day now to ask for the money that she is worth. Boüdi passes by and says, 'Keep the fish whole, don't cut off their heads.'

Sabita says, 'All right. Achha, Boüdi, can I take the entrails home? We can't afford fish, but we cook and eat the innards when we can get them. Patka, we call the dish. If you're going to throw away the innards, that is.'

'Yes, of course, take it with you.'

Then Sabita finds herself saying, 'My boy and girl will love it. I think they haven't eaten all day, save maybe for some paanta in the morning. And the poor children will have roamed around in this killing sun all day –' then she stops herself, not knowing how those words had occurred to her.

She hurries, as much as she can, on the walk home. Will she see Gauri and her children by the pond or will they have already gone back? It will be hours before the sun goes down. She should have bought some puffed rice and jaggery for them to take for their day out in the open. In the fields and woods beside the pond, she sees Gauri and four other cows, one of them a bull with huge curved horns ending on impossibly sharp points, sitting in the shade. The children are nowhere to be seen. There are crows and mynas making a racket up above in the trees. She calls out Sahadeb's and Mira's names, tentatively at first, then, as she walks into the colony of trees and bushes and undergrowth, hollering. Nothing. One girl, two, emerge from behind the trees, both holding bundles of kindling on their head with a raised arm. Sabita knows both of them – Parul and Mamoni. They live, like Sabita with her son and daughter, in the outermost scatter of huts at the edges of Nonapani. She asks, 'Ei, did you see my boy and girl?'

They say, 'No. But we haven't been here long.'

Sabita is too irritated with her useless children to quiz them further. Those wretched puppies, you couldn't ask them to do one little thing and breathe in peace that it would be done. You had to keep at them until you were foaming at the mouth. They were bloodsuckers, those children. The sudden hostility gives her, flagging at the end of the day, enough energy to think, 'I'm here now, let me bring Gauri home.' No sooner has she thought this than the presence of the bull and the three other cows asserts itself. Those horns. First, she calls out to Gauri, but the cow doesn't give any indication that she has heard. Sabita moves closer, gingerly, step by step, approaching from Gauri's rear, which is the end furthest from the bull.

'Ei, Gauri, Gauri, tchu tchu tchu' – as if she's calling a cat – 'Gauri, here, look, GAURI.' All the while Sabita is far more alert to any possible movement on the bull's part than on Gauri's. Gauri is oblivious; not even the swish of her tail or a sideways movement of her head. Sabita repeats her calls, this time impatiently. Nothing. In a flash of inspiration, she looks for a fallen branch, finds one, strips it into a makeshift switch, and strikes Gauri gently on her rump. The skin where it is touched quivers, as if a darting creature in the flesh under it has been momentarily startled, but other than that Gauri continues to sit like a stone. Does Sabita need a stick, something more substantial to strike with so that Gauri can feel the impact and understand that something is being asked of her? Isn't that how animals are kept in order or prevented from straying: a periodic impact of a stick on their bodies to remind them where to go? She has seen bullock carts being driven – the driver does not spare the animals the lash of his whip. Lured by the smell of the fish innards inside the plastic packet in her left hand, flies are beginning to form a cloud around her, and at least a dozen crows, and counting, are hopping around her, waiting for her to put it down on the ground. Half-heartedly, she hits Gauri again, a little bit harder; she cannot bring herself to use full force, but more out of fear than compassion – what if Gauri gets cross and stands up to kick her or attack with her growing horns? Miracle: Gauri gets up – it takes so long for her to do it, nimble these creatures are not – but the bull stands up too and advances towards Sabita. She drops her branch and runs pell-mell. When she has covered what she thinks is enough distance, she looks behind her – Gauri and the bull are still standing where they were, utterly uninterested in the human who enforced herself upon their world.

At home, Sabita finds both her children asleep. All the irritations of her day – the heat, the exhaustion, the manufactured scare, the unfinished business of bringing Gauri back, the sheer helplessness the cow's presence has plunged her into – crystallize around this sight. She wishes she still had that switch from earlier, but, resourceful as ever, she grabs hold of the broom and begins to strike the sleeping children with it, shouting, 'Burntface! Misborn! Nothing done, the cow still in the fields, the unun unlit, the yard unswept, and you're sleeping like pigs. Get up, get up, or I'll turn your bones and flesh black. Get up, go fetch Gauri.'

The children, barely awake, flee. Dazed with hunger and exhaustion, and still entangled in the net of sleep, they don't quite understand what is being demanded of them, and when they work it out, they are no nearer to having any idea how to achieve it. They find themselves by the pond again. Sahadeb takes a while to discover the rope, which he left under a tree earlier in the day. He has no expectations of himself, and the thought of whether he may or may not be able to bring Gauri back home hasn't crossed his mind. Taking Gauri to graze happened with ease, so if he assumes anything it is that leading her home will be a replication of that earlier action, but in the opposite direction.

Mira says, 'Look, she's looking at us. Do you think she's recognized us?'

Sahadeb says, 'Who knows?'

He approaches Gauri with the rope held out but cannot reach high enough to string it around her neck. Following her brother, Mira begins a steady patter of mostly meaningless words which she thinks will be soothing for Gauri. And who can tell, maybe the stream of repetitive sounds does comfort the cow, for she lowers her neck towards Sahadeb, as if asking for the halter to be put in place.

By the time the unun catches, Sabita's anger has somewhat dissipated. She fans the flames, gets up to pick a small handful of purple-black chillies from her vegetable patch and some green stalks of onions and garlic, sets the rice to cook, opens the packet of fish entrails, which shrouds her immediately in a miasma, and as she carries on with her chores, she tears up. She blames the smoke, which, however, is blowing in the opposite direction. Eeesh, bechara, fatherless while having a father, she thinks, letting that sentiment carry the weight of the feeling of smallness inside her.

Mira comes bounding along, almost singing – 'Ma, ma, we've brought Gauri back with us, she followed us like a good, golden girl.'

Sahadeb follows, holding one end of the rope, Gauri behind him.

Sabita, surprised at how quickly they've returned, asks, 'Did you not have to coax and cajole? She followed you easily? What did you have to do?'

She divides the fish innards fry-up entirely between her children – the cooked dish has reduced to barely a couple of spoonfuls – and leaves nothing for herself. The long day's abrasions begin to be soothed for her, or maybe she is just too tired. She gives Gauri her usual bowl of rice in its starchy cooking water. Her last thought before sleep takes her is this: the children are naturals at grazing Gauri, they can take charge of the whole thing now.

7.

'O Sahadeb's-ma,' her neighbour, Mamoni's-ma, says, 'people from the town came and waited and waited and waited for you, then left. I sent them to see the children in the field. They'll be able to tell you what those people wanted. They said it was something to do with your cow.'

Sabita has just returned from town. Before she has had a chance to have a cooling drink of water, Mamoni's-ma arrives with this news. It is the tail end of summer – all day long the earth is scourged by the unforgiving sun, then at night, the earth, as if in revenge, sends the heat back out. It is difficult to say which is more punishing, the day or the night. She will just have to wait until Gauri and the children are back to find out what the city people wanted. That old fear, that they've come to ask for the cow's price, shows its face again, but it's a different face now – the apprehension now is that they're going to take Gauri away because she hasn't fed her enough, because she hasn't looked after her properly, because her barn is just a chatai roof held up by four bamboo poles, asking to be undone with the first kalbaishakhi wind, which will come along any afternoon now, because she hasn't grazed her properly because, because.

An intense wave of anger for those people in fancy clothes almost topples her. She shrieks at Mamoni's-ma, 'Do they think I can sit at home all day, waiting for them to arrive at their whim? Will those whore's eggs, those fuck-courtesans, give me a job when I lose my work in town for not showing up because I was waiting for those sister-fuckers?'

Her head reels and feels light and her vision becomes dark and swimmy for a moment. Mamoni's-ma says, 'What good will it do to give me a tongue lashing? I'm just passing on what they said.' She leaves in a huff, muttering, 'Never do anyone any good. That cow is your death wish, you burntface, mark my words.'

There is a commotion nearby: Gauri, Sahadeb, and Mira come into the yard followed, a few steps behind, by two women Sabita doesn't know. The children's faces look shrunken like thieves'. The woman in the red sari says, 'This your mother?', then turning to Sabita, 'Your cow got into our garden and destroyed a banana tree. It ate most of the leaves –'

The other woman interrupts, 'Not just the leaves, it ate all the banana flowers. There were four banana flowers, I counted yesterday, four nice, tight, big ones. Your cow ate them all. It didn't spare a single one.'

The woman in the red sari takes in Sabita's yard – the dark hut, the handkerchief-sized vegetable patch, the risible barn, the smoking unun, the rows of cow-dung cakes on every available surface and the muddy round stains left behind from where they had been picked – in one raking glance and says, 'You don't give your cow enough to eat?', and lets the question hang in the air.

Sabita comes out of her daze. Her first response is to go on the offence. 'The cow has eaten a few banana leaves, and you're behaving as if she's eaten your head. Well, what is she supposed to eat?'

Red Sari lashes back, 'If you're keen on giving your cow banana leaves, why don't you plant your own tree? It ate *our* banana tree.'

The second woman adds, 'The whole tree, leaves, flowers, trunk. It won't grow back now.'

Red Sari ratchets it up: 'You hardly have enough to eat yourselves and you've allowed yourself the vanity of a cow?' She matches this with a bark-like laugh.

Now the second woman: 'And what were your useless children doing? They're supposed to keep the cow from getting up to such things.'

Sabita can see from the corner of her eye that her neighbours have all come out of their huts to take in the spectacle. She shouts back, 'Get out! Get out of here immediately. Whores! Father-fuckers! Get out, otherwise I'll use the broom to sweep you out. Build a wall around your fucking banana tree if you don't want cows to get to it. Get out.'

The women, who had expected contrition from Sabita, or at least some embarrassment, back out, shouting retaliatory abuse. 'Maidservant in profession, maidservant in language – all of a piece. You are the one who is a whore. Don't think we don't know what you go to that distant town for.'

They're not done, having flung that bucket of mud. Their final words before they retreat are: 'If we see that cow again, we are going to take it in our possession. Let's see how you can release her then.' With that, they are gone.

The spectators call out comments and advice: 'Keep her tied up.' 'Eeesh, the poor cow, the grass is all singed to straw in this heat, she was hungry, that's why she ate the banana leaves.' 'Teach your children how to hit the cow if it strays, then it'll learn not to do it.'

Sabita's face burns. The children have watched the confrontation in absolute silence, in fear of what awaits them. And it follows, as surely as the procession of months or seasons. Sabita turns to them. 'Why did you not stop her?'

Sahadeb stammers, 'We tried to, but she's so big, we couldn't physically steer her around. When I hit her hard with the stick, she kicked her back legs.'

This last addition is a lie, but Mira nods along, hoping her confirmation is going to save both of them.

Sabita attacks them first with a rubber slipper, then when that falls from her hand, she goes at them with her hands, fists, legs, finally resorting to the broom. 'The shame, the shame,' she pants as she goes about her business, 'you've brought shame upon our heads. We can't show our faces here. Why couldn't you have stopped her?' Thwack, thwack. 'Tell me, why, why?'

The children, in between their wailing, try to repeat that Gauri is too big for them to control, besides, they don't know how to manage a cow, they've never been taught, but they are too out of breath from the sobbing. The blows from the broom are especially difficult, delivering a stinging, burning, and cutting feeling all at the same time. Belatedly, it occurs to Sahadeb that telling their mother about the people who had come to see them when they were out grazing Gauri could distract her.

'There were people …' he sobs and hiccups, 'people came … from town. Phone, they will bring you a phone.'

Sabita pauses – she had entirely forgotten about that. But stopping instantly would mean conceding to what Sahadeb has just said, and that would be a loss of face, so she continues for a few more blows then shouts, 'Why didn't you say that earlier?'

The storm has passed, the children know. In between catching his breath, sniffling, wiping snot and tears, Sahadeb says, 'They asked me a lot of questions. I couldn't answer most of them. They asked if you have a phone. They talked a lot among themselves, I didn't understand what, but they mentioned grazing many times, and asked me what we give her to eat. What we eat. They'll come again, they said. Soon.'

'Phone? We can't get enough rice in our bellies and they asked about phone?' Sabita asks in the same tone of fury as before but now transferred to a different target.

'They said they can call you beforehand so that you know they're coming.'

Outside, the water from the rice has boiled over and partially extinguished the cooking fire. What still burns has scorched the rice. Gauri, her equanimity dented by the sounds from inside the hut, is waiting for everything to cool down before sticking her head inside the pot. They've forgotten to tie her to her post.

8.

The monsoon rain pelts the earth in a watery version of the revenge the sun was extracting a month earlier. For nearly three hours, Sabita is strafed by it; it takes her longer to walk back because the rain slows her down. She looks like a drenched crow when she arrives home. She has only one other set of clothes. If the rain continues tomorrow, as it is certain to, she'll get that set wet, while the soaking clothes that she's wearing now will not have dried, and she'll still have to hang out tomorrow's clothes to dry. Worry eats away at her insides steadfastly; the only reliable thing in her life. During the rainy season, Mira lights the unun inside the hut, and this evening is no exception. But the sight that greets Sabita this evening is new: the chatai that served as the roof of Gauri's shed has partially come off in the wind and rain and one side of it is lying curled on the mud while the other side is held aloft, just, attached to two poles. Gauri is standing at the entrance to their hut, her head inside, the rest of her sticking out. Sabita can hear the children inside trying to cajole and sweet-talk her into exiting.

'She has smelled all the leaves you've chopped to cook for our meal,' Sahadeb says to his sister accusingly.

'No, no, she's trying to come in to get away from the rain,' Mira argues back. 'The roof of her shed has blown over, can't you see? Cows don't like getting wet. Haven't you seen them stand under the trees when it's raining?'

Sahadeb cannot deny this. In fact, he remembers telling his mother about how whenever it started raining all the cows in the fields would gently, almost unnoticeably, gather under the trees for protection. One minute they were out in the open, the next they were all under trees; those with the densest canopies, he had noticed.

'They don't run for cover the minute it starts pouring,' he had said, 'but I couldn't tell how they had all got there.'

Mira had added, 'They know when it's going to rain, so they take cover before it starts. Whenever they start to move under the trees, we know rain is going to come down shortly.'

Sabita cannot get inside now because Gauri is blocking the entrance. It isn't possible for all three humans and a cow to fit inside their hut. Her husband isn't here to fix the roof of the shed and Sahadeb is too small to do it. There is a puddle at her feet from all the water dripping off her clothes. Soon the compacted earth inside will turn to mud.

'Get her out, get her out,' Sabita says impatiently.

'We can't,' the children say in unison.

'One of you come out and give her something to eat in her shed,' Sabita suggests.

'I haven't put the rice on yet,' Mira says.

'Push her out,' Sabita says. 'Hit her on her head or her nose.'

The children are silent.

'Ki re, did you hear?' she hollers again.

Reluctantly, the children gently push her head. Gauri turns it away, like a child refusing the food it's being spoon-fed, but refuses to move. Sahadeb says, 'Ma, you pull her by her hind legs.'

'Have you gone mad? She'll kick me. Hit her, can't you hear, hit her!' Sabita demands. She is at the end of her tether.

The children fall silent again. Mira says, 'Let me put on the rice and feed her some starch water instead.'

Sahadeb says, 'Arrey, she wants your taro leaves.'

The rain continues to drench Sabita as well as Gauri's rear half equally. 'Why didn't you tether her?' Sabita now demands, her anger rising. She wants to thrash the children and the cow.

There is silence, again, then Sahadeb offers in a small voice, 'It was raining so hard, Mira's hands were full with taro leaves, we found some on the way so she said we should bring some home to cook. We wanted to get inside as soon as possible, so we just ran in, thinking that we could tie her to the post later.'

The irritation suddenly lets go of Sabita. In its place, there is now a drowning exhaustion. All she wants to do is sit down and stretch her legs. The girl, who has been taught how to forage by Sabita, has had the good sense to pick taro leaves.

'Did you get the taro root too?' Sabita asks.

Mira says, 'No. We tried to dig, but it was enormous.'

The boy adds, 'We'll need a crowbar, or a spade, to dig it out.'

Sabita says, 'Give her the taro leaves if that'll get her out.'

Mira says, 'What will we eat then? Did you bring anything today?'

'No, nothing today.' The earlier thought, that she might have to give up her two jobs as domestic servant, returns, but this time with a variation: she has always collected the peelings and scrapings and all the stuff that would otherwise be thrown out in the homes where she works – cores of cabbages and cauliflower in the winter, peels of potatoes and gourds, the seeds and piths of pumpkins, old and yellowing vegetables, or those on the turn – and brought them back home to cook, and those have added something to their meals, but without the jobs, the perks would be gone instantly.

'Try slipping inside by going under Gauri then between her front legs,' Sahadeb says.

'What if she kicks?' Sabita asks.

'No, she doesn't kick, she's a good girl. Aren't you, sweet one? Do you want some taro leaves? You do, don't you? Look at you eyeing the leaves. Here, have some,' Mira says, offering the chopped leaves to Gauri to sniff then slipping out under the cow's legs with the dish, thinking that this manoeuvre will lure her away to her shed. It doesn't work. Now Sabita is joined by her daughter in the drenching. Mira crouches under the cow, goes inside, and tries the operation again. Nothing doing – Gauri is unbudging. The girl has mucked out the shed, Sabita notes, otherwise she'd be standing in mud mixed with cow dung, straw, dried grass, whereas now she's standing in mud mixed with Gauri's urine. Never mind, cow urine is supposed to purify everything, she thinks. The girl is barely seven years old, give or take, and has learned well. A thought goes through Sabita's mind, but she pushes it down for now.

Eventually, the standing in the rain outweighs the fear of Gauri's kicking, and Sabita, amidst much hilarity, manages to get inside on her hands and knees, using the same technique as her daughter. The physical contortions, the awkwardness, the mirth ('You look like a little calf under Gauri,' Sahadeb impudently comments as Sabita is wriggling beneath Gauri, trying to squeeze in), the ensuing laughter, all dispel, if only for the time being, the cloud of anxiety that is the future, whether it's tomorrow or the day after or a far distant time.

The cloud is back soon – Gauri laps away at her starch rice-water and some rice but remains standing where she is.

'Let her stay,' Mira says.

'But we have to tie her to the post. What if she goes missing while we're asleep?' Sabita asks. They have all eaten after a long, exhausting day, battling with their jobs, the weather, and sleep takes them before they can argue out a solution. When Sahadeb gets up to piss in the dead of the night, he finds Gauri's head gone from their entrance. He tiptoes out of the hut to relieve himself on one side in the open. Even in his half-asleep state he notes that Gauri is in her shed, standing under where the chatai still holds. It has stopped raining.

The morning breaks with sheets of water coming down from the sky. Sahadeb says that he saw Gauri in her stall last night then wonders if he has dreamed it all. Sabita cannot go to work in this weather; the matter of the wet clothes alone rules it out. The cloud of anxiety settles again. Will they fire her? Deduct money from her pay for the absent days? Pulak hasn't sent money for a long time … when will the next sum arrive? If she and her children are holed up inside for days because of the rain, is there enough rice and lentils to tide them over? In this weather, how will they take Gauri to graze?

As she knots and unknots these tangles in her mind, she hears a rustling followed by a sort of sliding sound, as if something is falling but not all at once, instead in stages. Suddenly, a small gap opens up in one corner of the roof. Rain starts pouring in. Sabita rushes out to see Gauri pulling at the straw roof and chewing peacefully as bits of the roof disintegrate.

9.

Both homes at Majharsharif dock Sabita's pay for the days she missed because of the rain. 'You didn't show up for four consecutive days. Four, four!' they complain in outrage. 'How do you think we coped? Heaps of washing all piled up, no help with the preparation of food, the floors unswept and unmopped … how do you think we managed? No notice, no nothing, suddenly, you stop showing up. And for four days, one after another. You've landed us in so much trouble.' And so it goes. She thinks of protesting, but beyond repeating her circumstances – a two-hour walk in the violent rain then the same distance back, having to wade in knee-deep waters, sometimes even hip-deep, the mud, the wet clothes, which they know well about (and can also imagine the little details that she leaves out, such as the problem of clothes) – she cannot do more.

On her way back, at the bend past the main village where three banyan trees stand like ancient sentry men guarding the Sitala temple under their shade, she is told by a woman she knows, 'You have visitors from town. I saw them accompany your children.'

And there they are, three women and two men, standing in the churned mud across from the hut, talking. Sahadeb and Mira are a few feet away, staring at them, almost unblinking, their mouths open. Not only has the chatai on the roof been fixed, but extra chatai has also been added to make two walls to the shed. Gauri, tethered, has her head in a huge wooden container and is chomping her way through whatever is in it. There are bales of straw, covered in plastic, standing next to Sabita's vegetable patch, or what used to be her vegetable patch since it's been washed away by the rains, leaving only a rectangular puddle with three or four green shoots of garlic or onion sticking out. There are a few heavy, bulging jute sacks lying around in the mud. There is also, surprisingly, a huge metal drum, the kind they use to transport oil. The first thought that goes through Sabita's head is: where will all this go? There's no space in their hut to accommodate even one of those jute sacks. And the first words to leave her mouth are: 'What are these?'

It's as if these visitors were waiting for a switch to be turned on. Information rains down upon Sabita. Mobile phone, with charger, so that they can get in touch with her. A hopeless and long explanation of how a phone works, which Sabita cannot understand. Grazing rules. Straw only as top-up food for the cow. Molasses in the tin drum to be mixed with the hay sometimes. Rules about keeping the shed clean. Who to call if the cow is ill. Injections and medicines. How to tell if the cow has enough food or not. How to get more out of the fuel-cake business. When they'll come to get the cow pregnant with an injection. Milking training.

At the last item, pregnancy, Sabita, already overcome with feeling intimidated, buckles inside. She wants to say – how will I afford the metal buckets to catch the milk? Even the bucket the children and I use to collect her dung was salvaged. She wants to say – there aren't enough hands to do the kind of work you've saddled me with. If you want to improve my lot, why don't you give me money instead? She wants to say – if the day had been twice as long as it is, and the nights too, maybe she would have managed, but she, like everyone else, is bound by the iron laws of god-given time. But she says nothing. Instead, she grapples with two feelings. The first is her fear and confusion and anxiety at not comprehending most of the information that these people are unleashing. The second, related, is her fear that they'll take Gauri away if she lets on that their advice and suggestions and rules are all flying above her head. The thought crosses her mind, very briefly, that that might not be such a bad thing – ever since Gauri arrived, she hasn't drawn a full month's pay, which keeps, barely, their body and soul together, and now she is in danger of losing that too while seeing none of the wealth – yes, wealth, that is what was promised, not just sustenance – that was supposed to flow from Gauri. And that fear seconds ago, of losing Gauri, is made murky by something else, maybe greed, maybe just the hope of slightly better days, of not having to live from hand to mouth, of not having to toil endlessly.

Then the people from town are gone. She has not been able to ask them the most basic question of where she is going to store all the stuff that they have left her with.

The phone rings while Sabita is wringing out the sheets and covers and worrying about where to hang them to dry because the skies have opened again. The loud ringtone is the thudding, jangling opening section of a bhangra song that is currently popular. Boüdi shouts from another room, 'E ki, whose phone is this? My god, so loud. Sabita, is it yours? Can you turn it down?'

Sabita, anxious that her phone is causing offence, hurries to get it. Her feet and hands are wet. There is only one number that calls her, and she knows how to answer it. That's it. She cannot read, so she has learned how to do this by rote. However, having no electricity at home, she can only charge the phone while she's at work. The son of Boüdi in the first house she serves has taught Sabita how to do this. Now, she answers the phone and shouts into it.

'No need to shout,' Boüdi calls out, 'they can hear you on the other side.'

Sabita lowers her voice then raises it again after two or three words: 'Yes … yes … no, how can I go, you think I don't have any work to do that I'll just sit and wait for you? After six … yes … no … that I cannot say. Yes … all right.' The call ends.

'Uff, shouting down the line like this,' Boüdi scolds Sabita, 'have you lost your head? You think people are deaf? Uff, someone's put a lock in my ear.'

'They called about the cow,' Sabita says.

'Yes, I can tell, you don't need to tell me. If you take a day off, I'll have to dock your pay. A thousand troubles with this cow – I'm getting tired of this now. If you want to tend to your cow, go, you needn't come back here again, I'll find someone else to replace you.'

This goes on for the next quarter of an hour. Sabita is simultaneously upset by and indifferent to it – she lets it all in through one ear and out of the other, but the fleeting middle section of its passage sometimes snags, causing anxiety. She doesn't have two bodies, she cannot be in two places at once. The work as domestic servant has clear and tangible returns – money at the end of the month – but Gauri has brought in nothing, instead has taken a lot: time, energy, peace of mind, food. The children no longer go to the village pathshala; Sabita, being illiterate, doesn't know that they were not learning anything there, but she had hopes. Hearing Boüdi go on like a leaking tap now, Sabita feels something turning in her and settling down into a hard residue: if it comes to having her pay deducted, or even losing her jobs in Majharsharif, so be it – she would much rather hold on to Gauri and find a way to make that generate money than do this bone-grinding work as a servant.

'And if you have to go,' Boüdi whines, 'you must find someone to replace you. It's very difficult to get hold of someone nowadays. Who will do all the work that needs doing?' She starts running off the jobs, one by one, oblivious of the fact that Sabita is the last person who needs to be reminded of the items on that list.

Sabita tries to make light of the complaints – 'Arrey, don't worry about it, that won't happen, I'm telling you' – then changes the topic: 'Boüdi, where am I going to hang all this washing? It's pouring outside ...'

The thought about her daughter that had occurred to her a few days ago as she stood outside her hut, unable to get in, returns, this time producing the same reactions as fear does – a hammering heart, the beginnings of coldness in her feet and hands, a slight unsteadiness. She pushes the thought down again.

10.

Most of Gauri's shed is now occupied by her food – the tin drum of molasses, the jute sacks of grass clippings and hay, the bales of straw – leaving the cow only a little corner in which she can sit or stand. Sabita, helped by Sahadeb and Mira, moved some of it inside the hut, fearing that if it were left in the shed Gauri would go through it all very quickly – the plastic wrapping was neither comprehensive nor secure and Gauri could easily find a way in. But there was no space inside to store the bales, so Sabita and her children had come up with the idea of using two bales as mattresses, one for the children, one for Sabita. What they hadn't foreseen was how the straw, not compacted and secured as any stuffing was inside a mattress, would start to loosen and come free under the weight of humans tossing and turning and moving on it in their sleep.

The inside of the hut is now a mess of loose straw, like a giant bird's nest, unravelling. Mira has to sweep it all up first thing in the morning, pick through it, then feed the loose straw to Gauri. The rotting, humid heat of the end of monsoon season begins. They take Gauri out to graze more often now. Sahadeb climbs the tamarind tree and plucks ripe pods of the fruit, which he throws down to Mira standing underneath. Mira brings the plastic bucket for picking up cowpats with them now. Her mother has taught her how to shape them into cakes, and the trick of the wrist-and-palm movement that will make them stick, the only problem being that Mira's cakes are much smaller because hers is a girl's tiny palm. Sabita has pointed this out to her, so the girl tries to spread her fingers as wide as she can, but this has a negative effect on the smooth movement of slapping on the cakes.

There is always a mental barrier Mira has to overcome before she can bring herself to scoop up the cowpats; today, she procrastinates for as long as she can. Brother and sister sit under the tamarind tree with his rich pickings and allow themselves to eat a fruit each; the rest will supplement the evening meal of plain boiled rice. The fruit is mouth-puckeringly tart, and both of them pull faces as they get used to it.

'Our teeth will feel funny,' Sahadeb says.

'I wish we had salt and chillies with us,' Mira says.

'We'll ask Ma to mash it with salt and chillies when we go back home,' he says.

The shadows refuse to lengthen. Mira says, spitting out the shiny dark brown seeds, 'Uff, now I have to go fill the bucket with cow dung.'

Sahadeb doesn't move. Mira gets up and starts looking for cowpats in the grass, under the trees, by the pond, but the afternoon heat is too much to bear. The children try to keep awake for as long as they can, but ultimately fall asleep under the tamarind tree just before it is time for them to bring Gauri back home.

When Sabita returns and discovers that neither the cow nor the children are back, she ventures out to the fields. There is a man and a woman standing under the trees, next to the cows.

Pointing to Gauri, the woman asks, 'Is this cow yours?'

Taken aback by the presence of the strangers, she can only nod.

The man says to Sabita, 'Do you know whose cows these are? They belong to the Purokayastha family in Nonapani. Do you know who they are? They even own this land we are standing on' – he flings his arm out in a wide radius to encompass the area – 'this pond, the fields, the paddies on the other side, this wood, everything belongs to them.'

Sabita cannot say anything in return, but the thought goes through her mind: is this man lying to deter her from grazing Gauri here? Less competition, so more for their cows, Sabita thinks, but she cannot confront him on this point. First, he's a man, and second, he could well be an upper-caste person, given that he is polite, using the most respectful form of 'you' for her, and that his words sound like those of a man who is educated.

The strangers take her silence for acquiescence. The man says, 'Good, then I have your word that you will graze your cow elsewhere. The anger of the Purokayasthas would be a terrible thing.' He delivers all this in a pleasant, affable tone.

Sabita leaves it for ten days before sending the children out with Gauri again. In the meantime, they try to think of other grazing spots.

'Khokababu's beel on the Chunirganj side?' Sabita suggests. Mira is too young to know anything about distances and location or even the place that her mother has mentioned. Even Sahadeb looks a little blank.

'I think I've seen cows grazing there,' Sabita adds hesitantly.

'What about the field in the main village?' Sahadeb throws out, not really knowing what he's talking about. 'Or farther along on your walk to Majharsharif?' he asks.

'Thinking. There are farmers' plots everywhere, and cultivated fields, so they won't allow any grazing,' Sabita says, trying to summon memories of cows grazing and fit them to exact locations.

They cannot come up with anything, and Sabita does not have the time to go on a reconnoitre first then send the children out to a new place. So they go back to their original grazing ground, Sabita trying to placate the children's anxiety, and her own, with frequent repetitions of: 'Nothing will happen, you can go without any fear. How can that land belong to anyone? If it did, wouldn't it be put to use? It's lying fallow. No one even goes there, no one washes clothes in that doba, no homes have come up on it. That man was lying.'

The children go with great trepidation. They let Gauri free, but they cannot decide whether they should remain in partial hiding within the copse or stay in the open so that they can see anyone approaching them from any direction. They try a little bit of both, and time passes, and there is no human apart from them and, occasionally, a few others who walk by in the distance. When anyone comes too near the pond, they hide themselves. While squatting behind a bush, Mira nudges Sahadeb and says, 'Ei, look, look, that big one with horns is trying to climb on top of Gauri.'

Sahadeb peers out. Yes, the bull is trying to mount Gauri. There are several false starts – its forelegs can't quite get a grip on Gauri's rump at first and they slip a few times down her side, the back legs stagger about a little on the earth. Gauri seems oddly unresisting. Sahadeb cannot quite put his finger on what is going on, but he feels an embarrassment tinged with a touch of shame, as if he's witnessing something that is not meant for his eyes.

'Are they fighting?' Mira asks. 'Should we go chase the horned cow away?'

Sahadeb lets out a weak smirky laugh. 'No, let them be,' he says, but he can't turn his eyes away from the sight.

11.

The aus paddies are turning colour, Sabita notes on her way to work; another two months or so, maybe less, and harvest will be upon them. This year, she has not been able to hire herself out for the transplanting of the seedlings, and god knows if Pulak will be here for the harvest. That extra money, or payment in rice, is now lost. Sabita wants a holiday for all five days of Pujo. Both homes are adamant that it should be four, so Sabita settles for that. Pulak usually comes home for the holidays, or he sends money. No money has arrived since he last left. Sabita knows she'll get a new sari from each of the homes in Majharsharif, but how is she going to buy new clothes for Sahadeb and Mira? And sweets for the children on Ashtami? It occurs to her to ask her employers for a Pujo bonus instead of the saris, but she knows she's going to get nowhere with such requests. Pujo, when the whole world is aloft, it seems, with joy and celebration and holiday, is a cause for even greater anxiety for people like her: festivals always mean more expenditure. The thought of sending the children to the main village to see the goddess's effigy, the lights, the drummers playing the dhaak, in old, torn clothes fills her with pity – whether for them or for herself, she cannot tell – and a feeling of smallness: she cannot give them what they are never going to ask for.

Cleaning out Gauri's shed, Sabita is struck again by the vastly diminished store of bedding straw. The people from town had said that the straw needed to be replaced every other day, but Sabita had made it stretch as much as she had dared to, waiting until it had gone wet and smelly and a greyish colour before drying it out in the sun and shredding it to mix with the cow dung. There are wisps and threads of straw everywhere, it seems they're swimming in it, even drowning, yet the thickness of the 'mattresses' indoors has been so reduced that they are all back to sleeping on the floor.

She says to Gauri, 'Move, move a little, Lakshmi-ti, move, I need to clean your bed.'

Gauri sits where she is, ruminating calmly.

'Arrey, sitting there like that – what good will it do?' Sabita continues. 'Move, move, I need to go to work after I muck out your barn. What it is that you chew all day long, god only knows. Is it the straw that you're eating? Didn't they say that too much straw is not good for you? Not enough hay, is there? Or grass? You too are half-stomach like us?'

Sabita's patter comes to an end when she kneels down to cut open a bundle of hay. A rat scuttles away. The hay has densely constellated pinpricks of mould all over it. She takes out bunches from the surface to peer into the depths of the bale – yes, there too, even denser, looking like sprinkled grey-blue sugar or dust. Would spreading it out in one thin layer in the sun get rid of it? Would it then be safe to give Gauri?

The cow stands up and breathes down Sabita's neck. She calls out to her children, still snoozing inside, 'Get up, get up, it's time to take Gauri out. I can't tell if I should give her this hay. You'll need to graze her today. I have to run now, I don't have all day. I have to break my body to bring in rice. Mira, Sahadeb, up, up! Mira, you need to make dung cakes today, the bucket is full. There are flies everywhere, they're getting into my nose and mouth with every breath I take. Gauri is flicking her tail constantly. Come on, get up!'

255

*

Mira nudges a dozing Sahadeb: 'Ei, get up, get up, there are two people near the cows.'

They see two men standing a little distance from the animals, talking to each other. Then the men notice the children; it is clear that they then begin to talk about Sahadeb and Mira. The children are afraid that they'll be punished for letting Gauri graze on private land, but they are too scared to run. Besides, the men are approaching fast and the distance between them is not enough for Sahadeb and Mira to run. The men ask, 'Is that white cow yours? What a nice cow. What's her name?'

'Gauri,' says Sahadeb.

'The other cows and that bull are ours,' says the dark man with the moustache and a heavy stick in his right hand. His tone seems friendly enough.

The second man, lean like a broom and wearing a blue lungi, says, 'We come to check on our cows, see what they're eating, and sometimes, if there isn't enough for them to graze on, like in the summer, we give them a little something.' Here he points to the jute bags each of them is carrying.

'Where do you live? What do your parents do?' the man continues.

Sahadeb tries to answer to the best of his ability, but he's not exactly forthcoming. Mira is silent and stands behind her brother, as if trying to hide.

'You're both shy, I see,' the chatty man says. 'But that's fine. Do you want to watch us feed the cows? We'll give Gauri something too.'

'We haven't seen you before,' Sahadeb musters up the courage to say.

'We were just saying to each other that we haven't seen the two of you either,' the thin man laughs.

The man with the moustache brings out hay and even what looks like the chopped-up trunk of a banana tree from his sack and puts them in front of their cows and the bull, while the thin man in the blue lungi offers the same to Gauri.

Sahadeb and Mira remain somewhat arrested in their suspicion and shyness, their initial fear of the men. They stay quiet as they watch the cows, including Gauri, and the bull calmly eating what has been given them.

At home, however, the children thaw and fall over themselves to tell their mother what happened in the afternoon.

'At first, we thought the men had been sent by the two people who warned us off from grazing Gauri there,' Sahadeb says.

'She chomped down what the man gave her,' Mira says.

Sabita says, 'Shall I not give Gauri her rice and starch water this evening then? Mira, go, give her some starch water first, see if she laps it up. If she doesn't want it, then we get to save more rice for the paanta.'

It is as Sabita has speculated – Gauri shows no interest in the food Mira pushes under her nose.

'Let it be, leave the starch water there, she'll have it later,' Sabita suggests.

But there is no later. In the dead of the night, something wakes up Mira, she is not sure what, but before she can fall back to sleep, she hears odd noises coming from outside. She is afraid to go out and check – it could be a ghost, a nishi, out and about to catch the souls of anyone who might be abroad at this hour, the unresting spirit of the brother who had died before she and Sahadeb were born. She shakes Sahadeb's shoulder and whispers, 'Dada, dada, get up, get up, there's someone outside.'

Sahadeb takes what seems to Mira a long time to be released from the cage of his sleep. The noise outside sounds like a thrashing, punctuated by a choking kind of noise. The children are goosebumped with terror.

'Can you hear?' Mira asks.

Sahadeb says, 'Let's call Ma.'

It seems to take forever to bring Sabita back to waking life; she is like a stone when she is asleep. When the three of them come out, they can barely see anything in the dark.

'Mira, light the kupi and bring it outside,' Sabita says.

In that smoking, flickering light, they see Gauri stretched out, thrashing her legs, her jaws gurning, her tongue hanging out like a long rag, now looking black, now lighter – and who would have thought there was so much tongue in her?

'Oh my god, hold the light closer,' Sabita orders.

In that light they see a foamy spill under Gauri's muzzle; the colour cannot be ascertained. There's a thin foam coming out of her mouth. Her eyes roll around in their sockets. Only the whites of the eyes seem to be visible to the humans around her.

Mira, clutching Sahadeb's arm, wails, 'Look at her eyes! I'm afraid. What is happening to her?'

Sahadeb is speechless, as is Sabita, too, for a moment, before she exclaims, 'Ki shorbonash. She's ill. My hands and feet are turning cold. What am I going to do now?'

Then, after a pause, she says, 'She's eaten something that is making her ill. Some poison or something. Why would she be like this otherwise?'

'What are we going to do now?' Sahadeb asks despairingly. 'Will she now die, thrashing about like this?'

'Don't say such inauspicious things,' Sabita says. 'Orrey, Mira, get some water, quick, get some water. Get the entire kunjo.'

'O ma, she's trying to bite her tongue,' Sahadeb says.

'Mira, pour water gently on her head. On her face. Use your hands,' Sabita instructs, as she strokes Gauri's head, her neck. The cow's body bucks and heaves, and with each of these motions, Mira cries out, as if they are hitting her face, causing her pain.

'Sahadeb, run to the well, get some more water. Mira, give her some to drink. She'll feel better if she drinks some water. Give it to her little by little.'

By the time Sahadeb comes back with water, the situation is unchanged. Both Sabita and Mira are now crying unrestrainedly.

Sabita says, 'Sahadeb, watch that she doesn't turn on her back, go hold her, support her there. Once she turns on her back and puts her legs in the air, that's it, it's all over. Hold her back, put your hands under it. Put some pressure, push against it so that she cannot turn upside down.' Sabita is beside herself.

Sahadeb says, 'We need to get a cow doctor.'

'Cow doctors don't grow on trees,' Sabita fairly shouts. 'Where am I going to get a cow doctor from? And at this hour too.'

'You have a phone. Call those town people.'

She had forgotten that she had a phone, but no sooner is the idea suggested than she realizes it is not feasible – she doesn't know how to use it. Fearful of the instrument itself and the complicated business of calling someone, she has never dialled the one number in the contacts list, and this lack of repetition of the act has resulted in the failure of rote action to take hold. The phone will be as useful in this situation as a lump of clay. But in the scenario unfolding now, even that lump holds hope.

She asks her son, 'Do you know how to run it?' That's the verb she uses, as if it's a machine or a mill.

Sahadeb shakes his head.

'What use is that then?' Sabita barks.

'If the phone is taken to Nonapani, maybe someone ...' he starts to suggest hesitantly.

'Who? Who in Nonapani? And at this hour? And who will take it there? Your burntface father?' she shouts. She wants to slap his face off him.

'One of the boys I knew at the pathshala may know how to,' he mumbles.

'I can't hear your min-min voice – you have leprosy in your throat?'

'Maybe a didimoni at the pathshala.'

'We have to wait until the morning. The sky is still coal-black. The cow will not survive the night.'

It is the longest wait in each of their lives. Sabita thinks that even the time between the search for her drowned son and his body floating up in the pond did not feel so long. That fearful rolling of the animal's eyes, with so much of the whites exposed. Mira says, 'She is thrashing a bit less now, na?'

'Her energy is dimming,' Sabita says. 'Her life is running out, that's why she is thrashing less. She has been poisoned. Someone has put poison in her food. It was those men who gave them food.'

At the first stirring of the birds, before streaks of dawn have begun to mark the sky, Sahadeb is dispatched to the main village with the phone. On the walk, his inhibition about knocking on doors – he doesn't even know which doors to try – and waking up strangers too early to beg them for a favour outweighs the risk to Gauri's life if he delays. He is nine years old – the present tense has far more weight for him than a possible outcome in the future even if that future is just around the corner. Who would want to be seen as a beggar, and that too at five o'clock in the morning? He sits by the sweet shop and waits for the town to wake up before he starts making enquiries. He cannot find a didimoni's house, but he has the nous to ask for directions to the homes of two or three of the children attending the pathshala who had looked better off. He is in luck with Tamal's house – it is made of bricks, so someone in there will know about phones.

But Sahadeb returns home with dispiriting news: the phone cannot be made to work unless he brings something with it, he forgets the name, something that can connect it to electricity. Gauri has stopped thrashing her legs – the calm seems more ominous than the wild physical restlessness earlier – but a thin green foam leaks out of the side of her mouth. Sabita and Mira look like ghosts of their former selves. A few neighbours have come out to see what's happening, give advice. Sabita still hasn't given up her patter – it's now changed to: 'We'll just have to get her to stand. Once she stands, she'll be fine. If she keeps lying down like she is now, the poison will go to her head, and that's it.'

Sahadeb returns to Tamal's home with the charger. He is made to sit outside as the phone returns to life. Tamal brings out a pocketful of beautiful coloured marbles and plays with them a few feet away from Sahadeb but doesn't invite him to join. Tamal's mother comes out, shouts at her son, 'Playing with marbles first thing in the morning? Come inside right now! I'll show you marbles.' Tamal goes inside after carefully collecting all his marbles, one by one. The door slams shut. Sahadeb feels the usual smallness when he understands that he is not deemed worthy enough for the son of the house to be friendly with him. A bald man with glasses, wearing a dirty pajama that is tied under his enormous paunch, comes out with the phone and says, 'I see there's only one number here. Is that the one you want to call?'

Sahadeb has no idea what he's talking about, so he nods.

The man calls the number and hands the phone to him with 'Here, it's ringing.'

There is a falling feeling in Sahadeb's stomach. He brings himself to ask, 'You, you talk to them?' with as much supplicatory humility he can muster. He wants the ground to open and swallow him.

'Why? You don't know how to use a phone?' the man asks.

Sahadeb is relieved – the man could have reprimanded him for being audacious enough to ask him to do something. Instead, he had settled on rubbing in the boy's ignorance; the less-smarting of the two. Sahadeb smiles foolishly and shakes his head.

'Ei, they've picked up. Yes, hello, hello. Hold on, hold on, let me ask,' then to Sahadeb, in a loud whisper, 'What shall I tell them?'

Sahadeb whispers too: 'The cow is sick. It's lying down, thrashing its legs ...'

'Wait, wait, stop there – can you hear? Hello, hello, can you hear?' He is screaming, the people in the neighbouring village will be able to hear him. 'The cow is sick. Sick, can you hear. Yes, yes. Thrashing her legs. Yes. Achha. Wait.' To Sahadeb, 'What's your name? What's your mother's name? And your address?'

Sahadeb supplies these, the man relays. The boy adds, 'The cow is vomiting and rolling her eyes.'

The man obliges by repeating the symptoms. Then he says to Sahadeb, 'Wait. They asked us to wait.'

After what seems so long that the man thinks the line has been disconnected, someone speaks on the other end. 'Oh. Achha, achha.' Then a long pause. 'So long? What if something happens to the cow?' Another pause during which Sahadeb is almost felled by a wave of nausea. 'Achha.'

He terminates the call and hands the phone to Sahadeb. 'Leave this on. They'll call you. They said they'll come with a doctor, but when, they cannot say. They'll have to find a doctor first, see if he is free, get him to come here from far. I understand much wood-and-straw needs to be burnt before this can happen. Don't forget to leave the phone on.' Looking at Sahadeb's blank face the man understands that the boy knows nothing about charging a phone, how to leave it on, so he takes Sahadeb through the necessary steps, miming which end goes into the wall socket and how, but does not invite him inside to demonstrate, so that he leaves with only a murky idea of what he's been told.

Back home, Sahadeb finds the drama unchanged, except more people have joined the throng of spectators, offering advice, solutions, remedies. This is entertainment to lighten the load of the dragging sameness of days weeks months years. Gauri is still prone, the ground looks as if there's been a straw-storm; Sabita, with bits of straw in her hair, is sitting with her legs stretched out, wrung out like the rag she uses to swab people's floors; and Mira is stroking Gauri's head and nodding off, pitching as far forward as to touch the cow with her forehead and then jerkily sitting up straight only to keep repeating the falling-and-startling-awake arc.

The tableau comes back to life with Sahadeb's arrival. However close to disintegration, Sabita has been hanging on to a fully assembled version of herself to hear the news her son will bring. In her mind, everything turns around that. When she learns that the visit from a cow doctor is open-ended, even uncertain, she lets herself go and starts to wail and mourn as if Gauri is already dead. The spectacle value for the people gathered ratchets up; they settle in for longer.

The dark settles in too. Mosquitoes feast on them with abandon, but both mother and daughter have lost the energy to slap them away. Mira lights the kupi again – she cannot tell whether it's a new night or the continuation of the previous one, when she had brought out the same taper to cast light on a largely similar scene. Sabita, spent to a husk of herself, says to Mira in a pleading whisper, 'Bechari has thrown up all day, there's nothing in her stomach except bile. Will you make some rice and give the starch water to her? Maybe she'll be able to keep that down.'

Mira, herself weak with exhaustion and hunger, obliges. Sahadeb notices that his sister is nodding off again – there is a real risk of her tipping face forward into the boiling pot of rice. He says to her, 'Why don't you show me how to cook rice?'

Mira is too surprised to react for a while then she says, with both affection and dismissal, 'Dhush, you won't be able to do it at all.'

'If you show me, I will. It's cooking rice, not hunting a tiger – how difficult can it be?'

Mira giggles and tries to appear important at the same time. The banter between them keeps her alert and awake. They put out the starch water for Gauri, who is still on her side, still leaking a thin greenish foam from the side of her mouth, as far as they can tell, or it could be the puddle of all that's come out of her for the last twenty-four hours. Her eyes have stopped rolling, but the exposed side is marked by long shudders at intervals. The children urge their mother to end her vigil and eat something.

'See, see how she's heaving and shuddering and drawing huge breaths,' Sabita weeps. 'She won't survive the night, the life is leaking out of her, can't you see, can't you see?'

The children force her to eat something. The rice in their stomachs, coming at the end of such a day, makes all of them, even Sabita, let go, and they all fall asleep before anyone can check on Gauri one last time. Only little Mira dreams: of a cow that keeps changing colour, from white to green to straw, and runs away from her as the girl follows.

Sabita is the first to get up in the morning, before sunrise. Her first waking thought is of Gauri. She comes out of the hut and in the watery light she sees the cow sitting up, her legs tucked under her, staring at nothing, lost in her world.

12.

The vet arrives, accompanied by two women who have been here before, three days after the phone call. Sabita doesn't remember the women's names or whether she was told of them in the first place. The vet checks the cow's teeth, tongue, eyes, asks questions about her food, where it is stored, where she grazes, what the symptoms were on the night in question. He takes a sample of the cow's blood; Gauri is impassive throughout. Sabita tells them that her children saw Gauri being fed by strangers. Sahadeb recounts the story for them. When the vet asks for a sample of Gauri's vomit, Sabita can no longer hold herself back.

'Vomit?' she begins. 'Vomit? Do you think I saved it for you? Is it pickle, or sweets, that you want it saved? And for you? Who took his own sweet time getting here? My cow could have died ... what good would coming here, after the cow became a carcass, do? Tell me, what good is you lot coming here now going to do? I sat here with the cow, my children sat here with me, when she was about to breathe her last, all night long, all night, and where were you then? We didn't see even the tiniest sign of your pigtail. And now you come here, three, four days after my cow came so near to going over to the other side, and you ask for her vomit?

'You have foisted a cow on us and now it's ruining me. You made it sound so shiny,' she begins to parody them – 'you'll make money, you'll move to a brick house, your children will go to a proper school, you can give up your job as servant – false, all false. You shoved the cow into our yard and then disappeared. What she will eat, where we will take her to graze, all these matters you left us to deal with, without giving any help. You're not supplying her food regularly, nor are you giving me money so that I can arrange to buy her hay. Now we can't even take her to graze because someone poisoned her.

'And what have you done instead? Asked me hundreds of questions, a whole fountain of questions, each time you've come here – what we are eating now, what we were eating in the past, what we were wearing, what we are wearing. A jungle of screeching questions. And wrote them down, to show to us illiterates that you can read and write. Why did you give me the cow? For your benefit, not mine. I cannot go to work today because you are here – they'll dock my pay. Tell me, will you pay me the lost wages?'

Here she runs out of breath. And because she has been shouting, she has, predictably, brought out the residents from the nearby huts who now listen, agog. The fury still courses through her blood. The women accompanying the vet say that they have tried to call her several times, but the phone is either switched off or no one picks up. If Sabita could learn how to work the phone, keep it charged and on, things wouldn't have reached this pass. It is only after the vet and the women have gone, having made assuring noises while retreating, that it occurs to Sabita that she may have alienated powerful people who, if kept appeased, would be in a position to change her impossible situation.

At work, there is the usual chiding and threats for her closely bunched two days of absence. She keeps her phone on, but days go by and she doesn't hear back from them. When things are once again settling into the same pattern of silence and disappearance, her phone begins to ring suddenly one afternoon, as she is walking back home from work, startling her so much that she nearly trips over. She thinks she knows how to do this – press the button with the green lines on it, the one on the right-hand side of the phone. There, she's done it, her heart beating faster as she holds the phone against her left ear. Yes, she has got it right – there is someone on the other end asking for her by name to tell her that Gauri is pregnant.

'Boüdi, can I ask you something?' Sabita says, not making eye contact with her employer.

'What?'

'You were saying, some time ago, maybe you don't remember, but you were saying that you wanted me, that you'd like a, that you wanted me to find someone who would take my place.' There, she's said it. She rolls the pestle up and down on the soaked dried chillies on the flat grinding stone with extra vigour.

'Oh my, why do you ask? Are you leaving?' Boüdi nearly shrieks.

'Nooo, but I was thinking, my daughter could come and be your live-in maidservant,' Sabita replies, concentrating furiously on the chilli paste.

'Your daughter? How old is she?'

'Seven or eight.' Sabita hesitates. She does not know years and months, she only knows the girl was born during the monsoon.

'O ma, a slip of a thing, then. What work do you think she'll be able to do?'

'No, no, she can do everything: make rice – she makes good rice – cut vegetables, clean and sweep and mop the floor, cook. I've taught her everything. She's the one who looks after everything when I'm here. She can even forage for things. I taught her how to identify nurnuri leaves, she brings back bunches and cooks them –'

Something catches at her throat, makes her eyes begin to water. The chillies she is grinding into a paste are potent.

Boüdi, oblivious, continues: 'There is some advantage to having a resident maid, I give you that. She can do all the little chores that are always cropping up.'

Sabita doesn't trust herself to speak, so she only nods.

'But the salary will be less, I'm telling you from now only,' Boüdi says. 'She's a little girl, I'll have to train her, and keep an eye out for all the mistakes that she'll be making … that's a lot of work for me. I can't pay her what I pay you.' Then something new occurs to her and she asks, 'Are you keeping your job at the other house?'

Still unable to have her face witnessed, Sabita shakes her bowed head, then says, 'I was going to keep only one of them, so I'm asking you first. I'll ask them at the other house when I go there later today.'

'Then you give your girl to the other house and you keep working for us here,' she says huffily, peeved that she might be put in second place, but it also occurs to her to weigh up the pros and cons of the new situation, so that if a choice has to be made, she wants to be the one exercising it, to her fullest advantage, and not have something foisted on her that is the result of other people's decisions, particularly a servant's.

Sabita broaches the subject to Boüdi in the second house. Here, too, the answers and calculations are similar: less pay for the girl, which of the two households gets to keep Sabita. But in this house, Boüdi asks, 'But why are you sending the girl away? Have you found another house to work for?'

'No, Boüdi, what can I say, that cow is making us see mustard flowers! The children are still small, they cannot look after all the things you need to do when you have a cow. Grazing, feeding, cleaning out the shed, collecting dung, making and selling fuel cakes, dealing with people who throw problems your way just because they want to put a stick in your behind. Someone tried to poison the cow a couple of months ago, you know, that's why I couldn't come for two days. It's not possible to leave everything in my children's hands while I come to work here. And now the cow is going to have a calf. The people from town are going to come and show us how to milk her. Then we'll have to sell the milk. Where am I going to find the time to do all this? I can't be in five places at the same time. They said the cow was going to make us money. Rubbish. All lies. The cow is costing us our blood. We have to give her our rice and eat half-stomach ourselves. We have been going to bed hungry every other night. I can tell that the children are hungry – I am a mother, I can understand these things, I can see it on their dry faces, I can hear their stomachs making grumbling noises all night. I bought muri and some cane-jaggery for them to take when they were out grazing the cow – a week's, two weeks' worth of jaggery was finished in two days. And now we have to give the cow even more food because she is pregnant. Where am I going to get all this food? I call the people who brought us the cow, they say, we'll come, we'll come, but they don't show up. There is no regular delivery of everything the cow needs, or we need, to look after her properly.'

It's as if a dumb person has been given the gift of speech. The words make her relive everything, and the frustration manifests in the energy she brings to scrubbing the steel and aluminium utensils with ash. Boüdi takes it all in, a little silenced by the torrent. Sabita says, 'Besides, if I send my daughter to you or to the other house, she'll at least get to eat two square meals a day.' The flash-and-spark in her voice is suddenly gone.

'Why don't you give back the cow?' Boüdi asks.

Sabita has never allowed herself to ask this question, so she's taken aback when it is posed to her, and so nakedly too.

'N-no,' she almost whispers, 'how can that be?'

Boüdi interrupts with 'Uff, this cow will be the end of you. So, which home gets your girl and which one you?'

13.

The new grazing ground is much farther away, away from the main village, in the direction of what they call 'the other bank', meaning the border with the other country. The border is miles and miles away, along the river, and there are towns and villages along it, but Sahadeb and Mira haven't ever ventured that far – it would be impossible for them to go there on their own, and they would need some form of transportation. There have been no cows in this enormous field, almost wild, in the short time they have been bringing Gauri to this spot. The only drawback with this place is that there is no pond here, and they have to walk another mile to get to the stream that cuts through. Closer to the stream, the ground is stony and unsuitable for grazing. To their children's eyes, everything in this new place seems vast, unknown, unexplored, as if they are close to a new country and its difference from theirs is beginning to show. The stream to them is the river that they have heard about, the river that divides the two nations. When they see the other side, they think it's the other country, although it appears to be indistinguishable from the ground they are standing on.

On a winter day, bright and sunny, pleasantly warm in the sun, Sahadeb says to his sister, 'From tomorrow I'll be coming here with Gauri on my own.' He looks into the distance while speaking, as if looking at that other country.

Mira doesn't say anything; there's nothing for her to say. A wind passes through the meadow, setting off a rustling in the grasses and bushes and trees. Sahadeb cannot bring himself to look at Mira.

After a long silence, Mira asks, 'Can you look after Gauri on your own?'

'You'll see, when you come to visit, that I am the best cowherd in this country,' he says, but the aimed-for lightness lands flatly.

Mira gets up and walks towards Gauri. The sun is long past its zenith in the sky; they need to bring the cow back home before the shadows start lengthening, which seems to happen earlier and earlier every day now. Sahadeb follows his sister at a little distance. He is about fifteen or twenty feet away when he sees her lean her forehead on Gauri's shoulder – that's the full extent of Mira's height – and stay still for a long time, both her hands outstretched as if trying to hug Gauri's neck. Something stops Sahadeb from advancing. When Mira turns around her face is wet.

There is no leave-taking, no packing, since there is nothing to pack – Mira simply accompanies Sabita on her way to work one morning. Only Sabita will return. The girl is shivering in the early morning cold – she only has a thin chador over her faded, dirty shift. The one woollen sweater, full of holes, that belongs to them is worn by Sahadeb. It is a hand-down from a home Sabita used to work for. The arms are now getting short – they end just above his bony wrists – and it is unravelling in several places along the hem, but it keeps him warm. Sabita takes off her own threadbare shawl and wraps it around the girl's shoulders, her eyes averted from the girl's face. The silence is like a third person walking between them. If only to dispel that presence, Sabita repeats what she has said before to Mira: 'It's only two hours away from home. I go there and come back every day. You'll see me every day, I'm only a few houses away from where you will be. You'll get two meals a day, and they'll give you new clothes, and warm clothes for the winter, a sweater like Sahadeb has.' The words are just empty sounds now to Sabita's ears; she doesn't trust herself to speak for the rest of the journey. Mira does not utter a sound; if she had spoken, said anything, Sabita could have been on the more stable ground of consoling, comforting. She is grateful that they are looking straight ahead and walking – this way, she does not have to see Mira's face. How will she look into this child's eyes when she says goodbye at the first boüdi's house?

The day after Mira leaves home, Sabita cannot lead Gauri to her grazing ground. She digs her heels in, turns her face away from Sabita, and when Sabita tries to pull her by the rope around the neck, the cow lets out a loud 'Hum-baaa' and resists with all her strength.

'Arrey, this is trouble,' Sabita says. 'What's up with you? Come on, we're going to get food for you, food. Food. Come on, tchu-tchu-tchu-tchu, come.'

Nothing doing; the cow doesn't budge, won't even turn her face.

'Orrey, cooome,' Sabita says and gives a big tug on the rope. Gauri does not move.

Sabita calls out, 'Sahadeb, come here, look at this cow, she's not coming out to graze. What to do?'

Sahadeb says, 'She is not like this at all when we take her. Let me try. Come, lokkhi-ti, come, so much tender grass and leaves and shoots waiting for you in the new field, come, golden cow, come.'

'You have to do all this pleading and coaxing every morning?'

'No! This is the first time I've seen her do this. I don't understand.'

'You have to take her today. I can't sit here all day, begging her to come grazing with me. Sahadeb, you cannot go to Nonapani to catch rice from the ration shop today, you take her to the meadow. All my plans have gone to the doors of the furnace. And we are about to run out of rice.'

Sahadeb is secretly relieved. A day spent idling in the meadows with Gauri, spared the jostling and hustling of the ration-shop queue, the hours of waiting, then walking back with the heavy sack on his head, is an unexpected boon.

In the fields, he lets Gauri go. Sahadeb sits in the sun, then falls to dozing. He wakes up at irregular intervals, looks at where Gauri is, then nods off again. At one such waking moment, he sees Gauri with her nose to the grass, not quite eating but sniffing, or looking for something, he fancies. At that instant, the cow looks up and turns her head around slowly, left and right and centre again, her eyes trained on the horizon, as if really looking for something. Or someone. He feels chilly even in the sun, a tightness in his chest. The field, with not a single animal, other than Gauri, nor a human in it, the stream in the distance, the other country beyond – it feels vast, frightening. This is the most alone he has ever felt in his small life.

Just after Sankranti, the usual messenger boy from Nonapani comes to tell Sabita that some money has arrived for her and is waiting to be collected. In all the time Pulak has been gone, Sabita has thought of him less and less, so that the arrival of this boy comes as a surprise. It is true that she has thought often, and bitterly, of his delayed, maybe even missing, moneys, so in that respect she has thought of him, but instrumentally: the money first, the man after, and only in connection to income.

274

Sabita is also coming to understand that in real terms her earnings have fallen: her two salaries are now one and a half since Mira is paid half the wages that Sabita was paid. Besides, she gets to bring leftovers from only one home now, not two. That deficit does not make up for the reduced number of mouths she has to feed. In any case, the girl consumed little, didn't take up much space; instead she gave a lot more than she received. All Sabita's choices and calculations are turning out to be wrong.

The town people visit again, bringing sacks of food for Gauri. There is no space to store them anywhere, so Sabita is compelled to surrender her vegetable patch with a lot of misgiving. There are plastic-wrapped mini-silos of oil cakes, sacks of hay, tubs of calcium tablets, crumbled pre-cooked pulses, giant bags of rice and wheat husks. They build a flimsy shed, then ask for more space where all the metal pails for the milk can be kept. All these small things, one dependent on another, that she, or even they, had never thought about, are now causing problems whose solutions hem in Sabita further, sometimes literally.

If she hadn't known, Sabita would not have been alert to any physical change in Gauri, but now she is primed to regard the cow's growing stomach, her swollen udder. What Sabita does notice, when she is feeding Gauri her ration, is how much her appetite has increased. It brings back the terror of the early days – running out of fodder and having to feed Gauri their own rice and dal, going to bed hungry themselves, the permanently hungry cow pulling at anything she could chew, in one instance, Sahadeb's shirt, which was drying on top of a bush. Mira had once seen Gauri eating paper that had been lying on the ground on their way to the field. And like a stubborn ghost who has managed to evade exorcism, the words of the town people return to her: 'This food is only until you can begin to milk her. After that, it's up to you to buy her food with the money from the milk and fuel cakes you sell. We'll stop all this after the calf is born.' And she feels a version of the earlier terror again. She knows she will have to use at least some of Pulak's money to buy fodder for Gauri, and she hopes the money will last until that time.

Shortly after this, one cool morning, as Sabita is mixing Gauri's food, Sahadeb asks, 'Is Baba here?'

'Baba? Baba is missing, gone in Allah's name.'

'No, I saw his chador on a bush where we shit. Just now.'

Sabita stops mixing for a moment then asks, 'Why didn't you wait for him?'

Sahadeb cannot give an answer to this; instead he smiles foolishly and begins, 'I thought, I thought ...'

'Enough thinking. Come and take over, misborn fool. Watching your mother reduce herself to black bones and flesh and you stand there bleating Baba, Baba.'

Half an hour passes before Pulak walks in.

14.

Sabita goes to see the boüdi in the home where Mira works now. 'I have come to ask you for something. Mira's father has returned – if she could come home just for one evening to see him ... I'll bring her back tomorrow morning.'

Boüdi treats Sabita like a stranger, or a stray come in to beg. All the casual informality from the time Sabita used to work there has been replaced by a cold aloofness. Through some perfectly placed 'tsks', the lift of her eyebrows, the touch of petulance on her face, Boüdi lets it be known that both Sabita and her outrageous request are extremely unwelcome. Mira is in the background silently swabbing the floor with a wet rag, her face down. She cannot betray any hope, yet her bent-over form seems to be the shape of pure expectation.

'One after another, these demands,' Boüdi complains. 'I'll have to do all the chores in the evening myself. You seem not to have given that any thought, you're so absorbed in yourself. All right, then, take her, if you must, but she's coming back here first thing tomorrow morning. If she's late, you don't have to bring her back ever.'

Mira continues with the floor-swabbing as if she hasn't heard anything. She'll only open her mouth on the walk back home.

'Has Gauri had her calf?' is what she asks Sabita when they begin their two-hour walk back to Nonapani.

When Sahadeb had asked two months ago if his father had returned, he hadn't asked with joy, anticipation, excitement, but as a straightforward empirical question that needed answering, something along the lines of 'How much does this weigh?' or 'How much does one candle cost?' And it was just as well that Mira came home for one night only since there was no longer any space for all of them inside the hut. On that first night, Sahadeb and Mira had slept outside in the cold, but after Mira had returned to Majharsharif the following morning, Sahadeb resumed sleeping indoors and his father slept outside. A coir khatiya from Nonapani arrived for this purpose. Father and son had carried it back on their shoulders from the village.

'You want to sleep in it one night?' Pulak asked.

'No, it's fine,' Sahadeb said. That slight awkwardness, that whiff of formality, again.

It's not that Sabita and Sahadeb sleep any better indoors – Pulak coughs almost constantly outside, disturbing their sleep. Sabita says to him, 'Come inside during this cold season, the cold air and the morning dew are making you ill.'

Pulak declines. When Sabita asks him if he is off again soon, he shrugs and says he doesn't know. He has come back thinner, more lined around his mouth and eyes, and his stubble has generous glints of grey. Sabita cannot quite put her finger on what it is about him that has changed, but she feels he is not just more haggard, but also different, quieter, distracted, elsewhere. He eats little, says little, and spends most of his time in his cot, staring at the cow, she had thought at first, but now she understands that he's looking beyond her at nothing. There is black under his nails that won't come off in the pond where they all bathe, even after scrubbing with soap. 'Coal dust,' he says, giving Sabita a rare peek into what his life is like when he is away.

'You dig up coal?' Sabita asks.

'Sometimes.'

'And at other times?'

'Building houses, roads, construction.'

He doesn't expand on that, or say anything else, even unrelated to his work, after those few words. He is not forbidding her to inquire more by being laconic, only expressing a sort of boredom, even fatigue. In any case, it suits Sabita well; her only interest in the subject is the earnings he will send home, not the means by which he gets them.

Spring comes and goes. The heat increases. There are clouds of flies everywhere; Gauri's dung has to be collected as soon as it is expelled to mitigate their onslaught; not that it makes much of a difference since they easily get under the dried palm leaves that loosely cover the bucket to gather thickly on the dung inside. Sabita shouts at Sahadeb to deal with the dung and not leave it lying around for her to pick up after she returns home from work, but Sahadeb ignores this and rides out her anger. Pulak complained about the smell and the flies in the spring, but it appears now that both have defeated him in their combined and increasing strength over the summer. Sabita sees him often dozing in his cot intermittently throughout the morning, his mouth open, a fly crawling on his lips, trying to enter his mouth. Sometimes, she swipes it away with her hand, wondering if he is asleep or unconscious.

One skin-scalding mid-morning in Baishakh, with flies everywhere in Gauri's shed, inside the hut, in the cow's feeding bucket, on her body, trying to get into Sabita's mouth and nose as she is mixing dung, while Pulak is staring into space, she says, 'You won't touch cow dung, fine, but you could mix her feed in the mornings. I can't look after everything.'

Pulak doesn't respond, it's not even clear that he has heard, so she repeats what she has just said.

'Ask Sahadeb to do it,' he says at last.

'Sahadeb takes her to graze.'

'He can do both, they are at different times.'

Sabita doesn't reply. There's nothing for her to say. Then, surprising her, he adds, 'I sent a lot of money, that should last us a while.'

She understands that he's not implying she could give up her job at Majharsharif to look after the cow full-time, but that the money liberates him from doing any work at home.

With the beginning of the monsoons, the flies abate, but mosquitoes begin their reign. Pulak can no longer sleep outside because of the rain. When he moves inside with his khatiya, Sahadeb has to flatten out the sacks of fodder as best as he can and lie on them. Sabita sleeps half under the cot. The corner of the roof that Gauri had pulled down last year, hastily fixed by the people from town, begins to leak again. The overpowering cloud of dung and cow-urine mustiness changes to its wet version and settles into a suffocating blanket.

Sabita feels herself fraying. She has to think about so many things that her mind cannot accommodate them. Fresh water, they had said, the cow must have a lot of fresh water every day, on top of her feed having to be mixed with a bucket of water twice a day. Pulak coughs all day, all night, and looks as if he is being consumed from the inside. Sabita asks him to go see a doctor, but he shakes his head. The only thing he says is 'Bring my daughter back. You should not have sent her away', but weakly, as if it's a trivial afterthought. It hits Sabita on a weak spot: her growing awareness that the trade-off between sending Mira away and Sabita therefore getting more time to manage Gauri at home is not working out as she had expected. She barks, 'And what money are we going to live off? Yours? You seem not to have enough hours in the day to sleep.' Pulak doesn't say anything; how her words have affected him she cannot tell.

The few feet from the hut to Gauri's shed is a churn of mud, dung remnant, cow urine, and bedding straw. Clean straw, clean, dry straw, especially when she gives birth, those people had said. How is she going to get clean, dry straw in this weather? As the monsoon rages, the fodder delivery is first delayed then becomes irregular. If the next delivery does not arrive in a week, maybe ten days, Sabita will have to begin to stretch out the rations. After that she will have to find a way of buying the food herself. There is still some money left from what Pulak had sent after Sankranti. She had checked, when Pulak was out in the fields, if he had brought home more, but that quick search had turned up nothing. Where did he keep it? It's not as if there are many hiding places or things belonging to Pulak, such as clothes, bags, pillows, in which he can have hidden it.

When Sahadeb comes in with sacks of oil cakes and hay on a cycle rickshaw from Nekurgram, Sabita is away at work. Pulak, catching a rare lull in the rain, is sitting outside.

'Where have you been?' Pulak asks. 'What's all this you're lugging in?'

'Nekurgram, to bring fodder for Gauri. We've run out, so Ma sent me to buy more.'

'Buy? She gave you the money or the people from town?'

'Ma gave me money.'

'How much?'

Sahadeb names a sum. After he has finished stacking the fodder inside the hut, Pulak gives him a few rupees and says,

'Get some bidis for me from Nonapani. Go now, before it starts to pour again. With the remainder, you can buy whatever you want for yourself.'

Sahadeb, who was about to grumble, is pulled in by the bribe. As soon as he is out, Pulak goes to the tin where Sabita keeps the rice, puts his hand in, digs under the six or seven inches of grain, and finds what he is looking for. He pulls it out, careful not to spill any rice: a small cloth bag. Inside, there's a bundle of notes, folded in half. He counts the money, peels off two hundred rupees, then puts the rest back. When he had looked yesterday, the sum of money was more by the exact amount Sahadeb mentioned a few minutes earlier plus the two hundred he has just taken.

When Sabita returns, Pulak gives her some time before he asks her casually, 'I saw Sahadeb bringing in fodder for the cow. Did he get it from the people who gave us the cow?'

Sabita is fanning the unun to get the dung cakes to catch. She says, 'Yes.'

'He gets it free?'

'Yes,' she lies. 'They tell the shop how much ration they should give him, he goes and collects it.'

'And you don't have to pay anything?'

'No,' she says forcefully, 'can't you hear me? How many times do I have to say it?'

Pulak gets out of his khatiya and kicks her on her back so hard that she falls face down on to the unun. She is lucky that it hasn't caught fully, lucky too that she falls not squarely on her face but partially, to one side. She screams. Pulak is transformed from the husk-like half-living creature he has seemed to be all these months to someone possessed. He pounces on his wailing prostrate wife and slaps and punches her while howling, 'I turn my blood to sweat to earn money and you spend it all on cow fodder? That's what you do with my money? Lying whore! Then you pack my daughter off so that her money can be burnt on the cow as well? You are not the daughter of one father. Tell me, is that how you spend my money, my blood?'

Just as suddenly, the fury leaves him. He goes back to being that dwindled, coughing man, silent, with that faraway look in his eyes, a stranger to everyone and everything around him. Had it not been for Sabita's split lip, black eye, a face singed from chin to cheekbone to temple, the whole episode could have been just a dream.

The monsoon is the heaviest in many years. News comes in of villages by the river entirely submerged under water, of people having to swim to safety with their belongings packed into one bundle on their heads, of old people and animals drowned. In Nonapani, the entire rice crop is ruined. Pulak cannot get any work in the paddies; not that he shows any energy or interest. One afternoon at the tail end of the monsoon season, when the rain has let up for a while, Pulak says, 'I'll go away for a few days.'

Sabita feels almost afloat with relief, followed very closely by the hope that there's going to be money coming in soon. She has never asked where he goes to find work and this time, too, she doesn't make an exception.

15.

Three days after Pulak leaves, Gauri gives birth to her calf. Sabita notices a viscous rope of milk-white mucus coming out of the cow's genitals and calls the town people immediately, as she has been instructed to do. Gauri is restless, sitting for a few minutes, then standing up again, repeated for what feels to Sabita like hours. She shouts out, 'Orrey, Sahadeb, Gauri is about to give birth.' The call brings out people from the nearest hut, then the news spreads and people from slightly farther come out to see this spectacle of calving. They are certainly quicker than the vet and the town people. Sympathetic shudders go through Sabita as she watches Gauri's abdominal straining and contractions, so powerful that the poor woman is convinced something is wrong. She is at her wit's end as suggestions and advice flow freely.

'Leave the cow alone, just let her be, they don't need any help, have you seen animals need help to give birth? One day you wake up and there are puppies or kittens.'

'Arrey, I'm telling you, you have to shove your hand inside to bring out the calf. I've seen it before.'

'No, only an animal doctor can do it. You're not asking *her* to shove her hand up the cow, are you?'

'No, no, I'm just saying.'

'The cow needs water in front of her.'

'Someone should massage her behind to help along the contractions.'

'Easier said than done – are you going to do it? Massage her behind, tchah!'

'Oh, look, look, there's a big gush of water coming out. It's yellow, like urine. She's peeing. What force.'

'No, that's her water breaking, the calf is going to start coming out now.'

Two hooves and a muzzle emerge first. Sabita has long lost track of time. There is nothing she can do except watch, like the rest, the birth, and hope and pray that it will follow its course without needing any intervention. Every episode in her life, every turn of events, brings her face to face with her own absolute helplessness. She has power over nothing, power to do nothing. She is resigned to it, but not indifferent. Inch by inch the calf emerges, then suddenly, all at once, it is out, deposited like a giant turd. A cheer goes up. Someone blows on a conch shell, marking the moment as auspicious. The calf lies there, inert. The sound of the conch, pushed away by the rattling in her chest, is very distant to her ears. If she looked closely, she could make out the barest tremble in the calf, shivering it all over. Sabita, too, finds herself shaking everywhere – her hands, her knees, deep inside.

'Arrey, you have to pick up the calf now and put it in front of the cow's face.'

'No, no, the cow will turn around and do it herself.'

And then the vet and town people arrive, all bustling, busy, urgent – taking charge, shooing the onlookers away, changing the straw, issuing orders, demanding hot water, disinfecting. Sabita tries to get up, but halfway through the motion, she blacks out.

*

In the fading light of the day, Sahadeb notices something resembling a long, raggedy piece of dirty cloth hanging out of Gauri's bottom. He moves forward a bit to free her from whatever it is that she has got stuck to her. Then he sees it: a wildly torn flag of skin, membrane, pink flesh. Rooted to the spot, he watches Gauri extend her neck as far back as she can and start to tug and chew on it. With repeated jerks of her neck, the thing comes detached. Gauri eats it up before Sahadeb can let the shudder go down his spine. With her bloody tongue, Gauri starts licking her calf. He heard someone say earlier that cows lick their calves to shape them into the proper cow form since the babies are born as shapeless lumps.

The calf is allowed to suckle Gauri for the first three days then moved to bottled milk; it falls upon Sahadeb to do the feeding. After what Sahadeb has witnessed, he is reluctant to go anywhere near Gauri or the calf, particularly to touch either of them. The calf is dark, a shade between grey and purple. It's going to change colour, they say, it's going to be a brown cow, or maybe brownish-black. They call him Gopal. Sahadeb is taught how to mix formula for the calf, how to hold the teat of the bottle to his mouth.

'He was doing fine, drinking milk from Gauri, why do I have to feed him from a bottle?' he grumbles.

'Because, stupid, the milk is for us to sell, not for Gopal to drink. He'll guzzle it all if he's let loose,' Sabita says.

Gopal is tied to a post driven next to what used to be the vegetable patch and is now the fodder storage silo. Mother and calf are within each other's sight, but not close enough so that either animal can reach the other even if they stretch out to the utmost length of their respective ropes. Milk will come to her udder as long as she can see the calf, they had said.

As a woman shows Sabita how to milk, Gauri kicks her. The woman steps back quickly, but she is used to this. Sabita, already apprehensive about the milking business, refuses to come near the cow, the fear overruling her familiarity with the animal. 'What if she kicks me? She has never kicked anyone in her life, she is such a gentle creature,' Sabita keeps saying.

'Don't worry, look, I've positioned myself in such a way that she cannot kick me. Look, I've shortened the rope as well, she won't be able to move around so much,' the woman says.

'But she can still kick sideways.'

'Well,' the woman confesses, 'the trick is to lull her by the milking so that she doesn't kick. She'll get used to you. She'll be restive only the first couple of times.'

But Sabita is unwilling to go anywhere near Gauri. The training woman has another idea: she unties Gauri, makes her face away from the calf, and ties her to a different post. Gauri lows loudly, face held up at an angle, kicks again when the woman gets near her udder, but seems to quieten after a few attempts.

Sabita approaches gingerly, ready to leap away at the first sign of recalcitrance on the cow's part. The nervousness delays what turns out to be a difficult education. Sabita feels that she'll never learn: the udder is far too big for both her hands cupped together – it keeps spilling over generously from almost every point in the circumference of that cup; the right movement of pulling one teat and then another, alternately, in the rhythm the woman tries to get Sabita to master ('hold two teats, diagonal ones, pull number one and simultaneously squeeze teat number two, as you relax your hold on number one pull number two, then squeeze number one again as you relax your hold on two') is beyond her dexterity. The udder slips out, the milk leaks on to her hands instead of falling in a thin jet into the bucket held between her legs, and that alternating one-two rhythm is just impossible. She simply cannot master the magic trick of the motion, as she had once done with getting wet cow-dung cakes to stick to a vertical wall. As she keeps trying, and failing, other instructions fly at her: wash the udder with hot water before milking; disinfect the milk pails; speak or sing to the cow while milking; feed the cow at the same time as you milk her first thing at dawn, when her udder is bursting with milk ... How is she going to do it all?

The question is answered for her. Four consecutive days of not showing up at Majharsharif gets her fired; the excuse of Gauri giving birth is ineffectual. She is paid for the days she has worked, and Boüdi repeats her refrain: 'This cow will be the end of you, mark my words.' Sabita feels relief; for once, she doesn't think of money lost but of time gained. She needs all the time in the world, the time of four people, five, given to her. She goes to the house where Mira now works and asks Boüdi if Mira can come home for one night.

'The cow has had a calf. Mira was so –'

Boüdi, incredulous, cuts her short. 'You want to take her home again? She went just a few days ago.'

'No, it's been several months since she was last there.'

'You're arguing with me? What cheek. Take her away and don't bring her back. I'm done with this.'

Mira's face shines as she walks back home; the double joy of a new calf and not having to work as a maidservant, living away from home.

'Will you milk the cow? They'll teach you how to do it,' Sabita says.

Mira agrees, without thinking, to everything that her mother asks of her; her thoughts are all consumed by the calf.

'But why is he black? Gauri is white,' she asks.

'Maybe his father was black.'

Mira dances into her old home, rushes to the calf and puts her arms around him. 'What a nice smell he has. Why is he kept so far away from his mother? Look at them, they only have eyes for each other.'

Sahadeb eagerly supplies the explanation. In all the chaos of homecoming, and Gopal's presence, and the new duties added to the old ones, in all the sprawling mess and density of three humans and two animals sharing the limited space that used to be inhabited by three people at most times, Mira doesn't think to ask, 'Where's Baba?'

16.

It is Mira's small hands that manage to acquire quickly the trick of milking Gauri. Sabita remarks, both as a kind of explanation and as a muted expression of pride in her daughter's skill, 'It's like swimming – you can't float for a long time, you try and try, then one day you're floating.' The morning milking fills up a five-litre pail and a little bit over a third of another; the evening yield is almost as much. The milk is foamy and warm. It takes so long to fill up a pail, thin squirt after thin squirt, that after the first flush of the novelty of milking a cow fades, the negatives begin to make their presence felt. Mira's hands ache by the time the milk reaches the quarter-mark so that she has to start taking increasingly frequent rests. Gauri stamps her hooves whenever Mira pauses to give some relief to her hands. For the morning sessions, she has to get up so early, sometimes even before the roosters in the main village have crowed, that she finds her head lowering to rest against Gauri's flank, then slowly nodding off … and awakened by Gauri kicking the ground. Sabita, who had kept from Mira the information about Gauri's kicking, notes that the cow is calm and pliant with the girl. Mira is also entrusted with the duty of feeding Gopal formula milk from a bottle, and not only because Sahadeb has proved to be useless at his sole task: Mira feels the milking of Gauri is a duty, but the feeding of Gopal a pleasure.

One useful thing the town people have done is to get a stable buyer for Gauri's milk – the sweet shop in Nekurgram. The price has been negotiated beforehand so that there's no scope for haggling or cheating. The shop is an hour and a half by foot, and Sabita and Sahadeb do both the morning and the late-afternoon runs.

'You're not diluting the milk with water, are you?' the sweet-shop man with the enormous belly asks. 'We'll know immediately if you're doing it. We can tell just by looking.'

Sabita is scandalized and protests vociferously. After about a month of delivering two rounds of milk daily, both mother and son begin to tire of the six hours of walking. But Sabita has money, for the first time in her life, so she decides, after a fortnight of internal debate trying to justify the expense, to hire a rickshaw for the final leg of the journey, the return home in the evening. She even says to Sahadeb, 'If I can save a little bit of the milk money every day, then you can have a cycle yourself and take charge of the milk runs.' Sahadeb is excited by the idea of owning a cycle, not so much about the work that he will be put to. Still, at this stage of dreaming, the cycle is far bigger in his mind than the reason for acquiring it.

On the advice of the vet, who comes in with the people from town to visit twice in one month, Gopal is weaned off milk and given grass clippings and hay. Sabita buys new clothes, slippers for Mira and Sahadeb and for herself, but always after painfully protracted consideration. They eat two meals a day now, and Sabita buys another unun so that Mira can cook rice and a vegetable or a dal simultaneously. On the milk-selling trips into Nekurgram, Sabita buys vegetables that she would never have thought of buying before, either because she grew them herself, such as onions, garlic, chillies, gourd, or because they were beyond her means – cauliflower, aubergines – and she didn't have the space to cultivate them.

She buys cooking oil, sugar, jaggery, spices, even eggs one day. She buys stainless-steel plates and glasses so that each of them has her or his own for the first time. Mira will no longer have to wait for Sahadeb to finish eating out of the dented and chipped, lipped, blue-rimmed aluminium plate that Sabita had brought back home from one of the homes she used to work for because they were discarding it. She and Sahadeb bring back Gauri's fodder together; a very heavy worry rolls off Sabita's shoulders with the ability to provide ample food for the cows twice a day. She no longer has to think of grazing them and all the attendant problems. She allows herself to think of having the roof repaired, maybe even having a bigger hut or, god willing, a home made of bricks.

Pujo comes around and Pulak returns home but this time with no money to show for the time that he has been away. Sabita doesn't dare ask him what has happened; besides, she doesn't need to, since Gauri, their goddess of wealth, is providing them enough. She tells him how their fortunes are beginning to turn at last.

'I'm thinking of going to the Kali temple in Nekurgram and giving them a little something in our name so that they can do a pujo and thank her for turning her glance at us smilingly,' she says.

Pulak says nothing, but behind his wife's words he hears a taunting tone, as if she's saying, *I have turned the tide of our fortunes, not you. We lived from hand to mouth while you were the main earner, but look at us now, when mine is the principal income.* He watches carefully all the work necessary to keep a milch cow, the daily routine, the labour of selling the milk, the great success they have wrung out of their blood-drying toil, and the food that Mira gives him, twice a day, no less, feels like ashes in his mouth. The cow has made him redundant. He does not offer to help with anything, doesn't

292

get involved in the labour, only watches, coughs non-stop, and toys at mealtimes with what to him are thorns and stones.

Then two things happen, the first of which is unimagined if predictable – the town people come to take away Gopal. Mira, overcoming her natural fear of strangers attired in proper clothes from a distant big town, throws herself in front of the calf and begins to weep. Sabita says, 'He's our calf. You had no hand in getting Gauri pregnant, she did it herself. The calf belongs to us.'

The people are taken aback by this line of reasoning, partly because their work involved getting the cows given as gifts to lift up people from poverty artificially inseminated so that the cows could provide milk that could be sold. They have always assumed that because the cow has been paid for by them, as well as the costs of the insemination, the resulting calf belongs to them too. This contingency of a gift cow producing a calf without any help from them is a novel problem, one to which they haven't given any thought at all.

But an asset is something no one gives up, not without putting up a serious fight. 'What are you going to do with him? He won't give you any milk. On top of that, you'll have to feed him and house him. He'll cost you money,' one of the people from town says.

Sabita doesn't understand the value of the bull-calf for the town people. If she were nimble in her thinking, she would have been able to claim Gopal for exactly the same reason. Instead, she says, 'Let him cost us money. We'll get a cart and yoke him to it. We'll find a way of making it work, you don't need to think about it, he's not yours to think about.'

Sahadeb says, 'We'll put him to farm. He can pull the plough.'

This goes on for a good while. Pulak watches silently, doesn't intervene. Both parties begin to get angrier and angrier.

The exasperated town people ultimately say, 'Fine, you keep the calf then, return the cow to us. She's been acquired by our money, she belongs to us entirely.'

It's an empty threat – their experiment in rescuing the ultra poor from poverty traps by asset transfers will not work if the very asset is confiscated – but Sabita doesn't know this. Her shoulders slump visibly, she is at a loss for words. Mira, who has been weeping softly, now lets out a loud wail. Sabita knows that she has been trumped. The best she can do now is to allow them to take Gopal away without too much loss of face. Gauri and Gopal both understand what's happening. They start lowing once they are out of each other's sight. The calls continue until Gopal's fade away as he is taken farther and farther, but Gauri's persist for longer, right next to their ears, until the intervals between the cries become longer and there is finally nothing but silence at the end of them.

The second unexpected thing that happens: the sweet shop at Nekurgram first asks Sabita if she can supply four times the amount of milk at nearly half the price, and when she says she cannot, asks her to reduce her rate anyway. She calls up the people from town to complain, but a week goes by in 'let's see what we can do about it' then another week of silence, during which time Sabita has to plead with the sweet shop to continue to buy her milk at the initially agreed rate. One morning they say to Sabita and Sahadeb, 'Today is the last day we are buying from you. We have found a wholesale place. They will be able to meet our rising demand at a much lower price.'

'So what am I going to do with all this milk?' she asks foolishly at last, after a long, pitiful pause.

'Drink it. Give it to your son here. Make sandesh,' they laugh.

Sabita cannot bear to throw out the afternoon's milk. She and Sahadeb go around to two or three homes in the main village in Nonapani to try to sell, knowing well that no one else can afford it. They manage to sell only two powas worth and have to bring the rest back. No one in the family of four has ever drunk milk apart from their mothers'. They don't know whether to treat it as a desirable or a suspicious luxury.

Mira says, 'If we boil it, it'll keep for another day. I've seen it in the house where I worked.'

'But so much milk? What are we going to do?' Sabita continues to say.

'What about making payesh?' Sahadeb offers.

The suggestion is so risible in the circumstances that it even shakes Sabita out of her despair. 'After two days we'll go back to eating boiled rice and salt, if we're lucky, that is, and you want to eat payesh on the eve of that?' she remarks acidly.

Pulak gives a dry laugh, seizes up with coughing, but manages to say to his son at the end of the fit: 'No skin on your bum, but your name is Hare Krishna.'

But the glut of unsold milk leaves them with no option other than what Sahadeb suggested, so Mira turns to cooking the celebratory dish for a disastrous occasion. On the wildly uneven flames of the unun, the milk catches and burns in the cheap pots; payesh is going to be impossible. Sabita feels that the milk is rebelling against its improper use. They are forced to drink some of it, unable to distinguish between its burnt taste and the smell in the air. Unused to the stuff, they get flatulence shortly afterwards and then the runs a bit later. It's only Gauri left in her shed, appearing to be calm, indifferent to the scene of desertion, as they all go into the bushes separately to suffer out the punishment of the milk.

17.

Just after seven in the morning, Sabita and Sahadeb knock on the doors of what appear to be better-off homes in Majharsharif, asking if they'd like fresh milk, straight from a cow, delivered to them daily. Look, it's still warm, still foamy, they say. It's rich, it'll fill your mouth. Sankranti is around the corner, you'll want milk for sweets and pancake fillings, for payesh. This is no better than begging, Sabita thinks, but her choices are few. She avoids the homes she used to work for, although she knows that they might be the kind of people who would buy at least some of it. By the time mother and son return home, having found buyers for all the morning's milk, it's around one o'clock. When they wake up from their afternoon sleep, Mira is preparing to settle down for the afternoon milking session. They are drained of every particle of strength, of will, of hope; seeing the pails fill up, and thinking of another four hours of walking the streets, this time in the dark, trying to sell to strangers who shut the door on their faces, makes their heads swim. Sabita asks Pulak to try out homes in Nekurgram, which is slightly closer – in fact, her calculation had been exactly this, that they would go to sell at the nearer place as evening fell – but Pulak barely registers this. When Sabita repeats her request, he gives voice to exactly her earlier thoughts, 'It'll be like begging. You think I'm a beggar?'

Sabita doesn't push; the memory of the last beating is close to the surface. She rages inside, and her mood is such that she fears she'll sour the evening's milk if she comes anywhere near it. In the dark, mother and son seek buyers in Nekurgram. There are no streetlights, so they are guided only by the lighted windows of houses that have electricity. Some of them don't even bother to open their doors; selling milk at this hour must be a ruse for some mischief or crime. Only one home takes in around half a litre. They bring back the rest in pitch dark; no more luxury of a rickshaw. Mira dutifully heats the milk, trying not to burn it, so that it can be stored overnight without risk of spoiling, but even her resourcefulness is no match for the iron laws of physics and chemistry. Their only hope is that the milk will lose its burnt smell by tomorrow morning. They dare not consume it themselves.

The next two months fall into this pattern of itinerant milk-selling and throwing out some of the evening's yield frequently. But the pattern keeps shifting, always destabilizing Sabita's life. Some regulars drop a day or two, leaving her with excess milk for which she cannot find a one-off buyer. Some switch time of delivery from morning to evening, or vice versa, causing mayhem in stock management and supply. There are days when Sabita asks Mira not to milk Gauri in the afternoon. Gauri grows restless and irritable during those nights, often lowing at all hours, even trying to kick Mira at the dawn sessions. Pulak goes away for short intervals, three or four days, but doesn't bring back any money on his return.

As Phalgun gives way to Chaitra and the heat becomes intolerable, one customer at Nekurgram complains, 'The milk you gave us yesterday was curdled, we won't pay you for this evening's.' Sabita has no way to dispute this, so she has to accept, with much grumbling, but a week later, as she and Sahadeb are walking back home at night with unsold milk, she catches a whiff of something sour from one of the pails. Yes, the milk has turned.

The milk begins to spoil with increasing frequency, and one day it happens to a half-bucket of milk they haven't been able to sell in the morning. Sahadeb notices it first: 'That smell is coming from the pail,' he says. Hungry, thirsty, drenched with sweat, dreading the hour of walking still remaining in the skull-splitting heat, Sabita feels an uncohering, of something coming loose inside her. She flings the bucket into some bushes – the milk flies in a splattering arc, some falling on the earth, where it is immediately sucked up, leaving no trace, some on leaves, barely marking them white – and the thought of Gopal goes through her head: all this milk, which he could have drunk, which he was forcefully restrained from drinking, going to waste. Where is he now? She sits down and lets herself go: she weeps with abandon, as if this is the last liberating action allowed her before the endless labour of her days extinguishes her.

The income from the milk begins to go down so much from its early peak of selling to the sweet shop that Sabita and her family slide back to their old ways of paanta in the daytime, sometimes only muri and gur, then something meagre cooked at night. Pulak taunts his wife: 'You thought you were going to eat and live like a queen, didn't you? Now you're back to paanta and muri.' It's as if even his own privation is nothing compared to the joy he gets from seeing Sabita's dreams crushed. And crushed they are, she feels in every vein in her body, every beat of her heart: she is possessed by shame when she thinks of all the plans that she had dared to make – a cycle for Sahadeb, a brick house – and how everything has evaporated, as if someone is punishing her for such lofty dreams. She cannot shake off the thought that this is payback for the way they treated Gopal. In her mind, there is a cruel symmetry to it: they have deprived a calf, a holy creature, of its mother's milk, now the gods are using that very milk to punish her.

The rationing of Gauri's food begins again, something Sabita never imagined that she would have to go back to. Sabita, old hand at stretching things to make them last longer, thinks she will be able to manage, but as Baishakh edges into dangerous Jyoishtho, when being in the sun for a few minutes can burn a hole in the middle of your head, Gauri's food reduces to such an extent that it becomes imperative to take her out to graze. But graze where, when all the grass has long turned to straw, when all the cow wants to do is sit or stand in the shade?

One afternoon, Mira says, 'Her milk is reducing. There's nothing in her. Look, I'm pulling, like before, but nothing comes out.'

'That's because you're giving her less to eat,' Pulak says.

Sabita feels a strange mixture of relief and dismay. When she and Sahadeb were running around trying to find buyers for the milk, and having to throw some of the yield away either for lack of enough buyers or because the milk had spoiled, she had often prayed for Gauri's udder to run dry, but now that her wish is being granted, she is brought face to face with the prospect of having to go back to work as a servant, pack off Mira to do the same. *This cow is going to be the end of you, mark my words*, both boüdis had said. The words ring loudly in her ears.

On a close evening, with Sabita fanning the unun, Mira mucking out Gauri's barn and collecting dried fuel cakes, and Sahadeb doing, as usual, nothing at all, Pulak says, 'I'll take her out to graze,' making Sabita nearly fall face down on the flames with shock.

'Where will you take her?' she asks calmly instead. 'Fields and banks are all dry as tinder, empty of all life.'

'I'll find some place, I know places that are not obvious or easily visible. You think every cow in the world is kept inside during the summer? Sahadeb and Mira used to take her out in the height of summer last year, you said.'

Sabita does not trust herself to say yes in case he is playing some kind of a cruel joke on her and takes it all back the moment she lets the 'yes' escape her mouth.

For the first three or four days she asks where he takes Gauri. He is vague – he points in a random direction and says, 'You won't know it, it's quite far away, you go past the jhil beyond Sukhmoti, then there is a stretch of paddies ... it's beyond that.'

'Why don't you take Sahadeb with you? He'll get to know the way, so he can take Gauri there when you have to go away again on work.'

'Naaah. It's too far for children.'

Gauri's milk production, however, doesn't pick up. In fact, Sabita thinks the cow is losing weight, looking bonier by the day. On the tenth day of Pulak taking Gauri to graze, neither of them returns.

Sabita and her children look for Gauri in bushes, brakes, fields, copses, any open green expanse they can think of. They visit the former pastures, and Sahadeb looks out to what he thinks of as the other country, which would have been easy to cross over to now since the stream is dry. They separate, searching individually, then come back together, each hoping the other person will have found the cow. They begin to search from the first break of light to the point when they cannot even see each other standing close by in the darkness. They are at their wits' end.

'She has escaped and gone to find her calf.'

'No, some Muslims have got hold of her and taken her to the other side. They'll kill and eat her. Or maybe even Muslims here.'

'Maybe she is hiding. We don't give her enough to eat, so she's cross with us, trying to teach us a lesson.'

'We'll have to report to the people who gave her to us … and what if they then ask us for the money?'

'Best not to call them.'

'But they may be able to send out more people to search, call the police. Do you remember, they took pictures of her and said that that was a new law, that all cows had to have their picture taken, have a number?'

'The number will feed your ancestors' ghosts! What good will a number do? If we can't see her in front of our eyes, what will the number achieve?'

And so it goes, round and round. They call out her name in the open air, shouting to the skies, the trees, the dry earth, the stony banks, the singeing air around them. They cry out her name till they're hoarse, till they think they've torn open the soft insides of their throats. In all these hours, no one calls out for Pulak or Baba, no one asks what has happened to the man.

18.

It is so dark that Pulak can see Gauri's white form only when he concentrates. If he didn't know where she was standing, he would take a few moments to establish her presence after taking his eyes away and returning them a minute or two later. He plays this game a few times just to pass the hours. Any minute now they are going to come and tell him to start moving. It will be done tonight. Tonight he will be paid in full. They've given him only five hundred rupees, half the rate, for taking Gauri over. The remaining fee and, most importantly, the money for the cow, of which he has been paid only a twentieth, has been promised him after he returns from the other side. He knows the price he has been offered for Gauri is half of what she would fetch if he could sell her on the open market, but that's not a possibility – besides, she is not his to sell – so he has to settle for the cut-price offer. On top of that, the hefty fee for the middleman will have to come out of it. He had demurred about this, but the man had said, 'You think it's all for me? More than half will go to bribe the BSF who guard the border. Looking the other side while we do our deed is a costly act, bhai.' Pulak wants to return tonight, or tomorrow night. In any case, that will have to be under cover of darkness since he is crossing at night, without handing his ID over to the BSF, so returning during ID-checking hours is going to be

302

impossible. Someone will be at the fence, helping Pulak to cross over with Gauri; that's what he has been promised.

When the call comes, it is not as a sound, but as a presence – of yet another nameless man, the one who is supposed to walk him part of the distance, ostensibly to show Pulak the way, although it's a straight line north-east from where he is, about a couple of hours' walk, one hour and a half if he were on his own, but he has a cow with him.

The man hands Pulak a pair of wire cutters as they begin their walk. The only thing the man says is, 'There are very few dark areas near the fence now. Up north, at Murikhawa, they've turned night into day with very powerful lights. They're like huge walls of lights. You walk in the direction that you're walking until you see the man waiting for you. He will be waiting, and you won't miss him. He knows you're coming. Just follow your nose from this point.' With that, he's gone. It's Pulak on his own now, and Gauri, until he is met by the man near the border.

The men Pulak had talked to when he was still sounding out his plans had said various things.

'East, east, you need to go east.'

'They've put a high barbed wire fence along the entire border. There are BSF guards in their sentry posts at regular intervals.'

'Why does he have to do it himself? He should give it to a cattle smuggler.'

'No, no, where there are rivers, it's easy to cross. How can they put fences on water?'

'Why do you think the BSF don't know this? They are extra vigilant at those watery crossings.'

'But there is no water now, or very little. The rivers are all shrunk to trickles. You can wade across in most places.'

303

'Wade across Ichhamati and Mahananda? Have you gone mad? You'll drown like a leaking boat, you fool. Even with this heat that we've been having, they're still rivers, not your local nala.'

'You've seen the rivers with your own eyes, huh, that you are speaking so confidently?'

'But smuggling there always is. The BSF are in on all the rackets. In fact, they run the whole thing. They control it. You need to pay them off first.'

'They catch only the naïve ones, crossing the border with a single cow, but the real smuggling gangs, with many people involved and hundreds of cows, they run themselves. Shooting these solo smugglers is just a way of showing to the government that they're doing their job. Behind that, it's business as usual. I have heard many stories.'

'He should take his papers with him. They shoot only Muslims because it's Muslims who are the smugglers and the criminals. They all come over from the other side, seething like worms, swamping us, looking for work. But your friend is not a Muslim, he'll be fine. But he must make sure to have his papers on him.'

Pulak had been careful to lie about his name, where he lived, the reason for his enquiries – he had maintained that he was asking on behalf of a friend. He had gathered the information from several people at different places, Chhatkhola, Nuagram, Bistarhaat, Najimbajaar, Chaporkhali, never engaging one man for a length of time that would seem anything more than casual, time-pass conversation, never lingering in any one place for more than a day. He knew what was at stake. If word got out, however unintentionally, to cow vigilantes, any number of whom patrolled the countryside, they would hunt down Pulak and lynch him. The downside of all this patchy and cautious information-gathering was that he had only anecdote, rumour, stories at several removes to go by, nothing very reliable. Still, it had led him in the right direction, to the place where he could try in a more purposive way, at the very least to somewhere where he wouldn't stand out, would be one among many who were caught up, one way or another, in the business of moving cattle.

The idea had come to him while he was a day-labourer at a building site in Raipur. He had told one of the labourers that he owned a cow.

'So why are you breaking your back working here? You must be wealthy to own a cow,' the man had said.

Pulak had said nothing, choosing to let his silence be taken as modesty.

'Do you know how much cows cost? If your cow gives ten to twelve litres of milk a day, you'll get at least fifty thousand rupees for her. At the very least,' the man had said.

The amount mentioned had stunned Pulak.

'How do you know?' he had asked.

'I know people who are cattle farmers near Bhagalpur. Take my word for it, I know about these things.'

Fifty thousand rupees. With that money, Pulak could move his family away from Nonapani to somewhere better, live in a brick-and-cement house with a tin roof, maybe even a brick roof, send the children to school, not have his little daughter packed off to work as a live-in maidservant. Fifty thousand rupees. An arrow had gone through him. Everything could change; would change, he had begun to think. And once he had started thinking about how the money could change their lives, there had been no turning back. He was tired, he wanted to be liberated from this life of his. He wanted to liberate his wife and daughter from the lives they had. The cow, supposed to improve their lives, was sucking their blood out of them instead. Fifty thousand rupees. They would all be free.

He thought more and more about it, until there was nothing else he could think about. He spoke to some men here and there in different towns where he showed up for loose-change work and, like the unexpected statement about the price of a cow from the construction worker in Raipur, someone in Chhapainagar mentioned cattle-rustling across the border. Pulak's ideas about leaving Nonapani with fifty thousand rupees for a better life elsewhere shifted and bent into something else. Two things, one old and one new, came together in his head into causality: he had found a way to sell the cow that would necessitate leaving Nonapani and going missing. Two birds with one stone. Liberation, finally. Freedom from being ground down to dust under the burden of responsibility, of the labour needed to provide for a family. He wanted to breathe again. The thoughts hardened into plans.

He has to cross a tar road before he can get to open ground. It feels to him as if a long time passes before he can even get to the road. Although dim and few and far between, there are lights along part of the road. The stretch appears to be without tea- or snack-stalls, small shops, huts. How can this be? In his few days here, there has been nowhere that hasn't been populated: large stretches of paddies; cultivated plots of jute, wax gourd, mustard; closely huddled huts with dilapidated roofs; humans, hens, ducks, cows. He had been told to make his face familiar to the locals by taking Gauri out to graze every day. The earth was both parched and lush at the same time. The river, unlike what he had been told, looked too wide to swim across. The water was a greenish-yellow, still like a pond until you looked again or saw the wake left by boats crossing the river, to and fro, to and fro. And the BSF at every place, at checkpoints, trawling the settlements and villages, their spies everywhere – it was impossible to discern who was an informant, who a smuggler, who worked both sides, or if there were any stable sides at all in the first place, everyone playing everyone else in a forever-shifting, dangerous game, going wherever the hope of money took them. Pulak felt at once noticed and hidden; in a place where the people saw so many daily crossings, the numbers swelling and reducing like the tides in the river, he could have been both a transient face, one among many, seen and instantly forgotten, and a new face, eliciting intense curiosity and suspicion – who was he, friend or enemy? Which side did he belong to, this or the other? He gave his real name whenever anyone struck up a conversation with him or asked him questions: the cost of being taken for a Muslim was too high. Besides, if papers were demanded, a false name would put him in a potentially dangerous situation.

He is now much farther north than where he has been staying and grazing Gauri and biding his time. But where is the river? He climbs the gradient giving on to the road, pulling Gauri behind him. A small section of the other side is now visible in the gloomy illumination: an embankment leading down to what he supposes is open ground. Could the river be farther along, the fallow ground giving way to it? Gauri has to be pulled up the slope. As Pulak stops at the edge of the tar road, gathering up resolve to cross, he hears a large vehicle coming. There is no place to hide; he and Gauri are visible to all four quarters. There is a falling feeling from the bottom of his chest to the lowest point in his stomach. Pulak's sphincter loosens then contracts again. He scrambles down the gradient, leaving Gauri still standing on the road. A truck goes by, its headlights turned off. What if Gauri decided to cross over to the other side on her own? What if she got hit by another oncoming vehicle? Before he can raise his head, he hears another truck coming. His heart, mouth, ears are all one, all pounding in unison. This truck passes too. Silence descends, then stretches over the night. He suddenly notices the sound of crickets – a steady, unchanging wall for a few minutes, then a slight flick in that sound-wall, as if a dent has been made in it, followed by a slightly different configuration of that wall, continuing in its monotone forever and forever. He raises his head above the embankment – Gauri is standing there with her back to him, facing the other side. Has she seen something? He reaches her, takes the rope, and almost pulls her down the slope on the other side, not considering that if the cow decides to be recalcitrant now, there is nothing he can do since she weighs much more than he does.

The other side is a flat plain, with intermittent areas of squelchy mud and darkness stretching ahead. This must be the area the river swallows every monsoon, surrendering it back in the summer. Where is the fence? Where are the sentry posts? Pulak doesn't know if he is thankful for the darkness or suspicious; surely if there were sentry posts around here, some light from them would have reached where he is? Or if not reached, then he would have been able to see the lit posts in the distance. Is he in the right place? He has that odd feeling in his sphincter muscles again. He is imprisoned in the choice that he has made – to get fifty thousand rupees, even though he's receiving less than half that sum. He has not given much thought to fitting the new life he has imagined into the diminishing amount; it's still a new life, a better life. Once the plans started occurring to him, there was no going back. He thinks of his daughter's silent face, her head turned away from the unun she is fanning because smoke keeps getting into her eyes. One dawn he had heard her singing some made-up little tune to the cow as she milked her, the girl's dark head resting against Gauri's white flank, and for some reason the tunelessness of the invented song had made a fierce sense of wanting to protect her wash over him swiftly then ebb out.

There is something pale sticking out of the mud about six inches from where he is standing. A concrete post, about a foot high, with writing on it; it's too dark to make out the marks. There is the ooze of mud under and between his toes. It feels ever so slightly ticklish. Even at this hour, the heat feels like it is choking all the breath out of him. The quality of the darkness is such that he can't see his hand if he holds it up to his face, but can make out shapes in the distance, see the sky, the undistinguished black expanse all around him. Then he almost falls into it, the river, or at least a branch of it: it doesn't seem very wide because he can make out, from the different shades of darkness, the other bank, and a few metres farther, the barbed wire fence, like thin dark black circles and scribbles on slightly less black paper. At the far end of that wall of scribbles to the right, there is what looks like a sentry post, but there are no lights in it. How is he ever going to swim or wade across with Gauri to get to the fence? No one told him that he had a stretch of water to cross. Where is the man who is supposed to meet him? He tries to swallow but his throat is too tight. He has been set up. Or Gauri is going to be taken away from him in this darkness and he is never going to be paid. He clutches the rope in his clammy hands tighter, as if to remind himself that she is still beside him, as if the sight and smell and sounds of the animal are not enough.

Then, knocking his heart out of his bony chest, there is a voice almost in his ear. 'Smuggling the cow, are you?'

Pulak jumps. His scalp tingles. As far as he can see, there are two men to his left, two to his right. No sound comes out of his mouth. From the darkness more men come running. He is surrounded by a circular wall of dark shapes. A torch is shone on his face, blinding him.

'Caught him red-handed, shala Molla-r bachchha!'

'Grab the cow first, grab the cow.'

'He has a wire cutter in his hand. Take it, take it first.'

He cannot see anyone's face. Above the shouting, and the abuse the men are flinging at him, he hears Gauri low once, briefly. He wants to say, 'I'm not Muslim, my name is Pulak Bera, my village is Nonapani, I'm a Hindu, I belong to this country, not to the one on the other side, I'm not a Molla,' he wants to shout, but he is trembling, and not even a whisper can emerge from his mouth. He wants to plead with them, beg them, pray to them to be merciful, he wants to say, 'I have a wife and two children at home, the children are little, they'll be cast into the sea without me, please spare me,' but instead he just pisses himself.

They push him down on to the mud, then drag him by his hair to the river.

'Keep the noise down, we don't want the BSF fuckers to come running,' someone says. The cow is lowing madly.

'Then we can't beat him before sending him over, we'll have to finish the business quickly.' They drag him back to where they were and pull him up by his hair. He has found his voice – it emerges as a cross between weeping and begging.

'Has someone got the cow? Where's the cow?' a man asks.

'Let me despatch him, I'll finish him off now,' another man says, sounding as if he is exerting himself.

Pulak feels something warm and wet on the skin of his stomach, then that warm and wet sensation, stinging and piercing at the same time, is strangely inside him. Suddenly, as if in answer to the question of where the cow is, the wall of people parts. At the end of it is a vague pale shape, but Pulak cannot put a name to what it is. He's still searching for the name, so familiar yet still so elusive, right on the tip of his tongue, when the paleness devours everything.

Acknowledgements

Monica Ali, Archishman Chakraborty, J. M. Coetzee, Carrie Comer, Michelle de Kretser, Emma Dunne, Lauren G. Fadiman, Susan Faludi, Karen Joy Fowler, Talia Goldberg, David Herd, Jenny Holden, A.M. Homes, Aravind Jayan, Meng Jin, Manan Kapoor, Jhumpa Lahiri, Dominic Leggett, Yiyun Li, Gabby McClellan, Barry McClelland, Janet McDonald, Niall MacMonagle, Paul Murray, Aditya Pande, Rohini Pande, Anna Pincus, Matthew Rabin, Ritwik Rao, Marie Rutkoski, Russ Rymer, Peter Sacks, Osman Salih, Namwali Serpell, Claire Sharpe, Akshi Singh, Tracy K. Smith, Celia Stubbs, Drew Elizabeth Weitman, Edmund White, Emily Zhao.

Jill Bialosky, Poppy Hampson.

Jessica Bullock, Sarah Chalfant.

The nucleus of Salim's story first appeared in *The Refugee Tales*, volume II, edited by David Herd and Anna Pincus (Comma Press, 2017).

'Here is a magnificently clear-eyed portrait of our times lit equally by sorrow and rage. Neel Mukherjee is a superb writer, and *Choice* is **his greatest work yet**'
Michelle de Kretser

'A magnificent accomplishment... In each panel of this masterful triptych **exquisite prose gradually crescendos to jaw-dropping revelations**'
Namwali Serpell

'**Burns brightly with fierce intelligence**, with wisdom and compassion, and achieves what so few novels even attempt: it makes the reader think deeply about how we've come to live this way, at what cost, and about those who pay the greatest price'
Monica Ali

'If the world were a patient, one would like to entrust it to a surgeon like Neel Mukherjee, whose keen eyes, formidable intelligence, masterful scalpel, and compassionate approach would offer us reassurance and hope without any illusion. A powerful novel about many of our contemporary dilemmas, *Choice* **will stay with the readers long after we finish the last line**'
Yiyun Li

'**Searing, poetic and beautifully brutal,** *Choice* reveals just how far the imagination – when buoyed by courage and conscience – can travel'
Tracy K. Smith